ELLEN ES CEELY

SON of KINGS

THE LEGENDS OF ZALE

a prequel
BOOK TWO

Copyright © 2023 by Ellen ES Ceely

All rights reserved.

No part of this publication may be reproduced, distributed, or transmitted in any form or by any means, including photocopying, recording, or other electronic or mechanical methods, without the prior written permission of the publisher, except as permitted by U.S. copyright law. For permission requests, contact Ellen ES Ceely at ellen.es.ceely@gmail.com.

NO AI TRAINING: Without in any way limiting the author's [and publisher's] exclusive rights under copyright, any use of this publication to "train" generative artificial intelligence (AI) technologies to generate text is expressly prohibited. The author reserves all rights to license uses of this work for generative AI training and development of machine learning language models.

The story, all names, characters, and incidents portrayed in this production are fictitious. No identification with actual persons (living or deceased), places, buildings, and products is intended or should be inferred.

Book Cover by Ellen ES Ceely

First edition 2023

eBook ISBN 978-1-962016-00-1
Paperback ISBN 978-1-962016-01-8
Hardcover ISBN 978-1-962016-02-5

10 9 8 7 6 5 4 3 2 1

To Hova:
For reminding me that
wisdom, kindness, and love
are always the answer,
and for choosing to protect
the weak and the vulnerable.

You are perfectly imperfect.

ZALE

DRYAD FOREST

NYAD SEA

Fresh

City Island

Salt Water

SALT LANDS

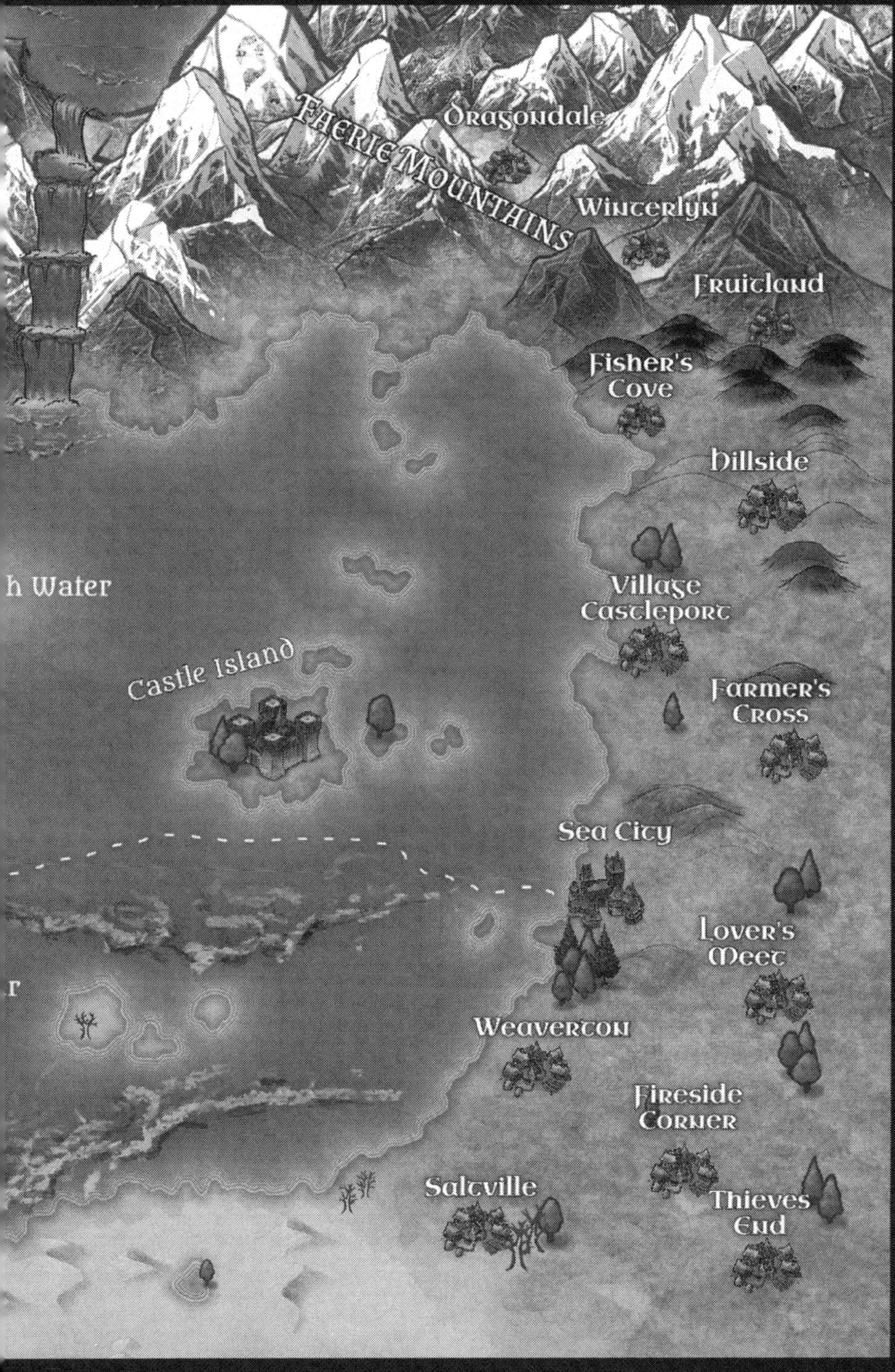

Faerie Mountains
Dragondale
Winterlyn
Fruitland
Fisher's Cove
Hillside
Village Castleport
Castle Island
Farmer's Cross
Sea City
Lover's Meet
Weaverton
Fireside Corner
Saltville
Thieves End

Trigger Warnings

This book contains content that may be troubling to some readers, including, but not limited to:
depictions of and references to death, suicide, generational trauma and abuse, homelessness, PTSD, and inferred rape.

While I seek to approach all topics with sensitivity and to keep the content of my work within the commonly accepted
bounds of YA literature, I cannot guarantee the complete comfort of all readers.

Please be advised that this story is not an HEA (happily ever after).

PROLOGUE

The Woods grow dark, hues of pink and gold shimmering through the trees as the sun sets. I sit, as always, by the small fire I've made outside of my hovel of branches, moss, and leaves.

I curse the day I was born.
I curse the day I met my father.
I curse the day my mother died.

Do I sound bitter? Good. This should never have been my destiny. Cursing is the only inheritance I have left - that and a life of solitude within the safety of these Woods.

I curse the ground I sleep on, the food I eat, and the silence surrounding me. I curse the weakness of my heritage, the blood coursing through my veins, and the treachery of destiny.
I curse the Shadows.
I curse Hadithi.
I curse Chiwa.

Most of all: I curse myself. Much as my mother and father did, I curse my very existence. Yet I am too much of a coward to end everything; too afraid to leave the only place I have left to hide.

ELLEN ES CEELY

Who are you to judge me? Who are you to say I should've done differently? Who are you to deserve my story at all? You are less than nothing. No one of importance. If I could, I would scream at you of how your opinion matters not at all, and how I did not ask for it.

I can see you now as you reach the end of my story, sneering at me, judging me, turning and walking away from me, not even bothering to spit in my direction. I would be a waste of your spittle.

If I could, I would wring your self-righteous neck with my bare hands, releasing all the anger boiling up inside my soul.

But, alas, I cannot.

This is not the way the plan was supposed to end. This is not how I was destined to survive. Instead of power, I possess a broken sword, a knife, and this quill for writing. Rather than glory, I endure loneliness, abandonment, and the company of my own inadequacy.

Do not pity me, as you walk away. Do not, even for a moment, imagine that I desire or deserve your compassion. Keep your distance to keep your life. Maintain your silence to maintain your voice.

Let me sink into wallowing as I sit here sleepless and self-loathing. Leave me to grasp my broken sword in my crippled hand as I scratch out with the hand that remains unblemished the truth of what events made me who I am today.

The light fades, and the fire's flame is not strong enough to see the page. I will take up this story, my story, when day returns. Perhaps you will judge me less harshly, reader, when you read the truth of the whole tale.

If you choose otherwise, then cursed are you!

Yuvraj: *Commander of the Shadows; Exile of Shantu*

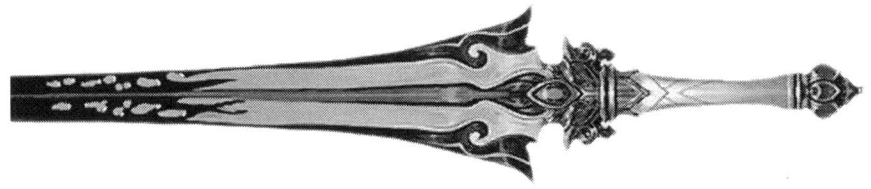

PART ONE

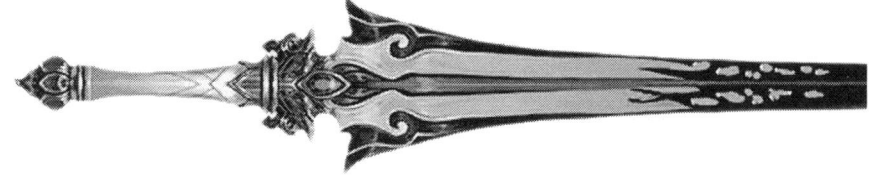

Chapter One

"GATHER 'ROUND, CHILDREN," I whispered through the rain as it hissed on the pitiful and poorly protected fire we'd managed to light in the alleyway, causing smoke to fill the space between us. "And I will tell you the greatest fairy tale ever to exist!" I wiped away the last of the unwanted tears escaping my eyes, thankful for the veil of smoke.

Only a few gathered tonight. Other children who, like me, had no parent to claim them and no home to stay dry in. Usually there were more, but on such an awful night most had probably tried to find shelter from the rain.

My stomach growled, reminding me that fairy tales only distract you from reality for so long. Reality has a way of taking over, of painfully forcing its way into the limelight.

"Once upon a time," I said, pushing past the loudness of my growling innards, "There was a little boy who defeated the evil emperor and became king!" I sat there, hugging my knees to my chest, allowing my mind to wander wherever it wanted as I stared into the depths of the smoky flames sputtering in the rain.

"This little boy was just like you and me: unwanted, unloved, and unseen." I spoke with passion, trying to make eye contact with the few cautious and ragged children that sat around the fire with me. "He begged for food, apologized for his existence, and hid from the rich and the strong." The five pair of eyes that met mine, regardless of age or gender, all gazed back at me with an understanding that could only come from mutual experience.

"But one day, he decided he'd had enough." I stopped hugging my knees and sat up on them, rocking back and forth, my voice growing in strength. "He decided he wouldn't live like a beggar any longer, wouldn't hide in the shadows like a coward." I stood up, a fire burning in my belly, a fire I'd come to know as anger, or maybe even courage.

"Instead of living out his days as an unwanted gutter rat, he became an unseen terror." The excitement and conviction in my voice were rising. I poked at the fire with a stick, watching it catch in the flames. "Rather than hiding in the shadows like a coward he decided..." I paused, trying to figure out what to say as the image of who I wanted to be flashed before my mind. "He decided he would become one with the shadows - a Shadow himself!" Excited, I pulled the glowing stick from the fire and gazed at it.

The children around the fire were looking up at me, eyes shining with hope and fear, then clouding over with hunger and fatigue. We'd survived this long, made it through so many years of beatings and starvation and cold. The older we got, the more likely we were to live long enough to fight our way into the world of the respectable Common People of Shantu.

Those of us who were boys knew one day we might manage to become an apprentice, a sailor, or a soldier. A hard job, a warm bed, and consistent food in our bellies was our dream scenario.

The girls had different futures, most of them much less appealing. They were more likely to end up in a brothel, or as a scrub maid to the Governor. If they were lucky, they might make a respectable marriage with a farmer looking for a sensible wife. If they were beautiful, they might aspire to become the mistress of a wealthy merchant.

Even those of us who managed to make it into the world of the Common People were still likely to find ourselves in a damp cell awaiting a strong noose, especially for a crime we hadn't committed. We were forever the scapegoats of society, mere pawns in the schemes of those who ruled our world.

Life so far had been survival of the shrewdest, the strongest, and the meanest. We'd been trained by our older and wealthier counterparts to fight with each other rather than band together and fight those who oppressed us. I'd survived by relying on my stature, leaning into the anger burning inside my soul. My wit had helped me outsmart those who believed they were superior to me. I'd always wondered if, maybe, there was a better, easier way.

The image of becoming one with the shadows cemented itself in my brain, stirring up a faint glimmer of hope. This wasn't how I'd imagined this fairy tale would go.

"The little boy decided," I continued, my voice rising and falling as I sank into the story. "He would disappear into the darkness, becoming one with the dark alleyways he called home, embracing as a friend what was meant to be his curse." My voice remained bold and strong as I waved my stick in the air like a sword. The rumbling in my stomach had quieted as my mind was distracted by the future I wished over myself.

"The little boy decided he'd had enough!" I shouted, eyes closed, my face turned upward in the smokey, damp alleyway, the children around me staring wide-eyed. I clenched the stick and stood up as tall as I could, the fire and the rush of adrenaline warming my tired, hungry body. My heart raced, the crackle of the flames the only noise to interrupt my thoughts. The children around me huddled together, holding their breath to see what I did next.

"I have decided," I said, softening my voice as I relaxed my arm and lowered the stick back to the fire. "I've had enough. Not only for myself, but for all of us." I sat back down and glanced around, earnestly, at each of my frightened, hungry, colleagues. "Have you had enough?" I whispered. "Have you had enough of hunger and beatings and being told you are unwanted? Unworthy?" I gazed into the fire, a rush of feelings bubbling up inside to form words. "Have you had enough of fighting to survive? Of stealing to not starve? Of sleeping in filth and skulking in the background of society?"

Silence. No one spoke. No one answered me. No one moved.

"Maybe," I said, choking at the hope that came to mind as I uttered the word. "Maybe the fairy tale could be reality?" I waited for someone to laugh at me, to smack me on the side of the head and tell me to stop dreaming. I half expected a soldier to overhear my words and rush us, breaking up our small gathering and smothering the flames of our warm fire in an effort to smother the flames of hope rising in my soul.

ELLEN ES CEELY

"What's your name?"

I jumped at the sound, shocked by the sincerity and boldness of the question one of the children across the fire from me asked: a boy about thirteen years old - only a year older than me - with a dark handkerchief covering his left eye, wrapped tightly around his forehead. I hadn't noticed him before. *When did he arrive? How could I have missed someone with a handkerchief over his eye?* I wondered to myself.

"Yuvraj." I answered, noting the protective arm he rested around a little girl who couldn't have been more than five years old. She sat close to him, wrapped in a cloak far too big for her, holding his free hand between her own. Her black eyes were bright and fearless, almost taunting. *What an odd pair.* I thought to myself.

"My name is Yuvraj." I repeated, puffing my chest up out of habit, trying to appear strong and intimidating.

"Son of the King." He spoke the meaning of my name with a dull interest, as if it bored him but he needed to know. "You believe you are the son of a king?" He stared out at me from his right eye, the bluest eye I'd ever seen. His question wasn't a challenge to fight, but rather a question within a question.

I glanced from him to the little girl and back again. Her eyes were jet black, her hair a short, curly mess of dark red, and her skin a deep brown. He was fair and blue-eyed; with the whitest blond hair I'd ever seen. They looked nothing alike, not their skin tone or their hair, and yet, they both held something in their appearance that was unmistakably the same.

"I know I am the son of a king." I whispered back at him.

"Then the fairy tale is already half true." He said, his face breaking out in a smile. "Go on. I'm listening."

CHANTREA MOTIONLESSLY WATCHED THE children gathered in the alleyway below from the shadows of the rooftop ledge. The thick black cloak wrapped around her tall but slender frame created an impenetrable barrier between her and any prying eyes. Their intense, childish voices wafted up to meet her ears as they sat around the fire.

SON OF KINGS

They're a pathetic sight. She thought to herself. *So common and beaten down, dirty and malnourished.* She looked on as a couple of the children drifted off to sleep, the chill of the rain finally leaving their poorly clothed bodies as the flames grew in volume. Some laid down next to the fire, curling up with their backs against its warmth. Others fell asleep sitting up, their heads falling forward onto the knees they hugged, either too exhausted or too afraid to lie down.

But their strength is undeniable. She conceded to herself. *To live so long in a world that does not want them, to survive through the good and the bad. It's admirable.* Her lips parted in a sad smile.

Only three remained awake, and they were the three Chantrea was interested in.

"My name is Tyr," The older boy with the handkerchief across his eye said, resting his free hand on his heart. "This is my sister, Hova." He motioned to the small girl sitting next to him, wrapped in the giant cloak. Chantrea squinted her keen eyes, searching for a reaction from Yuvraj. The boy glanced from one to the other, cocking his head to the side. His eyes settled on Tyr.

"Battle?" He inquired, clearly uninterested in Hova's less intimidating name meaning 'wind'.

Typical boy. Chantrea thought, her eyes zeroing in on the fiery little creature below. *She is a force to be reckoned with, a force he will one day have to reckon with if he's not careful.* She could practically see the wheels in the little girl's head turning as she jutted out her chin at the boy's snub and turned her eyes back to the fire.

"That's the name my mother chose for me," Tyr replied, solemnly nodding in Yuvraj's direction. "I suppose she had less interest in who my father was than she did in the future consequences of his actions."

Oof! Chantrea smiled in full, the boy's intelligence and boldness caught her by surprise. Yuvraj stared at his new companion, eyes slit, jaw tight, ready to pounce if needed.

"What are you saying?" Yuvraj asked, his voice quivering with excitement and anger.

Oh, come, child. Chantrea thought, shaking her head at him in disbelief. *You know what he's saying! Dumb is not a good look on you.*

"That you," Tyr said, calmly. "Are not the only son of a king. Your battle is my battle." His voice was steady. "I'm saying we are the same, you and I, in so many ways. We are the same because we are brothers."

Ha! Chantrea felt giddy in the tense silence. *Aepep has no idea what's coming his way!* The knowledge excited her. *I may have failed to defeat one son, but I will work to destroy the one I can find!*

"Then..." Yuvraj's voice broke the tension, hesitant but strong. "You agree? Tonight we find a way forward. Tonight we make a pact to discover how to become one with the shadows and embrace what was meant to be our curse."

"Yes." Tyr spoke in a loud whisper. "Tonight we find a way."

Chantrea listened as the boys talked far into the early hours of the next morning. Finding a comfortable way to lay down on the thin rooftop ledge was easy for the seasoned warrior. Laying on her side, she drifted in and out of sleep, her face toward the alleyway opening as the dim light of the fire glowed below. She felt stable and content, warmed by the many layers of her long cloak and expertly designed clothing.

"We'll make him pay!" Yuvraj's voice would reach her ears with Tyr's grunts of agreement not far behind. "We'll take back what's ours, our rightful inheritance!"

"We'll fight for each other, for ourselves." One would venture, expounding on the wonderful ambitions they had, entertaining imaginary battles as they fought the oppression with which they were all too familiar. "We can practice together, find a way to grow stronger so we can defeat his soldiers!"

"We'll leave no one behind!" The other would exclaim, motioning to the sleeping children around them. "We'll share our rightful wealth the way it should be shared and rule with justice."

"How many of us do you think there are?" The question came up more than once, followed by silence and the lack of a concrete answer. "How many mothers, like our own, has he thrown out on the street? How many children of his have died in the gutter while he sits in his palace?" Even in her sleepy stupor, Chantrea recognized the anger in Yuvraj's voice as deep and filled with a loathing that echoed in the darkest places of her own heart.

"I have long suspected we have more family than we ever dared realize." Tyr's steadiness always seemed to recover, excited by Yuvraj's passion but never overcome. "Too long we have been pitted against one another, taught to hate each other, told we're worthless and undeserving. All the while so many of us have been wandering the streets as heirs to a throne that will never be ours."

"And to think," Yuvraj spoke in a hushed, sheepish tone. "All this time I never thought of who else might be my own flesh and blood. I thought..." His voice trailed off.

"You thought you were the only one?" Hova's bright voice startled Chantrea, waking her from her stupor. "You thought you were the only one whose mother died on the streets after the governor threw her out for being pregnant with his own child?" Her obvious scorn for Yuvraj went above and beyond the five years she had spent on this earth. Chantrea sat up to watch the scene below, time slowing down as she fully woke up.

Silence. Deafening, awkward silence.

Chantrea saw Yuvraj staring at Hova in disbelief. The tiny creature hadn't spoken a word the entire time they'd been sitting there. Chantrea had nearly forgotten about her, believing she must've gone to sleep long ago.

"I, well, yes." Yuvraj managed, his voice betraying his frustration. "I thought I was the only one. At least, I never thought about whether there were others..." His voice dragged off again.

"Well, there are. There are a lot of children just like you: children of the governor of Shantu." Hova responded. Chantrea wished she could see the child's face, but it was hidden from her by the enormous cloak she wore.

"Hova, it's alright." Tyr interjected, giving her a quick squeeze of the shoulders, his voice strained with desperation. "What matters now is working together."

"Wait, what do you mean a lot of children like me? Don't you mean like us?" Yuvraj gravitated toward Hova's choice of words, latching onto anything that would help him fight back and defend his own lack of self-awareness.

"No, I mean–" Hova began with fire in her voice, but was cut off abruptly by Tyr in an effort to divert any of her pent-up aggression.

"She's my half-sister just as you are my half-brother," The older boy stated the strange facts like one would announce the weather. "But while you and I share a father, Hova and I share a mother. Her father took my mother in as his wife while she was still pregnant with me."

More silence.

"Like you said," Yuvraj finally replied. "What matters now is working together." He spoke through clenched teeth. After a few minutes, he held out a hand. "What do you say? Do we join as brothers of the unexpected? Brothers of the shadows?"

Tyr nodded in agreement, "Together we rise as brothers of the shadows." He said, holding out his own hand to shake on it. "Together we protect. Together we will use the darkness we've been abandoned to, to fight back and take what's rightfully ours."

Without another word, they laid down to sleep through what remained of the darkness, the fire dying as they ran out of wood scraps to fuel the flame.

High above in the waning moonlight, Chantrea watched them. *Steadiness, passion, and fury.* She mused. *They have all the spirit of a revolution, but none of the skill. This I will have to ponder.* With effortless efficacy she laid back down on her ledge and drifted off into a fitful slumber.

CHAPTER TWO

I RAN THROUGH THE streets of the slums in Shantu as the early morning sun rose high above the city. Spring had arrived and the humid, frozen bite in the air that had held on with a ferocity for months was losing against the South-Eastern wind and the lengthening days.

Spirits were rising as warmth increased. Spring was a time of hope and celebration for the slum dwellers like myself. It meant we'd survived another winter and life was about to involve more food and more restful sleep. Even for the most respectable common people of Shantu, spring was a time of relief.

The streets were uncommonly full as I headed toward the river that ran through the middle of our city, flowing from the great Rock Walls of the North-West into the great Sea of the South-East. I had to slow down and dodge out of the way, winding my way through the crowds moving in the same direction I was: the Governor's Grounds.

Several weeks had passed since Tyr and Hova had come into my life. We'd determined, through lengthy conversation and a few arguments with Hova, that we were much better off living together. There was safety in finding a place to live together.

ELLEN ES CEELY

We needed a home where we could invite others who, like us, deserved a different life; children whose father had thrown them on the street before they'd taken their first breath. We needed a place to train in fighting as we planned for how we would take back what rightfully belonged to us. It was important we learn to trust one another as we never had before. We needed a place to become, as we'd agreed to call ourselves, Shadows.

Tyr and I became fast friends, discussing the injustice of the man whose name we could hardly stand to speak aloud, the man whose blood ran through our veins - Aepep, Governor of Shantu. Though Tyr's mother had been taken in by someone kind and respectable, her fate had still ultimately been the same as my mother: death by plague and malnutrition. While I loathed our father, Tyr seemed inclined to regard him as a necessary evil, a resource to be used.

We'd discovered an abandoned shack on the outskirts of the slums close to the North-East Gate of Shantu nearest the Woods. The entrance to the shack had been boarded up long ago, but the giant window in the narrow alleyway was all we needed to access our new home. Inside we found a few worn out stools strong enough to hold our weight, a low table with uneven legs, and a couple moth-eaten blankets. Best of all, we found an old barrel stove still connected to a pipe that ran up and out the window that needed some cleaning out.

Hova was a hard sell from the moment Tyr and I decided to band together, but even she had to admit that our newfound home was better than living on the streets. The rats and the dirt were as bad inside the shack as they were out in the street, but at least the roof could be easily patched to keep out the weather. The stove would keep us warm.

We'd spent the last few weeks cleaning the place up and patching the leaky roof to keep out the freezing rain. We gathered firewood and searched for fabric scraps in the garbage heaps outside local milliners' shops. Now that we had a place to sleep and keep our belongings safe, we'd turned our attention to creating a hub of safety where we could grow and learn. Eventually, we hoped to add others to our efforts for justice.

"Yuvraj!" Tyr yelled for me as I slowed from a run to a weaving walk. The crowd trying to filter its way through the gates into the Governor's courtyard was thick and growing. People pushed this way and that, ever forward, hoping to reach the

SON OF KINGS

most opportune place to stand. Those who had arrived early pushed back from the front of the crowd, yelling at anyone who shoved them.

I scanned the crowd, my eyes moving in the direction of Tyr's strong voice. I found him perched in a maple tree high above the crowds, Hova glowering down at me from the branch supporting her. *She should smile more.* I thought to myself, clenching my jaw in offense at the look on her face. *You'd think after a few weeks I'd have gotten used to the unending judgment, or that she would have changed her mind and warmed up to me. But no. She continues to hate me.*

I worked my way through the crowded courtyard and climbed up the tree to join them. Maples were perfect for climbing and perching in with their multiple, thick branches. The Woods were largely made up of maple trees, most of which were tapped every spring to be drained of their sap to make delicious candies. My mouth watered at the thought as I climbed up next to Tyr, staying a respectable distance away from the fierce gaze of his sister. I ignored her and settled down comfortably onto my branch.

"Nice spot." I said to Tyr as I gazed out over the heads of the crowd below, a direct view to the soldier-lined platform running along the East side of the Governor's Palace, with all the towns-people gathered around.

The Governor had rung the assembly bell before the sun emerged from its resting place, while the streets were dark and the only people awake and about town were vagrants, servants, or bakers. The Governor usually called an assembly at the start of each season, but he'd already called the spring assembly a couple days before, which made today unique and a bit of a frightening mystery.

"Did you get it?" Tyr asked me in a hushed voice, nudging my arm. I turned to grin at him, nodding and pulling two stale sweet rolls out of my jacket and handing them to him to share with Hova. I studied her out of the corner of my eye. Her face softened as she took the roll. The hunger in her eyes grew into joy and she sent a halfhearted nod of gratefulness my way as she bit into it. I grunted in response and turned back to the matter at hand.

"What do you suppose he wants?" I asked Tyr, just loud enough to be heard above the ruckus of the crowd below. I took in the platform ahead, noting how the whipping block was empty, but the noose was ready with a strong rope, the Hangman standing next to it with folded arms and a grim expression upon his face.

"Looks like a hanging." Tyr stated drolly. He frowned but his voice carried a smirk. I grunted at him much as I had his sister, swallowing down my laughter in stubbornness.

The Governor's Guards, a unique group of no less than six bodyguards, emerged from the palace doors to the left of the platform. They were smartly dressed in black tunics and cloaks, shining silver chain mail glistened from beneath their cloaks as the sun caught on it. They swaggered, strategically holding back the left side of their cloaks to reveal long, sharp swords; standing tall in their thick, black, lace-up boots, their faces invisible inside their hoods.

A slight bulge over their right shoulder spoke of the swords they carried strapped against their backs, easily accessible if the need arose. All they had to do was shed their cloaks. Their commander, Jabez, followed up at the rear with all the same armor, distinguished, however, by a deep crimson cloak. The guards fanned out in front of the platform, Jabez standing at the center.

The crowd fell silent as the assembly bell sounded again. Governor Aepep strolled confidently out the doors of his palace and up the steps of the platform where he stopped in the middle to address the people. He was, by anyone's standards, a handsome man of medium build and strength. His dark blonde hair held no trace of gray, his fair skin was lightly tanned, and his blueish-green eyes flashed with intelligence.

The anger in the pit of my stomach swelled as he gazed out at the people he ruled over with a cold, calm serenity. The resemblance Tyr bore to our father was uncanny and obvious once you knew the truth. Other than the difference in hair color and the lack of green in Tyr's right eye, anyone could have sat them side by side and noted the family resemblance.

"People of Shantu," Aepep's voice interrupted my train of raging thought. "Today is a solemn assembly, one that pains me as your guiding leader." His tone was smooth and sorrowful, carrying over the heads and into the ears of every person in attendance. The tone was full of sorrow, but the light in his eyes was bright and frightening, a betrayal of his real sentiment.

"Today," Aepep continued. "I have gathered you together to witness what happens to those who would defy the laws of our incredible city." A motion from the palace doors drew my attention as he spoke. "This girl," the Governor motioned with his left hand to the small person being led out on a rope by a soldier three times her size. His voice cracked with pained anger. "A mere servant of my great household, has dared to defy the laws that keep us all protected."

I followed the pitiful creature with my eyes. She was older than I but not by much, maybe sixteen or seventeen. She was petite and frail, and you could tell she'd been smacked around by the bruises on her face and the split upper lip. She walked unsteadily, hands tied in front of her, a petrified look of shocked uncertainty stretched across her face. Her eyes were wide and she visibly shook as she walked.

My stomach churned. *What crime deserving of death could someone that pathetic have possibly committed?* The thought made me forget the other roll I had tucked inside my jacket.

My eyes settled on her belly, the odd roundness of it held a stark contrast to the undernourished frame holding her together. *Worms?* I wondered, confused by the odd shape of her body. Her tunic was uncommonly tight in the middle while sagging everywhere else. She reached the noose and stood beside it in a daze, eyes wandering bewildered over the faces of the crowd below.

"For the following crimes," Governor Aepep spoke the words boldly, his voice booming. "Aleira, daughter of no one, will be hung by the neck until dead!" The pleasure in his voice cast a chilling contrast to the stern expression on his face. *Am I the only one who can tell he's faking sadness?* I turned to Tyr. His jaw was tight and his good eye fixed on Aepep. With one hand he held onto the tree. With the other he held onto his sister, as if fearing her fate would be the same as the pitiful girl before us. I turned back to the matter at hand.

"For delivering false accusations of assault against a prominent person of the Governor's palace, I find you guilty." Aepep wasn't reading off a parchment. He had the entire thing memorized. Either that or he was making it up as he went along. "For illegal prostitution of self," He continued. "Among the high-ranking officers of the City of Shantu, I find you guilty." My jaw dropped as the words sunk in, bringing fresh understanding to the roundness of her belly. "For the theft of precious food and drink stolen from the larders of the Governor's palace, I find you guilty. And finally," Aepep turned to the side, facing the trembling girl who stood before the noose. "For conspiring to discredit the Governor and remove him from his rightful seat in the palace, I find you guilty."

ELLEN ES CEELY

The crowd was silent. So silent you could hear the leaves of our tree brushing against each other in the wind. The Hangman trudged up to the poor girl, the wood of the platform creaking under his weight. He placed a wooden crate for her to stand on over the top of the trapdoor, nudging her elbow and helping her up.

No one spoke. Not a sound emanated from the crowd below. I gaped in horror, clenching the branch beneath me with both hands, digging my fingernails painfully into the wood. I wanted to look away, but all I could do was stare straight into the poor girl's face as she stepped up onto the crate. The Hangman adjusted the noose around her neck, tightening it behind her head.

"Have you any last words, child?" Aepep's voice made me jump. I'd almost forgotten how the judge was standing nearby the judged. Aleira turned her face toward him, tilting her head in a daze, hands clasped tightly before her over her rounded belly.

"M-my..." She sputtered. "My baby?" It was halfway between a question and a statement of shocked realization. Her sad confusion was obvious to all. Aepep's body went rigid as a few gasps rose from the crowd.

"You should've thought about that," He finally responded, his tone sending chills down my back. "Before you became a lying criminal." He signaled to the Hangman who moved over to the lever of the trapdoor. "If there is a god, child, then I suggest you pray for mercy on your soul." He dropped his outstretched hand and the trapdoor fell.

Tyr, Hova and I waited until the crowd dispersed. We sat in silence on the branches of the tree, watching as Aleira's life was snuffed out from her body, the baby in her womb dying with her. We stared as the Hangman removed her from the noose and laid her down on the platform, drawing a ragged, dirty sheet over the limp shell of her frail humanity.

Aepep swaggered over to where the poor girl lay, bending down to peer at her ashen face beneath the sheet. He muttered something under his breath and threw the sheet back over her, waving his hand in disgust for them to take her away.

Aepep stood on the platform in the courtyard for some time, the Governor's Guards remaining close by. He stared out at the crowd as the people disappeared through the gate back into the markets. Everyone returned to work in a somber mood, the assembly bell ringing in dismissal. The high spring spirits had come crashing down. Aepep's mouth turned upward in a smirk as the people dispersed.

I turned to Tyr, biting my lip to keep from crying. I was overwhelmed by a mess of sadness, shock, and deep-seated rage. His face had turned an odd mixture of white and red, his jaw tight and a fire in his good eye. He nodded at me. We both slid down the tree, jumping from the lowest branch to the ground. Hova followed suit, dropping into Tyr's outstretched arms. He placed her gently on the ground beside him and held out a hand for her to hold.

I could feel Aepep's eyes on us as. Without a word, we all paused and turned to meet his gaze. No words, no actions, just a look. He moved his eyes over us with curiosity, as if seeking to probe our innermost thoughts to find out who we were and why we felt such boldness. His stare lasted only a few moments.

We must've been quite the trio: two dirty street boys, one with a missing eye, and a tiny, wild looking girl in a cloak too big for her. But it was all we had within our power to do. Before he could say a word or send a guard after us for questioning, we turned and walked away.

He'll pay for this! I swore to myself, clenching my fists as I walked beside Tyr. *For this and for all the other unjust deaths, all the murders of those he's used and abused. I'll make him pay for all the heirs he's conveniently killed off at the same time as a mother who's tried to discredit him and take what is owed her.*

The fire in my belly rose up into my throat as I thought of who the baby was and how helpless the mother, a mere child herself, had been to protect herself. One glance at Tyr told me he felt it as well. One glance at Hova told me she no longer needed to be convinced that we should join together.

Aepep walked through the front door of the palace, up the great staircase, and through the halls toward his chambers, reviewing the events leading up to Aleira's execution in his head. *The brat!* He thought as he stomped through the corridors. *The absolute, arrogant insolence of that girl!* He fumed inwardly as he recalled her threats.

"If you throw me out," She'd spoken so pitifully, angrily trying to muster up enough force in her voice to yell. "I'll tell everyone what you did, how you told me you loved me. I'll tell everyone who will listen it's your child!" She'd wiped snot and tears off her face with one hand, the other hand resting on her growing stomach. "I'll tell anyone who will listen!"

The back of his hand crossed her face as the last word left her lips, causing her to stumble backwards. She'd stifled a scream of shock, clasping the stinging cheek and wiping the blood away from the lip she'd bitten from the force of his slap.

"You tramp! You really think anyone will listen to you?" He'd said, sneering at her angrily. "You are nothing! You are no one! I am Aepep, the Governor of Shantu, son of Azai the great founder of our magnificent city! You are less than nothing!" He came close to her, hand outstretched, grasping her around the throat and pulling her face up to meet his, his breath hot in her face. "You were a gutter rat, an orphan given the privilege to serve in my palace and you dare defy me? You dare to threaten me?" She'd weighed so little that with one simple motion he'd tossed her aside, letting her crumple on the floor at his feet.

The rest had been easy. *No one would've believed her anyway. But she deserved it!* Aepep fumed, stopping at an upstairs window to stare out at the courtyard below. *Spirits are too high, the people are beginning to care a little too much for one another, believing they can take care of themselves.* The thought made him anxious. He'd worked hard to grow the slums, to create an atmosphere of utter dependence on his guidance and generosity, to incite fear as the core emotion of every resident.

Anyone who questioned his actions or pointed out the reality of what he was doing was swiftly silenced. It had been months since the last public display of discipline. Aleira had shown herself to be an easy scapegoat. *Stupid little rat!* He muttered, then smiled as he looked out at the empty courtyard. Her body was gone now, only the Hangman remained, dutifully winding up the rope for another day.

Aepep's eyes fell on the maple tree and his smile fell at the memory of the three children. Uneasiness rose in his chest. He shook his head, closed his eyes, and took a deep breath, letting it out slowly.

"Curses, Aepep," He said to himself in a hushed voice. "They're only slum children. Don't be ridiculous! What possible harm could they do to you?" The

SON OF KINGS

words made sense, but the feelings of unease continued to echo in the back of his mind as he walked away and shut himself up in his private chambers.

Chapter Three

The rain drizzled outside our new home. It was coming on midday. The clouds had been threatening all morning and had finally given way. Spring was in full swing with the early summer rains starting to pick up. Farmers who hadn't finished planting their crops were scurrying to finish up soon before the heavy rains took over. The seeds needed moisture, but they also needed time to take root so they didn't get washed away in a downpour or fried in an early fall drought.

My eyes studied the dripping water outside the window with a melancholy satisfaction. Rain meant cleaner air even if it also meant muddy streets and a cloudy river. Warmer weather meant less sickness, which meant less dead bodies gathering on the streets of the slums. The carts would finally be able to gather the waste that had accumulated all winter rather than focusing solely on carting away the dead to be burned or buried.

None of us were entirely sure where they took the dead bodies. I chose to believe they were burned or buried, even if it meant they all went together. There were rumors, of course. Some claimed the bodies were taken to the furnaces of the Governor's Grounds to be used as fuel. Others claimed they were all thrown into the depths of the Sea, never to be recovered. Still others claimed they were kept frozen in the winter air and shipped off to a faraway land with cannibals. The cannibal rumor always made me roll my eyes.

The last and most disturbing rumor was that the bodies were taken to less reputable butcher shops and sold as meat to the Common people when food was in short supply. I shuddered whenever that one reached my ears and shied away from anything meat related during the winter months. Meat was never offered to me frequently anyway. But still.

I took a deep breath, closing my eyes as I relished the sweet smell of rain, letting the freshness wash away the thoughts of winter. The weather had warmed up, but the rain had not. Not yet, anyway.

Behind me, Tyr and Hova stirred something over the barrel stove. We'd come a long way in our efforts to set up house in the abandoned slum hovel. Tyr and I managed to patch the roof and clear away the worst of the heavy dirt and filth caked onto the floor. We'd gone into the Woods to gather pieces of bark. Where there had once been gaping holes, now there was only soft moss and a damp, earthy smell. The thick layer of grime had been harder to get rid of, packed in as it was by years of water and hot fall sun. But once we realized there was a real, wooden floor beneath the filth, we worked tirelessly to get it up.

Hova kept busy with finding things while Tyr and I worked. She was ingenious at discovering piles of discarded scrap fabric, broken pots and bowls, and unwanted chairs. She'd taken to pulling around a small wagon she'd found in a back alley, throwing in anything she thought might be of use before hauling it home to unload.

Now that the weather was warming up, her tiny frame and large, beautiful eyes helped her beg vegetable scraps off some of the kinder Commoners. Carrot tops, shriveled beans, potato peels, and turnip greens had become the staple of our diet - supplemented, of course, with what bread I stole from nearby Bakers.

She'd even used some of the vegetable scraps to start a small garden on the roof of our hovel. Using the sturdiest part of our roof, she'd piled moss and dirt from the Woods on top to use as a planter. Every morning she would diligently climb up to check on it, pulling weeds and watering if needed. On the days that food was scarce, Tyr and I were still strictly forbidden to touch or disturb what grew there.

ELLEN ES CEELY

As much as I believed the small girl still loathed and judged me, we'd learned to live at peace with one another. Having begged a needle off a local seamstress, Hova cleaned and pieced together all the fabric scraps she found. It took forever, but the rough creations that emerged were both impressive and useful. She'd given Tyr her oversized cloak, having pieced together a wool creation of her own.

Roughly pieced together blankets appeared over time, neatly folded up for any of us to use. Cotton curtains hung in the window I sat by, the one and only entrance into our little home. The more she sewed, the better her creations became. I secretly hoped she would make a cloak for me by the time the next winter rolled around, but I was too stubborn to request she do so.

"Yuvraj," Tyr's voice broke my train of thought. I turned away from the window to look at him. "Food's ready." He said, nodding toward the pot on the barrel stove. I hopped down from the windowsill and walked toward the stove, plopping down on the short stool next to Tyr. Hova filled a poorly shaped, chipped clay mug with a soup concoction of vegetable stubs and beans and handed it to me.

"Thank you." I said, hoping I'd shown enough deference for her to be happy with me. She nodded, but did not smile. A nod was better than nothing. The food was nondescript. It was no failure on the part of Hova or Tyr, but our inability to flavor it very much. Salt was impossible to come by without money, so Tyr and I had walked to the South-East corner of the city to gather some salt water from the Sea that bordered Shantu. It had, at least, made our bland food more palatable.

I chewed on a stub of mushy carrot, pushing the hard piece of stem with my tongue so I could spit it out and swallow the rest. We sat there silently in front of the stove, all three of us eating our soup and drinking down the watery broth.

Hova's eyes studied me. "What was your mother like?"

I froze, tensing up at the sound of her little voice asking such a question.

"Hova!" Tyr scolded. "You shouldn't ask such questions." But the large, stern eyes never moved from my face. Hova wanted an answer. She was determined to get it. My mind raced, half inundated with sudden memories of my mother, half wondering how or what to say.

"Why," I spoke carefully, clearing my throat and fumbling over the words. "Why do you want to know?" I was buying time, trying to decide what I would say.

"You never talk about her unless you and Tyr are having one of your rant sessions about your father." The words smarted. They were true, but they sounded

SON OF KINGS

so harsh. I felt as if though all the layers of protection I'd worked so diligently to create to mask my weaknesses had been effortlessly ripped away by a child half my age. It was unnerving and unexpected.

"How can you expect anyone to care about your hopes of fixing wrongs when you don't talk about her?" Hova's tiny voice sounded so old. "If we're all in this together, as you say," There was a tone of mocking creeping in now. "Then I think it's about time you told us more about her."

I turned to face her. She sat there on a piece of dried-up old tree stump, her short legs just long enough to reach the floor from where she perched, arms folded stubbornly across her chest, eyes cold and determined with one eyebrow raised in defiance.

"Her name was Muna." I said, returning Hova's cold stare, my heart racing as I spoke her name out loud. "She was the daughter of a poor commoner who died when she was fifteen years old." I paused and looked back at the stove, all the old curiosity about my grandparents coming to the forefront of my mind. The slow pitter-patter of rain calmed my palpitations, and I took a deep breath.

"You want the truth? You want to know who she was?" My voice was strong. "I'll tell you who she was: she was a prostitute!" The anger welled up inside me. I wanted to stand, throw my arms up, and yell the truth at the curious child before me. But something about her small frame coupled with her cold eyes kept me firmly on my stool. Tyr sat nearby, tense and ready to defend his sister if needed. I nodded reassuringly at him and lowered my voice.

"She became a maid in the Governor's Palace when her parents died. By the time she turned seventeen she'd grown into a beautiful young woman." I could hear my mother's voice telling me her story as I told it to Hova and Tyr. "It wasn't long before Governor Aepep noticed her. She had fair skin, wavy brown hair, and dark brown eyes with green specks in them. She was tall and curvy. Most men gawked at her." The words disgusted me, but I didn't know how else to describe the woman who gave birth to me.

"Aepep showered her with compliments and flattery, giving her gifts and special treats. He seduced her. It wasn't hard. She wasn't smart or talented or well-schooled. No one had ever cautioned her against the attentions of a powerful man." My eyes smarted and I turned toward the stove, hoping my audience wouldn't catch sight of the tears fighting for release.

ELLEN ES CEELY

"He gave her nice clothes and a comfortable room next to his. He told her he loved her. He told her one day they'd be married. He told the rest of Shantu she was his ward and he'd taken her 'under his protection'. That way she could attend banquets and go on special outings whenever he wanted her to. Even if people didn't believe him, who were they to argue?" I shrugged my shoulders in resigned anger.

"Almost a year after he'd taken her as his mistress, she got pregnant. She thought he'd be happy and excited. She told him. He screamed at her about how she'd ruined everything calling her a whore, refusing to believe it was his child - that I was his child." I choked on the words and looked back at the watchful faces of Tyr and Hova. Tyr's expression was unbearable, full of pain and compassion and pity. I focused on Hova's unwavering stare.

"Governor Aepep gave my mother, Muna, a choice: she could leave of her own accord or be locked in the dungeon. She cried and begged him to reconsider. But it was no use. She left that evening, crying and wandering around Shantu with no place to go." I sighed as I thought about how pathetic and scared she must have been.

"She wandered around for days, begging food off anyone who would give it to her, sleeping in alleys, getting run off by soldiers. Then, one of the Upper Class gentlemen found her." I bit the inside of my cheek to keep from screaming and steadied my voice. "He made her a deal. He gave her a room in a hovel he owned in the slums. Not far from here."

"In return, she did him favors." I nearly choked on the words. "She also gave him a large cut of any coins she got from all the other men she did 'favors' for." Guilt and shame washed over me as I remembered all the times I'd been locked out of the room. Day or night, their perverted wishes knew no boundaries. Feelings of powerlessness returned as I thought about all the ways in which I couldn't protect her, all the times I'd found her crumpled on the floor bruised and bleeding.

"Yuvraj?" Tyr's voice made me jump. I'd sunk so far into the past I'd forgotten where I was. "Are you alright?" His compassion hurt my pride but reinforced my loyalty.

"I'm fine." I said, shaking my head as if the movement would somehow shake off the feelings overwhelming me. "She also gathered things in the Woods." I said, my voice flat and distant. "She taught me what was edible and what was poisonous, how to hide in plain sight if necessary. When it gets warmer, I'll be able to gather more things for us to eat." I said, looking pointedly at Hova.

"How did she die?" The little girl's voice was softer than before, but her eyes remained steady. Her lack of pity somehow gave me the strength to finish my mother's story.

"Malnutrition? Disease? Too many beatings?" I shrugged my shoulders, my gaze unwavering. "How should I know? I was nine years old. One morning I woke up and she didn't." I said, pushing away the memory as soon as I spoke the words.

We sat in silence again. The rain stopped and the only sound we heard was of water dripping off the roof into puddles.

"Thank you." Hova said, nodding at me as she spoke. I nodded back, noting the tiniest spark of respect lighting up her eyes.

AEPEP SAT IN THE great meeting hall of the Governor's Palace late at night, obsessively checking over the spring financial accounts. A quick tap on the door made him look up from his work, marking and closing the book so he could pick up where he'd left off once his unwanted visitors left.

"Come!" He shouted to the end of the great hall. The door creaked open, allowing a tall, well-built man in a light gray, wool cloak to enter, followed by a petite woman in a cloak that matched his.

"Ethan," Aepep said with a sly smile, disdain in his voice. "What a pleasure." The words were welcoming in theory, but stale and full of caution. "I see you've brought your daughter with you." Aepep nodded in the woman's direction. "Chiwa, you are most welcome as well." The cordiality was pleasant but cold. He'd remained seated at the long table that held the spring accounts.

Ethan and Chiwa approached the governor without a word, pausing a few feet from the table. They stood there, side by side, like two menacing reminders of a reality Aepep liked to forget. They lowered their hoods in unison, giving Aepep a chance to look them over.

Ethan's tanned skin, dark wavy hair with strands of silver, and deep gray eyes with a hint of a green circling the outer edge of the pupil were deceptively charming. He wore a bright smile. He nodded at Aepep and bowed, sweeping his cloak to the right in mock reverence. "Governor Aepep," he said, his eyes on the floor. "What an honor, sir."

Aepep resisted his urge to chuck the nearest candlestick at the man as his gaze moved to his daughter. Chiwa's almost translucent skin was an amazing canvas for the bright blue veins running down her neck and protruding from her hands as she swept her cloak back and curtsied. The young woman held Aepep's gaze as he stared at her long, wild, golden curls. Her cold, silver eyes with a ring of deep blue made the hair on his neck stand up straight. *Like an ice storm.* He thought to himself as he eyed her, trying to control the shiver ready to run down his spine. *It doesn't matter how many times I see her.* He mused. *I will never get used to her other-worldly look.*

"To what do I owe the pleasure of your company?" Aepep asked them, leaning back in his chair, folding his hands in front of his chin, and tearing his eyes away from Chiwa's face to look back at Ethan. He did not invite them to sit down. He did not offer a drink of water or a bite of bread. *The sooner this is over, the better.* He thought.

"Chantrea is on the move again." Ethan announced, his smile frozen over his face. "We've seen her. We tried to catch her, but she has learned how to make herself invisible." The frustration in his voice was evident. "Whether by magic or talent, we do not know, but -"

"Why should it matter to me," Aepep interrupted the man before him. "If your renegade Elf has eluded you?" All pleasantries had faded from his voice and face. *Is there to be more whining? More pleas for help with finding people who have nothing to do with Shantu or the future of my kingdom?!* Aepep glared at Ethan, tense and ready for whatever the response might be.

"It should matter," Chiwa's harsh voice caused Aepep to wince inwardly. She stepped forward, her veins flickering between blue and red. "Because word has reached us she is looking for your children." The young woman paused and glared at him, allowing the weight of her words to sink in for a minute. Aepep froze at the last word and stood up.

"Even if that is true," he said, his voice strained. "What could she possibly want with my – I mean, with a few gutter rats living in the streets of our slums?" He refused to admit parentage. Admitting it gave over a power he did not wish to release.

"Word has it, governor," Ethan's voice was mocking once more. "That she wishes to overthrow you. Her business here has worn on her already fragile mind." Ethan spoke with false compassion now. "Chantrea has decided to leave behind her past life and find a way to gain control over Shantu instead. Do you know the danger of a trained Elven warrior - especially a warrior such as Chantrea? She could upset all you have worked so hard to build. She might train and empower an army of those who would like to see you hung from the nearest tree." Ethan's voice betrayed the pleasure it gave him to think of such an event. "I warn you, brother," Ethan spat the word at Aepep, leaning forward and lowering his voice. "She has become as much a threat to you as she would be an asset to us."

"You go too far, Ethan!" Aepep shouted at the man across from him. "I renounced you as a brother long ago. It is by my mercy that you are tolerated to live and hide in the city our great father Azai built." Aepep's fury rose, a fire burning in his feet and hands. The image of the three children in the courtyard, staring boldly back at him, leaped suddenly into his mind. Out of the corner of his eye the governor observed Chiwa take a firm stand next to her father. Her veins gave way completely to a bright, burning red, the flames of the candles flickering eerily.

Fury made him wish to challenge her, to break his long-held rule and show them both how powerful he was. Caution reminded him to hide his true power for a more advantageous day, just as his father had taught him. He clenched his fists and glared at Ethan.

"Get out." He whispered fiercely. "Get out before I lose my temper."

Silence filled the room as the two brothers stared at each other.

"Remember this," Ethan spoke solemnly, eerily, no trace of a smile remained. His eyes glistened. "Remember this moment. Remember I tried to warn you." He said as he bowed his head and turned away, pulling his cloak up as he walked toward the door. Chiwa followed suit, hatred spewing from her look of distrust.

Chapter Four

Tyr and I walked briskly through the all but empty streets of Shantu. The moon was high and full above, but covered almost entirely by a thin layer of clouds. We wore dark tunics and had taken to smearing ash on our faces before we went out on our weekly efforts to aggravate the governor and his guards. Tonight was no exception.

The summer air was thick and still, a gentle, refreshing breeze running down from above all too rarely. Even though it was disgustingly warm out, I was thankful. Tyr and I both were. For once we did not freeze. For once we didn't need to wear anything that might impede our movement. Our bellies had grown larger and our energy was up. We'd decided now was the time to act. Now was the time when Aepep would be least expecting trouble and his guards would be less likely to report the theft of any food from the storehouses, or vandalism of the Governor's Grounds.

"Tonight we'll target the South-East corner of the Governor's Grounds," Tyr had said, drawing a crude map of them with a charred stick on the wooden floor of our home. Hova pursed her lips as he did so, her disapproval of both the plan and the dirtying of her floor clearly displayed across her face. I fought a smile.

SON OF KINGS

For someone who had spent so much time in the streets, she had incredibly high standards of cleanliness.

"I'll wash it off when I'm done." Tyr told his sister in an irritated voice, noticing her annoyance. "The wall on that side is neglected," he said, looking back at me. "They don't worry about it because it's up against the river across from the Eastern Upper Class sector. They like to keep dried meats and cheeses over there because they believe they're safer." Tyr grinned. "I plan for us to feast for at least the next month, possibly longer!" The glee permeating his voice at his own ambitious hope was contagious.

I paused, thinking through his plan, smiling at the thought of Aepep finding out his precious store of dried meats and cheeses had been invaded. My smile lost way to a frown as I thought about something else.

"But how will we escape?" I asked Tyr. "If we're spotted, the worst thing we could do is walk down the street carrying stolen meats and cheeses! They'll catch us before we make it out of the Upper Class sector!"

"Ever taken a bath in the river?" Tyr asked, his smile growing bigger. I stared at him and nodded, piecing it together as he spoke. "Well then, we're going to float our ill-gotten gains down the river!" His laugh was almost giddy. "They only have a few guards on this side of the Governor's Grounds and even fewer lights. They rely almost entirely on fear and lack of imagination!" His tone was half pleased with his own ingenuity and resourcefulness and half scorn at the lack of confidence Aepep and his men had in the intelligence of the people of Shantu.

"What if they catch you?" Hova spoke up. "What if your plan doesn't work?" Blunt as ever, she stared at Tyr with arms crossed, a twinge of fear in her eyes.

"They won't." Tyr said firmly, reaching out to grab one of her tiny, calloused hands with his own. "I promise. If there's the slightest chance of trouble, we'll drop our goods and run for it." He stared at her until she nodded back at him, a slight smile forming on her lips. Tyr was the only person I'd ever seen her give a genuine smile. When she begged for food or bartered for supplies her smiles were cordial but strained, and she never smiled at me. *Why do I care so much?* I wondered in frustration.

"They won't catch us, Hova. They won't even know we're there. I promise." Tyr was so confident, so self-assured. I believed him wholeheartedly, although a small part of me wished the guards would catch us. I had a few things I'd like to say to Aepep. *Then again, that would probably be the quickest way to die.* I thought to myself as we worked our way through the darkened streets, ever closer to the Governor's Grounds.

The streets of the Upper Class were quiet, clean, and well lit – so unlike anything we experienced in the Slums. We crept from shadow to shadow, hiding in dark corners and short alleyways whenever we heard a guard coming. My heart pounded in my ears as I tried to keep my breath shallow and quiet.

The fear of what might happen to us if we were caught kept knocking on the door of my imagination, trying to distract me from the mission at hand. I pushed it away, working in sync with Tyr as we reached the South-East corner of the Governor's Grounds. The deeper we got into the Upper Class sector, closest to the river, the fewer guards we encountered.

I could hear the rush of the river as we neared the end of the road. This road didn't have a bridge. The only way out of this neighborhood was to either go back the way we'd come or to swim the rapids that had steadily grown from the Spring and Summer rains. Few people living in the Common Sector had any interest in trying to get across the river unless they were using one of the bridge's to do business in another part of Shantu. Most people in Shantu weren't strong swimmers either, so the idea of swimming the river seemed like a foolish one.

Tyr and I had very little to lose, so much to gain in both food and pride, and the strong benefit of youthful bravery – which is also known as foolishness. We inched our way along the wall of the Governor's Grounds. The cobblestones beneath my feet were so smooth, so perfectly level. I'd never been this deep into the heart of the Upper Class.

I'd only ever ventured into the Governor's Grounds when the Assembly Bell rang out. Outside of that, it was too dangerous for a gutter rat like myself to dare show my face in a neighborhood so beautiful and well-off.

I stuck to the Slums and ventured only into the wider community of the Common Sector or the Woods outside the East gate. I'd rarely ventured over to the Sea, where the river flowed out at the outer edge of the South-East corner of Shantu. Too many soldiers. Too many stories of slum children, like myself, going out there to look and never being heard from again.

The wall beside us grew gradually shorter and more crumbly the closer we got to the River. *How did Tyr know this?* I wondered. Now that I'd been through the streets and seen both the distance as well as the numerous guards, I was in even deeper awe of my half-brother's knowledge. The courage it must have taken for him to scout out these streets ahead of time also impressed me.

Tyr stopped, suddenly, and pressed himself tight up against the wall, trying to blend in with the shadows. I followed his lead, listening intently.

"Oy!" A harsh, nasally voice on the other side of the wall said, a little too close and loud for comfort. "Why are we here, anyway?" I could hear a soldier shifting back and forth, kicking rocks and chucking pebbles into the river with a splash.

"Shut up." A deep, dead-inside voice answered him. There was a pause in the rock kicking and the pebble chucking as if the first speaker were assessing his situation.

"I'm just saying," He decided to proceed, another pebble hitting the water. "It seems like a waste of time! Who's going to come down here anyway? It's been three weeks since I was assigned to this corner of the Governor's Grounds and I haven't seen a soul out this way! I just think-"

"No one cares what you think." The deep voice responded, cutting off the first speaker. "No one wants to know what you think." The voice was getting louder with each word. "So listen to what I think about your thoughts: shut up!" As he shouted the last command to shut up, a rock hit something sharply, causing a nasal shriek to pierce the air.

Silence ensued, broken only by the intermittent hiss of cursing on the part of nasal voice. I wanted to laugh. I had no idea what the two guards looked like or what the rock had struck, but the conversation overtook my fear, and I was thoroughly amused. I swallowed my laughter and waited, wondering how we were going to get past the two guards.

We stood with our backs plastered up against the wall for what felt like ages. The cursing dwindled into silence and soon the sound of a deep snore reached my ears. I assumed sleep had overtaken the deep voice, but I had no way of guessing whether nasal voice was still awake and watching. I wondered if Tyr had a plan for guards. If he did, then he hadn't mentioned it to me earlier.

Tyr shifted around to face me. I could barely make out the outline of his face, the dark handkerchief hiding where his left eye should be. *Someday,* I thought fleetingly. *Someday I'll ask him what happened.* He stared at me and nodded toward the hole in the wall, holding up three fingers. I nodded back, believing I understood what he meant.

One. He counted off, turning back around to face the crumbled wall. *Two. Three.* Slowly, he rose from his crouched position and peered over the wall and the rubble surrounding it. I held my breath as I followed him, my left hand clenching the rock I'd picked up as a pitiful defense.

"C'mon," I heard Tyr's whisper, and my heartbeat slowed a bit. He climbed over the wall and I followed suit, setting down the rock I'd picked up to make it easier. The scene that met my eyes was comical, to say the least. Two soldiers, one big and tall, one short and skinny, sat slumped against the crumbling wall, both in a deep sleep. The deep snoring, to my surprise, came from the skinny soldier. It seemed to defy all reason. I stood there, frozen, staring from one soldier to the next, forgetting for a second what I'd come to do.

"Yuvraj!" Tyr tugged on my arm and I started forward, blinking as if I'd just woken up from a dream.

"Sorry." I mumbled, scrambling over the rubble and grass beneath my feet. There were several small, dilapidated buildings around us, all made from the same cobblestone and rock as the wall surrounding the Governor's Grounds had been. Tyr sank back into the shadows of one of them, catching his bearings and peering around the corner. I followed him like a puppy, excitement and confidence growing in my chest.

"We practically own the place!" Tyr whispered to me as he peered around the corner of the outbuilding. "No one else in sight. Let's move!" He walked quickly, but less cautiously, toward a short stone building with a wide wooden plank door. The roof of the building couldn't have been much higher than my shoulder, and I wasn't exactly tall for my age.

Tyr examined the wooden door closely. He turned to flash me a grin in the moonlight as he unlatched it and pulled it open. The rough metal hinges creaked ever so slightly, and he stopped, the smile fading. We held our breath and waited for the sound of any soldiers making the rounds. Nothing stirred.

"Spit on them." Tyr said. I looked at him in confusion. "On the hinges." He clarified and leaned over to show me what he meant by gathering up a disgusting amount of spit in his mouth and hurtling it onto the unsuspecting hinge. I followed his example.

SON OF KINGS

For the next couple minutes all that could be heard was the sound of us spitting on the hinges of the giant door. My mouth grew dry, and my cheeks started to hurt from trying to suck out every bit of saliva I possessed. Finally, Tyr seemed satisfied and nodded at me. He swung the door open with confidence, not a single sound met our ears.

We crouched down and peered inside the low building. Thick, ugly hewn stairs led down into a dark pit of cool air. My heartbeat quickened again as I gazed into the blackness, wondering what might be down there. *What if the soldiers wake up and find us down here?* I thought. My heart skipped a beat as memories poured, unwanted, into the forefront of my mind.

"Quickly now," Tyr said, climbing down the stairs and motioning for me to follow. "Come on in and close the door behind you." He was so confident, so unfazed by the idea of getting caught or venturing into a dark enclosed space without knowing what was down there. *He's so fearless.* I thought, hesitating to follow, but my desire to prove my own fearlessness won out. I scrambled down the stairs after him and shut the door gently behind me.

I sat on the stairs for a minute, blinking rapidly in an effort to see through the inky darkness. I tried to focus on my breathing, fighting not to return to the prison in my head. *One breath in, one breath out.* I told myself. *One breath in, one breath out. This is not that place. You are not alone.*

My eyes were starting to make out long rows of shelves piled high with stuff. Small, broken chinks in the walls let in welcome slivers of light. I could just make out Tyr's shape among the shelves, walking up and down the rows, looking at everything, pulling things into his arms.

"Yuvraj," The one-eyed boy hissed at me. "What are you doing?! We need to get out of here before they come by to change the guard."

I swallowed, trying to come up with something to say.

"Yuvraj? What's wrong with you? Do you have the sacks?"

I nodded instinctively and pulled the piece-meal sacks Hova had reluctantly made for us out of my tunic, stumbling down the stairs as I did so. "Sorry," I managed, my mouth still dry. "I, uh, my eyes were having trouble adjusting to the light." It came out even worse than it sounded in my head. Tyr ignored the excuse and grabbed one of the sacks.

35

ELLEN ES CEELY

"Hurry!" He whispered as he began to fill the sack with the food he carried in his arms. My sense of smell was kicking in now. Even wrapped in thick, waxed cloth the scent of smoked meats and cured cheeses was unmistakable.

I kicked myself into gear, breathing steadily as I rummaged through the shelves, trying to find the choicest cuts of meat and cheese. *It needs to hurt.* I thought, wishing it were something less petty than stolen food. *It needs to get his attention.* It only took a few minutes for us to fill up the two sacks. I tied mine off at the top and swung it over my back, the cloth strap tight across my chest. Tyr did the same and we climbed stealthily back up the stairs to the door above.

We listened. Footsteps sounded in the distance followed by muffled voices. We held our breath and waited, fully expecting the door to swing open at any moment as a soldier pointed at us with a sword or a bow and arrow. The footsteps faded away and there was silence again.

Tyr pushed gently on the door, and I exhaled with relief as it swung easily out at the pressure of his hand. The hinges remained silent as we cautiously took stock of our surroundings. No soldiers were visible. It was now or never.

We crept out of the dark hole with our ill-gotten gains and closed the door behind us, fastening the latch the way it had been before. Tyr nodded at me, and I pulled a scrap of fabric out of my pocket, tying it tightly around the latch. I smiled, proud of our success and our creativity. But there was no time to dawdle.

We walked back toward the opening in the wall, staying close to the shadows of the buildings. The sack across my back was getting heavier by the minute, slowing me down more than I'd expected. We paused to watch the two guards as we came nearer. To our dismay, the tall soldier was standing at the opening, quite alert and very much awake. The short, skinny soldier continued to snore from his propped-up position.

My pride dwindled as my heart sank. *What do we do now?* I wondered. *What if he stays awake the rest of the night? What if-* My thoughts were interrupted as a shadow right across from us moved. I nudged Tyr with an elbow and pointed with my chin.

We gaped in amazement as a tall, cloaked figure glided silently over the rubble toward the unsuspecting soldier. One swift knock to the head and he sank backwards into the mysterious figure's arms. The cloaked figure leaned the soldier up against the wall where he'd been when we arrived. With a wave of the arm the figure hopped over the broken-down wall and disappeared from sight into the alleyway.

Tyr and I exchanged a stunned glance and ran for it, stumbling over the rocks and heading toward the river. We grabbed pieces of driftwood and tied them together with rope Tyr had brought. Pushing ourselves into the water, the sacks of food lay tightly on top of our backs. The water was cool and refreshing, a welcome feeling to the adrenaline rush sweat we'd both broken out in. We floated down the rapids staying as close to the shore as we dared.

"Who was that?" Tyr voiced the obvious question we both had.

"Why did they help us?" I asked him in return. We shrugged in unison and continued in silence. The rest of our trip home was uneventful. We arrived home in the wee hours of the morning, soaking wet, to a relieved and watchful Hova.

As the sun rose over Shantu, waking the residents to a new day, Aepep stared unblinkingly at the dirty scrap of fabric on the table before him. His blood boiled just thinking about it. The fabric was dirty and torn with crude charcoal letters etched into it.

Into the shadows you cast us,
So from the shadows we rise,
Until, as Shadows, we emerge: victorious.
We're coming.

Aepep wanted to throw the rag into the fire where it belonged. He wanted to forget about it. It was only a few hams and some chunks of cheese. But the intentionality of it all, the forethought and planning it must have taken to succeed, and the brazen audacity they had to write and leave the stupid piece of cloth in front of him – it all made his blood boil in a way he'd never experienced before. No one had ever threatened his authority. Not like this.

The image of the three children in the courtyard flashed before his eyes again, causing his anger to turn to dread.

ELLEN ES CEELY

The two soldiers stood before him trembling, heads bowed. The tall man was rubbing the back of his head, wincing. The short man was glaring at his feet, dread and anger plastered across his face. Aepep gave them one last cold stare and waved for them to be taken away by the commander of the Governor's Guards.

"Ten lashes each, if you please Commander Jabez." Aepep announced flatly. "Followed by a day in the courtyard stocks. Perhaps they'll think twice, next time, about napping on the job?" Aepep's eyes blazed as his voice scorned the men in front of him.

Jabez nodded and marched the soldiers away. Aepep turned back to stare once more at the dirty piece of fabric before him.

We're coming. The words mocked him.

CHAPTER FIVE

I scrambled through the window of our home, hoping none of the soldiers had seen me. It had been two weeks since we'd stolen the meat and cheese from Aepep's stores. I'd hoped for a reaction, but I hadn't expected such a forceful one. Aepep quickly went from leaving the Slums deserted of any soldiers to marching pairs of them down every street at random times of the day.

He'd posted notices throughout the Slums and the Commoner's Sector indicating what would be done to anyone who was found in possession of the stolen goods. He was angry. I'd never seen him react this way before. We'd kept a low profile, only climbing up on the roof to check on our garden at night. So far, no one had perceived that our boarded-up shack was inhabited. Soldiers performed randomized searches throughout the neighborhood, but they'd found nothing. What they did find left most of them disgusted and eager to leave.

"They've probably never dealt with stench and bugs." I muttered bitterly to Tyr as we stood in a crowd watching them pick through a windowless hovel nearby. A widow and her three boys looked on in silence as the soldiers gingerly picked things up or nudged them with their feet. It wasn't out of reverence or respect that they dealt so gingerly with these things, but out of fear of what they might uncover or inhale.

"Bunch of weak stomached wimps." I hissed a little louder. Tyr elbowed me in the ribs as Hova gave me her classic, "shut up and be still" look. For the most part we all sat quietly at home for two weeks. Laughing and grinning at one another, we toasted chunks of stale bread and cheese over the stove, gnawing on beautiful bits of cured meat as the cheese melted.

"Did anyone see you?" Tyr asked as I brushed my hands off and adjusted the fabric over the opening. I turned to answer him. My smile froze as I caught sight of the three extra figures in the room.

"Uh...no," I sputtered as my eyes adjusted to the dim room. I leaned in close to Tyr's ear. "Who are they?" I asked, nodding toward the three new children, struggling to make out their faces.

"My name is Kaimbe," The older boy, perhaps fifteen or sixteen years old, spoke up. He was tall, with dark hair and skin, muscular underneath the too-small-for-him tunic and pants he wore. There was a gentleness to his voice I was not expecting. "These are my brothers, River and Ryder." He gestured to the two timid boys, twins who highly resembled their older, stronger brother. The two of them looked to be about ten years old. All three of them looked familiar, but I couldn't figure out why. I nodded at them, tilting my head.

"Their mother is the woman you call 'the widow' down the street." Hova broke in bluntly. "That's why they look familiar." I flushed and glared at her, embarrassed she'd discerned what I was trying to do and that she'd called me out in front of them.

"Thank you, Hova." I said, curtly. She ignored me as she continued to sew whatever she was working on in her corner of the room, leaning close to a crack of sunlight coming through a boarded-up window. I pulled Tyr further away from the others. "What do they want? Why are they here?" I asked him, my brain calculating how much food we had and how much they might use up.

"They want to join up. They want to be part of our group, to be 'a Shadow'." His whisper was loud and excited. I was certain everyone in the room could hear it. "Rumors have spread throughout the Slums, Yuvraj. The note we left for Aepep has been recited to anyone who will listen. Aepep is claiming there's a secret group of rebels hiding in the Slums, plotting for the overthrow of Shantu." Tyr's voice was oozing with enthusiasm. I looked over his shoulder at the three boys standing close by Hova, watching me with cautious eyes.

"Where will they live?" I asked, hesitant at the thought of squeezing them into our home.

"With their mother, of course." Tyr said, the tone of his voice fading into slight disgust at the question. "They're not about to leave her alone. They'll come here to organize strikes on Aepep and we can work with them to find food." Tyr said, his eye glazing over as he dreamed about all the things we could do together. "The more who join us, the stronger we become! Don't you see, Yuvraj?" He stared at me, reaching out to grasp my right shoulder and staring me in the eye.

"Of course," I said, nodding my head, trying not to wince at the strong hand digging into my shoulder. "Of course, the plan has always been to grow in number but..." My voice faded as I looked at the newcomers again. "Are you sure we can trust them?" I whispered it as quietly as possible, afraid of offending them. "What if they're only doing this to turn us in to Aepep for some kind of reward?" I asked, anxiety filling my heart as I tried to come up with a plan for what we would do if we were betrayed. "Are they even his children?" The words came out more defensive and demanding than I expected. Tyr pursed his lips as he looked at me.

"I thought, from the very beginning," My half-brother's voice was stern. "That the idea of becoming Shadows, of banding together, was for anyone who had been cast into the shadows and labeled a gutter rat?" The judgment in his expression caught me off guard. I knew he was right. "Being related to Aepep has nothing to do with being a Shadow."

"Well, how do you know they can be trusted?" I asked, shrugging his hand off my shoulder. *What if they were sent by Aepep himself? Am I just supposed to welcome them with open arms and ignore the fact that they might be spies?* I thought.

"How do you know they can't?" Tyr retorted, folding his arms in front of him. We stared at each other in silence.

"Ahem," Kaimbe cleared his throat. "If it helps at all, Governor Aepep's soldiers just destroyed the only home we have." He shifted uncomfortably on his feet. The twins stood on either side of him, grabbing onto his massive hands. His speech sounded odd to me. There was a harshness to the words even though his voice was gentle, as if he was clipping them short the way I'd seen a gardener clip the bushes in the Governor's Grounds.

"My mother isn't from Shantu." He said, uninvitedly pulling up a stool to sit down. He placed a protective arm around the waist of each boy and drew them close. As I watched him squat on the small stool, I couldn't help but think how much he looked like a frog with his long legs. "She was brought here a long time ago by a pirate king. She served as his maid and in return he set her up here in the slums." The gentleness never faded. We all knew what he really meant when he called his mother a maid.

"Does she still work for him?" I asked, curious to see how he'd respond.

"No." Kaimbe responded, shaking his head. "He gave up her services when Governor Aepep hired him to be the Commander of the trading barges that carry goods across the Sea." Kaimbe met my gaze without any hint of shame or embarrassment. "He got married. Settled down. You've probably seen him at Assemblies or down by the Sea if you've ever ventured down to the docks."

My mind raced as I thought through all the high ranking officials I'd ever caught sight of. Suddenly it dawned on me, and I asked, a little too loudly, "Is he the one with the giant hat that has an enormous feather stuck in it?" I was staring wide-eyed at the three boys now. "The one with the long, pointy beard? The one that never smiles and even Aepep seems to respect?" I hadn't seen the man in quite some time, but it was summer and that probably meant it was the peak time for trade and shipping across the Sea.

"Yes," Kaimbe said, nodding. "His name is Aruj." It was a simple statement. *Born of the sun.* I thought to myself. *Somehow it seems fitting for a pirate king to have a name like Aruj.* Kaimbe's desire to join our resistance was making sense now. The anxiety in my body dissipated. Maybe he didn't have a bone to pick with Aepep directly, but he certainly had a justified interest in causing as much pain as possible to the man who employed his father. *And by default,* My logic followed through my thinking, *to the father himself.*

"I have two more questions." I said, walking over to where Kaimbe sat, pulling up a stool to join him. "Why do you want to join us?" I glanced at the two young boys and then met the older boy's gaze. "And will you abide by the rules Tyr and I put in place to protect the Shadows?" I ignored the scoff I heard in response to my question from Hova's corner.

"My mother deserves better," Kaimbe's voice was quiet and intense. "River and Ryder deserve better." He said, still holding the boys next to him. "It's time, as you've both said," Kaimbe looked from me to Tyr, who had come to stand beside me. "It's time for us to emerge victorious!" The sincere passion in his voice was unmistakable. "It's time for them to tremble when they approach the shadows, rather than us hiding in them with outstretched arms, begging to be treated as the children of royalty we are." It was anger now, just a small flicker of it, but anger all the same that crept into Kaimbe's words.

"Your note brought us hope!" The boy leaned forward. "If one note and some stolen goods can make Aepep this nervous, then you must be doing something right. And I want to do that something with you!"

"I'm sorry to have doubted you." I said, holding out my hand and smiling. "Tyr was right to trust you." Kaimbe reached out and shook my hand. His grip was firm and strong. "Welcome to the Shadows." I said, butterflies hatching in my stomach as I uttered the phrase for the first time.

AEPEP STOOD AT THE open window of his regal bedroom chamber, staring out over Shantu City. The sound of the marketplace closing for the day echoed in the distance as the sun lowered over the horizon, vendors crying out last-minute deals on stale bread and leftover vegetables.

"Two weeks," He muttered. "It's been two weeks and still they cannot find the food or the thieves that stole it." He clenched his fists and jaw as he thought about the reported rumors that were reaching the soldiers.

"I can help you." The harsh voice made the governor's hair stand up all along his arms. He jumped and whipped around to face the intruder, one hand on his sword, the other outstretched, ready to use any magic necessary. "What's the matter, uncle," Chiwa cackled from beneath the hood of her cloak. She was sitting on the foot of the bed, her feet barely reaching the floor. "No warm welcome for your favorite niece?"

"Chiwa," Aepep managed, forcing himself to relax. "What a surprise." He'd thought about adding the word 'pleasant' in there but couldn't bring himself to utter the lie. "How did you get into my private chambers?" He couldn't help but ask the question.

"Oh, uncle." Chiwa said, leaning back on her arms as she did so. "If there's one thing my dearly departed father taught me," The emphasis was obvious and excessive. "It was to find my way in and back out of wherever I desire to be."

"Departed?" Aepep inquired, letting go of his sword and moving as calmly as possible toward the drink cupboard at the far side of the room.

"Yes." She responded, coldly. "He tried to take something from me. He paid for it with his life." Her tone sent chills down his spine, causing him to pause briefly as he poured wine into two glasses.

"May I ask what he tried to take?" Aepep asked, turning back around to offer her the wine, holding it out like an invitation a few paces from where she sat on the bed. Chiwa stood up and walked toward him with an outstretched hand. He stared at her wrist, bruised and scratched.

"My dignity." She replied through gritted teeth, snatching the wine away from him. Aepep's mind swirled as he put the pieces of the puzzle together.

"You mean..." His voice trailed off before he could finish asking the question. Caution voiced her opinion in his head as he turned back to the open window. "What can I do for you, Chiwa?"

"It's what I can do for you." She responded, curtly. "You have a rebellion brewing. Your soldiers are sorely incompetent. I can, obviously, get into wherever I want to be." She paused to gloat and sip on the wine."

"What do you propose?" The governor asked, sipping his own wine.

"I know the streets of the Slums better than your soldiers know the lumps of the mattresses in their bunks." Chiwa's disdain was obvious. "I'll help you find these children, these 'Shadows'," She cackled, low and slow. "And you'll help me find one, or both, of the Elves." She took another swig of wine.

"How do I know you won't use your powers against me?" Aepep asked, turning to face his niece. "How do I know you don't want to take over Shantu?" He waited, prepared for anything she threw at him.

"Uncle," Chiwa began, setting down her empty wineglass. "Why would I want this stinking, rotting, pitiful excuse for a city, when I might have an entire land to myself?" Although she meant it as an insult, it was a fair question, and the response Aepep had hoped for.

The Governor studied his niece, sipping his wine slowly. *If I agree and succeed in finding one of the Elven ladies, I lose nothing but information.* He pondered the idea, weighing what he might gain. *If I agree and fail, I may risk her anger, but I also gain a powerful ally in the streets.*

"There's no question about it." Aepep finally said, smiling and setting down his own wineglass. He grabbed a small knife out of his belt and slit his hand, offering the knife to his niece. "I give you my blood oath." He said, holding out the bleeding hand and solemnly bowing his forehead. Without a second's hesitation, the young witch lowered her hood and grabbed the knife from his hand, slitting her left hand to match his.

"I give you my blood oath." She swore, clasping her uncle's bleeding flesh to her own. Her freezing gaze pierced his eyes as he realized how warm her dripping blood was while her hand remained cold to the touch. *Fire and ice.* He thought to himself. *Ice and fire. It is the only way she stands before me. She sets fire to her soul and her heart retaliates with ice.*

"It was quite brilliant." The woman spoke softly, her voice strong and beautiful. It was the kind of voice that made me want to cry just listening to it. It was melodious and poetic. I stared at the mysterious figure that had appeared as if from nowhere. Swallowing, I shifted from one foot to the other.

"I, uh - I'm not sure I know what you mean?" I put the statement to her like a question, stuttering and standing up straight with my hands in nervous fists, ready to throw a punch if she decided to attack. She was leaning against the wall of the alleyway, closing me in. I'd noticed some scraps of wood and fabric and had wandered in to grab them. I figured both might earn me a cordial grunt from Hova. The woman had appeared as if from nowhere, blocking out the waning sunlight as soon as I'd bent over to pick up my treasures. Those same treasures that now lay at my feet in a heap.

"Are you frightened, Yuvraj?" Her voice contained something I didn't have a name for. An emotion, or a sentiment, or a quality I felt should tell me something about her. *Kindness.* The word passed through my brain as I mulled over her question, trying to decide how to answer it.

"Yes." I managed. There was something about her that made me want to tell the truth. She made me highly aware of how vulnerable I was and yet I wanted to do better, to live better, to be better, because of her voice. I wanted to tell the truth. The thoughts and feelings were uncomfortable and unnerving. "Yes, I'm frightened." I said, my voice shaking slightly as it uttered the words.

"Of me?" She asked.

I wonder what she looks like. I thought to myself. *Does her voice match her face? Is she beautiful? Is she old or young or somewhere in between?* I wondered silently. Then I wondered at my own curiosity over something so trivial at a time when my life might end at any moment if she proved to be other than what I hoped for.

"Yes. Of you. But also-" I stopped, biting my lip, shocked at the sudden urge I had to unburden my soul, to tell her about my life and my fears and my hopes and dreams.

"Yes?" She asked, still as ever, a mere dark cloak with the sun at her back a mere shadow. The idea of bearing my soul to her made my heart race as a new hope flitted through my mind.

"I'm afraid all the time. I'm afraid of being found by the soldiers." I gulped. "I'm afraid of being killed or beaten or getting my hand cut off for stealing. I'm afraid of life in general." I couldn't stop the words from tumbling out, faster and faster. "I'm afraid of you, but I'm more afraid of failing."

"Failing at what?" She prodded.

"I'm afraid of failing to defeat my father. I'm afraid of failing to get the justice I deserve. I'm afraid of failing to become a true Shadow." I was breathing heavily now, as if I'd just run a long distance.

"Good." She sounded secretly delighted and satisfied with herself. She pushed away from the wall and walked in my direction, kneeling in front of me so our faces were on the same level. I shifted uncomfortably. *Am I dreaming?* I wondered for the first time. The sun was at its most beautiful now, turning the skyline a beautiful shade of pink at the end of the alleyway. *They'll be wondering where I am.* I thought to myself as my eyes drifted momentarily away from the kneeling woman before me.

"Into the shadows you cast us," She whispered, reaching out with a hand gloved in black. "So from the shadows we rise," The words Tyr and I had written sounded different, fresh, almost inspiring coming from her. "Until, as Shadows, we emerge:

victorious. We're coming!" Her added emphasis hit my ears like music. It sounded more like a rebellious war call and less like a threat. I stared into the stranger's hood, searching for a face as I held out my hand to meet hers. She squeezed it in return to greet me.

With her free hand she reached up and lowered her hood. I blinked at first, wondering if my eyes were playing tricks on me in the fading sunlight. Taking a step back I gasped as my eyes latched onto her straight, thick, bright white hair pulled into intricate braids behind ears like none I'd ever seen before. They were long and pointed. My eyes traveled from her ears, across her smooth, dark skin, to her eyes. Such eyes I'd never imagined could exist, bright blue with flecks of gold.

She was beautiful, but not in the way I had imagined, rather in an almost sacred way. She was strong and poised, tall and slender. Her jaw and lips were like finely carved stone, and the tiny lines around her breathtaking eyes were the only betrayal that her age did not match her looks.

"Who are you?" I whispered, awe completely consuming me.

"My name is Chantrea." She said, smiling. "I want to help you become a true Shadow of Shantu."

Chapter Six

My heart pounded as I gasped for air in the pitch-black room. Sweat dripping down my forehead, I opened and closed my eyes, desperate to see something. *The glow of the hot stove.* I thought to myself. *The twinkle of a dying streetlamp or the waning moonlight and the star-studded sky...anything but this darkness.* I was hugging my knees to my chest, rocking back and forth, trying desperately to get a grip.

'Yuvraj,' I heard Chantrea's voice in the dark recesses of my mind, forcing its way through the panic and fear. *'Yuvraj, you are not alone! You must fight the fear, give into the very thing that paralyzes you. Only when you find the courage to face your darkest fears will you be able to unleash the magic living within you!'* I took a deep breath, clenching my knees with my hands, tired and dizzy from the lack of oxygen.

I knew where I was. I knew I was safe. I knew I could give up at any moment and Chantrea would stop the training. But it didn't matter what I knew. *It's so dark.* I thought on repeat. *I can feel the closet closing in around me.* The thought sent a shiver down my spine as I sank into the memories. My mother's voice came to me, everything from laughter to sobs to shrieks of terror to noises I wished I didn't understand.

SON OF KINGS

"Leave her alone." I whispered, hopelessness filling every part of my body, feeling frozen and limp all at the same time. "Leave my mother alone." My voice trembled. I wanted to stand up, to charge out of the room and strangle the men using and abusing my mother with my bare hands. I wanted to kick them, to slap them, to tie them up and hurt them in as many ways as I could imagine. *I want them to beg for me to stop the way I begged them.* I thought, filling with shame.

'Keep going, Yuvraj.' Chantrea coaxed me. I was still lying on my side with my knees curled up to my chest, burying my face into my knees as I rocked back and forth. I opened my eyes slowly. The darkness was so intense, so deep, so exactly as it had been so many times before. Ghosts of leather belts falling heavily across my back made me bite my upper lip to keep from crying out from pain that lived in the scars hiding beneath my ragged clothing.

'Deeper, Yuvraj.' Chantrea pushed again. *'Let out the anger and the sorrow. The magic will follow.'* I relaxed my arms, unclenching my fists and extending my legs so my feet reached the wall. I took a deep breath, pushing myself up to a sitting position. A lump formed in my throat as a tear slid down my right cheek.

"I don't want to cry." I choked out the words. "I don't want to cry, Chantrea." I knew she heard me, but silence met my voice. The rock in my stomach pushed its way up into my chest, the pain of it worse than all the memories and ghosts appearing in the darkness like white paint on a black canvas.

I rocked again. Back and forth, back and forth, urging the memories to go back to where they came from, pleading with them to disappear as quickly as they'd come. "I don't want to cry!" I screamed into the void on repeat, stumbling to my feet, feeling for the wall with my hands, leaning against it in exhaustion.

"Yuvraj..." The whisper met my ears, cutting off the scream that echoed out from the deepest recesses of my being. My mother's face floated in front of my eyes. Her sad, thin face smiling at me in disappointment. "Stop screaming. They might hear you." She looked away as she said the words, shame and defeat at the core of her tone. "Don't you care about me at all? Don't you care how I'm treated?" Guilt reared its ugly head as her question sank deep into my soul. "You need to be quiet, Yuvraj." She stared at me with an intensity I'd forgotten. "You need to stay hidden, in control, or you might get beaten again. I might get hit." She shrugged her shoulders coldly. I wanted to run, to escape her look of judgment.

ELLEN ES CEELY

"Mama, I..." My voice drifted off into the darkness as she disappeared and the belt fell, impossibly, across my back once more, cutting painfully into my skin. I curled up into a ball, losing control as a deep groan of pain came screaming out from somewhere I'd never known existed. *It hurts to cry*. I thought, clenching my ribs as I convulsed, sobbing uncontrollably. *But it hurts even more to hold it in.* My inner voice reasoned with me.

How long I lay there with my eyes closed, crying it out like a beast of the ancient myths, I do not know. It felt like an eternity. I was cold and alone, crying out the pain of wounds I'd never acknowledged in the closet in which I'd spent the better part of my childhood.

Suddenly, the sobs ceased. I sniffed and sat up, wiping the snot away from my nose with my tunic and rubbing my eyes as I tried once more to open them. Searching for any hint of light, I wondered where Chantrea was and what was real. I felt so free and unhindered, as if a significant weight I hadn't realized I was carrying had fallen off my back.

'Reach out for the light, Yuvraj.' Chantrea's voice was so calm, so beautiful and rich. I held out my right hand, palm up the way she'd shown me. *'You are the son of a powerful wizard,'* Her voice repeated for the hundredth time since we'd first met. *'You carry within you the ability for magic. Hold out your hand and speak the word. The light will come.'* She made it sound so simple.

"Kal." I spoke the word hesitantly, my voice weak, staring into the darkness in search of my outstretched hand. For a split-second a light flickered, my hand came into view holding a bright orb, fading just as quickly back into dark oblivion. I sat in stunned silence, wondering if I'd imagined it.

'Again!' Chantrea's voice urged me. She was excited. *'Louder. Stronger. Remember you do not command the light nor do you doubt its existence, rather, you request that the light reveal itself to you.'*

"Kal!" I spoke the word with a confidence foreign to me. I looked on in amazement as the orb I'd seen flash before my eyes came back into view, this time round and bright and glowing, hovering over my right hand. I brought it in closer, afraid it would disappear if I moved too fast. As if I could frighten it away. I stared as it flickered in my hand, holding my breath, my left hand protectively cupping my right. The door beside me creaked open. Chantrea kneeled next to me in the makeshift closet she'd insisted we build.

SON OF KINGS

"You did it." She said, the pride in her voice evident to anyone listening. I didn't look around. I couldn't speak. Fear rose inside me now the door was open. *How strange.* I thought to myself as I continued to stare at the miraculous light in my hands. *Not long ago the closed door was what sparked fear. Now, it would seem, the open door is the perpetrator.*

"Yuvraj," Chantrea said, gently touching my right arm. "It's time to rest now. Come eat some food. I have much to tell you."

"But what if I let go and the light never comes back?" I whispered to my teacher, verbalizing my fear. I heard her kind laugh, quiet and steady.

"The light will always be there, Yuvraj." She replied. "You just have to look for it." She waited for a few more seconds, allowing me a little longer to stare at the strange but comforting light in my hand. "It's time to let it go, Yuvraj. You can practice more later." She squeezed my arm. "Simply close your hand and the light will go to sleep."

Fighting against everything I wanted to do, I obeyed. The light disappeared as magically as it had appeared. I sighed as I lost sight of it. Chantrea stood up and held out a hand. I looked up at her and took it, surprised at my own wobbling.

My stomach growled furiously, awakening my mind to the idea of food. I looked around the room. Tyr and the other boys sat next to the window, as far away from the closet door as one could get, obviously avoiding my gaze by staring at the ceiling, the floor, or the fascinating lines of their hands.

I searched for Hova and found her in her usual seat, quietly sewing by the light of the dim fire. I squinted at her face, noticing the glint of water on her cheeks in the firelight. *She's been crying.* I thought, shocked at the sight. I'd never seen Hova cry before. I'd never seen her show any kind of weakness before. Hova was always so serene and strong and level-headed. Even as the youngest among us, she was still somehow the most mature person I knew.

"Hova...I...uh..." I fumbled over my words, trying to figure out how to ask her what was wrong. *Has she been crying...for me?* My question went unasked. She responded to my fumbling attempt by tossing aside her sewing, furiously wiping at her face and jumping up to stoke the fire unnecessarily. Her furious wiping suddenly reminded me that my face was covered in snot and tear-streaked dirt.

"Here," She said, pushing a bowl of something into my hands. "Eat. I'm sure you're hungry." She returned to her seat beside the fire without looking me in the eye, picking up her sewing with an intensity I'd never seen.

"Thank you." I spoke to her back, feeling oddly at peace with how messy I looked. Hova nodded in response. I sat down with my food next to the stove, across from the seamstress. It was hot, but I didn't mind. Plus, there was nowhere else to sit unless I wanted to sit on the floor. The sound of rain reached my ears, a slow, drizzling rain.

"You did well, Yuvraj." Chantrea's rich voice broke through my thoughts as I attacked the lentil and ham soup in my hands, dipping a wedge of bread into it and looking around for cheese. "You are progressing well. Do you have any questions?" She stared at me as she asked.

"How did you know?" I asked, louder than I expected, my hands poised over the bowl in my lap as I turned to meet her stare. "And why won't anyone else look me in the eye?" I was shocked at my own blunt openness.

"Didn't you believe me?" She responded, the firelight causing me to notice her strange, beautiful eyes. I'd grown more comfortable with her appearance, but I still didn't know what to make of her. I shook my head in response, chewing rapidly.

"Then why did you agree to have me train you?" She asked, still not answering the questions I'd asked her, the questions she'd invited me to ask. I chewed and swallowed hard. "Why did you trust me, Yuvraj?"

"You told me I was the son of a wizard!" I said, sputtering. "I thought maybe you were crazy. But I know we need help if we're going to change Shantu." I shrugged my shoulders. "I didn't think I could actually wield magic. I just, that is, I just went along with it. The only reason I believe magic exists is, well, because you exist." She looked sad when I said this, so I stumbled quickly on. "Plus, you talk inside my head!" The smile returned to her face.

"Do you believe me now?" She asked. "Do you understand how much I have to show you?" She sounded desperate, excited. I took another bite of my food, thinking through everything I'd just experienced.

"I believe you." I nodded. "But you still haven't answered my questions. I have so many more." As I spoke, I broke off a piece of cheese, stuck it on top of my bread then laid the bread on top of the metal grate of the stove to toast. I watched as the cheese quickly bubbled up.

"I'm sorry." She said, laughing at my honesty. "You're right, I haven't answered your questions. Your friends," she said, gesturing in the general direction of the evasive Tyr, Kai, River and Ryder. "Are embarrassed and slightly afraid. They don't know what to do. They've never heard someone sob before, and they've definitely never seen someone hold a hovering orb of light in their hand before!" She laughed as the boys twisted in their seats.

"And Hova?" I asked in a quieter tone. The girl never looked up; her hands never paused. A tear slid down Hova's face and I grew agitated as I watched it fall. It surprised me that Tyr didn't seem to notice, that he wasn't sitting next to his sister, comforting her. Chantrea's laugh faded.

"Hova has her own reasons." Was the cautious reply I received. It was unsatisfactory, but I knew it was all I would get. *For now, anyway.* I thought to myself, determined to get the truth out of Hova if it was the last thing I did. I moved on.

"Who are you?" I asked Chantrea, sliding my bubbling piece of toast off the stove and tossing it from my left fingers to my right then back again, blowing to cool it down. I'd been afraid to ask her questions, partly because I'd been afraid of what answers I might receive. Even Tyr, my fearless half-brother, had been too afraid to ask the question. The room went silent, and I looked around to see everyone watching Chantrea, waiting for her answer. Even Hova's industrious fingers were still.

"Gather 'round children," Chantrea whispered, causing the hair to stand up straight on my arms. *She's using my lines.* I thought, realizing she must have been in the alleyway with us, unseen. "And I will tell you the greatest, saddest, fairy tale ever to exist!"

A SMALL FIGURE CLAD in gray stood motionless underneath a crumbling awning in the Slums as the moon rose in the clouded, rainy sky above. The weather had chased anyone other than the most desperate off the streets. The few who remained, sat beneath awnings much like this one, waiting for a random stranger to come along and do business.

Chiwa had been watching from her spot all day, but no one went in or out of the dilapidated excuse for a home. The boarded-up windows and doors gave off the appearance of vacancy, but the plants that peaked up from the slanted roof and the slivers of light she thought she saw through cracks in the boards all led the witch to believe she was on the right trail.

"Curses." She muttered under her breath, her veins glowing bright red beneath her gray cloak as she seethed with disgust. "Where are they?" She had to admit that even she was growing tired and hungry. They'd have to come out eventually unless she had the wrong place. But she was almost positive she'd seen that strange little girl disappear when she'd reached this corner.

Her mind wandered to her last exchange with her father, the catalyst for her solitary life of working with Aepep. Her stomach continued to churn, and her skin crawled once more. Ethan had whispered into her ear, towering above her slight frame. She hugged her arms beneath her cloak and leaned back against the alleyway wall, closing her eyes briefly to stop the memory from returning.

"You've gone mad!" She'd exclaimed in shock, stepping quickly away from the only parent she'd ever known. "I will not do it." Her defiance was weak at first. *Surely he's playing a sick joke on me?* She'd thought to herself. *No father would demand such a revolting thing of his daughter.*

"Mad?!" He'd exclaimed, the green in his eyes glowing wickedly as he laughed and took long steps in her direction, reaching out to grab her wrist. "You swore your loyalty to me!" He'd screamed the words into her face, his nails digging into her skin. "Need I remind you of your apprenticeship vows?" He'd hissed, pulling her face roughly up to his. "You pledged your life to me: body, mind, soul, and spirit. You swore an oath sealed by blood, fire, and ice!" Chiwa had tried to pull away from him, tried to remind him of his own oath sealed by the same blood, fire, and ice. But his grip was impossible to get away from and he'd gone beyond the point of reason.

"If you wish to become all I have destined you to be, if you wish to leave apprenticeship behind and embrace your full power as a witch, you must obey!" He'd screamed the last few words, slamming Chiwa's body up against the wall behind her as one hand clawed roughly at her dress and the other reached around her neck to hold her still.

The next few minutes had gone by in a blur. Something deep inside of Chiwa had broken free – or maybe just broken – rushing up into the forefront of her mind as a means of protection. A power, an anger, and a fear unlike any Chiwa had ever known had all mixed into one powerful feeling she had no name for. One minute she was choking against a wall. The next minute she stood over her father, shrieking at him to stop as she threw a constant stream of fire from her hands, the veins of her entire body burning a bright, fierce red.

The memory faded and Chiwa opened her eyes to the alley where she stood. She replayed how she'd tossed Ethan's warped and lifeless body into the depths of the river, watching until he'd disappeared underneath the slow current that carried him out to the Sea. The witch looked once more at the Slum house in front of her, tired and cold from the memory that wouldn't leave her alone.

"Curses." She muttered again, sighing and releasing her arms from their hug to push herself away from the wall. Turning to leave she stopped short as a muffled sobbing moan reached her ears. She sucked in her breath at the sound of it tumbling through the growing shadows, picking up speed and depth with each rain drop it absorbed. Each sob that followed communicated a different woe, a separate grief that had never been expressed until now. The soul that unleashed the sobs made Chiwa's heartbeat race, her adrenaline rushing as the pain of it all filled her with energy and a renewed sense of purpose.

Chantrea. The witch smirked as she turned back around to cross the road silently, ducking under the sliver of roof overhang outside the dilapidated building.

CHAPTER SEVEN

"Gather 'round children," Chantrea whispered. "And I will tell you the greatest, saddest, fairy tale ever to exist!" The boys sitting near the entrance came obediently nearer the fire, joining Hova and me where we sat. Chantrea looked around at each of us, her bright, blue-gold eyes staring into our very souls. A slight smile hovered at the corners of her mouth. She was leaning forward, pausing as we all waited for her tale of magic. The steady downfall of rain ensured we wouldn't have any unwanted visitors.

"Once upon a time," The beautiful voice began. "In a magical land called Zale, there lived a wizard named Azai. Azai was a kind man who lived in a castle and ruled over the inhabitants of what had, unimaginatively, become Castle Island." I found myself a little indignant as I took a bite of my cheesy bread. *This magical land doesn't sound so impressive.* I thought to myself as I listened. *Also, what does a wizard in a faraway castle have to do with us?*

"Azai was a kind and well-meaning man. He was also a powerful wizard and he ruled the land of Zale with other powerful leaders. Among the leaders of Zale were the Elven Queen of the Dryad Forest, the Faerie King of the Faerie Mountains, the Nyad goddess of the Nyad Sea, and the great Dwarf Elder whose people dwelt deep beneath the surface of the far, Northern peaks of the Faerie Mountains."

SON OF KINGS

Chantrea had my attention now. I stared at her, my mouth stuffed with bread, trying to figure out if she was making fun of us.

"Azai, as I said, was a kind man and an exemplary leader who cared deeply for the people who depended on him. Due in part to his great power as a wizard, he was able to establish a peace treaty with the other rulers and worked hard to build up another of the islands in the great Nyad Sea which came to be called City Island." My faith in her words wavered between complete disbelief in the existence of such fantastical creatures and the firm admission that such boring names for important places would never be chosen in a made-up story. *Only real people could think of such mundane names for the places they inhabit.*

"Yet for all his wisdom and impressive power as a wizard, Azai had one flaw: he was foolish in believing he knew best." Chantrea stared at me as she said this, making me squirm uncomfortably in my seat. I felt the remark aimed as a rebuke or a caution specifically for me. "As the land of Zale grew in wealth and prosperity, Azai feared what might happen if anyone were to find them and try to take the land from them. High in the tower of his castle, tucked away in his magnificent library, Azai came across an ancient manuscript of myths and legends.

"As the wizard read through the crumbling manuscript, he found a myth about a powerful witch who used dark magic to control her enemies through their dreams. This witch cursed any who stood against her with unending nightmares, nightmares that plagued them until they went mad or died. In his fear, and without the knowledge or permission of the other rulers of Zale, Azai worked tirelessly to create the greatest weapon he could think of. He used this myth as inspiration and guidance.

"Azai worked for months on end, piecing together a book of strong, dark magic, hiding it from anyone who came to see him, refusing to divulge what he spent his days doing. Castle Island and City Island continued in daily life as always, but the other rulers of the land worried about the state of the wizard's mind. Each time they saw him at the great council meetings, he looked more tired, paranoid, and distant than the time before. His gentle smile, keen mind for business and fair treatment had always been an exceptional asset to the council, but he had grown strange and distrusting.

"Soon, rumors spread from Castle Island and reached the ears of the other rulers. Rumors of people going mad, and inexplicable acts of cruelty and violence grew in number. Concerned for the well-being of Zale, the high council called a secret meeting without inviting Azai. They agreed it was time to call the wizard in and question him.

"The Nyad goddess sent word to Azai, requesting his presence at the next council meeting. Little did the council know that Azai was planning to have a demonstration of his new weapon for them, to show them how his creation might protect them from the enemies he'd come to believe Zale had.

"In creating the book, Azai went to dark places deep within his own mind and soul. As he'd practiced using the book on the inhabitants of Castle Island, their fear had gone from terrifying him to fascinating him. He'd grown obsessed with how to manipulate their dreams so that the deepest amount of terror would enter their souls. He'd discovered he could cause them to dream even when they weren't sleeping." Chantrea paused for a second, reaching for a cup of water and listening to the rain outside. We all continued to sit in silence, staring at her, waiting for the rest of the story.

"The night before the council meeting, as Azai was practicing his power on his subjects, something in the wizard's brain fractured. In a fit of paranoia, rage, and bloodthirsty glee, the wizard unleashed the full power of the book he'd created. Everyone in the castle turned on each other in fits of anger and terror." Chantrea took a deep breath and let it out slowly through clenched teeth. Her eyes were distant, as if she'd traveled far away from us and was looking at something we could not see. "We heard the cries of the inhabitants far across the water where we lived in the peace of the Nyad Forest. Their screams of terror and pleas for help sent a chill into my heart and I watched them in my mind's eye as they killed each other."

Silence continued for a few moments. I had so many questions I was practically bursting, but I bit my lip and remained still as Hova shook her head at me disapprovingly.

"By the time we reached Castle Island with the Nyad gods and goddesses and the Faerie King and the Dwarf Elder, Azai was nowhere to be found. The sight that met our eyes haunts me to this day. The bodies strewn about the castle, the look of terror in the eyes of all who died, the people who had jumped from the walls of the castle to their death, the hands around throats and the bloodied shovels - it was horrific. I have never witnessed such gruesome quiet before in my life."

Our companion fell silent again. I fidgeted in my seat, longing to hear more. Hova, to my surprise, stood up and walked over to Chantrea. The little girl took one of the Elf's hand's in both of her own.

"What happened next?" She asked. It was such a strange sight, the small child in a pieced together outfit of scrap fabric standing before the tallest woman any of us had ever seen, cloaked in black. One portrayed raw grit and stubbornness while the other revealed unmatched elegance. Chantrea's eyes watered as she focused on Hova and a smile broke across her face.

"We tried to find Azai. We climbed high to the tower he'd used as his library, the stairs lined with dead bodies. The door was ajar when we reached the top of the stairs and we walked in, hoping to find the wizard with an explanation. But no one was there. He'd vanished."

"Where did he go?" I blurted out. I believed I knew the answer, but I needed her to say the words out loud.

"When he came to his senses, Azai was horrified at what he'd done to his own people." Chantrea turned toward me as she spoke. "He took the book he created, ran down from his library tower, and transported himself by magic to another world. We don't believe he had a plan other than to get away. He was afraid. He realized he'd be banished or put to death for what he'd done. He also knew we would destroy the book if we ever found out about it. The mind of a broken wizard is a strange and dangerous thing. As much as he regretted his actions, he could not bear the thought of watching his precious creation be destroyed.

"Yes," Chantrea nodded at me. "He came here. Long before Shantu was a town, much less a 'great city'. Azai, the powerful wizard from Zale, opened a magic doorway and traveled to this land. For many years, we had no idea where he'd escaped to. We stopped looking." Regret came into her eyes. "We thought maybe he'd somehow journeyed through the Faerie Mountains to a land we'd never known, or that he'd taken to the Salt Lands to live out his days in exile.

"It was the wrong choice, but the choice we made just the same. There's no going back to fix our mistakes. We all know that. The damage has been done." I got the impression she was talking about something other than the dead bodies strewn all over Castle Island. But I didn't care about that in the moment.

"What did he do here?" Tyr asked, beating me to the question. "What happened to the book he created?" Chantrea looked at my half-brother with a strained smile.

"He united the land, of course!" The sarcasm in her voice startled me. "I'm sorry." She said, inclining her head in apology. "He appointed himself the ruler of this chunk of territory, gathering the scattered farmers around him. He was charismatic and charming. The local people were easy to convince he was the best thing to ever happen to them. He spoke of wealth and comfort, of how great the land could be if they joined together and followed him. Soon, there was a town. Not much later it grew into a city.

"As for the book..." Chantrea's voice drifted off. "Yes," she said after a momentary pause. "It still exists." We waited for her to say more, but she refused and switched back to Azai.

"Azai built the Governor's Grounds. He is the one who divided the city the way it is now: Rich, Common People, and Slums. He fell in love with the daughter of a neighboring nobleman, a simple girl named Kesava. Kesava was beautiful and vain, but not very intelligent. Her simplicity as well as her beauty are what won Azai's heart. He wanted a lady that would look good in his house, but one that wouldn't ask too many questions. Kesava was the perfect match for him.

"Soon after they married Kesava became pregnant. She gave birth to Aepep, our current governor," Chantrea glanced between me and Tyr as she spoke. "Your father."

We all sat in silence. I wasn't sure why. None of us could be shocked by the connection, and yet it was a lot to process all at once. Chantrea had said I was descended from a powerful wizard. *But a wizard who went crazy and created an evil book and came from another land to establish the city of Shantu?*

"Does this mean..." My question dragged off as the realization hit me.

Chantrea nodded. "Aepep is a powerful wizard. Azai trained him from a young age in strong, dark magic. He hides his powers well. Most of the population of Shantu has no idea their governor possesses magical powers. He rarely needs to use them, but when he does it's not a pleasant sight." Chantrea's face was like stone.

"Why don't...that is..." Tyr shook his head at our tall companion with confusion and a little disappointment.

"You want to know why you don't have any magical powers?" She asked him. Tyr nodded and I found myself suddenly just as curious. Chantrea shrugged her shoulders. "The ability for magic doesn't always pass from parent to child. It could be delayed in showing up, but it might also not show up at all. It's unpredictable." Chantrea studied the boy's crushed face as he looked away from us. I flushed with pride and embarrassment and guilt. *Why did I get magical powers when Tyr didn't?* I wondered, unsure of what to do with the question.

"Magic is not everything, Tyr." Chantrea said with kind sincerity. "Magic alone will not help you defeat the system you're fighting. Magic is only a tool that can be used in your battle against oppression. Magic is also rarely a sign of a good leader." The words smarted, striking down the pride swelling inside my chest. "You will make an excellent leader. You have already shown that. Don't ever feel embarrassed or apologetic about what you are not. Do we understand one another?" Her voice was firm but kind. Tyr nodded in agreement.

"What happened to Azai and Kesava?" Kaimbe asked, distracting me from my discomfort and annoyance.

"Kesava had another son a few years after Aepep. They named him Ethan. Azai trained him in dark magic as well. He became a powerful wizard, though not as strong as his brother or his father." The tone of Chantrea's voice changed when she spoke about Ethan. It held an emotion akin to hatred. "Kesava herself never learned of any of the magic or of the book. She never once suspected Azai possessed magical powers. He was careful and she was simple. She knew how to get him to give her whatever she wanted.

"Outside of spending time with Azai for her own personal amusement or gain, Kesava lived out much of their marriage looking in a mirror and flaunting her wealth. Several years after Ethan was born, when Aepep was still a young teenager, Kesava became pregnant with a third child, a little girl. The baby was stillborn, and Kesava died giving birth to her.

"Kesava had never been a particularly kind or attentive mother. She was cold and aloof and only cared for her sons when Azai was around. She was especially indifferent toward Ethan. I believe she saw a piece of herself in him and she hated him for it.

"For all his faults and failures, and in spite of all of Kesava's vanity and selfishness, Azai truly loved her. When she died, the last bit of his ability to love died with her. Over the next ten years Azai sank into darkness, drinking and poisoning himself to death. He continued to train his sons in magic and cut himself off from the day-to-day running of Shantu. Before he died, he gave Aepep a choice as the oldest child: he could have Shantu or he could have the book for his inheritance. Whatever Aepep didn't choose would be given to Ethan.

"As you can see, he chose Shantu. Aepep had no desire to try returning to Zale. Though a powerful wizard, he prefers tricks, lazy days, women, and status. In short: Zale sounded like too much work to win over when you already have a kingdom. His key desires are lust and luxury. Though he's naturally prone to violence, he's learned over the years how to control his temper when others are watching, as doing so only increases his status and power. The less involved Azai became in Shantu, the more Aepep took over. By the time Azai died, Aepep was already running the city on his own."

"What happened to the book?" Hova's brow was furrowed. I admittedly hadn't even thought about the book or the fact I had an uncle. I was slightly shocked at Hova's boldness. Tyr had already asked about the book and received a non-answer to his question. Chantrea studied the little girl with a sense of admiration and annoyance.

"You're going to ask whether I want to answer or not, aren't you?"

"What happened to the book?" Hova repeated, brow still furrowed, lips pursed, arms crossed in defiance.

"I suppose you need to know at least part of the story." Chantrea's sighed one of those deep sighs full of pain and regret. "Ethan took the book. He and Aepep grew up ambivalent toward one another. They neither hated nor loved each other. They were willing to help when it was convenient then turn against for personal gain. It was always that way and has continued that way ever since.

"Included in the book on a slip of paper were instructions on how to return to Zale. The book doesn't work here in Shantu. Its magic, unlike the magic of wizards, is tied to the land it was created in. It answers only to the voice of any person powerful enough to wield it. Though not as strong as Aepep, Ethan was still a powerful wizard. He followed the instructions and found his way back to Zale, bringing the book with him.

"I - it's difficult." Chantrea stopped, as if at a loss for words. I swallowed hard, feeling a rock forming in my stomach. "Ethan deceived us all. He came to Zale, settled in the land, married, then unleashed the power of the book. He destroyed lives, peace – the land of Zale as it once was." Chantrea's voice trembled as the detail she left out overwhelmed her. "Today it is a cold land haunted by nightmares that can overpower you at every turn. The book answers to no one and wreaks havoc on the inhabitants.

"We tried to stop Ethan. We tried to stop the book. But we were too late, and we failed." Chantrea's voice was growing more distressed with each word, her eyes were glowing with a depth of grief and shame and sadness I'd never witnessed before. I wanted to look away, but I couldn't.

She continued. "He left the book in Zale and fled back to Shantu, taking with him the child his Faerie wife bore. We came after him. We searched for years on end, trying to catch him and the child, to bring him to justice, to figure out how to destroy the book that holds our country and its people captive, but then..." Her voice faded. Suddenly, Chantrea drew her hood up over her face, hiding it from our view.

"Ethan has destroyed many lives." Chantrea's tone was steady, cold, and detached. "Much like his father his mind has warped with age and the book twisted an already greedy and vain existence. He longs to return to Zale, to rule the land through the power of the book. But he's a coward. He's waiting until his daughter is strong enough to help him return."

I wanted to cry. Instead, I looked over at Hova again only to find her crying softly. Tyr had moved over to his little sister's side and was holding her reluctant hand as she turned her face away from him.

"What's her name?" Tyr asked, calmly. "That is, what's my - my cousin's name?" The word sounded funny. *Cousin. I'm not sure I want to know anything more about my family.* I thought, dread filling my chest.

"Her name is Chiwa." Chantrea answered.

Off to the side, River raised a hand and waited to be called on. It was sweet and comical, a relief in the midst of so much information.

"Yes, River?" Chantrea asked the boy.

"Are you...are you an Elf?" The child's eyes were wide with amazement. What he'd chosen to latch onto was refreshing. Chantrea's chuckled again and she lowered her hood.

ELLEN ES CEELY

"Yes, River, I'm an Elf. A Night Elf. If you ever see me in the moonlight, you'll notice my skin glows blue. I'll show you sometime." She reached out a hand and ruffled his hair.

CHIWA STOOD STILL, HER mind wandering as the group inside the boarded-up hovel continued to talk. The rain was falling, and the moon had risen high above, its light barely burning through the hazy clouds of rain covering the city of Shantu. The witch's body ached with fatigue, as if hearing the story of her father, grandfather, and uncle had somehow drained her of the fire that normally ran through her veins.

At least the fool Elf doesn't know yet that Ethan is dead. Chiwa mused to herself, taking a deep breath and exhaling. *But why the secrecy? Why the failure to mention the bastard boy and his mother? Is her shame so strong she cannot speak the name of the Elven warrior who fell into the hands of the great wizard Ethan?*

Chiwa's lip curled as she thought through the bits of the story Chantrea left out. She wanted to believe it was because of the Elf's own shame, but it seemed like something else was holding her back.

Curses. I need time to think. The witch decided, pushing herself away from her listening spot and walking off into the rain. Working with Aepep was a gamble and a game. She knew where the Elf was and where the children were.

Chantrea was right about the lack of brotherly love and fidelity between Ethan and Aepep. If I tell Aepep where the children are hiding, he'll double-cross me and kill them all. Chiwa thought. *The odds are in my favor for now. What my fool of an uncle doesn't know won't hurt him. Well, not too much.* She thought as she wandered through the deserted streets, heading to her own, now empty, hideous refuge in the Slums of Shantu.

Chapter Eight

"Good. Now, as I lunge, I want you to twirl to the side and aim your sword to swing down and meet mine." Chantrea said, coaching Tyr as she taught him the art of defense and attack with a blade. The Elf had taken to training us in the Woods outside Shantu. Every day after breakfast, we'd spend the morning in a clearing in the Woods. Chantrea taught all of us how to wield a sword and disarm an enemy, but she focused on our specific talents as well.

Tyr was the most adept at sword fighting. It came naturally to him. His footwork was perfect and his ability to guess what his attacker would do next came easily to his calculating brain. At times I envied him as I stumbled through the steps, but my ability to wield magic always reminded me that I had something special to offer.

Kaimbe was gifted with the sword, but Chantrea focused on building his strength. He towered over all of us as a gentle giant. She had him pick up logs, climb trees without any equipment, move rocks, and catch things thrown from halfway across the clearing. His muscles grew every day, bulging through the seams of his clothing until it was almost comical to look at him. The twins, still young and small, were given more lessons in trapping and self-defense.

ELLEN ES CEELY

Hova's training was almost more intense than any of the rest of us. Chantrea gave her a knife and taught her all the self-defense moves she taught the rest of us. Hova's disgust for the sharp little blade was evident, but Chantrea didn't seem to mind. Instead, the strange woman took Hova under her wing and spent most afternoons walking the Woods with the little girl. I would often find them kneeling down to observe something growing in the underbrush. As much as it bored me, I still resented the extra attention Chantrea gave Hova, wishing to join them and understand what they were talking about.

"Good, Tyr," The lesson continued. "Feel the movement throughout your body. As you ground and balance yourself with your feet you must follow my eyes just as much as my hands. What will be my next move? How can you get ahead of me or throw me off my game? You are slowly mastering the art of defense, now it's time for you to develop the strength of attack." Chantrea continued to move through some of her regular moves, giving Tyr the opportunity to come up with something new to do instead of merely blocking her blows.

Sweat dripped down Tyr's forehead as he glanced back and forth between his teacher's eyes and hands. As she swung downwards toward his head, Tyr chose to somersault out of the way instead of blocking her blow. Chantrea's eyebrows rose in surprise as she whirled around to block his incoming lunge toward her.

For the first time since his training began, Tyr had the Elf on the defense. He'd turned the tables. None of the rest of us had managed this. We'd all grown better at protecting ourselves, but it was all I could do to remember my footwork right now much less think ahead to where she might attack next.

"Well done!" Chantrea exclaimed, obvious in how pleased she was with his work. She lowered her sword and bowed to him, signaling the end of their training session. "You are a protector, Tyr. Your very name means battle and I do not take that lightly." Her proud smile fell as she spoke. "Your entire life will be a battle for what is true and right and good in the world. Just be sure you don't become distracted with battling for what you most desire instead. You have it in you to become a great leader in Shantu. Only remember that leadership often involves very little glory or comfort, and so much sacrifice." Her ominous words hung about us as we all waited to see how Tyr would respond.

His eyes never left her face. "I will try." He said, nodding as he sheathed his sword. "But..." He hesitated and turned away.

SON OF KINGS

"What is it?"

"Will Aepep be overthrown? Will we get to enjoy our rightful inheritance?" He asked, biting his lip and avoiding eye contact. Chantrea studied him for a second before looking around at the rest of us, her jaw flexing.

"I cannot tell or promise you any of that. The future is still uncertain." She motioned for us to all draw nearer. We gathered around her in the clearing, the sun rising higher in the sky overhead as it kissed the damp leaves beneath our feet to create the warm scent of the season.

"It's important for you all to understand that I am not here to overthrow Aepep." Chantrea continued, glancing between all of us but focusing on myself and Tyr as she spoke. "All I can do is teach you how to defend and care for yourselves. I cannot tell you whether your hopes of one day running the city of Shantu will be fulfilled. I can promise you, however, that you will have it within your power to help and care for the people of the Slums. Your power will grow and so will your number. Whatever you do, I want you to promise me one thing." She waited for us to nod, the gold in her eyes flickering in the sunshine. I glanced at my companions before following their lead, wary of whether I wanted to make a promise without knowing what it was.

"Promise me that you will pursue the following no matter who joins your ranks or how strong you become. As Shadows of Shantu, you must pursue discipline over pain and honor unto death. Whenever you face an enemy, you must hit hard but show mercy. And always have each other's back. You are family. You are the only family most of you and any other Shadows will ever have." Her voice grew quiet. "Do not forget that."

I turned to my right, sensing someone was watching me. Hova's piercing eyes locked on mine. I wanted to turn away but felt entirely unable. She was so small and fierce. *What is she looking at?* I thought to myself. *Or rather, why is she staring at me?* Swallowing the lump of nerves in my throat, I fidgeted with my tunic. *She's only six years old.* I told myself. *Just turn the other way and ignore her. Why do you care what a little girl thinks about?* I couldn't explain it.

"Yuvraj?" Chantrea said, breaking my concentration and Hova's incessant stare. I turned back, confused and annoyed. The twins snickered quietly.

"Yes?" I stuttered; my voice slightly too loud.

ELLEN ES CEELY

"Do you swear, Yuvraj? Do you swear to uphold the creed I've laid before you as your teacher?" Her mouth smiled but her eyes were dangerous. I briefly contemplated saying no just to see what would happen, but panic rose in my throat before I thought of a challenging reply.

"Yes, sorry." I said, fumbling over the words. "I swear to uphold what you've said." I wasn't sure whether I meant what I said, but I no longer cared. *We need her help.* I thought to myself. *I can't say no even if I want to.*

EARLY MORNINGS IN THE Woods were unmatched by anything I'd experienced. Sometimes, when the voices in my head became too loud and the chaos at home too stifling, I'd rise and leave before dawn. Stuffing a bit of bread into my pocket, I'd grab a small canteen and fill it with fresh water by the river. If I wanted more to eat there were always wild berries and mushrooms to be found.

I explored the Woods outside Shantu until I knew them by heart. They drew me in, casting beautiful shadows around me as the light rose over the tree line. I discovered every hiding place, path, and danger zone that lay within the comfort of those trees. Before Chantrea came along, I'd been too afraid to venture very far outside the gates of Shantu. Her training had given me the confidence I needed to leave my well-known home and make the unknown a source of comfort.

One late Summer morning I made my way through the Woods, winding around the trees with an outstretched arm. The unending tension burning inside me cooled as I walked, the trees seeming to quiet the conflict I experienced within my soul.

I want to be good. My thoughts slowed. *I want to be everything Chantrea expects of me: a strong, kind leader who raises up the people of Shantu. She wants me to be a protector, a guardian, and a servant.* I paused, my arm wrapping around one side of a large maple tree as I leaned my head against it. Closing my eyes, I took a deep breath. *But I want revenge. Surely power would allow me to do more for the people of Shantu than self-sacrifice, wouldn't it?*

Breathing deeply once more, I opened my eyes as the internal battle waged. Small streams of light drifted through the trees. For a moment I forgot the arguing inside my brain and stared up at the leaves as they danced in a slight breeze. The tree I embraced remained solidly in one place, bringing me a comfort I'd come to crave.

"What do you need? Are you in trouble?" An unknown woman's voice sounded not far off. I froze, the air catching in my throat as I lowered my eyes to scan my surroundings. *Is she talking to me?* I wondered, anxiety swarming my brain as I considered what I should do.

"No, I just wanted to give you some food and some news." Chantrea responded, her voice simultaneously enveloping me with relief and curiosity. I continued to search the Woods for a glimpse of Chantrea and the strange woman. Though the light rose steadily, the Woods were dense, and I could not see them. I stopped trying and relaxed against the maple tree, focusing on what I might pick up from their conversation.

"Have you found out where he might be hiding?" The strange woman's voice drifted through the trees. Her tone suggested eagerness and dread all at once.

"I don't believe he's hiding anymore, Estel." Chantrea said.

Ah, Estel. I thought. *Who is Estel?*

After a brief pause, Chantrea continued, "I believe he's dead."

"How do you know?"

"Rumors are circulating among the Governor's Guards. They speak in fear of a small woman who wields fire. They claim to have seen her dragging the body of a man to the river. Chiwa is the only woman who fits their description."

"That doesn't mean he's dead." Estel's voice cracked as she spoke. "She's killed many a man over the years."

Chantrea's silence was interrupted by the laughter of a small child and the gentle sound of running feet. Instinctively, I moved behind the large maple and kneeled, the thick foliage surrounding the tree embracing me in shadow.

As I peered around the trunk, a little boy came into view. He wore a dark green linen shirt with a hood sewn onto the neckline. Laughing, he pounced on a rabbit as it tried to escape, catching it by its back foot. I gazed in amazement as the hood drifted off his head to reveal a curling mass of beautiful silvery-white hair. His skin was a deep brown and his ears pointed toward the sky. Hazel eyes shone in the soft sunlight as he wrestled with the rabbit. He continued laughing as he lay on the ground, the joy of his voice bouncing off the surrounding trees.

"Hadithi!" Chantrea and the other woman came into view. I'd never seen a woman taller than Chantrea, whose forehead came no higher than Estel's nose. Chantrea was slender and elegant, and I knew firsthand that she was nimble and powerful. Estel, however, made the breath catch in my lungs again. She appeared strong enough to toss a boulder and yet gentle enough to rescue a drowning kitten. There was something majestic about her and the way she carried herself.

I stared at her as she sat down beside the boy and pushed her hood back. Just like the boy, she had deep brown skin, pointing ears, and silvery-white hair that had been intricately braided. Her eyes, however, were a rich purple.

"Look, mama!" Hadithi said, still laughing as he drew the yielding rabbit into both arms. "I caught a rabbit!" He sat up and held it on his lap, patting its motionless head.

"I see." Estel replied, a slight smile breaking out over the corners of her lips. "What are you going to do with it?" She asked him, reaching out long, muscular fingers to stroke the captive's head.

Hadithi frowned. "I don't know. I just wanted to catch him and say hi." He shrugged his shoulders and hugged the creature more closely to his chest. "Can I keep him?" He asked, dubiously.

Estel threw her head back and laughed in such a way that I almost began to cry. *My mother never laughed. At least, not like that.* The realization flitted through my head. Jealousy rose within me for this child with a mother whose laugh contained more love and joy than I imagined existed. I wanted to look away or cover my ears. Her laugh warmed my heart, making me lose track of the moment. Her joy made me wish that I could give up my chosen mission to live with her instead.

"No, dear love. You cannot keep him." Estel's laughter quieted back to a smile, and she reached out to pet the terrified rabbit one more time. "It's time to let him go." She whispered, leaning forward, and kissing the child on the forehead.

A sob caught in my throat as an unmistakable expression of sorrow flitted into her eyes. *Who is this woman who makes me want to laugh and cry all at once? Why does she make me feel like my soul is coming undone?* I drew my hands over my mouth, smothering the sobs that fought to come out.

The little boy did as he was told, reluctance written all over his face as he watched the rabbit hop away into the underbrush.

SON OF KINGS

"Why don't you go practice what I showed you?" Estel told him, smiling again and motioning toward a tree a little way off. He nodded, stood up, and walked away. Estel continued to sit on the ground, her eyes trained on her child.

The boy took up a stance, picked up a leaf with his right hand, and held it between two fingers. He stared at the leaf intently until, to my amazement, it began to rise. I blinked my eyes, rubbing them to make sure I wasn't seeing things. The leaf floated, following his hand back and forth until he launched it at a tree the way one might throw a rock. He did this on repeat as the two women looked on.

"I need to be sure he's dead, Chantrea." Estel's voice was quiet. "I can't go back unless I know for certain that he's gone."

Go back? My mind spun. *Back where? Zale?*

"I'll try to find you proof." Chantrea said, still standing beside the seated Elven woman. "But I believe she killed him. Chiwa killed Ethan." She spoke the last words with a clenched jaw, as if it pained her to say his name.

Ethan? The evil wizard with the book? The Governor's brother? Why would Estel care if he's dead? Pride? Why aren't they saying more? I need more information!

"Why didn't you go back with the rest of them?" Estel continued to stare at her son as he practiced his magic. "Why did you stay here? Why work so hard to help these people?"

This question caught my attention. I'd wondered the same things several times since I'd met Chantrea.

Chantrea sighed and shrugged her shoulders. "Zale is not the only place in need of or deserving of help. You know that as well as I. Shantu is what it is today because of an inhabitant of Zale. The rulers of Zale may not want to acknowledge the connection, but I can't ignore it. Besides," she paused and took a deep breath. "I failed you. How could I return where my captain is no longer welcome, but blamed for something that's not her fault?"

After a brief, awkward silence, Estel stood up and brushed herself off. "It's not your burden to bear, Chantrea. They were right to send me away. I failed them, and I failed you. The consequences are mine and mine alone. I knew he was dangerous. I should've stopped and waited for you or Einar to catch up. But I believed I was stronger than him. I believed I could defeat him. I was a fool." Her face hardened, and she looked away from Hadithi to meet Chantrea's gaze.

"He's so much like Einar when we were little." She smiled for a moment, but it was soon gone. "Sometimes I forget who his father is. Or, if you're correct, who his father was." She paused, mulling over Chantrea's ideas once more. "But then I watch him practice his magic, or I catch a certain gleam in his eye, and it all comes back to me. Ethan's blood runs through his veins and it brings me unending fear, Chantrea." She stopped, a sob forming in her throat.

The two Elven women stared at each other in silence. My mind raced as I digested what she'd just said. *Ethan's blood runs through his veins. That means - no it can't be! That would mean Hadithi is my cousin and Chiwa's half-brother.* I leaned forward a little further, straining to catch a better glimpse of Hadithi and what he was doing. Instead of seeing him better, I lost my balance and crashed into the foliage. Fighting to untangle myself, I heard Chantrea sigh as her boots came to stand beside me.

"What are you doing, Yuvraj?"

"I, uh, I was just-" I finally managed to push myself up and out of the brush. "I was looking for mushrooms." I said as I tried to appear casual, leaning against the maple tree and painfully aware of the fact that I held no mushrooms.

My face was hot, and my cheeks flushed as I looked up at her. She studied me. I wanted to turn to see what Estel and Hadithi were doing, but I couldn't. I swallowed and tried to gather up some saliva in my mouth to speak.

"Go home, Yuvraj." Chantrea said as I opened my mouth to ask a question. She turned away from me, breaking the gaze that held me hostage.

I turned to search for the boy and his mother as my body instinctively obeyed her command. Estel now stood where she'd been sitting, her hand hovering over a knife strapped to her side. Hadithi peered at me from behind his mother's legs. His smile had disappeared, replaced by an expression of worry.

I stopped in my tracks, unable to resist the question begging to be asked. "Why don't they come stay with us?" My mind was racing with all the possibilities, all the potential an alliance with Estel and Hadithi might hold.

Chantrea froze for a second before turning around to face me. "Go home, Yuvraj. You do not understand what you are asking." She turned to leave again.

"I'm not stupid." I yelled, clenching my fists in anger. "I understand more than you give me credit for." I took a step forward, pride welling up as my face flushed and the veins in my arms began to tingle. "They could help us. We could use their talents, Estel's knowledge. Why are you hiding them from us? Why didn't you tell me there was another child with a gift of magic? It's just a simple question, why won't you answer me?" I was desperate, feeling I might explode if I didn't get the answer I desired.

To my surprise Chantrea turned, walked swiftly back to me, and lowered her face to my level. Her eyes flashed, betraying the anger so carefully contained.

"They are none of your business." She hissed, her spit hitting my face. "They are not tools for you to collect for your arsenal as you plot your revenge against the Governor. I have never and will never accuse you of stupidity, child. Your faults lie not in a lack of intelligence but in a surplus of arrogance and conceit." She paused, her eyes burning into mine. I'd never seen Chantrea so angry, so alive and seemingly undone. Fear screamed at me to run and hide, but I bit my lip and stood my ground.

"Chantrea," Estel's voice came from behind, a gentle hand falling on the Elf's shoulder. "Let me talk to the boy."

Chantrea closed her eyes and turned her head away as she straightened.

"Hello Yuvraj." Estel said, quietly standing in front of me. I stared at the ground, somehow more afraid of the calm stranger than the raging mentor. "Look at me." Her voice was hard and commanding. I looked up at her, unsure of what to expect.

"You have your mission in life, and I have mine." Her purple eyes unnerved me, bearing witness to a depth of pain I did not understand. "Hadithi and I are not part of your mission. Is that understood?"

I wanted to defy her, but instead I felt myself nodding in agreement.

"Go home, Yuvraj. Go home and forget all you heard and saw here today." Without another word, the Elf turned away from me and walked back to where Chantrea sat on the ground beside Hadithi. I chanced one more glance at the boy and turned to leave, my mind spinning as I walked away.

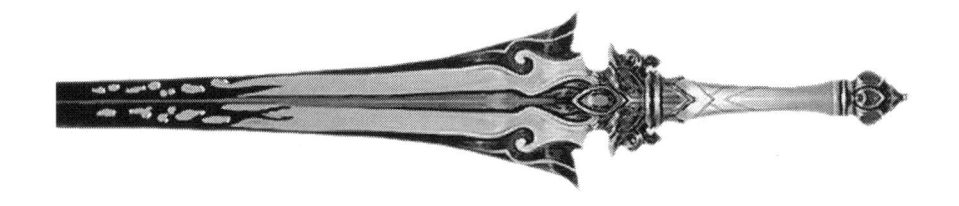

PART TWO

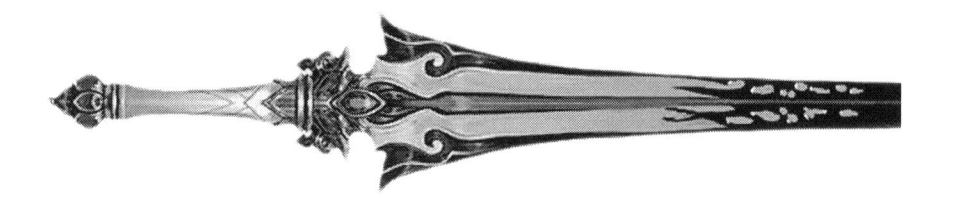

CHAPTER NINE

They say through fire and trial and war, heroes are born. I know this to be true. I've met one. I helped raise one. But I am not one of those heroes.

Eight short years had passed since the first time Tyr, Hova and I had gathered around the sputtering fire, determined to overthrow the man who persecuted us. We'd all grown up together; older and stronger in every possible way. As we'd grown, my longing for Hova's approval had deepened.

Tyr I appreciated for all the ways in which he benefited me. He was, quite possibly, the only person I both trusted and respected. Hova, however, I longed for, even - dare I say it - loved. Her benefit to me, to the cause of the Shadows, was great. I noticed it, spoke of it publicly, went out of my way to express my appreciation to her. But my affection was not returned. I was met with cold stares, short sentences, and eyes that burned through every mask I created.

But I digress.

I'd been biding my time, watching from a distance as the boy grew up. One look from his mother was all it took for me to realize she would never allow for a friendship or an alliance to form between us.

So, I waited for him to grow up.

SON OF KINGS

As I waited, Chantrea taught me all she could about magic, training me to fight with weapons and agility as my knowledge of magic developed. My body grew stronger, and so did my magic. But I was no wizard. I would be no match for Aepep on my own. I would never, as my Elven teacher so bluntly told me, be able to defeat Chiwa in a fight. Not yet anyway.

Tyr had grown in strategy, strength, and his ability with a sword. He could outmatch any of the Governor's Guards - something he'd proven time and again as we'd repeatedly raided their food storage and treasury. Tyr was steady, reliable, and ever trustworthy.

Hova had taken her place as a kind of guardian and nurse of all the children who joined us over the years. Her word was law. She was a fierce force of nature. Her hands were always busy finding or preparing food, sewing clothing, and gardening. Her tongue had cut down many an orphan, including those older and larger than her. Her wit could not be matched, and if push came to shove, she was the most unexpectedly ruthless enemy.

Chantrea taught her to fight in a way none of us understood. Though they would never admit it, soldiers looked away when she passed by them on the street. Some even crossed over to the other side. They all had stories of encounters with Hova, stories they told each other in hushed whispers.

And still, I waited. I waited for the day I would finally be able to contact that little boy. I waited for him to grow up. I waited, it seemed, as the only child of Aepep to have inherited any magical powers. I waited for the only other child Chantrea had found with strong abilities for magic – other than Chiwa, that is.

Little did I know I'd been waiting for his mother to die.

Flames enveloped the Slum cottage by the time I arrived. Hova saw it first, a strange, deep red fire. Her keen intuition and that strange ability she had of sensing another's distress warned her of the danger. It was as though she'd heard the cries of pain and sorrow long before any of us saw a hint of smoke. I cursed her ability because it stripped me of my capacity to hide anything from her. Her deep understanding of my innermost thoughts was of no gain to me or my unwavering affection for her.

It was late in the night. The fall rain hissed as it met the blazing fire inside the Slum cottage. I raced through the streets to the crumbling cottage, cursing the time I'd waited. All that waiting would seem foolish, stupid even, if I found nothing but the child's corpse.

Soldiers stood at a distance around the area closest to the Common People and their markets. They'd formed a watchful but unmoving wall of men ready to beat out the flame if it should creep up toward those the Governor deemed worth fighting for. He would only fight for those who added value and served the Governor's quality of life better than the people of the Slums.

Neighbors stood outside the burning cottage, trying their hardest to save the homes around it. Kaimbe stood on one side, shouting orders to those who were willing to help. He'd thrown off his cloak and was beating back the flames with a damp sack he'd found.

"Kaimbe," I yelled, running up to him. He'd grown into a giant of a man; his physical strength was unmatched within the Shadows. Only Tyr was strong enough to match him. "Is there anyone inside?" I shouted over the noise of the crackling fire. "Has anyone come out?"

"No," He shouted back, his eyes fixed on the fire as he rhythmically beat back the red, angry, unnatural flames. "I haven't seen anyone come out. A neighbor claims she saw a small, slender woman in a gray cape exit before she realized the home was on fire." His tone was grim. We both knew who the slender woman was.

Without another second to lose, and before Kaimbe could stop me, I threw off my cloak and ran into the cottage. The heat of the flames dried my damp clothing instantly and the smoke made me cough and wipe my eyes as I tried to see my way through. I paused as I reached the middle of the room. Holding my hand up to shield my face I gasped out, "Nen."

Water drenched me before I'd finished saying the word, cooling my face and clearing my eyes to see through the smoke. I looked around, desperate to find any sign of life. *Maybe they weren't here when she came.* I thought. *Maybe she just burned the place down out of spite, as a threat.* The idea was silly and I knew it. She'd burned the place down to cover her tracks. Such an intense fire on the inside of a building was not a common occurrence, especially when rain was still falling.

A small, seemingly lifeless body off to the left caught my eye, buried beneath smoldering ceiling beams. I ran toward it, tripping over something as I did.

Pushing myself up, I uttered the Elvish spell for water again as I turned around to see what I'd stumbled over.

I stared in breathless horror, the image of the woman's burned flesh searing itself on my memory forever as the underlying scent of the smoke made my stomach churn. I turned away, crawling over to the teenager buried beneath the burning wood.

"Kaimbe!" I screamed as I wrapped my arms around the heavy beams and started to pull them off. The Shadow was suddenly by my side, his bare arms dripping with sweat from exertion as he reached down to help me. I uttered the water spell to drench him and together we pulled as the walls began to crumble inwardly. Soon, the teenager was free. I scooped him into my arms, uncertain of whether he was still breathing, and ran outside.

The cool, rainy weather was a welcome change. I saw Hova on the other side of the street and crossed to meet her. She kneeled in the mud, cradling the young teenager's head on her lap, shielding his face from the rain by leaning over him. She sucked in her breath as she peeled back the hood of his cloak. I looked toward his face, struggling to see through the dark as someone threw my cloak over me. The fire behind us seemed to be dying out, Shadows and desperate neighbors continuing to beat it down.

"Is he...is he alive?" I whispered to Hova, longing for the answer to be yes.

"Barely." She replied. Her voice trembled. "These burns, they're deep." She was carefully peeling back the neck of his cloak now. "We need to get him home. This is not the place to treat him." She said, motioning to River and Ryder.

"No," He coughed and struggled, crying out in pain as he came-to. "Please, she's still in there," He gasped, pointing toward the cottage. My stomach churned again as I noticed the melted flesh of his hand.

"There, there," Hova whispered to him, leaning down close and stroking the top of his head gently. "We'll find her." Her voice cracked with pity and sadness as she spoke.

Jealousy rose in my throat. I wanted to scream and throw the teenager off into the gutter. I wanted to trade places with him. I wanted her affection. Instead, I looked away and helped River and Ryder tie the corners of my cloak to some nearby pieces of wood. Together the four of us carefully lifted him and placed him on top of my cloak. He whimpered in pain. River and Ryder picked him up and walked as quickly as possible in the direction of our home.

They faded into the dark streets, my eyes fixed on the strong, slender hand holding his, trying to shake off the thoughts filling my mind.

What if all this waiting was for nothing? I wondered, anxiety overtaking my mind. *What if he dies? What if he lives but wants nothing to do with the cause? What if his magical abilities aren't as strong as Chantrea led you to believe?* I paused as the darkness enveloped them completely.

"What if," I whispered under my breath. "What if he leaves and takes Hova with him?" The thought both terrified and enraged me. "Don't be stupid." I muttered to myself, wrapping my arms around me as I realized how cold and wet I'd become. "She won't leave Tyr. Besides," I comforted myself with the thought. "He's just an injured teenage boy. She's only doing her job."

I turned and walked back to the other side of the street to stand beside Kaimbe. We watched as the roof of the shack fell in, smothering the already dying flames.

"Where's Tyr?" I asked my companion as I realized I'd not yet seen him. Kaimbe shrugged his shoulders and looked around for our strategic leader, but Tyr was nowhere to be found.

HOVA SANG QUIETLY AS she went about treating the young teenager's wounds. Ryder and River held him down on the cot beside the stove where they'd laid him, looking away as she cleaned away the soot and dirt with a clean cloth that had been thoroughly boiled and dipped in lukewarm water. Their stomachs could barely handle the smell, the look, and the screams all at the same time. The deep burns stretched all along his right side, starting at his forehead and ending at his torso. His legs, somehow, had been spared.

He begged for her to stop. He cried for his mother, pleading for them to find her and bring her to him. When the pain would surge and overwhelm, he would plead to be left alone to die, trying his hardest to get away from the two strong boys holding him as still as possible.

SON OF KINGS

All the while Hova sang. She sang of hope and sorrow, of summer breezes and better days. Softly, gently, she cleaned the wounds and finally put the rag aside, reaching for a clay jar as her songs continued.

The teenager whimpered as he watched her, relieved she'd stopped touching his wounds. His left arm and shoulder ached, but it was a different kind of ache. Hova rinsed the clay jar with boiling water and walked over to her shelf of herbs. She crushed a generous handful of dried lavender in the jar. The smell of the lavender was a welcome contrast to the stench of smoke and burned clothing.

Next, she reached for honey, a precious commodity among the Shadows. She poured some in with the lavender, mixing it carefully. Staring at the mixture for a second, her song paused as she thought, resuming as she reached for amber, glass bottles with faded labels pasted on them.

"This will help ease the pain," Hova spoke kindly as she returned to his side. "I promise I will be as gentle as possible. I just need you to be brave for a little bit longer." She locked eyes with him, waiting for a response. He blinked rather than nodding, turning to expose the burned side of his face and closing his eyes.

Hova's song continued as she spread generous amounts of the homemade salve over every burn mark. His breathing eased and became less erratic as the salve sank in. River and Ryder let go of him and stood off to the side. When she was finished with the salve, Hova fixed a tight lid on the jar and put it up on the shelf. Walking to her sewing basket, she grabbed large, clean pieces of cloth. She bound the wounds loosely and walked around to his left side to examine his arm and shoulder.

Without a word, she twisted his arm up over his head and pushed on his shoulder. He screamed briefly as an audible popping sound came from the shoulder. Carefully, she placed his left hand on his stomach. "Don't move it." She said, grabbing a tin of peppermint salve and rubbing a small amount onto his sore shoulder.

Hova continued to hum, cleaning things up and putting other things away. River and Ryder were dismissed with a nod and disappeared through the window, Yuvraj's cloak in hand. Having finished her tidying, she sat down on a stool beside the bed.

The teenager was staring at the ceiling, his breath quiet and his eyes distant. The burns had marred his otherwise perfect, deep brown skin. His eyes were a bright hazel color with undertones of jade. His hair was a ragged, scorched mess of white, and his ears, much like Chantrea's, were pointed. The more Hova watched him, the more she understood his existence.

"She's dead." He whispered.

"Yes." Hova answered him, even though it wasn't a question.

"My home is gone."

"Yes."

"Someday," he said, his teeth clenched. "I'm going to find her. I'm going to find her and I'm going to kill her."

Hova paused before answering, her own heartbeat increasing as she realized who he must be talking about.

"Who? Who are you going to kill?" She asked.

"Chiwa." He said, choking back painful tears. "My - my sister."

Hova remained silent for a few minutes, her mind catching up as she read his face, her heart overflowing with a depth of sorrow beyond any she'd ever experienced.

"What's your name?" She asked, almost afraid of the answer. He hesitated for a second, then looked her straight in the eyes.

"Hadithi." He said, his eyes filling with anger.

"My name is Hova." She said, trying to smile. "You're safe here, Hadithi. You need rest." She sang again. This time it was no lullaby, but an ancient, nostalgic song Chantrea had taught her, haunting and soothing only to those who understood the depth of its meaning.

As Hadithi drifted off to sleep, Hova's voice faded. She silently wept for the new orphan in front of her, and for the mother lost in the flames.

TYR RAN THROUGH THE maze of alleyways in the Slums, streets he'd come to know better than he knew his own face. No one paid any attention to him. All eyes were either closed in sleep or trained on the flames and smoke rising high into the damp night sky.

SON OF KINGS

He'd heard her cries as he was walking home but had struggled to figure out where the cries were coming from. Reaching the house soon after it burst into flames, he'd noticed a light gray cloak disappearing into the night. He'd sounded the alarm and took off after the woman. Pausing to catch his breath, he peered into the hazy, rain-filled darkness, listening for any sounds. The street was still, the only noise the drip of the rain sliding down every roof until it fell to the ground, forming puddles in the dirt and trash of the alleyways.

Tyr sighed and turned back, discouraged by his inability to catch the culprit. He arrived back at the smoldering ruins of the small shack Hadithi had once called home. Most of the soldiers had been dismissed by their commander, free to go back to their warm barracks while a few sullen, unfortunate men remained to keep an eye on the undeserving poor.

"Tyr," Yuvraj exclaimed when he saw his brother come into view. "Where have you been? We could've used your help." He said, nodding toward the collapsed building.

"I know," The tall, young man said. His voice was cold and distant, his black cloak hiding his eye-patched and unremorseful face from view. "I was trying to catch her."

"She could've killed you." Yuvraj replied, lowering his voice as he pulled Tyr aside. "We need you, Tyr. You are more important than the witch. We can't win without you."

They stood together in silence, neither brother giving way to the other.

"Did anyone survive?" Tyr finally broke the silence.

"The boy." Yuvraj responded, nodding. "I pulled him out of the rubble." He said, omitting Kaimbe's contribution to the heroic endeavor. "Hova took him home to treat his wounds." He couldn't help but sneer as he said it, jealousy rearing its ugly head once more. Tyr paid no attention, his eyes fixed on the smoking ruins.

"Did you find her?" Tyr asked, the sound of her painful cries repeating themselves in the recesses of his memory.

"Yes." Yuvraj said, turning pale at the thought. "She was already dead when I got there. The fire didn't kill her, Tyr." His voice grew shallow as he leaned in towards his brother. "The person who started the fire killed her and burned her home down to cover it up. There was nothing we could do." His compassion was a mixture of genuine pity for his brother and feigned care for the dead woman.

"We need to bury her." Tyr made it clear he was not suggesting or requesting a burial, he was commanding. "She deserves a proper burial." His voice was firm.

"I, uh, how?" Yuvraj stumbled, glancing over at the wreck of the house as he remembered the body he'd found in his search for Hadithi. "Tyr, I agree with you, but I don't think-" His voice broke off as Kaimbe came up to the pair with something in his hand.

"We found this by her body." He grimaced as he spoke, holding out his hand to Tyr. Yuvraj felt slighted and annoyed but tried to ignore the feeling as he leaned over to view what was in his brother's hand. Tyr stared down at a thin, silver chain with a matching flower pendant, marred slightly by the heat of the flames. Yuvraj reached for it, but Tyr quickly tightened his hand, as if having read his younger brother's mind. He glared at Yuvraj.

"I just, I was just thinking, it looks expensive." Yuvraj muttered, avoiding Tyr's gaze.

"This belongs to her son now. I'll take it to him." Tyr said. The words were firm and final. Yuvraj knew better than to try arguing with him.

"Of course. Absolutely. I didn't mean..." Yuvarj's voice trailed off as Tyr abruptly turned and headed in the direction of their home. Kaimbe turned back to the embers of the house, Yuvraj following him soon after, jaw clenched in embarrassment.

No matter. He thought to himself. *The important thing is that we have Hadithi with us now. And he can't go anywhere. Even if he had somewhere to go, it would be impossible for him to leave us.* The thought comforted him as he helped Kaimbe comb through the ruins for anything else of value, avoiding one very specific area of piled up rubble. They would wrap up that pile with whatever cloth was available and dispose of it in the river.

DEEP IN THE DUNGEONS of the Governor's Grounds, a wail rose from the lips of a prisoner. The guards covered their ears and tried to drown out her cries with a song as the sound of her grief caused tears to rise in their eyes even though they didn't understand why she wept.

Chantrea kneeled on the filthy, cold floor, her arms stretched up and out. She swayed back and forth, intermittently beating her chest with her fists. The emptiness, the sorrow, and the love overflowing from her broken heart found relief in tears where words would not suffice.

When the guards told the tale to others, they swore her weeping lasted all night, that it was, "not of this world...just like her!" No amount of cursing or threatening or begging made her stop. Her anguish and her curious powers were more than enough to deter their following through with any threats of beating. They resorted to plugging their ears with their fingers, singing until their voices were hoarse, and then weeping along with her.

As the sun rose the next morning, her wailing turned to sobs, and her sobs turned to silence. Chantrea rose from the floor and walked on shaking legs over to the weak light coming through the grate above, throwing off her cloak to reveal swollen, closed eyes and a tear-streaked face. Her words were spoken soft and clear, somehow echoing through the dungeon hallways.

"In fire she died,
in water she is put to rest
.A warrior from birth,
a mother to the very end."

Chantrea took a deep breath, picked up her cloak, put it back on, and laid down on her bed with her back to the light. The silence the guards had longed for was suddenly more torturous and undesirable than the painful weeping.

Chapter Ten

"It's been two years since she disappeared," I said with a raised voice, tired of having the same old argument with Tyr, wishing that for once he would just give in. "We know Chantrea was captured by Aepep. We know he keeps her locked up. We know it's impossible to help her escape. What more do you want, Tyr?" I asked him, arms open as if I were ready to receive any direction my brother gave me even though I had no intention of changing my mind.

"We need her, Yuvraj!" Tyr yelled back. "We need Chantrea to train the young recruits. We need her to guide us, to help Hova with her gifts. We need Chantrea," He lowered his voice to a whisper and nodded in Hadithi's direction. "We need Chantrea to teach Hadithi how to use his powers." His bright blue eye stared me down. I flushed with anger.

"I am doing my best with him!" I hissed through clenched teeth. "It's not my fault she got caught before she taught me more about my own abilities." I lied.

Truthfully, my training had ended almost a year before Chantrea had gotten caught. She'd taught me everything anyone ever could about magic and how to use the powers I was born with. Unfortunately, it didn't seem like I'd been born with a particularly strong ability. But I wasn't about to tell Tyr or any of the other

Shadows I'd likely reached my utmost potential. I needed them to believe I was much more powerful. I chose to believe it myself.

"Besides," I turned to stare at the teenager, still whispering to my brother. "There's only so much I can do with someone who mopes around our home." We both observed Hadithi. He sat next to the stove, gazing into space, completely unaware of Hova cooking beside him or our heated discussion on the other end of the house. He'd hand things to Hova before she even requested them, holding up a spoon or a spice or a bowl of vegetables, his eyes betraying a distant mind.

A year had passed since I'd carried him out of the burning house. It was late fall again. Hova had nursed him back to health, forcing him to use his burned arm once the wounds healed, massaging his scarred face with her herbal remedies to relieve the nerve pain. She'd begged him to make the most ridiculous expressions so he could regain muscle strength on his right side.

Hova spent hours with Hadithi every day. She was the only one he would talk to about anything of substance, the only one who made him smile or laugh. Outside of Tyr, Hadithi was the only person I'd ever seen Hova care for with anything other than a sense of duty.

And he just sits there! I thought to myself, disgusted at his lack of interest in the teenager who clearly adored him. *What I wouldn't give.* My thoughts drifted off as I watched her cook, a bitter pang in my stomach, wishing she would turn to look at me and smile.

"We need Chantrea, Yuvraj." Tyr sighed beside me. "If nothing else, then we need her to help guide us. We, the Shadows, need Chantrea. We need you. We need Hadithi. We'll never be able to face both Aepep and Chiwa unless we can free Chantrea."

"Then I suppose you should start planning a rescue." I replied, resigning myself to Tyr's wishes. I watched Hova out of the corner of my eye as she tried to coax Hadithi into tasting whatever she was cooking for our lunch. His apathy irritated me. *If he were anyone else.* I thought to myself, going through a list of all the ways I'd like to smack him and show him who's in charge.

'If he were anyone else then he wouldn't be a threat to you.' The hairs of my arms stood on edge as a voice much like Chantrea's echoed in the back of my mind. Even in prison she still kept hold over us.

ELLEN ES CEELY

AEPEP SAT IN HIS chambers, muttering to himself as he tapped his fingers on the table beside him. His glass of wine shook to the rhythm his fingers created as they drummed the wood.

"I've tried everything." He muttered to some invisible condemning critic. "I made them outlaws." He spoke defensively, slouched to one side, leaning his head on his free hand. "I put more guards on watch and combed the streets for them. I captured the Elven woman. I put bounties on their heads and made examples out of the ones I caught." He stopped his muttering and drumming as he came to the same dead end as always.

"Still!" He shouted, pounding the table beside him and upsetting the wine so the cup clattered and spilled out on the floor. "They grow in popularity! After all I've done for those ungrateful Slum swine, still they will not give up their precious Shadows!" He gagged on the word.

The nagging in the back of Aepep's mind, that annoying sense of "I told you so" came back to visit, always with the voice and face of his brother accompanying it. He remembered the three small children in the courtyard, such malnourished creatures, staring up at the Governor's Palace. He remembered the defiance he'd seen, the fire burning deep inside their souls.

"What do you know?" He hissed at the memory. "You were killed by your own daughter! At least I'm still alive." The statement was meant to reassure his own mind, his own sense of control and power. Instead, it made him unbelievably nervous. The idea of being killed by one's own child unsettled him.

"Don't be stupid." The Governor said to himself, shaking his head and bidding the memory of his brother to go away. "Soldier!" He yelled at the door. A skinny young man came in, visibly nervous but trying to make a good impression as he stood at attention.

"Yes, Governor Aepep, sir. How can I be of service?" The young man's voice was unsteady, cracking as he spoke. Aepep stared at him in silence for a moment, a sneer forming on his lip in disgust. All the armor and clothing in the world couldn't hide how pathetically weak the man looked. *No wonder the Shadows thrive.* He thought to himself, massaging his forehead with one hand as he looked the soldier over. *With guards like this and training from that woman, how would they not feel they can and will succeed in overthrowing me? Especially with the continued protection the people of the Slums provide.*

"Call a servant to clean up this mess," Aepep barked at the man. "And tell Commander Jabez I'd like to see him in my chambers immediately. And," His voice faltered as he continued to survey the shaking man before him. "And eat some food, do some push-ups, do something, man!" He told the soldier, exasperation taking over entirely. "You look like a stiff breeze might blow you over!"

"Ay sir. Yes sir. Will do, sir." The soldier gulped and his face flushed, then went white with fear and embarrassment as he turned to leave.

Governor Aepep continued to sit in his chair, brow furrowed, lips moving silently as he cursed the gutter rats who'd grown up to defy him. A servant, a young woman, crept in and out of the room as quickly and quietly as possible, eyes wide with fear and fixed on the spill of wine. Mopping up the wine with some old rags and picking up the cup, she curtsied and left the room, hoping he wouldn't even notice her.

A few moments later Commander Jabez knocked on the door.

"Come." Aepep yelled. The commander of the Governor's Guards entered the room and bowed. His posture was impeccable, his uniform always as it should be, his red cloak hanging regally from his broad shoulders. Aepep studied the man's face for a moment, fury welling up inside him.

"Tell me, Jabez." He said, dropping the man's well-earned title as he always did when angry. "Why is it a man such as yourself – with all the vast resources I've graciously provided, at least a hundred common soldiers and six of the most elite soldiers our great city of Shantu has ever known – why is it you cannot rid our streets, my streets," Aepep added for emphasis. "Of these simple, common-place gutter rats?" His voice was deep and dangerous. The threat within the words was not lost on Jabez, nor was it a new one.

"Sire," Jabez said, a sense of calm overwhelming his voice. He knew Aepep could destroy him if he wanted to. He also believed the Governor would be hard pressed to find a suitable replacement for him. "Even though we've caught the woman, the Shadows continue to grow in number as the oldest ones grow in strength and tactics." His answer was simple and true, but he knew it would hardly be enough to satisfy the raging man before him.

"I don't want your excuses, man!" Aepep shouted, rising to his feet, his eyes glinting dangerously. Jabez was aware of what it looked like for Aepep to lose his temper. He was one of the few who'd kept the Governor's secret safe. He'd also trained himself extensively in case the Governor ever turned on him. *Time to give him the information he doesn't want.* He thought to himself.

"Sire," He began again, bowing once more, his voice steady and smooth. "The Shadows are not mere children. They are no longer untrained, unwanted gutter rats. Many of them are men. I would even venture to say they are soldiers. The Slums run rampant not only with stories of their strength and ability, but also of their kindness and generosity to those around them. The people of the Slums, even some of those in the Common Sector, not only admire the Shadows, but also adore them." He paused, checking to see what the Governor's response might be.

"Go on." Aepep spoke through gritted teeth. He'd turned to look out his window, hands clasped firmly behind him.

"Sire," Jabez continued. "I've seen them fight with my own eyes. One who wears an eye patch, they say his name is Tyr, can match any of the Governor's Guards. He's strong and strategic. Some say he's the leader of the Shadows. Another, they call him Kaimbe, is built like a giant. They say he can lift a grown man over his head and throw him on the ground the way one might toss a rabid cat in the river. I've never seen him do this, but I have seen him fight. He is no longer a gutter rat."

"Is that all? Two giant men? You have six highly skilled guards at your disposal – take these men out!" Aepep shouted at his commander, turning his back to the window, hands still clasped tightly behind him.

"Sire," Jabez faltered. "They are only two of the unknown number of Shadows. There's one they speak of in hushed tones. Less beloved, but still respected and feared. His name is Yuvraj." He stopped, holding his breath to see what would happen. Aepep clenched his jaw but said nothing. "Yuvraj, well, they say he has magical powers." Jabez practically whispered the words.

Upon hearing this rumor, Aepep did the most unexpected thing Jabez had ever known him to do: he laughed, dark and dangerous. Jabez started and stared at his leader.

"But then there are the women." Jabez said, awkwardly.

SON OF KINGS

"What woman?" Aepep asked him, still smiling. "The one who trained them? The one who started this whole mess? I have her locked in my dungeon right now."

"No sire," Jabez shook his head. "Not just one woman, several women. There's the woman who was burned to death in her cottage last year – the woman your prisoner wept for, whose weeping was heard throughout the Palace." The memory gave both an unsettled feeling. Jabez continued. "There's the woman who works as one of the Shadows, a tiny thing, beloved by the Slum and Common People alike. They say she has the gift of healing and can read your thoughts." He tried to hide his intrigue when he thought about her. "And finally, the woman who burned the first woman to death." He paused. "You know of whom I speak, Governor Aepep."

"Yes." Aepep groaned, unclasping his hands from behind his back and rubbing his forehead. His anger had faded to disgust. They stood in silence for a moment, Aepep staring at the floor beneath him as Jabez watched his master closely. "What exactly are you saying, Commander Jabez?" Aepep asked. His tone had changed with his demeanor.

"It is no longer a matter of simply removing the Shadows or of outlawing them or of making a public example of any of the ones we catch." Jabez spoke delicately. "They may have begun as a renegade group of annoying gutter rat children, but they're no longer children. They've grown up. They've learned new skills, skills no average person in this city would ever learn or teach." Jabez hesitated.

"Go on." Aepep said, sitting back down. He closed his eyes, interlacing his fingers in his lap, conveying a certain level of peaceful acceptance of whatever Jabez might have to say.

"The Slums have grown exponentially over the last few years. They're over-crowded and crumbling. The Shadows thrive in their midst because they come from there. They know every alleyway and side street better than I know the veins on the back of my hand. Whatever else they hope to accomplish, the Shadows take care of their own." His tone was one almost of respect and honor. "This is why they are so beloved, respected, and protected in the Slums." He paused, trying to figure out how receptive Aepep might be to his next point.

"And?" Aepep asked, eyes still closed and hands still in his lap.

"If the inhabitants of the Slums were the only ones who cared for the Shadows, our answer would be simple: kill them off." Jabez said, shrugging his shoulders at the thought. The idea made Aepep open his eyes and smile. "Unfortunately, the Shadows are also well-loved and respected by the Common People." Jabez continued, causing the smile on Aepep's lips to fade into a frown on his forehead.

"But how?" Aepep asked him, bewildered by the thought. "What have the thieving Shadows ever done for the Common People of Shantu?"

"They've helped them when no one else would. They've fixed leaking roofs when landlords would not, carried heavy buckets for young and old alike, shared food in times of drought, and sworn to never take from them again. The children the Shadows once were, the thieving gutter rats who stole food from the Common People to survive another day, have reformed their ways. Instead of stealing from the Common People, they trade goods, labor, and whatever they've stolen from the Upper Class. They protect the vulnerable against those who would take advantage." He paused again, wondering if his point had been made yet.

"So what you're saying, Commander Jabez," Aepep said with annoyance. "Is that the Shadows are more popular and beloved by more people than I am. Is that what you're saying?" He stared the man in the eye.

"Yes, sire." Jabez replied, unflinching. "I'm saying if you want to rid yourself of the Shadows it will take more strategy than trying to catch and hang them all one by one. If you want to rid the city of their presence forever, then we must move beyond the desire to burn the Slums down. Any attack we make on the Shadows could cause most of your people to turn on you. Idiotic as their beliefs may be, it might destroy Shantu altogether. We must find another way."

"I see." Aepep said, nodding. "What do you propose we do instead?"

For the first time since he walked into the room, Jabez smiled.

"Are your scars hurting?" Hova asked Hadithi. He sat beside her as her nimble fingers worked on piecing together the cloak in her lap. The house was quiet. The other Shadows were out at various places helping farmers, scoping out houses in the Upper Class Sector, and repairing roofs in the Slums.

"A little." He replied, which Hova knew meant they hurt more than he cared to admit. The wounds had healed within a month of Hadithi being burned, but the nerves had yet to accept their new configuration. Hova set aside the cloak and reached for the salve. Hadithi pulled off his tunic and closed his eyes.

The wounds had healed better than Hova hoped they would. Rather than severely disfiguring his face as she'd assumed they would, they'd healed in a long, thin, intertwining configuration that started on his forehead, spread down the side of his face, and continued down his shoulder, ending at his torso. The scars often reminded Hova of the intricate branches of a tree or a growth of ivy. They'd turned a surprising shade of blue as they healed, which had almost faded back to the rich brown of Hadithi's unburned skin.

Hova gently worked the ointment into every bit of scarring, starting at Hadithi's torso and working her way up, spending more time on his face and shoulder where she knew the most pain occurred. She always sang as she massaged the ointment in. Hova couldn't help but sing when she worked at healing. Her songs always came from somewhere she couldn't otherwise access, a piece of her heart changing the song depending on who she was caring for.

"Oh, faded days of life beyond the graveWhat do you see that I might face?Your light shines bright but beckons meTo hold, for now, to this dark place."

The song bothered Hova, but she couldn't change it. It came out of her lips on repeat as she worked the ointment into Hadithi's scars. It was mournfully hopeful, speaking to her of Hadithi's desires and of his uninspired resignation to his current fate. By the time she finished, Hadithi had relaxed. His skin was shining with oil, and the nerve pain had subsided.

"Thank you." He said, grateful as ever. He pulled his tunic back over his head as she closed the jar of salve and put it away. Leaning forward, he rested his left elbow on his knee and cradled the left side of his face with his hand. Hova loved when he did this because it smashed his face in a sweet and childish way, but she wasn't about to tell him. She sat down again and picked up her sewing.

"Hova?" Hadithi said, picking at a thread in his pants with his right hand.

"Yes?" She replied, noting the sadness in his voice.

"Will the pain ever go away?" His voice cracked as he asked the question, and he wiped away a stray tear. Hova's heart had grown with love for Hadithi more quickly than anyone else she'd ever met. His honesty, integrity, and depth of feeling were like a cool drink of water in a desert full of hard hearts and schemes. He was the only person she knew who wasn't actively seeking revenge or power. This question broke her heart as she realized he wasn't talking about the nerve pain.

"My mother died when I was very young." She spoke in a whisper, her fingers still grasping fabric and needle. "I miss her every day. I suppose I always will. But," She emphasized. "Every day it hurts a little bit less. Just like your scars will never go away, the loss of your mother will always be with you. But with time, and patience, the ache of her loss will fade a little bit every day. Just like the nerve pain."

They sat in silence for a minute, Hadithi wiping away silent tears, Hova choking back the tears of empathy rising to the surface.

"I miss her." He said. "I don't want to be a burden. I just miss her, and it's all my fault." He couldn't hold in the angry, aching tears any longer. Hova set aside her sewing again and hugged him, rocking him back and forth the way one would a baby.

"You're not a burden." She whispered repeatedly. "Your mother's death is not your fault."

Yuvraj witnessed the interaction from the window entrance, jaw clenched as tight as both fists. His mind reviewed all the times he'd cried in pain and Hova had never reached out to hug him. *She avoids all physical contact with me.* He thought to himself, biting his lip as the offense of it sunk in. He'd come back to grab some tools and had chosen to wait and see what happened. *Damn that boy!* He raged inside, hating his second-rate magic that made him dependent on the child.

Sensing Yuvraj's presence, Hova looked toward the window from where she sat, still holding the sobbing Hadithi in her arms. Their eyes locked. Yuvraj couldn't conceal the anger, the jealousy, or the longing. He didn't want to.

'How dare you!' The Shadow heard the words in his mind, and he took a step backward as if he'd been struck. *'I am not yours. I have never been yours. You have no right!'* He took another step backward in horror as he realized what he'd always suspected was true: Hova could see inside his mind. He wanted to run, but he couldn't tear himself from her gaze. Finally, she looked away and started singing to Hadithi instead.

Yuvraj ran, stumbling along the alleyway, like an insect that had just been released from a trap.

Chapter Eleven

"Good!" I said as Hadithi leaned on his staff and took a deep breath of spring air in the Woods clearing where we'd chosen to train. "Now, do it again!" Hadithi bit back a groan as he picked up the staff and came to face me. He was tall for his age, and he was learning fast. Our staffs knocked together rhythmically as he worked his way through the training session one more time.

Step, step, step, turn, lunge! Soon he'd be ready to combine his fighting with his ability for magic. Tyr and I had finally convinced Hova to let us train Hadithi instead of allowing him to sit around the house all day. Truth be told, Tyr had done the convincing, I'd merely stood to the side with my mouth shut and my eyes on the floor, trying to make my mind as blank as possible. After our encounter a few months ago, I'd taken to avoiding any confrontation with Hova. As much as I loathed her attachment to the young teenager, I needed the most influential person in his life to be on board with our desire to train him.

"Hova," Tyr had said, towering over his sister. "You know he cannot continue like this. He needs to be active." He spoke in a tone of respect only Hova brought out in him. Her stubbornness was stronger than his. Any hint of patronizing behavior would make her refuse him immediately. I noticed her eyes begin to turn toward me and I instantly fixed my own on my feet. *These shoes have been good to me.* I forced myself to examine the thick brown leather, the laces that tied above my ankle, and the way the heel of the shoe was still wearing well.

"Fine." Hova said, after a long stare. My heartbeat increased. *She's always refused, saying he was too sick or too weak or too young or too sad.* Tyr started to thank her and got cut off.

"But," she said in a loud voice, drowning out her brother's thanks. I glanced up to see her standing there with her right index finger pointed at Tyr's face, much like a mother would warn a naughty child. "If I observe anything I don't approve of," her voice was stern, bordering dangerous. "If I hear him crying unnecessarily, if you use any excessive force, if I witness any unnecessary pain or fear, if I find out about any verbal berating or belittling," she turned and pointed the finger at me. "The training will stop, and I'll skin you both alive while you sleep."

I nodded without lifting my eyes, half terrified, half amused.

"Hova," I heard Tyr say and felt her eyes shift back to him. "I give you my solemn oath I will not do anything to purposefully harm him. But you must let us push him, just a little, when necessary. He needs to be able to think quickly on his feet and it's going to take a while to get his physical strength up to where most his age already are."

"Not," I inserted hastily, glancing quickly at Tyr as panic overcame me. "Not that it's Hadithi's fault. He was wounded. Tyr isn't criticizing or blaming him for being behind." I faltered. Tyr nodded vigorously as he realized the implication of his words. Hova grunted in response.

"Agreed." She said, turning away from us back to her chores. "Now get out of here. I have work to do. Hadithi went to fetch water with River and Ryder." We turned to leave, allowing for one short glance of triumph to pass between us.

'I'm warning you.' Hova's voice intruded on my mind as I walked away. I paused to look back at her, breaking out in a cold sweat. She was sitting, calmly folding new pieces of scrap fabric. She didn't even look my way. *'I'm watching. I see everything. I'll know if you break your promise.'*

Hova's words echoed in my brain every single day, and every day a different emotion rose inside me when I heard them repeated in the background as I helped train Hadithi. I often wavered between indignation and anger, sometimes sinking into fear and curiosity of what she would do if I broke the promise. Other times I felt hurt, almost betrayed - offended she would not love me while doting on and defending him.

"Very good!" Tyr's voice rang out from the sidelines as Hadithi finished the steps. I heard the smile in my half-brother's voice. "Go on back to the house." He said, kindly refraining from calling it Hadithi's home. "Eat some food and check if Hova needs any help. Tell her we'll be along shortly." Hadithi nodded and pulled the hood of his cloak up over his head, hiding his other-worldly ears and hair. He took off at a half walk half run, tired from his training but compelled by the idea of food.

"He's a quick learner," Tyr said to me, staring after the teenager as he disappeared through the trees. "He gets stronger every day and he's grown tall. I think it's time for me to start trying to convince Hova to let him go on a mission. Just a simple one. Hadithi needs more experience." I nodded and grunted in agreement with my brother.

"His magic is still slow. He has an amazing, natural ability for it, but I can't seem to help him move past something, to truly let go and unleash his inner strength." I said, thinking through my personal training sessions with Hadithi. "I can't tell if it's fear or apathy. Fear I can work with, apathy..." I allowed my voice to fade away before I betrayed what I'd like to do to Hadithi if a total lack of interest and ambition were holding him back.

"Patience, Yuvraj." Tyr said to me, his hand squeezing my shoulder as he sensed my frustration. "We've come this far," He cautioned. "We don't want to lose him. I have no doubt you'll find a way to get through to him."

"Thank you, brother." I nodded and forced a smile. *Ever the noble heart.* I thought with a twinge of disdain and envy. *What must it be like to be always optimistic?*

"Go back." I whispered to Hadithi in the Woods clearing. A few days had passed since his combat training with Tyr. It was early in the morning, early enough that the moon was still high in the sky. I'd brought Hadithi out alone, determined to figure out what was standing between him and his natural ability, hoping to use the half Night Elf blood coursing through his veins to my advantage.

"Close your eyes and go back to your earliest memory." I whispered to him, flashing back to my earliest memory of him as I spoke.

Hadithi obeyed, closing his eyes, his breath becoming shallow. He stood still in the middle of the clearing, swaying slightly to keep his knees from locking.

"What do you see?" I asked him, pacing slowly around him. Waiting as I allowed him to center himself and unlock any memories he may have hidden away.

"I see," He faltered. "I see my mother." His voice cracked. *Good.* I thought. *I can work with this.*

"Embrace the grief, Hadithi, do not turn away from it!" I urged him in a low voice. "What is your mother doing? Where are you? What are you doing?" This was the first time I'd tried this method. Even though Chantrea had used my memories countless times to help unlock my abilities, I'd worried the grief might be too much for Hadithi, that it might make him become even more recluse and silent rather than opening up and letting go his restraint.

"We're in the alleyway outside our home." His voice cracked again, and he swallowed hard. "I've just fallen down." He managed to continue. "My hands are stinging, I've bitten my bottom lip, and I'm crying." The words slipped from his lips, full of raw, unbridled grief. *We're getting closer.* I thought.

"Don't give up yet." I encouraged him. "What happens next?" I waited, still pacing around him, trying to control the excitement welling up inside me.

"She's picking me up now, holding me and singing, carrying me back to our home." Hadithi was crying. He couldn't keep the tears back any longer, and the memory was spilling out with the tears. His skin was the faintest glowing blue, outlining his features perfectly as he stood in the moonlight. Chantrea's skin had fascinated me, it had fascinated all of us. Even after we'd grown used to the glowing, we still always wondered how and why. Hadithi's glow, though much fainter, also fascinated me.

"What do you feel, Hadithi?" I asked him, resisting the urge to reach out and touch the glowing blue skin of his face.

Silence ensued as Hadithi, I assumed, gathered his thoughts. I continued to pace around him, trying to maintain a sense of rhythm and entrancement.

SON OF KINGS

"I, I feel cold." Hadithi said, tears still falling. I stared dubiously at him in his long, warm cloak, wondering for a second if he was messing with me. "Not physically," he said, sensing my doubt. "I feel cold inside. As if my heart and stomach are frozen and unable to find the heat of the sun or the warmth of the moon."

The moon is warm? I wondered; half tempted to go down this path to satisfy my curiosity. *He can feel the moon. The moon warms him.* I filed this away in case it might benefit me later.

"Go on." I coaxed him. "What else do you feel."

"Afraid." He said, his voice faltering into a sob as he spoke the word. "And ashamed to fear so much. I'm afraid, always afraid." Another sob escaped him, and he reached a hand up to wipe away some tears. *Good.* I thought again, smiling. *I can work with fear!*

"Anything else?" I decided to push one more time, hoping for the one emotion I knew I could use better than any other. The one emotion that drove my own power and ability.

"I..." Hadithi started and stopped, hesitating to say it. His breath quickened and another sob came out. "I feel angry!" He practically shouted the word at me, gritting his teeth as he spoke.

There it is! My heart raced with excitement, and I stopped in front of him, staring into his face, those strange eyes still closed.

I leaned forward and whispered into his ear. "Tell me about your anger, Hadithi. Let it out."

Hova watched from the edge of the trees, torn between love and fury. *He's already broken his promise.* She thought to herself, wiping away an angry tear as the scene in the clearing unfolded before her. *I warned you, Yuvraj! I warned you what I would do if you hurt Hadithi!* She wanted to strangle him, to throw him on the ground and stand over him with her foot on his neck.

The lies! The blatant manipulation and withholding the truth of who you are to each other - it all makes sense now. She wished Chantrea were with her. She wished she could ask for advice, for a strategy on how to give Yuvraj the beating he so richly deserved while protecting Hadithi.

'What's stopping you from stopping him?' A voice that sounded remarkably like Chantrea's came from deep within Hova's mind. *'Why not reveal yourself, walk into the clearing right now, take Hadithi home, and slap Yuvraj across the face?'* Hova continued to stare as the scene before her eyes unfolded. Yuvraj circled a closed-fisted, weeping Hadithi like a feral cat playing with its dinner.

'Why don't you tell Hadithi who Yuvraj is? Tell him who Aepep is and how they're all connected. You have the choice. The option is yours, Hova. So, what's stopping you?' Chantrea's blunt honesty stabbed at the girl's conscience as she continued to stand there, motionless.

"Because," Hova whispered into the darkness, knowing Chantrea would hear her. "I'm also afraid." She looked away from the two in the clearing, closing her eyes and leaning against a tree.

'What are you afraid of?'

"I'm afraid..." Hova's voice disappeared when she tried to articulate the pain welling up inside as she acknowledged the weakness. "I'm afraid of losing him. I'm afraid of losing Hadithi. I'm afraid he'll run off and leave us, that he'll feel betrayed by me and try to return to his mother's land." She paused for a second, her voice quivering. "I'm afraid he'll go where I can't follow. Because I can't leave Tyr, and-" She stopped, clenching her jaw.

'Go on. Say it! Admit the truth and be done with it.' Chantrea's voice had an edge to it, a harshness.

"And I realize he does not love me the way I love him. Hadithi would never ask me to go with him." Defeat washed over Hova as she confessed what she knew Yuvraj admitted every day of his life: she loved someone who did not love her back. *Not like that anyway.* "But maybe..." She hesitated, sinking down to the ground in exhaustion and leaning her head against the tree trunk.

'You think perhaps, with time, that reality might change? That he might grow to love you in return?' Chantrea asked her. Hova nodded. *'Perhaps.'* Chantrea admitted reluctantly. *'I cannot see so far ahead. It is possible Hadithi will grow to love you. It is also possible he might grow to love another.'* The idea of Hadithi returning the affections of some unknown other girl made Hova cringe.

SON OF KINGS

'Hova,' Chantrea spoke the name affectionately. *'You cannot keep Hadithi from fulfilling his destiny, from experiencing pain and grief and disillusionment any more than I can keep you from doing whatever it is you choose to do. All you can do is make choices.'*

Silence ensued as Hova continued to watch Yuvraj and Hadithi.

'Just remember,' The Elvin lady said to her, unmasked grief in her voice. *'You must live with the outcome of whatever choices you make.'*

I watched Hadithi as he sat on his cot in the corner of the room, intently carving a piece of wood he'd brought back from the Woods. He had an entire collection of wooden figurines he'd carved all standing in a row along the wall. I'd suggested selling them as they grew in number, but I'd quickly retracted my suggestion when I saw the look of panic on Hadithi's face and the glare on Hova's.

"His training went better today than it did on all the other days combined!" I whispered eagerly to Tyr, who sat beside me. It was late, the fire in the stove next to us was dying and Hova had already laid down for the night. "We made progress. He managed to unleash some magic." I made my report as vague as possible, unsure of how Tyr would react if he knew the truth of my methods, convinced he wouldn't approve.

"How?" Came Tyr's excited and dreaded question. "What did you do differently that made him open up and try?" My half-brother also watched Hadithi from where he sat.

"I..." I faltered, trying to find the right words. "Just trust me?" It came out as a question rather than the statement I'd intended. "What I did worked, but I don't think you'd enjoy watching it." I turned my gaze to Tyr's face. He frowned. "I promise it won't hurt him." I lied. "Nothing I did today would go against anything Chantrea taught me." I switched to truth, knowing it would gain the approval I was looking for. "She would approve of my methods." I waited.

"If that's how Chantrea would do it, then you have my blessing. No need to fill in the details for me." Tyr said, nodding his head. "I trust you, Yuvraj. You've always acted in the best interest of The Shadows." He turned to make eye contact and smile at me. I felt a twinge of guilt looking at the trust and pride in his face, but I quickly dismissed the weakness as I found comfort in his words. I nodded in return and we both turned back to observe Hadithi.

Of course, I always act in the best interest of The Shadows. I thought to myself, reasoning away the guilt I felt for lying to Tyr when he trusted me so completely. *After all, I am the co-founder of the group. Obviously, I also know this is what Chantrea would do.* My reasoning continued. *I'm the only one who would know. No one else understands how she trained me. No one else has my abilities.*

Hadithi folded up his knife and put it in his pocket then laid down on his cot, the newly carved wooden figurine still grasped tightly in his hand. I couldn't tell what he'd made this time and it annoyed me for reasons I couldn't explain or understand for myself.

"It's late." Tyr said, squeezing my shoulder and standing up. He stretched. "Rest, Yuvraj." With that, he walked to his cot near the entrance and was asleep within seconds of lying down.

I continued to watch Hadithi as he slept, leaning back against the wall. Extending my legs so my feet could feel the heat of the stove, I wrapped my cloak tightly around me as my bones grew heavy and my eyes drooped. The fire in the stove crumbled into warm, glowing embers. *Why am I watching him? He's asleep.* I wondered as I began to drift off. I couldn't keep my eyes open any longer, but I also had no desire to move. I gave into the fatigue, my chin falling forward onto my chest.

My dreams were riddled with Chantrea's unintelligible voice and Hadithi's face. I tried asking Chantrea to speak more clearly, to let me see her face, but instead a faint blue light came into view. I couldn't figure out where it was coming from, all I could see was how it clouded out Hadithi's face.

'Wake up, Yuvraj.' I heard Chantrea clearly now. I opened my eyes slowly, blinking as the blue light continued, struggling to separate the dream from reality, but no matter how much I blinked the blue light wouldn't disappear, it only faded. I glanced around carefully, wondering if someone had found and entered our home, poised to jump up and fight them while calling for the others to wake up. It was dark by the window where Tyr lay, his quiet snores rising methodically. The door we'd installed over the window entrance looked to be undisturbed. I

SON OF KINGS

turned back toward the left where Hova lay, barely able to make out her small frame.

My eyes adjusted to the room and my brain finally registered what I was seeing. Hadithi lay with his blanket drawn up over his head, a blue light emanating from beneath it. I watched carefully, afraid to move or make noise. *What is he doing?* I wondered, trying to figure out the shadows beneath the blanket. *Is he playing with his toys?* The idea disgusted me. He was far too old to be playing with toys. *This will need to be dealt with somehow. I may need to take them all away and sell them when he and Hova aren't looking.*

Even as I nodded to myself in agreement, I knew it would never work. Hova was always looking, always watching. The moment the carvings went missing, she would turn those beautiful, stone-cold, jet-black eyes on me and stare into my soul until I curled up into a ball and begged for forgiveness. *Besides,* I thought. *He can always make more.* This somehow comforted me, and I pretended it was the real reason I wouldn't take away the figurines. No need to waste my time on something that could so easily be undone.

But something still needs to be done about this. He can't successfully train if he's staying up all night playing with little pieces of wood he carved into shapes. The disgust continued as I watched. Suddenly I realized Hadithi's hands were nowhere near the moving figures beneath the blanket. I blinked some more and rubbed my eyes, leaning forward in shock. The hair on the back of my neck stood up straight as I watched little wooden figures move clumsily around in the blue light – the blue light that could only be coming from the young teenager who glowed in the moonlight.

He...they...that is...magic. I stared in awe, rescinding all the threats I'd uttered in my mind about taking the figurines away. *How long has he been doing this?* I wondered. *Does Hova know?* I managed a quick, jealous glance in her sleeping direction. *Doubtful.* I thought. *Surely she'd be watching him too if she knew about this.*

I settled back, continuing to observe into the wee hours of the morning when the blue light faded, and the figurines fell still and Hadithi drifted off to sleep. I slept fitfully until dawn, my mind racing with the excitement of this new find.

Chapter Twelve

THE GIRL SHOWED UP sometime later that year, on a summer afternoon with the sun high and bright. Tyr found her, as he found most of our orphaned group of unwanted children. He watched from the shadows in the Common Sector closest to the Sea as the thin teenager slithered her way into the crevice between two cottages built too close together. He waited to see why she'd done so, smiling to himself as a few soldiers came crashing down the street, breathing heavily and scanning around for any sign of her.

"She went that way." Tyr muttered at one of the soldiers, pointing down a random street as he slumped against the wall to hide his impressive build.

"Of course. Thank you. I knew that." The soldier insisted, dripping in sweat, obviously offended a Commoner would believe he needed help. Tyr folded his arms and allowed his chin to slump over his chest. As soon as their voices and stomping feet disappeared into the distance, the teenage girl emerged, brushing herself off.

"Thank you!" She said, smiling directly at Tyr. To this day, I am convinced her smile alone won him over and made him invite her to join us for supper. They walked home together, her hiding behind him at a moment's notice as she laughed and told him her life story. Tyr's inability to refrain from helping someone he saw in trouble and his strong tolerance for mindless chattering and personal stories were among his greatest strengths and deepest weaknesses. It baffled me on a daily basis how he took such interest in complete strangers and had so much compassion for people.

I saw them from the roof of our home as I tended to the garden. I hated the muddy work, but I was forever trying to win Hova's approval, and this was one of the only ways I could guarantee she would spend time with me. Even if she remained silent. Tyr's cheerful voice wafted down the alleyway. The teenage girl's voice was too young and happy to hear it very well, but I watched them as they got closer.

She couldn't have been more than fourteen years old. She was of average height, wearing a light, blue, summer cloak and a plain brown dress underneath. Her brown hair was cut short, curling slightly about her ears. Her face was tan and freckled from the sun. From where I sat, she struck me as quite ordinary. There was nothing about her that grabbed my attention or made her stick out as special. If I had passed her in the marketplace, I doubt I would've even noticed her existence.

"Yuvraj!" Tyr called up to me as they neared our home, and he felt my gaze. "Come down and meet our guest. She's staying for supper." With Tyr it was always a matter of him asking for forgiveness rather than permission. But I'd be hard pressed to complain about the food seeing as how it was summer and we had no need to ration.

Standing up on the slanted roof, I brushed the dirt off my pants. I made my way down the ladder and met Tyr and his new friend at the entrance window.

"Yuvraj, this is-" Tyr began.

"Shantha!" The teenager said, cutting him off and sticking out her hand to greet me. Upon closer inspection I could see her freckles were even more pronounced than I'd thought. Her pale green eyes stood out to me as some of the kindest eyes I'd ever seen. The kindness had a strange effect on me, however. I struggled to smile back and shake her hand as feelings of disgust welled up inside me.

"Welcome, Shantha." Her handshake was firm and strong, stronger than I expected. "What brings you to our part of Shantu?" I asked, studying her well-made clothing. She was too well-groomed, too well cared for to have come from the

Slums, causing both curiosity as well as suspicion to creep into my mind. Shantha's face fell, and her smile faded as she opened her mouth to answer.

"Shantha can tell us about that after supper." Tyr interjected, glaring at me with his good eye as he smiled. I glared back but decided this wasn't a battle worth fighting with my half-brother. He'd clearly taken a liking to the girl, and I had to admit he'd never been wrong before about who to take in.

"Of course!" I said, shaking my head and smiling at Shantha. "Come in, it's getting late and I'm sure you're hungry. Hova should be done with our lentil and vegetable stew soon." I beckoned toward the open window, bowing slightly to indicate she was welcome to enter. The girl glanced at Tyr for reassurance. He nodded and she promptly jumped through the window.

"Tyr," I whispered as Shantha's voice sounded from inside our home where she cheerfully introduced herself. "Are you sure about this?" I had a nagging feeling she belonged in a much wealthier world.

"Trust me, Yuvraj." Tyr whispered back, his voice betraying his exasperation with me. "Wait until she tells her story. We need her more than she needs us." He had the same look in his eye he'd had when he brought back Kaimbe, River, and Ryder.

"I trust you." I admitted, shrugging my shoulders and sighing. "But..." I hesitated. Tyr looked at me with a half-smile.

"You can't stand her cheerful kindness, right?" His accurate description of my feelings impressed me. *He knows me better than what I give him credit for.* I thought to myself as I wiped my forehead with my sleeve and shook my head.

"It's just so annoying!" I said, still whispering but letting out a small laugh. Tyr patted me on the back in an understanding way.

"So are you, brother." He replied with a twinkle in his eye. "So are you."

"It was a dark and stormy night!" Shantha began, eyes wide and twinkling, hands poised in the air above her bowl. The lanky teenager had already downed two bowls of stew and had accepted a third serving after Tyr insisted and Hova solemnly scraped the bottom of the pot to fill the girl's bowl. I looked around the room as she started to tell us her story.

Tyr and Hadithi sat enthralled, the first with a gleam of adventure and amusement in his eye, the second with a gleam of infatuation as his deep brown cheeks glowed with a new pink hue rather than a blue tint. I made a mental note of this new infatuation and moved my eyes around the room.

River and Ryder sat on either side of Kaimbe. The three of them were quite the picture of classic suspicion and distrust, their arms folded over their chests, their backs against the wall, and their jaws clenched. They stared at her through slitted eyes as if they half expected her to become a sword-wielding warrior, attacking in the blink of an eye and slaying us all one by one.

Hova behaved as Hova always behaved: aloof and disinterested but listening. Always listening. Most of her glances were reserved for Hadithi, her one and only deep gaze having been when Shantha introduced herself. One look was all Hova needed to pass judgment. One look was all Hova ever seemed to give anyone who wasn't Hadithi or her brother. Hova's eyes remained trained on the stove, her sewing, and almost anything but the newcomer.

"I knew if I wanted to discover the truth about my father and his cursed wealth, then I had to follow him to the docks!" I tuned my ears back into whatever fantastic tale the girl was telling. She looked about the room with excitement, thoroughly enjoying the opportunity to spin her ridiculous story. "I went to bed as usual. Climbing the carved wooden staircase to my bedroom, I got ready for bed, laid down, and dismissed my maid, blowing out the candle as she left." Shantha's eyes locked with Hadithi's. In him she found an enraptured audience.

"My fireplace hissed as rain hit the bright, hot coals. I waited for hours, pinching myself to stay awake, rehearsing in my head all the steps I needed to take to get out of the house without being seen. I was determined to find out what my father had been hiding from me my whole life, why everyone who knew him was so afraid of him: the true source of his wealth!" The dramatic telling of the story halted for a moment as Shantha stuffed stew into her mouth and swallowed.

I wasn't sure if I was amazed or disgusted. I tried to keep my lip from curling. *Surely Hova disapproves of the girl.* I thought to myself. I needed this idea to be true. *If Hova disapproved then we could share in something, agree about something.*

I pushed away the aching in my heart and focused my attention back on the dramatic storyteller before us.

"As the moon rose high above the clouds pouring down rain upon our house, I crept out of my bed and quickly dressed in the clothing I'd laid over a chair next to my bed." Shantha was so clearly caught up in her own story that she couldn't read the room. Biting my tongue, I resisted the urge to roll my eyes and yell at her to get to the point. I slouched against the wall behind me, arms crossed in front.

"I listened at the door of my bedroom before carefully opening it and peeking out into the corridor. It was dark out there and I couldn't see any maids or guards. I slipped out and closed the door softly behind me, sliding silently down the banister as I'd done many times throughout my life rather than risking the creaking stairs."

Who exactly does this girl think she is? I closed my eyes, listening and running a list in my head of all the people in the Upper Class sector I knew might have multiple servant girls as well as access to guards. *If she's telling the truth she can only be the daughter of a very select group of men.*

"I knew I could never make it past the guards at the front door, so I stuck to the shadows, working my way through the house to the kitchen. The cook sat sound asleep on her chair next to the dying fire, snoring gently." Shantha paused. I opened one eye to see what she was doing. Apparently, the word 'cook' made her hungry again. I sneered inwardly, closing my eye again as the she finished off the rest of her stew. *I wish I could read minds like Hova.* I thought, sighing at the realization that this story would likely last much longer than I imagined. I longed for bed.

"I crept carefully past the cook," She hadn't forgotten where she was at in the story. *Small mercies.* "And placed my hand on the doorknob. I held my breath as I turned it and pulled the door open, hoping my efforts to grease the hinges a few nights before had not been in vain. The door opened without a sound. I looked back at the kitchen, giving it a good look over and walked out into the rain, closing the door behind me." A quiver came into her voice and quickly left. I cracked an eyelid to study Shantha's face, but no tears or sadness could be seen.

"Once outside, it was easy to find my way through the dark streets toward the docks. The rain had kept everyone indoors. I ducked between overhangs to find relief from the rain and stuck to the shadows as much as possible just in case some unfortunate soldiers had been sent out on regular rounds." Her knowledge of the hierarchy of soldiers and the misfortune of being found at the bottom of the pyramid were no surprise to me. Everyone knew that. I was still waiting to understand why Tyr thought she was so amazing, why she was such a great addition to the Shadows.

"Finally, after weaving in and out of the streets, I crossed into the dockyards. I kept my hood tight about my face and bent over like an old woman, afraid that anyone who saw me might recognize me and tell my father. The rain was letting up and a deep fog had overtaken the Sea."

I cracked an eye open to see if her face was still as intense as before. *Yep.* I thought, closing my eye again. The night she spoke about was coming to mind. A week back we'd had heavy rain and thick fog. *Where has she been sleeping?* I wondered, assuming the story would go the way I believed it would. *She's too clean and tidy to have been sleeping in the streets this whole week.* I wondered again if she was lying, if there was any validity to her story at all. *Is she a spy?*

Shantha continued. "I made my way to where my father's ship regularly docks." She paused and looked around at us, quizzically. "Have you ever been to the dockyard?" The hope in her voice made me unexpectedly sad. I opened my eyes and shook my head in response, looking around to see how everyone answered. A chorus of 'no' rose from my companions. As a group we'd always steered clear of the docks. Too many important, rich people. Too many weapons and sailors. Too much of a risk we might get grabbed.

We never worried about the soldiers, but we always avoided the sailors. Soldiers were young, predictable, and conditioned to being controlled. They were all single men, not allowed to marry, most of them just trying to make a living and stay out of trouble. They knew one way of fighting, one set of rules. Sailors were older, hardened, and well aware of the fragility of life. Some of them had families, others had lost their families, most were far more seasoned than any of us – even those of us with the darkest past – could ever imagine. Rules did not apply to their way of fighting. I'd never realized the humor in it until now.

"I have." Hova said. Her voice was quiet and flat, as if trying to hide deep emotion rather than being devoid of it. We all turned and stared at her in stunned silence. I was appalled, angry, frightened even. *Of all the places to go.* I didn't care if she read my thoughts. *What if one of them grabbed her?* I thought, my mind spiraling with all the fears of what might happen to Hova, coming to all kinds of unrealistic conclusions about how she'd never be allowed to leave the house again unless she strictly promised never to go there again. *As if Hova would ever do what Tyr and I tell her to do anyway.* I thought bitterly.

"Do you know it well?" Shantha asked her, eyes wide and anxious. Hova nodded. "My father's ship is the tallest one, right near where the river meets the Sea." She waited.

"The one with the pitch-black hull and the bright blue stripe running around it?" Hova asked, her eyes lighting up with curiosity as she realized which ship it was.

"That's the one."

Hova stared at the girl with a mixture of wonder and horror, glancing in Kaimbe's direction then back at Shantha. We all looked on as her eyes welled up with tears and she looked away. "I'm sorry." She whispered to Shantha. "I'm so sorry."

Tyr looked at me, bewildered, and reached out to comfort his sister. By now I was leaning forward, uncomfortably rubbing the palms of my hands against my knees, confused by the odd turn of events.

"Shantha," I said, remaining as calm as possible. "Maybe it would be best if you hurry up with your story so we can better understand who you are and why Hova is crying." The irritation welling inside me came through in my tone. I couldn't help it, noting how Hova continued to cry quietly off to the side.

"I'm sorry." Shantha said, her face showing her bewilderment at Hova's response. "I don't understand, that is, I didn't think I would make her cry." The young teenager looked like she was about to start crying herself.

"It's okay." Hadithi spoke up, shooting a glare at me as he rose from his seat and sat down next to the newcomer, reaching out a tentative hand to rest on her shoulder. I noted that she didn't push him away. "We're just worried about Hova." He said, looking with concern over at Hova as she tried to wipe away the tears and calm herself. "She understands things we don't. She knows things." He faltered. His earnest face betrayed confusion.

He doesn't know. I thought to myself in wonder. *He has no idea she can read his mind. I hold more power over Hova and Hadithi than I realized!*

SON OF KINGS

"It's okay," Hova said, sniffing as she wiped her eyes and nose with a handkerchief. "I'm okay. Please, Shantha, finish telling them your story." She smiled at the girl, giving her an encouraging nod. My heart sank as I recognized this gesture as one of kindness, one indicating Hova not only tolerated, but liked and trusted our newcomer. There would be no closeness, no bonding over a mutual dislike. Shantha nodded back and took a deep breath.

"I went over to where my father's ship regularly dock," The enthusiasm had gone out of Shantha's voice. She sounded sad now. "The rain continued at a steady drizzle. I hid behind some crates by the hull, waiting for a glimpse of my father, or of anyone I'd seen before." She paused. "You have to understand that he'd always told me he was a merchant, the wealthiest merchant in Shantu." She stared at the ground as she spoke.

"I had no reason to doubt him. He was a good father to me, a kind father. It wasn't until my most recent birthday, when I turned fourteen, that I started to wonder if he was telling the truth." She wouldn't look any of us in the eye. "He'd been gone for over three months, the longest he'd ever left me alone, returning the day before my birthday. I was so excited for him to come back. I'd begged my servant girl to take me down to the docks to meet him when he got in. She'd taken care of me ever since I could remember. She staunchly refused, becoming angry every time I asked. So, I stopped asking and went out on my own.

"I'd only ever gone to the docks when my father took me. Sometimes my servant girl went with us, but usually she stayed at home. I never questioned it, never wondered why things were the way they were, but I always sensed the fear of others when they looked at my father. It wasn't until I got to the docks the before my birthday that I realized why." She sighed, still looking at the ground. I was starting to form theories about what she'd seen, placing bets against myself as to the cause of her distress.

"My father is many things, but he is not a merchant." Shantha's voice was hard and angry, but it never quivered. "That day I went to the docks to greet him I arrived on board the ship just as he finished beating a child tied to the rails as the rest of the crew went about their business without a second glance. They unloaded countless items, all with different trademarks on them. Then they unloaded coins, all different shapes, and sizes, pouring them into cloth-lined boxes before taking them down the ramp to shore. The man I saw that day was not the man I knew as my father.

"I'll never forget the look on his face when he saw me, standing there, staring at him." Shantha was hugging herself, still staring firmly at the ground beneath her feet. "He wore a fine, black leather hat bleached by the sun and re-finished countless times. The whip in his hand was a perfect match to his boots and the hat. He wrapped it up without wiping the blood off it and stuck it snuggly next to his sword at his right side. His clothes were made of a thick, black linen, embroidered with what I can only imagine was pure spun silver.

"He shouted my name when he saw me, and I ran. My father is many things." She repeated. "But he is not a merchant. He is a pirate and a slave trader." She stopped. Her jaw tensed and released. The story I'd imagined she'd tell was not the story I was hearing.

"He came home that night dressed the way he always dressed, in a soft gray tunic and trousers, his beautiful gray hat with the feather propped casually on his head." My mind was spinning as I realized why Hova had glanced at Kaimbe. I glanced over to see Kaimbe's face hard as stone.

"Your father, is your father's name, Aruj?" Kaimbe interrupted the girl. She looked at him in shock and nodded. "Then I am your older half-brother. So are River and Ryder." He spoke the words in his usual, gentle tone, his face sullen.

Shantha stared at the three of them as they stared back at her, unsure of how to respond to this familial connection.

"Shantha," I said, my impatience rising. I wanted to hear the end of her jumbled story. "What happened next?"

"He chided me gently for coming to the docks alone." The teenage girl continued, breaking the stare of her new-found family. "I said nothing. I could barely look him in the eye, flinching every time he touched me. A few days later, my servant disappeared, and a new girl was in her place. When I asked where she'd gone, he said she'd quit. But I knew he was lying. He had to be." Hova was crying again. My heart pounded as I realized where the story was going.

"That's the night I snuck out and went to the docks again. I was looking for my servant because I finally understood where she'd come from. I found her. But I was too late to save her." She stopped talking and hung her head, closing her eyes.

SON OF KINGS

"That night I watched as my father brought her out from below deck, beat her, hung her, and threw her over the ship."

We sat in sad silence with Shantha, processing what she'd said. *Pirate. Slave trader.* My mind was spinning. *Murderer.* My stubbornness was giving way to compassion and a sense of loyalty.

"Please," Shantha said. "Please let me stay." She wiped a tear away from her closed eyes, then looked up at me. "My father is good friends with the governor. I want to help."

What else could I do but nod? *We're coming for you.* I thought, wishing I could speak to others the way Hova did.

CHAPTER THIRTEEN

Chantrea sat on the floor in the corner of her cell wrapped in her cloak, blending into the shadows. She smiled to herself as she sat, legs crossed and back straight. It always put the guards on edge when she did that. But their fear of her outweighed their annoyance. They'd figured out early on she couldn't leave the cell, but she could defeat anyone who entered the cell to confront or beat her.

There was so little to amuse the Elven warrior in this dungeon and so much time to sit and think. Whispering in the minds of the witless guards and putting them on edge always got their tongues wagging, which gave her much needed news of the outside world.

"The Gray Merchant came to see Governor Aepep," One guard whispered to another as they both watched her, shifting nervously from side to side. "I heard tell they had a terrible shouting match and The Gray Merchant left looking angrier than when he first arrived."

"What did he want of Governor Aepep?" The other guard asked, grunting. He always grunted. He grunted when he spoke, when he sat down, when he stood up, even in his sleep. It was the only mystery in the dungeon Chantrea had not been able to figure out.

SON OF KINGS

"He was here about his daughter. He claims she ran off and left him and he can't find her. He claims," the man lowered his voice as much as possible, unaware that if his prisoner could read his thoughts then she would hear whatever she wanted to regardless of how quietly he tried to whisper. "He claims his daughter ran off and joined the Shadows."

Another grunt.

"He claims it's Governor Aepep's fault they exist and was threatening him with what he'd do if the Governor didn't get rid of those gutter rats once and for all."

"Why do you call him, 'The Gray Merchant'?" Chantrea's rich voice made the men jump to attention and reach for their weapons. They stared at her in confusion for a moment. A grunt was heard, but no response. "I have my ways, you know." She whispered. In truth, Chantrea had never done anything to any of them except in self-defense, but she'd trained them to believe she could and would, at the slightest provocation, torture or kill them with her mind.

"I, uh, that is," the guard stammered, unwilling to test her. "He always wears, well, gray." He shrugged his shoulders, looking at his companion the grunter for confirmation. A nod and another grunt were eagerly given.

"Ah, and he's a merchant?" Chantrea mocked them from the corner where she sat beneath her hood. They both nodded, their faces flushing in the dim light with embarrassed anger. "But what is his name?" She asked, still sitting in the corner. "Does he not have a proper name? Or does he call himself 'The Gray Merchant'?" She asked, letting out a short laugh.

"We, uh, we can't tell you that." The grunter interjected. "Private information, top secret." He nodded at the other guard. "Against the rules to discuss it with criminals like yourself."

"Ah," Chantrea laughed. "You have no idea what his name is!" Their faces betrayed the truth as soon as she'd said it. She stood up and walked up to the bars of her cell, grasping one in each hand, and bringing her face up to the opening in between. "Come closer and I'll tell you a real secret." She goaded them. The light from the grate behind her created an eerie effect where they could only see the outline of her hood and her hands. They backed up a step, looked at each other, and came closer, just out of arms reach.

"What secret?" The first guard asked, accompanied by an annoying grunt from his companion, both brandishing their weapons to discourage any trickery they believed she might have in mind.

"I know his name!" Chantrea laughed again. "Better get ready, there's a storm brewing!" She turned around and walked back to her silent seat in the corner on the floor, leaving the guards to alternate between begging her for more information and cursing at her silence.

I crouched by the bridge that crossed beside The Governor's Grounds, Hadithi and Ryder beside me. It was a dark but clear night, the moon brightly shining through wisps of cloud high above us. A couple of months had passed since Shantha had arrived and fall was in full swing. The air was cool and damp, but comfortable enough for a dark, long-sleeved tunic to be enough to keep off the chill. The less layers we had to wear the faster we'd be able to move. Hova had been working for the last two weeks on creating the perfect scrap leather hoods and gloves for us to wear with our tunics, so we didn't have to use a cloak to keep from being seen in the moonlight – especially Hadithi.

Tyr had taken Shantha and River with him down the road to an area of the wall to the East that had recently decayed while Kaimbe waited in the shallows of the river, lying flat on his stomach on a raft, tethered to the underbrush, waiting for our hopeful arrival.

"We've got to get her out of there!" Tyr had been on the rampage to get Chantrea out ever since she got caught. "It's been two years. She deserves better from us, Yuvraj. She deserves for us to at least try!" His kindness and loyalty were an endless source of annoyance, causing me to both admire and despise my half-brother at the same time. *There will never be a good time for me to try to explain to him why I discouraged any kind of rescue mission every time he brought it up.* I'd thought to myself. *I'd have to explain too many of my hopes and desires, my plans for Hadithi and the Shadows.*

"Besides," he'd said, further trying to convince me it was the right thing to do. "Aepep won't be expecting it. He's let his guard down by now, gotten sloppy with guarding her. He might even assume we've forgotten about her, that we think she's dead and have moved on. Regardless of what he thinks, we've got to try!"

"Then let's try." I'd finally agreed.

Tyr had planned the escape for well over a month. All his time had been spent on late night scouting missions, staring at his homemade maps of the grounds, and watching - so much watching. The rest of us had gone about our normal preparations for the winter: harvesting what we'd grown, purchasing extra lentils, flour, and fat. We'd harvested as many mushrooms in the Woods as humanly possible, setting our traps and emptying them almost daily to catch, kill, clean, and then dry all the bird and squirrel meat possible. All while helping as many of the residents as possible with patching roofs and chopping wood.

Hadithi's training had continued. In the early mornings, when the moon was still bright, I would take Hadithi out to our clearing in the Woods to rehearse the spells I'd taught him. He'd easily mastered water, fire, and light. He could hold the light in his hands like a small moon, taking it a step further than I could by throwing it to wherever he needed light then pulling it back to hover in his hands again.

I always felt caught between envy and awe, half-tempted to tell him we were cousins just so I might feel bigger in his eyes. But I kept silent. I might not be strong enough to defeat my father, but the two of us together – along with all the rage and hatred I managed to stir up in Hadithi's mind with a single word – together we would be more than a match for the magic of my father the Governor of Shantu.

Tyr would always join us after Hadithi's magic sessions, taking precious time away from his plans to rescue Chantrea because he needed Hadithi to be combat ready for the plan to work. Hadithi learned quickly, something I expected from the son of an Elven warrior. He was quick on his feet and precise with his hits.

The last week before the rescue, Tyr and I decided Hadithi needed to work on combining his magic with physical fighting. Admittedly, we were all apprehensive. It was one thing to throw fire at a blade of grass, it was another to practice throwing it at us while still giving us enough time to duck. But the training went surprisingly well.

"Hit, two, three, four, fire, two, three, four, hit, fire, three, four, fire, two, three, four." We stood on either side of Hadithi, Tyr chanting rhythmically as we circled around. He started the chant slowly, then sped up as we went along. By the time the sun had risen, Hadithi had a good grasp of how it should go, but no idea what it might be like to throw fire at an enemy. By the end of the week, I could only hope our strict rhythm wouldn't confuse or restrain Hadithi if charged suddenly by a guard ready to kill.

Standing next to the bridge in the dark with Hadithi beside me, I still worried about what would happen if things got ugly and we got caught even while hoping Tyr's plan would be flawed and we wouldn't make it inside. If Chantrea and Hadithi met I had no doubt that my long-term plans for my cousin would be ruined.

I glanced at the small hourglass Tyr had perched on a rock beside us. Time was almost up. If all went according to Tyr's plan then he, Shantha, and River would be in position by now, ready to crawl through the opening in the wall. Tyr had timed himself, rehearsing his steps from every angle, allowing a few extra seconds in case any unexpected guards came by.

"It's time." Ryder whispered, pocketing the hourglass, and nodding at me. I nodded back and we moved toward the wall. I peered around the edge that met the river, where they hadn't bothered to rebuild what the water had naturally eroded over time. The water was shallow right now, making it easy to wade through, ankle deep, and walk around the wall into the Governor's Grounds.

A single guard was marching in the opposite direction, his back toward us. I waded silently through the shallow water, knowing Ryder and Hadithi wouldn't be too far behind me. We crossed the open ground without a sound and paused beside the wall of an outer building. The dungeon was near the center of the Governor's Grounds, beneath his mansion. With any luck, and if Tyr had timed it correctly, we'd be able to make our way there completely unseen and without disturbing any of the guards.

We zig-zagged our way through the grounds the way Tyr had drawn out for us on the map based on his calculations of when guards were changed and what route they took. Staying close to as many walls as possible, we stealthily peered around corners. We were in the heart of the soldiers' barracks, but most of them were sound asleep inside.

The rear of the Governor's Palace loomed in front of us, lantern lights twinkling from a few windows and all visible watch towers. The dungeon spread throughout the entirety of the level beneath the mansion. There was no telling whether Tyr or I would find Chantrea first, or if we'd find her at all.

"You have to recognize the very real possibility," I'd whispered to Tyr as we got ready to leave our home. "That Chantrea might already be dead. He could've killed her in private to avoid showing the people someone from another world." I knew it was unlikely. Aepep loved making a public example out of those he considered his enemies. But it was my last-ditch effort to discourage the rescue mission I didn't want to happen in the first place.

"She's alive." Hova said. I jumped and took a step backward, not having realized she was beside us. She'd handed me my hood, looked me straight in the eye with a fierceness and a fire that made me both love and fear her and repeated, "She's alive. Believe me, I would know if she were dead."

I shook my head as we reached the rear of the palace, trying to focus on the task at hand, trying to decide what I would do if we found our Elven legend. We kneeled in the shadows of the back wall. I looked around for guards. We would be hard-pressed to fight our way out if we were seen here. One cry for help and the entire compound would explode with half-asleep soldiers ready to attack.

Thankfully, the mansion itself was highly under-guarded on this side as Aepep didn't expect a threat because anyone approaching had to make it through the barracks first. Tyr was approaching from the entrance, which meant he had to make it through a much more heavily guarded area. As the stronger fighter and mastermind of the entire plan, he'd made the executive decision which entrance he would take.

"According to Tyr's map, there should be a grate to the dungeon somewhere close by." Ryder whispered to us, inching his way forward, staying low and close to the wall. Hadithi followed him and I brought up the rear, eyes open for any passing guards.

'Ah, Yuvraj! You've come to rescue me at last!' Chantrea's voice echoed in the back of my mind, just as Hova's had done. Sweat broke out on my forehead. *'What? No sweet greeting in return?'* I tried to ignore her, continuing to move forward as I scanned behind us for any guards. *'You should trust your brother. He was very thorough. No, don't worry, I didn't tell him any of your dirty little secrets. I didn't even speak to him.'* She paused as Ryder and Hadithi stopped in front of me.

"I found it!" Ryder whispered excitedly. I walked around the two in front of me and peered in through the grate. A dimly lit, grim looking hallway met our eyes. The grate was rotting and could easily be removed if Hadithi and I used our fire powers strategically. The danger was that we might be noticed. Red flames in the dark of night tend to catch the attention of guards, even guards who might be half-asleep at their post. But there was no other way.

'Poor Yuvraj. Have you decided how you will sabotage this mission? Or are you still trying to figure that part out?' Chantrea wouldn't leave me alone. I signaled to Hadithi, pointing at the top joint I wanted him to work on as I slowly burned through the last of the rotting bottom joints. With any luck it would bend out once we'd weakened enough of the bars. Ryder sat close by between us, his back to the grate, his eyes focused on the dark compound, watching for any sign of life.

'Have you ever wondered what Hova thinks of you? Truly and completely, as someone who can read your thoughts better than she can read her own?' The Elven voice rang in my ears, seeming to grow louder by the minute. I tried to focus all my attention on the thin stream of fire I was aiming at the bars with the palm of my right hand, determined not to answer her in any way. *'You claim to love her yet lie to the ones she loves. You have a choice, Yuvraj. You can choose to become a man worthy of her affection, proving yourself to her and creating a margin of chance for her to love you in return. But only if you really want to.'*

Chantrea's sympathetic advice made me angry. I burned through the bottom bars more quickly than expected and turned my attention to the top ones. *'Is it my fault I don't understand how to love the way everyone thinks I should? Is it my fault I want something greater for my life than a stinking, rotting house in the Slums? Don't lecture me on love and lies. You made your choices. You and I both know how that worked out for you.'*

I couldn't help myself. I knew I was one of the only people Chantrea had ever told the full story of why she'd left Zale. *'Who else did you tell?'* I asked her, blazing through another bar in the grate with unexpected ferocity. *'Kind, compassionate Hova?'* Silence was my only response, my mind quiet. *'You are as much of a hypocrite and liar as I am. Someday I'll make sure the others know.'* I wished I could look her in the eye as I said the words in my mind.

'You have a choice, Yuvraj. No matter how poorly a job I have done in teaching your heart as I trained your magic, you still have a choice. Make sure your choice

SON OF KINGS

doesn't cost you all that you love the way it did me.' I flinched at her rebuttal as I burned through the last bar. I nudged Ryder. He turned around. Together, while the bar was still warm, the three of us carefully bent the grate up so that, what had been the bottom, pointed straight toward the sky. I was shocked at how effective and quiet our strategy had been.

I signaled to Ryder and he quickly slid through the opening, followed by Hadithi. I glanced around and slid through. We found ourselves in the grim hallway, which stretched on to the left or the right. No signs, no soldiers, no sounds. Worst of all, there was nowhere to hide if a soldier did appear. My heartbeat quickened as I looked up at the opening we'd used to get inside. We could climb out, but it wouldn't be easy.

"Which way do we go?" Ryder whispered, glancing between our choices with the same slight panic in his eyes I was sure resided in my own. *For all his planning, Tyr didn't figure out where she was being held.* I grumbled to myself, knowing full well it was an unfair thing to have expected in the first place.

"We'll just have to pick." I whispered to my companions, shrugging my shoulders. "Hadithi, which way do you think we should go?" I wasn't sure why I asked him. He was staring down the right side of the hallway, in the direction of the river. Without a word he started walking that way, Ryder and I following quickly behind him, trying to mimic his silent footsteps. We passed two more grates before increased light formed ahead of us. The sounds of gentle snoring echoed down the corridor. We paused as we rounded a bend in the hallway, all three of us sticking as closely to the wall as possible.

I peered around the corner. A large, circular room with a single, long cell stretching from one end of the room to the other lay before us. Two guards sat slumped over, arms crossed, snoring. *Apparently, things haven't changed all that much in the last eight years.* I thought, remembering the first night Tyr and I had set out to steal from Aepep's storage rooms.

Something moved from the corner of the cell. Chantrea emerged from the shadows, tall, face uncovered and glowing a faint blue from the gentle moonlight streaming in through the grate above her. *She looks haggard, tired.* I thought, annoying pangs of guilt flooding the pit of my well-fed stomach. The Elf pointed to a ring of keys hanging on the wall close to where we stood. I nodded to let her know I'd seen them. *Now for the guards.* I thought, wishing there was an easy way to escape so I could accidentally wake them. But the only ways out were the way we'd come in and the grate above Chantrea.

Ryder pointed at one of the guards, indicating which one he'd take. He pulled out two large handkerchiefs and handed me one along with a string of braided twine he carried on his belt. It only took a few seconds to subdue and silence the two of them. By the time they woke up they were lying face-down on the floor with a handkerchief stuffed in their mouths and us sitting on top of them, tying their hands and feet together. They tried to speak and shout and sound the alarm, but they soon gave up.

I turned around to face Chantrea and froze. Hadithi stood in front of her cell, his hood lowered, his eyes wide and watering. I hadn't realized what might happen if and when he met her. There was no way of knowing if he would remember her from his early childhood, or if seeing her might conjure up the memory buried deep within. *What might Chantrea tell him?* I wondered, breaking into a cold sweat.

"I grant you peace." The Elven warrior whispered and extended her hand toward Hadithi, palm pointed toward the ceiling. The seconds seemed to drag as Hadithi hesitated, then awkwardly extended his own hand, palm down, to rest on top of hers.

"Peace I receive."

Chapter Fourteen

Earlier That Night

Tyr kneeled at the foot of the wall where the stones were crumbling, Shantha and River close beside him.

"It's best if we split the children up for their first raid." He'd told Yuvraj, much to his half-brother's relief. "We know how well River and Ryder work together, but the children might easily be distracted." That was Tyr's way of acknowledging the deepening friendship between the two. As oblivious as he was to Yuvraj's or Hova's feelings on the topic because they hid it so well, he knew putting Shantha and Hadithi together could make for a disastrous mission. *They need more training before they can be trusted to go onto the grounds together. Or anywhere, for that matter.* He thought.

The Shadow peered through the opening to see if it was time to move. The soldiers on guard were sitting by a small fire, perched on small stools. One was fiddling with a coffee pot and the other with a couple of wooden sticks he'd tied food to and now held precariously over the flames to cook. Best of all, they had their backs to the very space they were guarding.

Tyr smirked to himself. *They have to be large in number in order to make up for the size of their brains and the lack of dedication to their job.* Chantrea had taught him that strength in numbers only held specific advantages if those numbers were as dumb as the rocks they guarded. He glanced back at Shantha and River, nodding for them to follow him.

He'd chosen Shantha on purpose. He knew Yuvraj had a fascination and soft spot for Hadithi and he didn't mind. Shantha was quick on her feet and already understood how to use a sword – the one advantage to having a pirate as a father. She needed more training, but she was already better at hand-to-hand combat than Hadithi, and she was smaller. She would be unexpected and underestimated by an opponent if they ran into any trouble, and the unexpected was an advantage Tyr always enjoyed having.

The three Shadows slid noiselessly over the stones and steadily crept along the inside of the wall. The soldiers never even turned around.

Ryder and I stood there, unsure of what to do or say, staring at two, slightly blue, Elven people resting their palms together.

"We don't have much time." I said, clearing the nervous knot in my throat as I broke the silence. "We need to get you out of that cell, Chantrea." I grabbed the keys off the wall so I didn't have to look at her while I spoke. "Then we need to get all of us out of this dungeon." I fumbled with the keys as I eyed the grate inside the Elf's cell.

"Who are you?" Hadithi whispered, his palm still touching Chantrea's palm. She smiled and backed away, a tear glimmering in the dim light.

"Someday I'll tell you, child." She responded. "But not right now." She wiped the tear from her cheek and turned away from Hadithi's penetrating stare to look at me. "Right now, we need to get out of here. Just as Yuvraj said." I rolled my eyes and opened the cell door.

"Hadithi," I said, trying to hide the irritation in my voice as I pointed at the grate above. "I need you to help me. That's our best and easiest way out. I don't relish the idea of going back the way we came." I motioned for Ryder to join me in the cell as Hadithi seemed to gather his wits and walked through the door as well. Ryder and I easily hoisted him up, one foot in each of our hands, so his stomach was level with the bottom of the grate. He took a deep breath, peered out into the dark night, and started to burn his way through the iron bars just like he'd done before.

Chantrea stood watching us, silently. Time ticked by and I could hear the soldiers we'd tied up struggling with their ropes. The more they struggled the more the braided twine would dig into their wrists and ankles. I cranked my head around to catch a glimpse of how much they could see. Their eyes were wide with fright as they fought against the knots we'd tied. I felt oddly satisfied to know they must be terrified. *Good.* I thought. *The stories they tell will only add power and lore to the reputation of the Shadows.*

I turned back when I heard Hadithi grunting and struggling as he tugged on the grate.

"I can't bend it the way you did back there." He said. His voice was tired. He'd practiced his magic, but he'd never had to concentrate so hard on burning through so much before. "The angle's all wrong and I'm not strong enough." It puzzled me how he didn't seem to mind admitting he wasn't strong enough.

"Don't worry about bending it." I encouraged him. "Just burn through the last bar and be done with it. It's okay. Can you manage one more?" I asked him, ready to jump up and do it instead if needed.

"I can do it." Hadithi spoke with resolve as he shifted and started again.

"Hold onto the grate with your free hand." I told him. "Just in case it starts to fall out when you're done." He made no response, but I didn't fault him for it. He soon finished and grunted once more, pushing the grate outwards. It made a quiet thud as it hit the dirt outside.

"Now what?" He asked, looking down at me.

"Put your hood back on and climb out." I told him. "Be careful." I added, hastily, as he began to pull himself out and lifted off our hands. The idea of him being grabbed while we were down inside the dungeon was more than a little bit anxiety inducing.

"All clear." He whispered down to us as he wiggled his way out the opening and onto the dirt on the other side. I could hear him dragging the grate off to the side and leaning it up against the stone wall.

"C'mon." I said, nodding to Ryder and hoisting him quickly up through the opening. He hardly even needed the help; it was just the extra boost for height. I turned to Chantrea as Ryder reached down.

"After you." I said the words with as much accommodating kindness as I could muster, my ears picking up the sounds of approaching guards. To my surprise, the Elf smirked, closed the door to the cell, locked it, and brought the keys with her. I braced for her weight as she stepped into my hand, still trying to figure out how I might possibly sabotage a rescue that had gone so smoothly. She was lighter than I expected, causing me to realize how much weight she must have lost since she'd been locked up. Ryder helped her through the opening, then threw down the end of a short length of rope tied into a handle, holding tightly to the other side.

I eyed the situation as the rope hung just out of reach. The voices and stomping of guards grew closer and the soldiers we'd tied up were starting to gag out noises to accelerate their companions. I pulled my hood up and took a few steps back, lunging toward the wall, one foot stepping up it as I grabbed the handle. Ryder pulled the rope at just the right moment, grabbing onto my outstretched free hand as I scrambled up the side of the cell wall.

Once outside, we quickly dusted ourselves off, trying to catch our bearings. I looked up to find the moon as means of figuring out where we were and how many hours of darkness we had left, but the moon had disappeared somewhere behind a dark cloud. *Ideal for moving unseen.* I thought. *Not ideal for finding our way out.*

"Which way are you going?" Chantrea whispered as commotion erupted inside the dungeon.

"The river." Hadithi whispered back, beating me to it. "Kaimbe is waiting for us on a raft."

"Ah. Good plan, Tyr." I could no longer see the Elf, but I could hear her smile in approval and admiration as she spoke the words. "This way." Without another word, we ran, single file, ducking in and out of the shadows, following the Elf.

SON OF KINGS

Tyr, River, and Shantha had made it past five soldier patrols and had quickly overpowered the single guard standing next to the outside entrance of the dungeon when they heard the noise coming from the other side of the Governor's Mansion.

"I think we found them." River whispered to Tyr and Shantha, nodding toward the noise, and pausing his efforts to pick the lock on the dungeon door. Shantha's heartbeat quickened with anxiety for the first time all night.

"What if they're still inside?" She asked Tyr, wishing she could simply force the door open with her mind. "We need to go in there, we need to make sure they can get out!" She was trying to maintain her calm and lower her voice. Tyr reached out and grabbed her by the shoulders and leaned down, pulling her face close enough to his so she could see his good eye, even with his hood on.

"We have to go, Shantha." He spoke calmly, staring her down. "I swear to you by all that is good in this world, if they are still in there, we will get them out. We'll find another way. If Hadithi is still in there," he said, pointedly, knowing who she was most concerned about. "And everyone else escapes, believe me: we will not rest until we help him escape. We don't leave our own to die."

The girl nodded in response, took a deep breath, and stood up a little straighter. Without another word, they took off running along the wall of the Governor's Mansion, pausing to shrink into the shadows whenever a group of soldiers came close, all running in the direction of the dungeon doorway.

As they drew closer to the noise, Tyr signaled them to follow him, crossing over to the shadows of a storage building opposite the Mansion wall. Chaos from inside the dungeon was evident. An opening with bright torch light and a bobbing head came into view. Tyr took in the severed grate, leaning carefully against the wall and smiled. The bobbing head changed every few seconds to a different soldier, all trying to climb out of the hole or peer into the darkness for the escapees.

The sheer madness of the noise emanating from within the dungeon told Tyr that most – if not all – of the soldiers had chosen to enter the dungeon in response to a call for help, rather than running out to search the grounds for someone who had attacked or escaped.

"We won't find them in there." He whispered to the younger two. "They've gone. It's time for us to meet them at the river with Kaimbe." They dodged through the shadows, picking up speed as they got further away from the dungeon.

"Oy!" A voice shouted as they passed by one of the storage sheds. "Stop! You, what are you doing? Stop there!" Heavy footsteps sounded as the soldier shouted for others to join him. *If there are any others to join in.* Thought Tyr to himself, wondering how many soldiers had entered the dungeon and clogged up the passageways. *Why would I stop? Why would anyone stop?* The questions took over the Shadow's mind as the soldier continued to shout his feeble order for them to stop, obviously running more out of breath with each command.

Tyr fell back to take up the rear in case the soldier caught up to them, leaving Shantha in front with River close behind her. Up ahead a figure stepped out from behind a building, sword, and armor glinting in the light. Shantha didn't even hesitate. As soon as the glint of armor hit her eyes she dodged to the right, did a somersault, landed on her feet, and stabbed both of the man's legs from behind with her knife. Then she kept on running.

The soldier yelped in surprised pain and staggered. River dealt him a blow on the side of the head, knocking him over behind a storehouse. Tyr felt a sense of deep satisfaction as he watched them, running past the now-unconscious man without a second glance. He heard the soldier behind them pause, and further behind that soldier the sounds of multiple feet and yelling voices quickly catching up to them.

"Hurry!" He yelled ahead, preparing to turn and face the onslaught if necessary. As they neared the river they saw five hooded figures, one balancing precariously on a floating raft, struggling with over half a dozen soldiers. Fire sprang up sporadically from two of the five, a beautiful glowing light held in the hand of a third who masterfully disarmed and booted a soldier into the river.

Woosh! The well-known sound of an arrow whizzed past Tyr's head. *Time to get out of here, magic or no!* He thought, turning, and running nimbly backwards as he loaded his bow and shot into the group of armed and torch-bearing soldiers. A yelp confirmed he'd met his mark.

Turning back toward the river, Tyr saw all but one soldier had been disarmed and overpowered. Chantrea's tall, thin figure came into view as the light she held steadily in her hand helped them all board the raft Kaimbe had dislodged from the bushes, even as he balanced gracefully upon it, sword in hand.

"Yuvraj!" Tyr shouted. "I think it's time we got out of here!" He saw Shantha embrace Hadithi then jump carefully onto the raft, his hand tucked into her own. *Young love.* He wondered at it. *I'm not convinced it has a place in the Shadows.* He turned to face the soldiers again, sword poised, finding his place next to Chantrea. Kaimbe, River, Ryder, Shantha, and Hadithi had all boarded the raft.

"It's now or never, Tyr." Kaimbe warned as he dodged to the left, allowing an arrow to splash harmlessly into the water behind him. He steadied the raft with a long pole. Shantha and Hadithi were told to lay down as Kaimbe's brothers crouched low and loaded their bows, firing them off as they were able.

Yuvraj stood on the other side of Chantrea, throwing a flame into the middle of the oncoming soldiers. The soldiers yelped and held back, kneeling to assume a fighting position.

"Tyr," The Elven lady spoke decisively. "It's time for you to go home." Tyr threaded an arrow onto his bow, noting he only had a few left.

"You mean it's time for *us* to go home." He said, knowing full-well what she meant. He fired into the crowd of soldiers once more. They were growing in number by the minute. Any second now and they might change tactics and rush them all. If they did that, no one would escape.

"No, Tyr." She answered in the patient, loving voice she'd used when he was still a child and didn't want to obey her commands. "It's time for you and Yuvraj and everyone on that raft to go home. It's time for me to go back to the dungeon." She ducked as an arrow whizzed by her head. "You did a good job, and I could go with you, but if I do they will search every house in the Slums until they find me. Rather than being organized, we'll be fugitives, run out of the Slums by the very people we work hard at preserving."

"I'm not leaving without you, Chantrea." Tyr said, threading his bow again, wishing she wouldn't argue while wondering why Yuvraj said nothing.

"Go home, Tyr." The Elven lady said, taking a step forward, her light glowing brightly in her hands. She turned her back briefly to the soldiers so he could see her face. "Take your maps and go home." She stepped backward, edging closer to the soldiers. "Now!" The Elf screamed at him, turned back toward their enemy, and ran into the mob.

Tyr stood, watching in horror as the soldiers knocked Chantrea to the ground and climbed on top of her, tying her hands and feet together as the magical light died out.

"Tyr, we must go!" Yuvraj was screaming in his ear and dragging him toward the raft. He felt himself pushed onto it, water lapping at his feet as he was shoved into a sitting position. Arrows went by but Tyr didn't duck. Kaimbe pushed off from the shore into the current. Within seconds the yelling faded, leaving the Shadows with nothing but the sound of the running water beneath them and the muffled crying of a boy whose face glowed blue in the light of the moon.

WE SAT AROUND THE fire at home, boots off, things drying out while wrapping ourselves up in light blankets. All but Hova and Hadithi. He couldn't stop crying. He'd walked up to where she sat, quietly sewing with tired eyes as she waited for us to return. Kneeling, he'd thrown off his hood, buried his head in her lap, and sobbed.

I wanted to pull him away, tell him to leave her alone, to straighten up and stop crying over a woman he didn't even remember. I wanted her to stop smoothing his hair, resenting the way she'd pulled him up to sit beside her, hugging him and rocking him back and forth while humming.

No one spoke. Hova didn't ask questions or demand why the mission had failed or why Chantrea wasn't with us. Hadithi's tears and one look at the rest of us while failing to catch any sight of the Elven lady were all she needed. The details could be filled in later. Truth be told, her gentle humming soothed all of us.

Tyr was the first to wander off to his bed, leaving his boots and other clothing to dry by the fire. I caught a glimpse of a small flask tucked into his elbow. I'd never seen Tyr drink before. He'd pulled the blanket up over his head, hiding most of his face from our view.

One by one the others all drifted off to their beds as well. Shantha was last, waiting until Hadithi's sobbing stopped and the gentle rise and fall of his chest could be seen as he drifted off into oblivion. His head still rested on Hova's lap; his legs curled up in the fetal position. Shantha stood up, grabbed the thick blanket from Hadithi's bed and carefully covered him up. To my surprise, she also grabbed a blanket from Hova's bed and brought it to her with a sad smile. Hova thanked her with a nod, her face showing relief as the girl helped wrap the blanket around her.

As Shantha started for her bed, Hova grabbed her hand and held it, drawing her in to whisper something in her ear. The girl nodded, flashed another sad smile, and wandered off to bed.

I stared bleary-eyed into the fire, replaying the events of the night in my head.

'How did you do it?' I started at the sound of Hova's voice in my head. I continued to stare at the fire, afraid of what my eyes might betray if she could see them.

'What do you mean?' I asked her, resentment welling up inside me. I didn't care that I'd wanted to sabotage the rescue. I didn't care that in an altered state of events I would have done everything possible to ruin Chantrea's escape. I cared that she thought so badly of me; that she viewed me as the one at fault without ever asking what had happened. *'I didn't do anything! I'm the one who found her. I'm the one who helped get her free. I'm the one who saved your precious brother when Chantrea charged back at the soldiers like a crazy person instead of climbing onto the raft with us. If anything,'* I faltered, the mental screaming lowering to a dull roar. *'You should be thanking me. I kept your precious Hadithi safe as well.'*

Hova's silence, to me, was a deafening condemnation. I'd hoped my words would exact an emotional response, an apology, something to make me look good.

'He's going to have questions, Yuvraj.' She sounded tired. The kind of tired that reaches deep down into your bones and settles in your soul. *'When are you going to tell him the truth?'* My heart beat faster as she asked this question, inferring by default that I'd lied to him.

'You may like to play mother.' I decided to go a different route with my response. *'But you're not his mother.'* I turned to look at her. *'And you will never be his lover.'* I snarled, watching the hurt flashing in her eyes with an odd sense of satisfaction. *'I don't owe you an explanation. I don't owe you an answer. I don't owe you anything. You've made that very clear.'* I stood up and walked over to my bed, expecting the

conversation had ended; that the intrusion into my private thoughts would be done for tonight.

'Someday he's going to find out.' Hova's voice whispered in my brain as I curled up and tried to shut it out. *'Someday he's going to figure out the truth. I fear it will cost you more than you imagine.'*

Chapter Fifteen

"We need to find her." The witch muttered to her companion. He was a tall, thin man with a chiseled jaw and jet-black hair that matched his eyes. Thin lines around his eyes had started to form, signaling excess exposure to the sun, making it hard to guess his age.

"We will." He soothed, his voice like warm honey dripping off freshly cut comb on a summer's day. They were sitting together in a small, grim looking shack on the outskirts of the Slums, not far from the docks. The smokey iron stove between them, the roughly hewn chairs they sat on, and two cots pushed as close to the stove as anyone could safely dare, was all that could be seen. The walls that enclosed them dripped with humidity, a thick moss covering over the holes the rotting boards had created.

"Why do you stay with me, Efah?" Her eyes of arctic silver and the non-stop fluctuating of her veins between blue and red were the most enthralling and beautiful things he'd ever seen. The harshness of her voice seemed irrelevant to him.

"Ah, my dear," He spoke the word with caution, a sad smile breaking out of his face, causing the lines around his eyes to deepen. "My story is a sad one that I will not burden you with. Not all of it, anyway." He wanted to hold her, to embrace the witch and show how deeply he loved her. But he resisted the urge, determined to win her over with attention and loyalty.

"As I've said before," He continued. "My father is a bitter man, distrustful of so much. Like you, I come from the faraway land of Zale. It is my home, the place I most long to be. I once lived a happy, though hard life, on the edges of the much-feared Salt Lands. But, alas," He sighed on cue.

"My father rejected my love of magic and my thirst for knowledge. He didn't approve of my desire to grow in my understanding of the talent I possessed. In his anger and fear, he appealed to the Elves, and they honored his request: banishment from the only home I'd ever known to this horrible wasteland. I was still very much a boy when I arrived here, finding myself with nothing more than the cloak and clothing on my back and enough food to last me a few days." The man sighed again and stared at the flames in the stove, feigning a far-away look of sadness and apathy.

"What in the curses does any of this have to do with why you're here?" Chiwa asked him, her eyes still studying his face with suspicion. "How does this explain what you gain out of being with me and fighting my battle for me?"

"You," he said, steadying his voice as nerves rose from the pit of his stomach. "You are the rightful heir of Zale now that your father has passed." He hesitated, trying to decide which word would be the best choice. "You are the rightful heir to the Book of Nightmares."

"What's in it for you?" Came the cold reply.

"You want to gain what you have lost; what has been stolen from you. I want to gain that as well: the life I deserve, the home that has been taken from me. So, I propose the following." He stood up and paced slowly back and forth in front of her in the cramped space. "I help you find the Elven woman. Together we either make her tell us how we can return home, or we make her take us home." He shrugged his shoulders to show his indifference to Chiwa's preferred method. "I help you find your rightful inheritance so that you can help me settle in Zale as your right-hand servant."

Servant. Chiwa thought to herself. *I've never had a servant before. Of course, I know he means that he would be a man of some importance in Zale, someone who can gloat over his father.* She studied him. *But to be honest, I wouldn't mind.* She could never admit it to anyone, not even herself, but she missed the companionship of her father. The witch was lonely. Having an attractive man around to flatter and help her, who also knew something about magic, didn't sound like such a bad idea to her. Plus, she'd seen him knock out a nosey soldier without anyone else noticing.

"Very well." Chiwa rasped out after keeping him waiting for several minutes. "You can continue to stay here with me." She tried smiling. It felt strange. "But," she interrupted his immediate attempt to thank her and bow. "We must seal our agreement with a blood oath. I must have your fealty." She stood up, realizing once more that the crown of her head came well below his chest. Pulling out a small knife from the belt around her waist, Chiwa pricked the palm of her hand. Bright red came spilling out as Efah followed suit.

"Efah," she said, solemnly extending her hand to his. Their palms entwined, the small cuts meeting, blood smearing. "Do you swear on your life to be faithful to no one else but me, to defend my life as more precious than your own, and to never raise a finger against me?" Her harsh voice faltered a bit as she spoke the last part of the vow, memories of her father flashing across her mind.

"I swear." The man gazed down into her silver eyes, feeling his heart quicken. Her pulse met his as they pressed their palms together.

"Do you pledge to forsake all other leaders, to do as I ask without question, and to serve as my right-hand man?" The witch felt her power growing over him with each pledge and promise he agreed to.

"I pledge." Efah spoke with conviction, his free hand across his heart. "You are power and beauty and magic itself. I give you my blood oath to serve and treat you as my mistress, to give of my whole self without a care. You are Chiwa, powerful heir of the land of Zale. You are my witch, and you are my queen." He inched closer as he spoke the words, bowing his head and closing his eyes, hoping one day he might make her understand his depth of feeling for her. "I give you myself." He whispered. "I give you my blood oath."

CHANTREA STOOD AT THE far end of the great meeting hall, hands and feet shackled tightly together, eyes closed, head high, breathing in the room around her. The door closed behind her with a slow sense of reluctance, growing at least half a dozen pairs of soldier ears as soon as it was sealed shut.

"So," Aepep said, sitting comfortably on his chair at the other end of the hall. Jabez stood solemnly beside him while his six guards had been placed strategically throughout the room. "You tried to escape." He couldn't help but smirk, holding up a goblet of wine as if to toast her. "How did that go?"

Chantrea opened her eyes slowly, enjoying the privacy of her hood. Truth be told, she ached all over from a dozen soldiers piling on top of her and taking out their anger on her with a punch, a kick, and a slap. If Jabez and his men hadn't shown up when they did, she'd probably be at the bottom of the river by now. But the ache went much deeper than her skin and muscles. She ached for the children she loved.

"Tell me, Aepep," she said, filling the room with the richness of her voice. The sound of it sent chills down Jabez's spine. "How many of your soldiers died that night and what were their names?"

Anger flitted into the governor's eyes. He took a sip of wine and pushed the anger back down. "Their names are not important." His tone was cold and calculated, honest even. The expression on Jabez's face never changed. "They did their duty by me. They have fulfilled their vows to honor and protect all that I ask of them." He waited, wishing he could see her face.

"You're playing with fire, Aepep." She said, shaking her head slightly. "How long do you think it will be before Chiwa hears her cousins tried to save the lady she seeks from your dungeon?" She took a careful step forward, hands still clasped in front of her. "Who will protect you then? Who will fight the witch when she comes for what she obsesses over? Will Jabez and his men be enough to defeat her?" She paused for a second. "You know as well as I do that her magic goes far beyond that of her father. Are you strong enough to face her wrath?"

Aepep stood up and launched his goblet in her direction, knowing full well it would never reach her. It hit the floor with a thud, wine scattering over the floor.

"Shut up." He said, blue eyes flashing a warning that a storm might break at any moment.

"You're out of practice, Aepep." The Elven lady continued, taking another step in his direction. "You've kept it inside for so long, hiding the power you possess. I wonder," She tilted her head to one side much like a cat sizing up its prey before pouncing. "Do you even remember how to wield the powers you hold within you?" She waited for the repercussions of her words as the guards turned to watch his response.

Aepep inhaled sharply. *If I had any sense at all I'd get rid of her now.* He thought to himself, imagining how satisfying it would be to watch her hang after a good sound beating. The mental image of it all made his pulse quicken with excitement.

"If the time ever comes," he said, placing great emphasis on the first word. "I will deal with Chiwa. Do you think," he took a step in her direction, trying to see into the darkness of her hood. "Do you think I don't know that she's already broken our blood oath? Do you honestly think I don't realize my niece found the home of your precious Shadows years ago and has been holding that information hostage, pretending like she's still searching because she was looking for some woman that she finally found and burned to death?" It was a cruel question, and he savored every word of it, sensing Chantrea's discomfort as he stepped even closer.

"What makes you think a witch who doesn't keep her blood oath won't hold you to keeping yours?" Chantrea asked. The Elven lady's question made Aepep pause. "Do you know who it was she killed in that fire? Do you understand who survived it?"

The governor hated to admit he had no idea who his niece had killed or that anyone had survived the deadly flames.

"What does that have to do with anything?" He asked, searching in his mind for any rumors that might help him guess before Chantrea answered.

"Ah, Aepep." Chantrea shook her head gently from side to side. "Ever the strategist, ever the game-player. Ever the fool." She hoped her last comment would elicit the response she was looking for. She wanted him to see her eyes when she told him. She wanted to whisper danger into his ear and watch as the blood drained out of his face. It worked.

In an instant, Aepep pulled her hood down with one hand, tearing a few strands of white hair out as he did so, the other hand closing tightly around her throat. They were of equal height, both tall and strong. His breath was hot, rank with the stench of meat and wine. His eyes burned with fury, and his skin was beginning to tingle.

"I asked you a question: what does that have to do with anything?" He screamed the question at Chantrea, causing her to wince in pain and close her eyes as it pierced her ear drum.

"That woman," she said, pulling her mouth close to the governor's ear and whispering into it just loud enough for him to hear. "Was the mother of your nephew." She paused. Jabez moved forward, hand on his sword, eyes narrowed, watching for any physical threat to his rule. Aepep leaned back to see her face. The Elf smiled as she watched the wheels turn in his head.

"Nephew?"

"Yes. Nephew." She nodded. "You and your brother had more in common than you think. However," she said, trying to find the right words for what she was about to tell him. "Your brother's offspring both had mothers from Zale. Chiwa's mother, as you know, was a Faerie. It's what makes her so powerful and deadly."

"And the boy's mother?" Aepep asked, tightening his grip on her throat, wishing he could crush her windpipe and throw her body into the river.

"Ah, his mother was an Elf. The best, most powerful and talented warrior I've ever known." Chantrea contained the emotion welling up within her.

Aepep was piecing it together. The grief of Chantrea on the night of the fire, Chiwa's actions, Chantrea's mocking. Panic rose in his throat, his breath quickening as he tried to remain cool.

"Where is the boy now?" He already knew the answer to the question, but he had to be sure.

"You know where he is. He's training with your sons. Strong in magic and in fighting, even at such a young age. Passionate, angry, grieving." The Elf spoke each word slowly, savoring Aepep's discomfort. "Your nephew is a Shadow. I saw him." Aepep let go of her, his mind spinning as he backed up. "Yuvraj and Tyr may not be strong enough to defeat you and Chiwa together, but your nephew." Chantrea let the lack of words finish her thought for her.

"What's his name?" Aepep asked, catching Chantrea off guard. She was curious why he would even care.

"Hadithi." She smiled at him, reveling in the power of her knowledge, his name warming her heart as she spoke it. "Your move, governor." She sneered and laughed.

SON OF KINGS

"Throw her back in her cell!" Aepep yelled at the guards as he smacked her viciously across the face with the back of his hand, causing her to bite the inside of her cheek. Chantrea stumbled and spat the blood out, laughing again as they walked her back to the dungeon.

KAIMBE AND I DRANK the graciously offered tea the woman offered us as we sat crowded inside the tiny hovel we'd just helped repair. Dirt floor, leaning walls, but at least the holes in the walls had been patched and the roof had been repaired. Snow would be unable to build up inside, and the woman would no longer have to worry about freezing to death from icy winter winds and non-stop exposure to the elements.

We sat in silence, sipping the warm tea and smiling at our host, a mute woman whose name we didn't know. While she'd never shown us to confirm it, we suspected her tongue had been cut out by the governor or one of his guards, rendering speech close to impossible.

Patching homes was work I didn't enjoy, but the reward of loyalty and protection from those we helped was a wonderful pay-off, and well-worth the effort. Tyr and I had spoken frequently about our desire to slowly raise up those in the Slums so they could live and thrive without fear and without resorting to humiliating acts of desperation that further ostracized them from everyone in Shantu. It was a bold desire, an insane hope, but as much as I disliked the work, I couldn't imagine taking over our rightful inheritance and not transforming the Slums that had been our home all our lives.

"Thank you." Kaimbe said, smiling and setting down his empty cup. I downed the rest of my tea and followed suit. Kaimbe fished out a couple of loose coins he had in his pocket, and I reached into the sack I carried with me. I laid a bag of lentils, some dried meat, and a large bunch of carrots on the table.

"If you ever need anything, you know where to find us." I told her, squeezing her outstretched hand. She nodded; her eyes hungrily glancing at the food. Kaimbe bowed his head and ducked out the low doorway, closing it behind us.

"She might survive the winter now." Kaimbe muttered as we walked through busy alleyways, heading in the direction of our home.

"We'll add her to the regular's list." I replied. "Check in on her every now and then and make sure she's okay. She's old and frail. I can't begin to imagine how she's survived this long." That, of course, was a lie I liked to tell myself and others chose to believe. We all knew how to survive in the Slums, and nothing about our forms of survival was dignified.

We ducked down a quiet, narrow alleyway to avoid the midday crowds. A small beggar woman stood off to the side, leaning on a staff, the only person around. Kaimbe dropped a small coin into her gloved, outstretched hand and moved on. I started to pass her, but a strong hand detained me.

"I wish to speak with you, Yuvraj son of Aepep." The harsh rasp of her whisper startled me. Kaimbe looked back and paused near the end of the alleyway, watching to see if I needed any assistance. I rested a hand on the sword beneath my cloak and turned to face her, my back to Kaimbe.

"How do you know my name?" I whispered back, stepping away from her and throwing off the grip of her hand.

"Come now, Yuvraj, don't pretend you don't know me. Chantrea warned you about me. I heard her. I am, after all, your cousin." She chuckled, the kind of chuckle that made my skin crawl out of sheer repulsion.

"Chiwa." I said, hand tight on my sword, ready to use magic if needed, nervous about my odds.

"Relax." She said. "I told you, all I want to do is talk."

"About what?"

"I need certain information." She hesitated. "Information Chantrea has. I tried to get it from the other Elf but that," she chuckled again, anger entering the tone. "That didn't go well. Now Chantrea is my only hope."

My heart pounded. *Tyr's suspicions were correct.* I thought. *I should turn and walk away. I should ignore the witch completely. But I want to know what's in it for her.*

"What is this information?" I asked. "And what makes you think I can help you find it, or we can get it for you?"

"Yuvraj?" Kaimbe interrupted in a loud voice. "Are you coming?"

SON OF KINGS

"Yes," I said, turning to flash him a smile. "This old woman just needs some information. I'm almost done." I turned back to Chiwa. "Better make it quick or I'll walk away now." I said, fully aware of the fact that she could do some serious damage to my person if she wanted to.

"You want your rightful inheritance, correct?" She asked. I nodded in response. "As do I. The only person I know of who can get me to my rightful inheritance is Chantrea, and she's locked in Aepep's dungeon." She leaned on her staff with one hand and took the crook of my arm with the other, walking slowly in the opposite direction of Kaimbe. I followed. "Rumor has it you and Tyr broke into the dungeon and almost got her out."

"Yes." I responded, hesitant to give her any other details.

"Had I known she was there I would've gone to her myself. But, seeing as how my uncle has betrayed me," there was an unmistakable sneer in her voice. "And seeing as how your failed attempt to free her has made him even more cautious, I've decided our allyship is the only one that might work out.

"If you help me get to Chantrea, then I'll help you get the information you need to take down Aepep. Secrets about Commander Jabez, the names of his guards, when they're all most vulnerable." She paused at the end of the alleyway and took my hand between both of her own, as if thanking me for my assistance. "Once you've gathered a larger group of Shadows, earned a little more respect and loyalty from the Common People, and grown stronger in your magic, then we'll attack. You'll get Shantu, and I'll get Chantrea."

"Why should I agree to this?" I asked. "You're a murderer. You just admitted it. What makes you think I'll help you?" I said, excitement filling me. I wanted to say yes without hesitating. But my conscience fought me as I remembered the flames surrounding a burned little boy that Kaimbe and I had rescued.

"Because Yuvraj," she lowered her voice even more. "I know you're smart, and I know you're more loyal to yourself and your own desires than to anyone else. You know I can help you win. And you want to win!"

"It could take years." I said nervously, glancing at Kaimbe. He stood still, at attention, like a soldier waiting for a command.

"Doesn't matter. Just make sure your brother and his sister don't find out." She let go my hand. "I'll be in touch. Make sure you don't disappoint me, Yuvraj." Her voice was dangerous. A wave of indignation and disdain washed over me. *She has no idea Hadithi is with us, that he exists and is capable of much stronger magic.* I thought, the idea sparking inside me as the witch walked away.

"Same goes for you, Chiwa: don't disappoint me." I muttered, turning to rejoin Kaimbe.

Chapter Sixteen

"What was your mother like?" Shantha asked Hadithi in her quietest voice. Several weeks had passed since the failed attempt to free Chantrea had transpired. It was well into Winter, but the day was unseasonably warm, and the two children were sitting on a cot they'd dragged in front of the open window entrance. Chins propped up on the window, they soaked up the warm sunlight sneaking through the narrow alleyway to meet their upturned faces.

Shantha didn't look at him, hoping her question wouldn't scare him away or ruin the peace between them. They were home alone - a rare thing - just waiting for Hova to return so they could help her with dinner. Shantha had never asked before. She'd never felt she could and always hoped he'd tell her himself when the timing was right. But today she'd decided to stop waiting.

"She was amazing." Hadithi answered, his eyes steadily trained on the dilapidated wall in front of them. "Her name was Estel. She was the kindest, strongest person I've ever known. So full of life, but so sad." Tears formed and he wiped them away.

"She was my first teacher in every area of life - including fighting and magic. She sang to me, loved me, and never hid the truth from me. I know who my father was. I know what he was like and what he did to her and the rest of Zale. She never tried to hide that from me. But she always reminded me that his being my father didn't mean I would be like him or that she loved me less." He hesitated for a moment. "It's hard to explain."

Shantha sat in silence, allowing him time to sit with his pain. She had so many questions she wanted to ask, but she chose to wait and see what more he might tell her first.

"She was a warrior, you know." Hadithi began again, pride in his voice. "She was the best warrior they ever had. She climbed trees faster than anyone else, jumped from greater distances, and her arrow never missed. If she wanted to disappear, no one could track her. She told me that to become the leader of the Elven warriors she had to face several challenges. Her final challenge was to face ten of the best fighters and disarm them without hurting them or getting caught." He turned to smile at the teenager. "She did it faster than anyone before her." His face glowed, happiness spreading over it in a way Shantha had never seen before. She smiled back, remembering how she'd felt about her father before she found out the truth, wondering if anything her father told her about her mother was true.

"Did she ever take you to Zale?" She asked, curiosity winning out. "What did she say about it?"

"She did take me once." He said, turning away with a slight frown. "I was very young, and I don't remember much about the trip. She took me to meet my family, the Elves." He stopped short, leaning his chin on the edge of the window, squinting his eyes as if he were trying to remember. It was hard for Shantha to be patient. This world of magic and Elves was the most interesting thing she'd ever heard of before and she was dying to know more.

"What were they like? Did they all look like you, or like Chantrea?" She leaned a little closer to him.

"They were a lot like humans: all different skin colors. But they all had pointy ears, more so than mine." He said, touching his ears as he spoke. "Cool eyes too. And tall. They were all very tall. Like Chantrea, and my mother." His voice became sad again.

"Why did you come back?" She wished she'd kept the question to herself almost as soon as it left her mouth.

"They didn't want us." Hadithi whispered. "The Elves told my mother to leave and take me with her. They couldn't stand to look at me."

"I'm sorry." She said, leaning to rest her head on his shoulder, hoping the gesture would communicate what she couldn't put into words. They sat in silence again, Hadithi's cheek resting against the crown of Shantha's head.

"My mother always said it was wrong of them. I know it hurt her to have them turn their backs on her - on us - like that. She always talked about how one day we'd find my father and defeat him, maybe even take him back to Zale and make him fix everything he'd destroyed there. She was just waiting for me to get a little bit older."

"What was Zale like? Do you remember?" She believed she could ask him anything right now, as if he'd given her permission to ask.

"I remember vivid colors." He said. "Beautiful, vivid colors all around me."

"Was it warm?" She asked, closing her eyes as she soaked in the rare Winter sunshine.

"No. It was cold. Always cold. Even when the sun was out like this, I don't remember ever being able to feel its warmth. The wind was always chilly, even when flowers were blooming. We never took off our cloaks or slept without a blanket. Nights were especially cold."

"Why was it that way? Has it always been cold there?" Shantha frowned as she tried to imagine what it would be like to see a bright sun and blooming flowers but not feel the warmth of its rays.

"No, it's all part of the curse." Hadithi said, hesitating.

"What curse?" She sat up and turned to look at him.

"I, uh..." He looked down as if embarrassed by what he was about to say. "The curse my father brought upon the land. He used magic to release the power of an awful book of nightmares over all the land. Then he fled and came here. This happened a long time ago, right after Chiwa was born."

The witch's name always made Shantha's skin crawl. It was hard to believe the person she'd grown to love most in the world was the half-brother of the person she'd come to fear almost as much as Aepep and her father.

"Now everyone in Zale has nightmares." Hadithi continued. "All the time. Awake, asleep, it doesn't matter. The book manipulates their thoughts and feelings and causes them to fall into a sleep-like state while seeing the most horrible things they can imagine. Everyone lives in constant fear of their dreams, their loved ones, their neighbors, and themselves."

"Can't anything be done to break the curse? Can someone destroy the book?" Shantha asked, intrigued and horrified at the same time.

"I don't know." Hadithi shrugged. "I suppose they've already tried. My mother told me they all believed my father, Ethan, was the only one who could do it. But..." His voice dragged off. "I'm pretty sure he's dead now."

"Why?" Shantha asked.

"I only saw Chiwa the night my mother died. She was alone in the house with my mother." His voice quivered slightly as he said the words. "I think if he were still alive, then he would've been there with the witch. I think she killed him."

A dark apprehension came over Shantha as she listened to her friend. Somehow even the horrors of her own parentage couldn't compare with the twisted nature of his.

"Sometimes," He continued, un-urged. "Sometimes I think I might be able to do something. You know, because I'm his son." He choked on the last word, a sour look on his face. "Maybe, since he's dead, I might be able to do something to stop it. If I knew the right words or phrase or magic spell."

Shantha witnessed his face waffle between earnest desire and consuming anger.

"It's not your fault." She had to say it. He turned to meet her gaze for the first time. "You didn't choose him as your father. You're not responsible for what he did. It's not your fault." She leaned in close, one hand on his arm. "I just want you to know that. Even if you don't believe me."

Unable to help himself, Hadithi leaned forward and kissed her on the cheek, innocently, gently, and ever so sincerely, then touched his forehead to hers, taking the hand resting on his arm into his own.

"I know." He whispered. "My mother always told me that her mission didn't need to become my mission if I chose to walk away. But..." He stopped as he struggled to find the words. "But what if I'm the only one who can help them? What if no one else can break the curse, or defeat the book or wield the power of the book – or whatever it is that needs to be done? What if the only two people who can do it are the children of the one who unleashed it? And..." He was shaking. "And what if Chiwa gets to it before me?"

Shantha nodded, unsure of what to say, still blushing from the tingle of his kiss as it lingered on her cheek.

SON OF KINGS

"I'd given up the idea of going back." He said, straightening up and absentmindedly pushing his companion's stray hairs behind her ears. "My mother knew how to get there but never told me. I believed when she died that it would be impossible to figure out. Chiwa doesn't know." His anger was as abundant as his pain. "That's obvious. But then..." His voice dragged off again as he turned to look at the sun.

"Then you met Chantrea?" Shantha asked him.

"She was like the unexpected warmth of the sun on the coldest winter's day." He said, his voice cracking with hope. "I knew when I met her that she could tell me, maybe even show me, how to get back to Zale. I knew because I recognized her. I met her before."

Shantha nodded, absentmindedly caressing his hand.

"If I find out how to get there," he said, still looking at the sun. "Would you come with me?" He swallowed, nervously.

"You know I would." She replied, her face breaking out in a smile as she leaned her head back on his shoulder.

Down the alleyway just around the corner, unseen and unexpected, Hova leaned against the front wall of their home. Sobbing silently to herself, she listened to the two teenagers – not much younger than herself - dream of the day when they'd go to Zale and right the wrongs done by Hadithi's father. She'd seen their earnest faces as she'd been returning home, basket in hand, hood thrown back as she reveled in the unexpected warmth just like everyone else.

Now she stood, hood pulled over her face to hide the streaming tears, holding her sides, bent over, screaming silently at the basket of food at her feet.

'Sometimes it is too much to bear.' She reached out for the only person she believed would hear her. *'I don't want to let go. I don't want him to leave. How can I?'*

'Do you really believe you can keep him here? Keep him from his destiny?' The Elven lady's voice answered her. *'Could you live with yourself if you did? Do you honestly believe, Hova, that you could wake up every morning and see yourself any differently from the way you see Yuvraj?'* The question stung.

Hova sank down to a seated position, the sobbing almost over, too tired out to continue standing.

"No." She whispered; eyes closed.

147

'I'm sorry, child.' Chantrea's compassionate tone was rare. *'Heartbreak is a terrible thing, even when you know it's inevitable. But it's up to you to decide what to do with it because your heart has only begun to crack.'*

"I know." The young woman whispered in response as her breathing started to normalize. "Why didn't you come with them?" A tear ran down her cheek as she asked the question, her lip quivering beneath her hood.

'It wasn't the right moment, and it wasn't Yuvraj's fault.' Hova heard a sarcastic smile in the Elven lady's voice. *'He wasn't disappointed by my decision, but it wasn't by his desire. My presence would be a danger to all of you, including Hadithi. Hadithi would go back to Zale right now if I told him how to get there. He'd probably die within two days of returning. The problem is I wouldn't be able to resist telling him if he asked me. No, it's not right for me to be out there with him.'* She sounded resigned and sad.

'Hadithi needs more training and discipline, something both Tyr and Yuvraj can give him. He needs something and someone to fight for: me and the knowledge I hold. He needs your wisdom, Hova. I believe your wisdom and advice on life, along with your knowledge of food and herbal remedies will sustain him through times I cannot yet see, but fully expect. Shantha will be with him when he goes.' The words were honest and direct, leaving no room for sensitivity. *'They need more time to grow in deeper friendship, trust and love if they're going to make it.'*

Silence ensued as Hova pulled her knees up to her chest and leaned her forehead on them, the sun dipping down far enough to reach her for a few minutes before its warm rays disappeared below the surrounding buildings. She sighed, stood up, brushed herself off, and picked up her basket.

'I miss you.' She reached out once more before wiping her eyes with her pocket handkerchief and strolling energetically down the alleyway to greet the teenagers waiting for her. Through their cheerful "hello's" and offers to help with dinner, Chantrea responded in the far recesses of Hova's mind.

'I miss you too, child.'

SON OF KINGS

I arrived late that night. Kaimbe and I had gone to check on our mute woman to make sure she was alright, and to see if our handiwork had withstood the early bad weather. Everything had remained intact and, to our surprise, she not only smiled and offered us tea, but also showed us some rough sewing she'd picked up. We assumed this meant she'd found a way of bringing in a little extra cash. Anything that kept her from selling herself to the depraved and desperate soldiers was enough to keep us happy. Her cheeks looked a little fuller and I noticed a pot of soup cooking on the stove while we were there.

Pleased with my work and feeling we'd saved one more person from complete desperation, I'd arrived home hungry and anxious to share my triumph with the only person I still desired to prove myself to.

"Where's Hova?" I asked Hadithi and Shantha. They were sitting by the stove, whispering, and laughing as Hadithi carved out a new figure on a block of wood, his shavings piling up in the kindling box nearby. They looked up and around, surprised by the question.

"She must've gone out." Hadithi said, frowning slightly. "She was here just a bit ago. We made dinner and ate together. Maybe she went to check on someone?" I could tell he was concerned, but I didn't want him to go looking for her. Tyr was still out with the twins.

"I'm sure it's nothing." I said, calmly. "I'll go look for her. It's a pleasant night, so she might've gone for a walk."

"Do you want me to go with you?" Kaimbe offered. I waved my hand at him to sit and eat and shook my head in response. Turning to exit the window, I grabbed a chunk of bread to take with me. I climbed out and looked toward the street.

I'm up here.' Hova's voice entered my thoughts and stopped me before I reached the corner of the alleyway. I turned around abruptly and climbed up to the roof. She sat at the very top of it, her silhouette framed by bright moonlight. She was wrapped in her cloak with a blanket placed strategically beneath her for added comfort and warmth.

"I didn't ask you to come up here." She whispered as I sat down a couple feet away from her, maintaining a cautious distance. "I just wanted you to know where I was so no one would worry." She sounded sad, the kind of sad that made me want to cry in response.

"I, uh, I'm sorry." I apologized, swallowing the lump forming in my throat. I couldn't tell if she wanted me to leave or not. I sat there for a few minutes, silently staring at the sky. "I've never been up here at night before." I said, realizing how beautiful the stars looked on a clear night. "It's beautiful." I wanted to reach out, to hold her hand and sit on the blanket with her. But I knew it was a bad idea to test. Instead of reaching out for her hand, I wrapped my cloak tightly around me and pulled my knees up to my chest as she'd done.

"Where were you tonight?" Hova asked. Her voice was uncommonly neutral. It held a gentleness that was usually reserved for those we helped. I sat in shock for a second. *She's never shown any interest in me or where I've been unless it was out of anger or concern.* I thought, realizing she might hear the thought as soon as it came to me.

"Kaimbe and I were checking on a woman in the Slums. We helped fix her roof a couple weeks ago." I said, trying to calm the nerves rising inside me. Even when she wasn't upset with me, I still felt like I was on trial.

"The mute?" She asked.

"Yes, that's her." I replied, nodding absentmindedly.

"I helped her get some sewing work from a Tailor who owed me a favor." Hova said. "Did she show you?"

"Yes." I said, feeling a little silly for not having guessed as much sooner. "She looked happy. Healthier." I found myself wondering at what kind of favor the Tailor must have owed her. "Hova, why?" I couldn't fully formulate the question and I wished I'd held my tongue almost as soon as it left my lips.

"Why do I love him and not you?" The teenager beside me asked, her voice quiet and steady, the sadness still overwhelmingly obvious. "Why can't I give my affections where they're desired and obsessively asked for?" The question stung. "You might walk this earth a hundred years, learn all the magic it contains, win every battle you've ever hoped for, but until you learn to love unselfishly, you'll still feel unsatisfied, unwanted and alone, Yuvraj." She paused, turning to look at me. I kept my eyes trained on the sky above as my heart sank in despair and my face flushed with mortification.

"It's not so much that I hate or despise you, it's that I can't respect and don't trust you. I know your deceit. I've seen the greed in your eyes. Every time you look at me your longing for power and importance are betrayed. My brother loves you.

SON OF KINGS

What's more, he trusts you, Yuvraj. So does Hadithi." Her voice was gentle, so gentle it hurt me deep inside. "Kaimbe and the twins – they all think of you as their equal, their comrade, and their leader. But you see them as your playthings, your soldiers and puppets to be manipulated and used for your own glory."

"You didn't mention Shantha." I interrupted her, hoping to distract from where I knew she was going, wishing the mention of Shantha's name would wound her into silence. Instead, Hova laughed.

"Shantha trusts and respects you as much as I trust and respect Aepep." Her words bit into my mind as fiercely as a hungry street dog bites into a low-hanging piece of food. "She knew you the moment she met you." I turned to look at Hova, angry and desperate to avoid the inevitable. But the look of sadness in her eyes made me forget all the arguments I'd formulated.

"Tell me, Yuvraj," She continued after a moment, standing up and brushing herself off before gathering the blanket she'd been sitting on. "How does it feel to partner with the woman who killed Estel?" She turned and left me there, climbing down to the window without even pausing for me to answer.

I sat on the roof, shivering in the cold as temperatures dropped and clouds gathered, trying to figure out how Hova knew something I'd been so careful to hide. Trying, without success, to figure out why she hadn't outed me. Wishing I might forget her and move on.

But I couldn't forget her, and I couldn't figure out how she knew.

Chapter Seventeen

Heavy, wet snow started falling early the next morning, with temperatures plummeting quickly. We did our rounds and gave away as much food as we could spare, exhausting Hova's stash of pieced rag quilts and tunics. The sun rose, but its light couldn't shine through the dark clouds that hovered, unmoving, over Shantu. The daylight we all longed for never came. Streets remained silent and shops stayed closed as the snow piled up undisturbed, clinging to the fragile roofs we'd worked so hard to patch.

    I trudged through alleyways with Tyr, my back and arms sore from carrying bags of supplies. The moisture from my breath mixed with the frozen air, creating a thin layer of ice within the fibers of the homemade scarf I wore wrapped snugly around my head, neck, and face. My feet were numb, and my fingers tingled within the thick leather gloves Hova had so strategically lined with finely knitted wool. The bottom half of my cloak was frozen stiff with snow that had melted into it at each stop we'd made, making it almost twice as heavy.

    I longed for the fire and blankets at home, where we'd sent the others, but Tyr and I had one last stop to make. We knew there was a small camp of street children, much the same as we'd once been, not too far from the city gate leading into the Fields. Whenever things got bad, they'd huddle together under collapsing buildings around a pitiful fire, wrapped in rags, hoping to make it through the storm. As much as I wanted to go home, I wanted even more to know they had a fighting chance.

We were getting close, moving unhindered in the deserted, snow-filled streets. We gave little attention to whether there were any soldiers about, knowing they were most likely all huddled in their barracks or around campfires inside the Governor's Grounds. Even if a few unfortunate soldiers did happen to see us and realize who we were, we doubted they would have the energy or ambition to do anything about it. Now was not the time to wage war on us, no matter how much Aepep hated us.

Tyr stopped and held up his arm for me to stop. I stood close beside him, listening and looking around silently. Outside of the pale, unfortunate corpses that had given up on their search for shelter, and the sound of our feet crunching on the fresh snow, the alleyways appeared empty and silent.

"What is it, Tyr?" I whispered, but even the muffled sound of my whisper was a loud contrast to the quiet around us.

"Someone's following us." He responded. I could just make out his good eye, the only thing visible on his face beneath his cloak and scarf. We moved forward, both of us resting a hand on the weapons strapped to our sides, both straining our ears to hear better. As we rounded the corner, we dropped our bags and unsheathed our swords, waiting for whoever was following us to appear. My ears picked up the crunch of footsteps that paused then began again.

My heart raced as I wondered whether it was Chiwa, worried she might say something in front of Tyr about the agreement we'd made. I'd been expecting her to contact me again, but not with Tyr around. The camp of children wasn't far from us. A few hundred feet more and we'd probably be there.

A well-built figure rounded the corner in a soft, thick, and tightly woven dark gray cloak. The color was nothing special, but the fabric stood out as far superior to anything we, in our piece-meal clothing, could ever hope to own. The figure stopped and stared at us, sizing us up as I tried to guess who it might be. The awkward tension hovered in the cold air as the falling snow and dim light played tricks with my eyes, blurring the person who'd followed us.

"What do you want?" Tyr broke the silence, his voice steady and commanding as always. The alleyway bounced his voice around, sending an echo in the direction of the children's camp. If the children did hear him, I hoped they would take it as a warning to remain hidden.

"I want you to leave." The smooth voice replied. Tyr and I instinctively put one foot firmly behind the other, ready for an attack. The relief I experienced knowing it wasn't Chiwa following us was quickly swallowed up by the shock that overtook my mind as I realized who stood before us.

"Aepep." I whispered. The name tasted like a bad word that I wished I could spit out.

"Is that any way to greet your Governor?" He sneered, still unmoving.

"You govern as well as you father." I choked in anger, longing to throw off the caution restraining me and attack him without mercy.

"I never have been, and never will be, a father." He laughed, not even a little bit annoyed by my insult. "Whatever delusions of importance you may have, whatever lies your whore of a mother told you, I can most assuredly say that no one I know would ever call me a father."

I glanced at Tyr, trying to figure out why he was so calm and quiet. I wished I could see his face.

"Do you know who I am?" Tyr asked, his voice unaffected and void of any strong emotion. For the first time since he'd rounded the corner, Aepep shifted on his feet, as if pondering the unexpected question.

"Am I supposed to know who you are?" Was the only reply offered. It seemed like a calculated stall for time. "Am I supposed to care who you are?"

"Once upon a time," Tyr began. "Over 22 years ago, you became bored with your life in the Governor's Mansion." He took a small step in Aepep's direction. I was unsure of where this was headed, unconvinced this was the best strategy for dealing with the man in front of us.

Tyr continued, "You decided you'd go out and find something fun to do, find someone new to amuse you for a few weeks. So, you walked through the Markets and kept your eyes open for the first pretty girl you could find. Of course," He added. "You didn't go out as the Governor of Shantu. You went out much as you are now: more plainly and commonly dressed, much like an Upper Class merchant might dress if they were doing business.

"You could've picked anyone that day. With a tongue as slick as yours and the power to buy or command companionship at any moment, you could've had any girl you wanted. But you were bored of those choices. You wanted someone unsuspecting, someone who would buy your lies and believe whatever story of flattery and love you spun."

My brother took another small step in the direction of our father. I'd never heard this version of the story. I'd never heard Tyr speak so many words all at once either.

"You found your victim, a simple farmer's daughter seeking to sell a meager harvest of vegetables and wild berry preserves. Her name was Demi. She was as sweet as the preserves she held up for you to taste, and as unsuspecting and innocent as you could've hoped for. You flattered her. You bought her preserves. You courted her for weeks on end, showering her with flowers and gifts, waiting for the right time to convince her of the love you'd declared so many times."

Tyr took another step forward. I noticed, in surprise, that Aepep had taken a step backward.

"She gave into you, believing your declarations and intentions. But a few weeks later, the moment she told you about me, you laughed in her face and tossed her aside." Another small step was taken. "The game was over, complete. She wept and stumbled home to her parents with the parting beating you'd given her as her last present, your twisted fantasy now complete. She knew no one would believe you were the father. She was afraid of how you might retaliate if they did believe her.

"But, as luck would have it, I believed her. Much as my true father believed her while I was still in her womb. When they both died of plague and malnutrition, leaving my sister and I to manage on our own, I found my way to your Mansion on a cold and dreary night." Tyr took another step toward him. The gap was growing steadily smaller. I could feel my heart pounding, wondering if Tyr was about to explain his missing eye.

"We were cold and hungry, and I knew you had plenty to spare. I've always been good at planning and scouting, but I underestimated how many guards you would have in your kitchen larder. They caught me, hands full of bread, pockets full of apples, and they brought me to you." Tyr took another step. His voice had grown stronger, deeper, and darker with each word. "Do you remember me now?" He asked, hands resting on a sword strapped to his hips.

Oh, to be Hova and be able to read the minds of those I'm around. I thought to myself as I watched them.

"You didn't beat me for my thieving. You didn't hang me or put me in the stocks or throw me in the dungeon or send me off on a ship to be some merchant's slave as my punishment. You'd grown as bored of those punishments as you had of your average nightly companions when you sought out and groomed my mother." Tyr took another small step, now only a few feet away from the man he knew to be his father.

"I'll never forget the delight that came into your eyes as you stoked the fire with the poker, twisting it in the hot flames. I could feel the guards holding me become uneasy. They knew what you were about to do. They knew and they wished they could be anywhere but there. Their discomfort and my complete unawareness only added to the thrill you experienced as you ordered them to hold me still and then ground the poker into my left eye." Tyr whispered the last part.

The truth made my skin crawl and my stomach turn over as I envisioned the event that had created the Tyr I was familiar with.

"Do you remember me now?" Tyr whispered again, still poised a few feet from Aepep.

"You must think very highly of yourself to believe I would take any time to remember you." Aepep replied. "I remember only a rat from the gutter, who believed what's mine should be his, getting what he deserved. I also remember three children staring at me defiantly, children I should've beaten and thrown out of my courtyard. But, like a fool, I ignored your impudence. I remember stories of a man parading around with an eye patch, pretending to be a hero. I can only assume that's you."

I stood in stunned silence, the tension between the two men in front of me building stronger.

"Perhaps," Tyr said, barely audible now. "This will make me impossible to forget." He threw off his cloak in true fighting fashion and attacked, his sword clashing with Aepep's. The Governor did not remove his cloak, but he turned and ducked and blocked each blow almost as gracefully as the son attacking him. I stood by, trying to figure out what to do, where my place in this fight was.

I can't join in. This is Tyr's battle. I thought. *But, what if Aepep overpowers him?* They turned in the alleyway, Tyr leaning on the older man, backing him slowly

SON OF KINGS

toward the corner, every ounce of skill and precision he had acquired coming into play. Aepep grunted with exertion as he blocked the heavy blows Tyr dealt him.

All I could see were Tyr's strong shoulders, rippling beneath the layers of clothing Hova had demanded he wear. The closer Tyr pushed him to the corner, the more erratic Aepep's work with the sword became. Tyr saw his chance and took it, smacking the man sharply across the knuckles and stabbing him in his upper, right shoulder.

Aepep groaned and leaned back against the wall as his cloak began to soak up the blood spilling out from his shoulder.

"You have ruined the lives of so many." Tyr's voice was calculated and cold, colder than I ever believed it could be. "Look around you. These buildings, this poverty, it's all your creation. The bodies of those frozen to death in the alleyways of the Slums, they're all your handiwork. You destroyed my mother. You've denied me as your son. You take delight in torturing and hurting any who stand up to you or get in your way." He paused for a second before posing his final question, his sword still poised to take a final blow. "Tell me, Aepep, Governor of Shantu, son of Azai the great wizard, why should I let you live?"

I watched as Aepep pushed himself up to a standing position, sensing deep down that Tyr should've finished him without delivering the speech I knew he'd wanted to deliver for most of his life.

"Eye patch," Aepep spoke in an odd voice. "Good fighter, great swordsman, but not the one who wields magic." Before I could open my mouth to warn Tyr to move to one side, the Governor's bare left hand shot out, pushing Tyr away without even touching him. Tyr tumbled through the snow, his sword falling beside him. Aepep walked toward him, hand still outstretched. I fumbled at my gloves, my mind racing with all the possible outcomes there could be.

If I help him, we have a chance of surviving. The thoughts flew through my head as the scene before me unfolded in slow motion. *If? When did it become a possibility?* I could hear myself arguing with this sudden unknown other self. The same self that urged me to sabotage Chantrea's rescue. *If you run and let him die, then you could lead the Shadows on your own. Tyr would never interfere, never contradict what you do or say or believe. The Shadows would look to you.* The idea intrigued me.

He's your brother. He's your friend. He's fought for you time and again. The arguments raged quickly in my mind as I fumbled with my gloves, dropping them on the ground. *Without him, you'll struggle to plan and strategize. You'll lose your best fighter.* Still, I hesitated. I looked on in horror as Aepep stomped on Tyr's knee, causing Tyr to scream out in pain. The Governor then kneeled on top of Tyr's chest, reaching for his throat with his right hand. My brother struggled against the force of his father with one hand while fumbling for the knife strapped to his side.

"Not so strong now, are we." The Governor's hand glowed red as he taunted Tyr. His right arm remained limp and hanging, the dark stain of blood growing larger in the pale light. "Your mother was an idiot, a whore, and a liar. I have no son. If you wanted to make a difference, then you should've stayed home with the rest of the bastard gutter rats who follow you. I should've hung you from the gallows when I had the chance." Tyr was groaning in pain, the heat from Aepep's hand burning through the scarf and reaching his skin as Aepep choked him. The Governor leaned a little closer, his face still hidden by his cloak.

"I took your eye, now I will take your life. With your death my goals will be reached. The snake that sought to kill me will have no head. It will wriggle and struggle and die. With your death, I will kill the very soul of the Shadows."

"Yuvraj!" Tyr gasped, turning to look at me. One look from his pain-filled, blue eye was all it took to remind me that I needed him. *Hova will never forgive you if you let him die. She won't hide it from the others.* I threw off my cloak as I threw off the hesitation and sprinted clumsily toward my father, one hand grasping my sword, the other outstretched and on fire.

"Ruinë!" I screamed, the flame striking Aepep on the back as he turned in surprise. He tumbled to the side, releasing Tyr. My brother gasped for breath and moaned in pain. I leaped over him to shield him from Aepep's expected retaliation. My sword met the governor's as he crouched on the snow, holding the blade above him with his good hand as mine swung down. I pushed, leaning all my weight on him, but his arm would not give way. Behind me Tyr still struggled to breathe. My hopes of killing Aepep once and for all vanished as I realized my only choice was to tend to Tyr. I took a step back and threw another flame as Aepep stood up, this time hitting him close to where Tyr had stabbed him in the shoulder.

"Curses!" Aepep screamed at me as he dropped his sword and took a step backward. "I will find you," he muttered, holding his right side. "You caught me by surprise today. But mark my words, I will find you, and I will make an example out of every single one of you!" Without another word he ran, turning the corner of the alleyway and disappearing into the darkness.

I sheathed my sword and turned around to help Tyr. To my surprise, a large group of children had gathered behind me. One held my brother's head in his lap while a little girl had gathered Tyr's cloak to cover him up. The others stood around him, staring at me.

"Take the bags we brought." I instructed them as I gathered my wits. "Take the food and the blankets back to your hideout and stay there. I need one volunteer to run ahead of me and call for help at our home." I hesitated. "Do you know where we live?" I asked, glancing down at Tyr. His breathing was weak and slow, burned flesh peeking through the singed scarf still wrapped around his face. His eye was closed.

"'Course we do." The little boy holding Tyr's head replied. He couldn't have been more than six or seven years old. "We all know where the Shadows live." The other children nodded in agreement.

"We ain't leaving you to go back alone." The little girl said, crossing her arms in front of her. "The youngest will stay here, but us older children, we're all going with you to make sure you get back safe." Her stubborn, pursed lips were a light shade of blue, her skin as pale as skin can be. I wanted to argue, but I knew it would do no good. I walked over to one of the bags and pulled out the small blankets and cloaks we'd brought, handing them out and pulling them over their shoulders. The tiniest of them, about five children in total, grabbed the sacks and dragged them toward our original destination, leaving seven children gathered around me.

"Who's the fastest?" I asked. Two children raised their hands. "Run. Tell Kaimbe I need his help." They did as I asked, blankets tied in knots around their shoulders, disappearing down the alleyway. The falling snow had all but stopped, leaving behind enormous piles of soft, wet snow and even colder temperatures.

I pulled my gloves back on, then reached down to pull Tyr up and across my shoulders. He groaned in pain as I groaned in effort. The children threw his cloak over him as best they could. Holding onto both of his arms, I allowed his legs to drag behind me. I made my way through the alleyways, each step becoming heavier and more labored. Tyr's breath grew more and more shallow as the children helped guide me through the Slums.

My legs grew unsteady, and a cold sweat broke out all over my body. Just as I was about to give up and fall to my knees to wait for help, a shout sounded up ahead. Kaimbe bounded up to me. With one smooth motion, the giant of a man flipped Tyr into his arms and carried him back to the house. I paused in relief for a second, leaning forward to catch my breath.

"Thank you, children, but you need to go home now." I said. "It's getting late and it's time you sat around a fire and had some food." They looked up at me dubiously. "I swear, I will be back to check on all of you as soon as I can. Tyr will be alright." I promised, unsure if the last part of the promise would come true. Hesitant, but obedient, the children nodded and ran back in the direction of their hideout. With the weight of my brother no longer on my back, I was soon home.

A somber scene greeted me when I arrived. Hova was tending to her brother on a cot by the fire, Hadithi assisting her. I threw off my frozen cloak and scarf and wrapped myself in the blanket River offered me, then took the hot soup Shantha held out, my fingers tingling with pain as they started to warm up. My ears felt funny, and I realized I still couldn't feel my feet. Ryder kneeled and helped me with my boots, wrapping my feet up in a hot blanket when he was done. I told them what had happened in hushed tones, watching as Hova mended and bound Tyr's crushed knee and Hadithi treated his burns.

When I was done with my story, no one said a word. I sipped on the soup in my hands, and we all sat there, listening to the whistle of the wind and the crackle of the fire in the stove.

'Thank you, Yuvraj.' Came Hova's whisper in my mind. She sat beside her brother, singing gently, and holding his hand. *'You're not alone and you can't and don't have to do this alone. Become the Shadow you always hoped you could be. Live for more than the vengeance and the power that call to you. Those children look up to you and need you. Become the hero they believe you to be. They want to follow. Lead them.'*

That night I fell asleep and dreamed of a world where I was Governor of Shantu and Hova stood lovingly beside me as the Shadows grew into an uncountable force to be reckoned with.

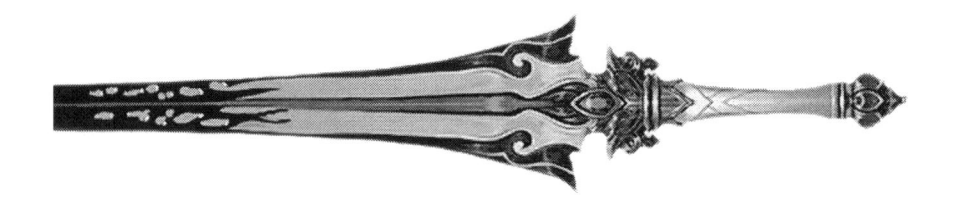

PART THREE

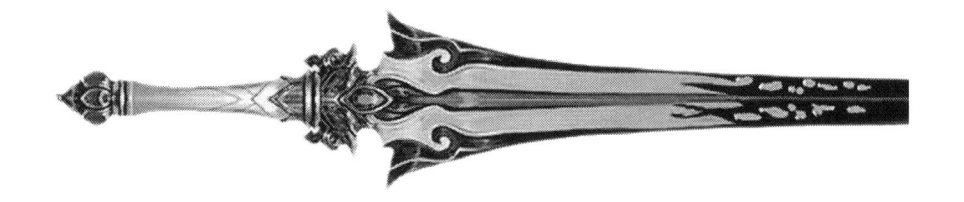

Chapter Eighteen

"Hit, hit, turn, hit, turn, excellent!" I watched as Hadithi worked with the group of young Shadows, training them in our way of fighting. He enjoyed the training, often taking on three at the same time to help them work on their group fighting skills as he worked on fighting multiple people at once without using any magic, something that made no sense to me.

"The ability for magic is a tool to be used, not hidden." I often told him to no avail. He always shrugged his shoulders and looked away, muttering whatever excuse he fancied at the time.

Seven years had passed since the cold night in the alleyway with Aepep and Tyr. The children who helped save our lives quickly became part of our order, bringing with them dozens more over the years. There were far too many Shadows to live in our Slum cottage, so we created a new strategy. As soon as the weather turned warmer, we scouted out another abandoned building to fix, teaching the children how to do what we'd learned on our own.

The children followed us eagerly, responding positively to the slightest hint of kindness or generosity. Hova held them under an unbreakable spell where they all instantly fell in love with and obeyed her without question, often whispering rumors they'd heard about her to one another. She never disputed even the most outlandish of rumors.

"I heard she fought off a whole group of Sailors by flinging them into the Sea with a wave of her hand!" I'd heard one say in the loudest whisper in the world. Hova had continued sewing, not even a twitch of amusement crossing her lips to refute the outrageous story.

I'd witnessed her mother and discipline and listen to all of them, all the while hoping one of them would grab her loyalty and attention away from Hadithi. I had no doubt she cared for every child that came our way. I also knew she still loved Hadithi in a way that she would never love me.

The emotion in her eyes, the softening of her face, and the smile that came all too easily to her lips when she was around him made her feelings obvious. Her affection for Hadithi went far beyond any sort of motherly affection she may have formed for those in her charge. There was, after all, only a couple years difference in age between them.

Every year, we found more children, our numbers growing slowly but steadily. We had to adjust how we functioned. Living with them for a couple weeks in their new home, we'd discern who the best leader would be for each group, planning surprise visits with longer and longer periods of time in between.

The young Shadows were kept under strict watch, never sure when one of us would show up to check on them. They were expected to do chores, help forage or hunt in the Woods when asked, and to be on time for training in the clearing every morning. As they got older and stronger, we'd teach them how to plant their own rooftop gardens and drag them along to help those in the Slums that reached out to us.

It became easy, over time, to figure out who had an aptitude for strategy, strength, or skill with a bow. The twins, River and Ryder, would teach hunting, bow skills, and knife throwing. Tyr would choose those he believed would do well against the Governor's Guards and more advanced soldiers. Most of Tyr's group consisted of group leaders, strong, intelligent children who weren't afraid to take risks. Their training was precise, intense, and both physically and mentally demanding.

Kaimbe often took a few under his wing to pick up boulders and climb trees without any ropes or equipment. Much like their leader, they were strong, deadly, and unfailingly kind. Truthfully, I'd grown to trust Kaimbe and his follower's abilities more than I trusted anyone else. Even more than I trusted Tyr. They were self-sacrificing, brave, and loyal to a fault. Just as Kaimbe had rushed into a burning building without question, his students followed.

Hova was the most particular in her choices. Several of the children she trained in self-defense and healing herbs would have done equally well in other groups, but she recognized in them something very specific: the ability to do what was necessary for anyone sick or wounded. Those she taught were like her own little gaggle of coldly compassionate caregivers.

Like Hova, these children had an aptitude for understanding others and being kind and gentle, even if warmth of emotion was not present. At the end of the day their word overpowered every leader Tyr raised up and I always suspected they could overpower anyone before their opponent realized what was happening.

Whether even a fraction of the rumors about Hova were true or not, I knew Chantrea had trained her and it would be foolish of me to believe Chantrea's training was anything less than effective.

Shantha surprised us as she grew up, slowly proving she was invaluable both as a spy and as a teacher to others on how to become invisible. Her choices were light-footed children who easily slipped in and out of small spaces regardless of their height or weight. There weren't many she picked, and those she did choose were trained by Hadithi and me as well.

While the others gave special training and classes, Hadithi and I trained all the beginners. These children were the youngest, the weakest and the few that didn't end up in any of the other groups. Our charges were either young, simple, or just plain ordinary.

At times, I felt as though we got the leftovers, those no one else wanted to bother with. However, I soon realized we had the first influence, and the longest standing trust built with each new Shadow that came our way. No matter where they ended up or who became their mentor, they were always glad to see us.

Our numbers had grown to over fifty Shadows, all living somewhere around Shantu. The Slums trusted us to provide support and protection, the Common People often called on us for help, and the Upper Class feared and despised us.

Being a Shadow had become synonymous with living in the shadows, being unknown as an individual. Although rumors circulated about many of us, especially us who were older, very few people were privy to our names or what we looked like. Being a Shadow was a way of life, a code of conduct, and an honor.

A few of those we raised grew up and left, sailing off to seek their fortunes on the Sea. Others set up a small living for themselves in the city market or married into one of the families that lived in the Common Sector. None left in bitterness, but with a sworn oath to carry our secrets to their graves.

"What is the choice of a Shadow?" Hadithi asked his three exhausted trainees, pacing in front of them to relieve the fighting adrenaline racing through his veins.

"Discipline over pain." One of them answered.

"Honor unto death." Another chimed in.

"Hit hard but show mercy." The last replied.

"And always, always," Hadithi said, stopping to look them each in the eye. "Always have each other's back. You are family. Some even by blood." His comment was obvious, even though it had become impossible to keep track of how many known children of Aepep there were in our numbers, much less how many others were mere possibilities. "But whether you are family by blood or by choice, you are Shadows. Now and forever. You stick together. You fight it out. Never leave one of our own to fight alone."

The three flushed faces nodded in agreement.

"Alright." Hadithi smiled for the first time all morning. "You've done well. Go and get your breakfast. We'll pick up here first thing tomorrow morning." The children's eyes lit up as they ran off in the direction of our Slum home, where Hova undoubtedly waited with hot porridge and toast.

"They're doing well." Hadithi said, picking up his cloak from the ground where he'd thrown it and slinging it over his shoulder. Late summer had arrived, when chilly mornings and hot afternoons were to be expected, making it awkward to dress efficiently for the day.

"Do you think they'll be ready to move up in their training by this Winter?" I asked as we fell in step.

"All but the youngest, Ava." He answered, pulling the light linen hood attached to his tunic up over his face as we neared the road. I was reminded every summer of the vast difference between our physical appearance and ability to pass through the city unseen. I often wondered if Hadithi ever resented needing to hide his foreign ears, hair, and eyes from the sight of Shantu. His mother had taught him

SON OF KINGS

to hide from an early age. We'd quickly realized no good would come of Aepep, Chiwa, or any of the soldiers catching sight of him.

"She's not strong enough yet. She's small for her age. I plan to speak with Hova and Shantha and see if either of them believe she'd be a fit for their training. If not, then we might need to reconsider how we train her depending on how the next month or so goes. No use trying to make her into someone she's not." He shook his head.

"Good." I agreed. "Hadithi," I hesitated as I found the right words for my question. "Do you ever think it odd that none of the children we've taken in have shown any gift or ability for magic?" I had my own reasons for being concerned about this, but I was curious to see what he thought. In all our seven years, not one child under our protection ever revealed any signs of having inherited Aepep's powers.

"There are times when I do." Hadithi spoke quietly as a forager and his son passed by us, nodding amicably in our direction. "There are times, I admit, when I wonder if there are some who have the ability but don't know it. Unfortunately, I don't know how to call it out of them, even though I sense the possibility sometimes."

"How did your mother teach you?" I asked carefully.

"She didn't have to." Hadithi replied. "As far back as I can remember, I've always understood and used my powers. She taught me to contain and control the magic."

I glanced his way as he shrugged his shoulders in feigned indifference. As the years passed, I'd never mentioned what I knew about his powers or how I'd seen him take his wooden carvings and made them play out the stories in his head. I held onto the knowledge, waiting to see how I might be able to use it - too in awe of what he could do to mention it in passing.

We continued our way down the road and into Shantu in mutual, comfortable silence, reaching the cottage as the sun rose above the tree line. Inside, eleven small children aged four to twelve sat around the room, gobbling down food as if they hadn't eaten in days. Hova's gaze skipped me and went directly to Hadithi as he came through the window behind me and lowered his hood.

"You both must be hungry." She said, handing us a mug of hot tea and chunks of toasted bread with cheese. "As soon as a bowl becomes available, I'll give you some porridge as well." She glanced my way, her eyes dull and distant.

"Thank you." I said, leaning against the wall as the breakfast scene unfolded before me. Hadithi patted Hova gently on the shoulder and smiled at her. Sitting on the floor in front of the children, he readily listened to their childish fantasies as he fed their stories with his own imagination. I often suspected breakfast was his favorite moment of the day.

While the older children would return to their own homes after training, the youngest would return to be mothered and taught by Hova on basic cooking, gardening, and hygiene skills. At lunchtime, they'd be sent off to their homes to eat and do as they were asked by the older children.

As the children finished their breakfast, they brought their plates and bowls up to the large buckets of water Hova had set up, scrubbing them clean before presenting them to her. Once the cleaning was approved, she set them up with basic household tasks.

Some tackled the mending and sewing, their little legs swinging over the edge of the bed as they concentrated earnestly on the needle in their fingers. Others were sent to the roof to weed in the garden. Some were pushed in the direction of a pile of laundry to wash and hang on the line we'd strung from one end of the room to the other.

Hova grabbed one of the clean bowls, filled it with porridge, and handed it to me, turning back around to do the same for Hadithi.

"What's on the schedule today, Hova?" I asked, trying to strike up a conversation.

"It's been a while since I made them bathe." She replied, without looking away from her ladle. She walked the bowl over to Hadithi and handed it to him, then returned. "The weather is cooling down so it might be best if I take them to the river for a thorough scrubbing before the ice sets in and the water gets too cold." She dished out more porridge, getting ready for Tyr and the others to return from their training with the older children.

I loved watching Hova work as I stood eating my porridge. For a few brief moments every morning I pretended the woman before me was my wife and the children she gently directed were our own. The dark red curls covering her head in chaos seemed to be the only thing in her life she could not tame. Her solution was to chop the unruly locks short and tie scrap pieces of fabric around her head to make the tangled mass appear somewhat contained and out of her eyes.

The few brief moments of fantasy always came to an end when she would glance up from her work, look me straight in the eye with her indifferent jet-black gaze and break the spell with a shake of her head.

"Yuvraj!" Tyr came bounding through the window, breaking my train of thought, helping me shove away the well-known rejection I felt. He was in a particularly pleasant mood this morning, signaling that training must have gone better than normal. I returned his smile and started on my porridge as he turned to Hova. Kaimbe was close behind him, the twins and Shantha climbing through the window a few minutes later.

Tyr's face had been spared from the burn marks Aepep left on him in the alleyway, leaving it easy for him to move about without a hood the way Hadithi did. Under Hova's care, the scars on his neck had healed quickly and faded over the years. They would never fully disappear, so he'd taken to wearing high collars or rolled up handkerchiefs to deter any sight of the awful markings.

I found it amusing. His eye patch made him stand out more than any scarring ever could, but Tyr had worn the eye patch for so long he no longer realized how it set him apart from others. I frequently thought that, with the handkerchief tied around his throat, all he needed to look like another pirate king was to throw on a big hat. But I would never be so foolish as to voice those opinions.

We ate breakfast together, the younger children running in and out of the house and interrupting us as needed. Hadithi and I listened to the others as they talked eagerly about the skills their students had mastered or the funny ways any of the children had tried to do something.

Once all the stories were told, Tyr, Kaimbe, and the twins all disappeared through the window again, off to walk the city and see what might be needed that afternoon. Shantha grabbed a wooden bucket from beside the stove and started for the window.

"Wait a minute, Shantha." Hadithi called to her. "Yuvraj and I need to speak with you and Hova."

The skinny girl had grown into a slender young woman of medium height and build. Like Hova, she chopped her wavy brown hair short and pulled it out of her face with random scraps of cloth. Her face was covered in freckles and her uncanny, light green eyes always lit up the most when talking to Hadithi. Swinging around, she tossed the bucket in his direction. She threw her head back to laugh as he shook his head in feigned disapproval.

Their public displays of affection and flirting always made me want to curl my lip in disgust. They'd remained close over the years, seeming to share a depth of relationship none of the rest of us were capable of duplicating. From whispered conversations to silent moments by the fire, through times of discouragement and heartache, their mutual love never wavered. We all assumed one day they would leave us to live on their own in a nearby cottage.

In his love for Shantha, Hadithi appeared oblivious to Hova's loyal affection and treated her much like a younger brother would treat his favorite sister. Hova seemed quietly content with her situation. Despite everything, she never raised her voice or her hand against Shantha. Quite the opposite. She took the girl under her wing in every way imaginable, always around to console and comfort, never failing in her encouragement or appreciation for what Shantha was capable of.

I didn't understand, but I didn't dare ask Hova why she treated so well someone who had stolen Hadithi away from her. Instead, I assumed she had a reason for treating Shantha well, just like I had my reasons for treating Hadithi well.

"This morning we were discussing Ava and her future," Hadithi spoke in a quiet voice so any children passing by would be less likely to hear him. "While she's come a long way, she's small for her age and still very weak. Which means the other children are almost ready to move forward in their training, but she isn't. Do either of you believe she would be a good fit for your skills?"

The two women stared at us and then at each other as they thought through the request. I could feel Hova probing my mind, searching for some ulterior motive, no doubt. This was something I'd grown used to over the years, but I still resented my inability to block her out.

There are no secret reasons for this, Hova. I decided to tell her myself, staring her down, irritated by her constant suspicion that every move I made must be somehow self-serving and morally wrong. The cold stare turned away from me and back to Hadithi without a response or acknowledgment from Hova.

"When the time comes for the others to be chosen by Tyr, Kaimbe, and the twins, we will take Ava into our care and see how she does." Hova took charge, speaking for both of them while Shantha nodded along in agreement. "If she does well with a few training sessions of spying, then Shantha can continue with her until she's ready to help on missions. If she does poorly, then I will keep her with me and find a way for her to succeed. That might mean getting her the training and job opportunities she needs as a local seamstress or basket weaver."

"Who knows," a sly smile crossed Shantha's face as she spoke. "Maybe her placement as a local would be of more benefit to the Shadows than if she were to become the greatest spy we've ever seen. The wealth of information she might feed us could be invaluable."

The matter had been settled more quickly than I'd imagined. We all nodded in agreement and the young lovers left through the window together, Hadithi grabbing two more buckets from beside the stove. As Hova went about her work, I considered picking a fight and questioning her automatic response to me when Hadithi had been the one to make the request. But as much as I wanted to get a reaction out of her, I decided it best to leave and let out my irritation on an unsuspecting plant on my way out.

It was a beautiful day outside, warm, and sunny but not too hot or humid. The alleyways were bustling with activity and the activity only increased as I made my way to the edge of the Common sector.

"Yuvraj." A well-known harsh voice grabbed my attention as I passed by a dark, narrow crevice between houses. Stepping back a few paces, I peered into the shadowy space and blinked a few times as my eyes adjusted to the lack of light. The outline of Chiwa's small figure clothed in gray stood out to me.

"What do you want?" I whispered, glancing around me to see if anyone had noticed before leaning against the wall outside and pulling out a pocketknife to whittle at a stick.

"Ah, Yuvraj," The witch said, coming closer to the opening. "There's a spy in your midst and you don't even know it. Every time Aepep sends one in, you're fooled. What is it about these pathetic children that makes you lose your ability to discern whether they are who they claim to be?" She let out a low cackle that made my skin crawl.

Chapter Ninteen

"Well, out with it." I demanded of the witch. The stick I was carving had become a dull arrow.

"Not so fast." The push back was expected, but still annoying. I waited for her demands and gave my surroundings another quick glance as I noticed her coming closer to the sunlight. One arm was now just barely visible, clad in a long, soft linen gray sleeve with matching gloves. Much like Hadithi and Tyr, Chiwa had a harder time hiding herself in the heat of summer.

"When are you going to move?" She growled. "I'm growing weary of all this waiting, Yuvraj. Efah and I are *both* growing weary." The mention of her odd companion made my eyes roll in their sockets as I wondered if he might be watching from a distance.

"Soon." My reply was short and to the point as there was no possible way for me to guarantee a specific date to attack. *Not yet anyway.*

"You've been saying that for the last two years. If I didn't know any better, I'd assume you've decided your Slum cottage and a small group of do-good gutter rats is enough for you. However," The words matched the witch's overly calm tone, causing me to shift uncomfortably against the wall. "One glance at your mind shows me all the discontentment I need to see."

The knife in my hand froze as I wondered for the first time if everyone around me was constantly reading my mind.

"We'll move as soon as we're able, and when we do, you'll be the first to hear." I replied through gritted teeth. "Now, who is the spy?"

"Why, it's your favorite little gutter rat: the small, weak, innocent and failing Ava."

"And then, during our training, they have us repeat this mantra about how we'll always be loyal to each other and never leave another Shadow behind." The Governor's Guards listened to the rambling child in icy silence as Aepep leaned forward to listen to the girl devouring everything set in front of her.

Clothed in a short, piece-meal dress and thin leggings that reached just below her knees, Ava looked like any other street orphan with her wild hair, dirt encrusted fingernails, and diminutive stature. At twelve years old, she still looked much younger.

"What exactly do they have you say?" Aepep asked in veiled disgust, already half bored with the child.

"Discipline over pain, honor unto death, hit hard, but show mercy, and always have each other's back. We are family." The child recited while stuffing her mouth full of leftover roast beef and spiced potatoes.

"How, exactly, is this going to help us defeat them?" Aepep whispered to Commander Jabez. "We've been working with this little rat all summer, and she still hasn't told us anything useful! What assurance do we have that she isn't pretending to help us just so she can eat free food?"

"Sire," The Commander replied, leaning down closer to Aepep's ear. "We must be patient. There's no way of knowing whether she's being truthful or not. Time. We need more time, Sire." They glanced back to find Ava studying their faces, her mouth full, her hand poised over the plate in front of her as she strained to hear what they were saying.

"I am many things." Food spewed out of her mouth as she spoke. "But I'm not a liar." Chewing hard, she swallowed, threw the meat in her hand onto the table, crossed her arms in front of her, and lifted her chin. "If you don't trust me and you don't want my help, then I'll leave right now and never come back to bother you." Her indignant stare was enough for Aepep.

"Nonsense, child." He smiled at her and stood up. "You're the perfect little spy. Don't be silly. I was testing you." He moved around the table and spooned some more potatoes onto Ava's plate while refilling her glass with milk. "Eat, and please tell me more of what you do in training."

Ava eyed Aepep for a few seconds before reaching out for her glass of milk and draining it.

"Just remember," The Governor said, leaning in to whisper in her ear. "The moment you fail to tell us what we want is the moment you sign your death warrant. Do you and I understand one another?"

Ava nodded and continued to eat, seemingly unphased by the threat.

Aepep regained his seat and leaned back. "Carry on." He said, with a wave of his hand.

"Before I do," The girl said, in between bites. "How do I know you won't kill me even if I do tell you everything you need to know?" Her question surprised the Governor and made Commander Jabez smile, as if congratulating himself on a choice well-made.

"You don't." The answer was blunt and bold. "You'll have to trust me. I give you my word, on the life of my mother, I will not kill you if you tell me what I ask." It was a weak promise at best, but it was the best Ava supposed she'd receive.

"And what do I get if I help you defeat the Shadows?" The food was rapidly disappearing. Aepep paused to consider her question.

"Your life." He replied. "And a modest cottage in the Common Sector along with a small sum of money to live off of. Will that do?"

"Agreed."

Few deals had been made in that great hall, but this was by far the cheapest deal Aepep remembered making.

I still might kill you. Aepep thought to himself as Ava prattled on about her training and the daily habits of the Shadows. *Then again, I might make use of you before I do. The Witch has no idea that I have yet to deliver on a pact I could've fulfilled long ago. If she had she would've acted on it by now. If she's this easy to manage, then I doubt you'll be much trouble to take care of.*

SON OF KINGS

I mulled over the information Chiwa had given me for over a week, watching Ava closely. I followed her when she was sent off to do chores at the river, or when she was dismissed for free time and ran off by herself. Though I doubted Chiwa was lying or mistaken, I needed to be sure that her information was current and worth acting on.

Finally, at the end of that week, late in the afternoon, I followed her to the Governor's Mansion and watched from across the street as she spoke with the guards and went inside, returning a couple hours later.

It's now or never. I thought to myself, still unsure of what I would do when I confronted her. Following the girl into an alleyway of the Common Sector's busy marketplace, I quickened my pace to catch up to her.

"Hello, Ava." I said. She whirled around to face me, freezing in her steps, eyes full of ferocity, hands up as if she expected a fight. "It's me, Yuvraj." I laughed, trying to disarm her. "I'm not here to fight with you. I just want to ask you a few questions."

Fists down, but still curled by her side, Ava relaxed slightly and eyed me, taking a few steps back and glancing behind her to see how far it was to the end of the alleyway.

"What do you want? Hova told me I have free time." She said, defensively. "Am I in trouble?" She edged backwards a little further.

"That depends." I leaned against the wall; arms crossed in front of me. "Stop trying to escape, stand still, and answer my questions." I commanded her, her body instantly freezing in place. She was only a couple arm lengths away from me, and she'd never make it into the busy street in time to get away from me, but it would be so much easier if I didn't have to chase her or use any excessive force.

"I'm curious, Ava. Do you consider yourself a Shadow?" I waited, locking eyes with her.

The child visibly gulped and nodded her head, opening her eyes wider like a scared owl.

"If you consider yourself a Shadow, then why do you break the rules we set in place? Why do you betray us all for a few measly bits of food and a promise of comfort that Aepep is sure to break as soon as he's tired of you?"

"I-I don't," She stammered, her voice trailing off as she swallowed and tried again. "What are you talking about?" The look of horror on her face surprised me. "How could I betray my family?" Her bottom lip quivered as she spoke. "You're all I have and I'm so grateful. I would've starved on the streets if you hadn't found me and taken me in when you did." A single tear slid down her cheek. She didn't move to wipe it away.

I studied her, trying to figure out if she was playing me, wondering for the first time if Chiwa's information had been wrong.

"Then tell me, what were you doing at the Governor's Mansion?" I asked, pushing myself away from the wall and taking a step in her direction. "What would a Shadow have to do in there for over two hours?"

The calculating look that passed through Ava's eyes was all I needed to confirm that Chiwa's tip had been valid. *What a little traitor!* I thought, the anger boiling up from somewhere deep inside me as I contemplated finishing her once and for all. Unlike the other spies Aepep had used to infiltrate our small but ever-growing circle, Ava was intelligent and calculated. *Not to mention an excellent little actress.*

"All right, you figured it out." She smirked, shrugging her shoulders, and executing a mock curtsy in my direction. "What are you going to do about it?"

The challenge was obvious. I stared at her, contemplating my options, amazed by the difference in her demeanor and tone.

"I could kill you." I said, leaning back against the wall and crossing my arms over my chest.

"True." She replied. "Or you could let me live and I might help you get what you want."

"You think you know what I want?"

She smiled at me and cocked her head to one side. "Only an idiot would fail to see what you want. I know you want to be governor. You want to kill your father. I'm simply proposing to help you achieve these wonderful goals."

"Why would I need your help?"

"I can tell you things. Sleeping habits, the Governor's Guards schedule, and where Commander Jabez sleeps."

SON OF KINGS

"Do you really think we need your help?" I asked, walking toward her. "You've seen how organized we are, you know who we are and what we do, and you think we need *you* to help us defeat Aepep?" My face flushed with anger. The scrawny child clenched her jaw and backed away from me as I grew closer. *The impudence. The insult of it all.*

"I can help you; I swear." Ava said, hastily backing further away, one hand out front, the other on her knife. "I won't tell them anything useful. In fact, I haven't told them anything useful. I just blabber on about food and chores and training - I've never told them where we live or anything like that. I would be helpful, tell them lies. I like the fancy food they give me, that's all."

Taking a giant step forward, I grabbed her wrist as she drew her knife on me. Crying out in pain, she wriggled and dropped her weapon, simultaneously landing a swift kick to my gut and clawing at the hold I had around her wrist. The breath escaped from my mouth as I winced and doubled over, but I held on.

"Why you little - I should end you right here and now!" I growled at her, pushing her against the wall and wrapping my free hand around her neck. A familiar sense of pleasure washed over me as I squeezed her throat, feeling my power and watching her eyes fill with fear.

"I've done it before, you see. Killed. You think you're the only spy Aepep ever sent our way? Idiot. Your predecessors never stood a chance against me." I squeezed a little tighter as Ava clawed at my hand, gasping, and trying to speak.

"Yuvraj." Hova's voice rang out behind me.

Surprised by the sound, I froze, battling between what I knew she wanted me to do and longing to snuff this traitor child out with a few more seconds and double the pressure.

"Let go, Yuvraj. Let go or I swear on Hadithi's life that I will destroy you." She spoke so quietly, her tone dark and dangerous in a way I'd never heard before. "I will rip away your power and status one word at a time and I will never look back or shed a tear on your behalf. My word will trump any lies or excuses you make to Tyr or Kaimbe or Hadithi or any of the others." A hand rested on my shoulder. "Release her."

As I stared into the pained eyes of the child choking in front of me, I knew Hova was right. I let go. Ava fell to the ground on her hands and knees, coughing as she gasped for air.

"I have no other choice." I said, turning around to face Hova, my fists clenched. "If we let her go, she'll go straight to Aepep and tell him everything she hasn't yet exposed about us. She might compromise everything I've worked so hard to accomplish!"

The look on Hova's face transformed the fury boiling inside my chest into terror. I shrank away from her, my hands loosening. Her black eyes burned into mine, painful to look at but impossible to look away from. Brushing me aside, she kneeled beside Ava, turning her neck one way and then the other to check for any permanent damage. I stood by, shifting from one foot to the other, my fingers twitching and tensing as if I were still holding the child's throat between them. An odd sense of having been robbed of something washed over me.

"Sit up straight, Ava. Lean against the wall." Hova propped the child up as she spoke, the coughing slowly easing. Tears started to stream down Ava's cheeks, and she glanced anxiously from me to Hova and back again. I glared down at both, disgusted by my inability to defy Hova.

If I loved her less, it would be so much easier. I thought, loathing myself for this weakness. Her oath came back to my mind: I swear on Hadithi's life. It stung that my love for her enlisted my obedience and submission while her love for Hadithi was the dearest thing to her, the emotion that most clearly communicated how she would destroy me.

I wanted to punch the wall, to kill, to hurt someone. Instead, I stood there, hands at my side, waiting for Hova to look at me again.

"Ava," Hova said, pulling the child to her feet. "Why? Why did you do it?" Her voice was kind but stern.

Ava let out a slight sob. "I don't know." She said, sticking out her bottom lip and staring at me with defiance in her eyes as she massaged her neck.

"Look me in the eye and tell me the truth." Hova shook the girl gently until she met her gaze. "Why did you do it?"

Ava's defiance melted away, and she physically shrank as she stood there, glued to Hova's eyes.

"I-I want more than this." She said, sneering at the woman with the fiery red hair who'd saved her life. "You think you have it so good, acting like your life is complete when you sit about sewing and cooking and *helping* people. But I don't want this life! I want to be comfortable. I want clothes that match, not piece-meal rags! I want to eat rich cheese every morning and drink fine wine every night. I don't want to slave away at the whim of someone else or forage in the Woods for a few scraps of food so I can curl up in the corner of a hovel under a ratty old blanket!" She was screaming by now, half rage, half shame.

"And you believe Governor Aepep will give you these things?" Hova's voice remained calm, her hands still firmly placed on the shoulders of the sobbing child in front of her. Ava didn't answer. She looked away and wiped her nose with the back of her hand.

"Go home, Ava. Go home and stay there until I come to you." Hova released the child, and she took off running. I stared after her, wishing I could fling some fire her way and be done with her. But Hova's hold over me was too strong.

"You had no right, Hova." I growled, clenching my fists once more. She turned toward me, eyes flashing, nostrils flared, her short red hair shifting in the light breeze.

"How dare you!" She hissed at me. "How dare you try to tell me what right I have over the life of a child in my care." She inched toward me. "Do you think I just happened to come across the two of you? Do you believe for a second that it was chance or good fortune that brought me here in time to save that foolish girl?"

We stared at each other, my heart both bursting and cowering at the same time.

"How many, Yuvraj? How many have gone before Ava? Two? Three? Ten?" She was getting closer to me, a dangerous anger overtaking her entire face. "Did you hide them at the bottom of the river, or did you simply fling their bodies onto the closest rubbish heap to be carted off later? No one would notice, right?"

I kept backing up, searching for the words to respond, wishing for the ability to lie to her as the lifeless eyes of seven children passed through my brain.

"Are you saying you followed me?" I said, finally managing to stutter something out in reply.

"You? No. Do you think you're the only one whose thoughts I can see at will? I asked that child for answers to give her a chance at honor, not because I need the truth. Her mind is an open book that I read every day as I go about my work."

"If you know the depth of her deceit, if you knew all along, then why didn't you let me do what needs to be done?" I said, staring down into her piercing eyes. I was leaning against the wall, having backed up as far as possible as she came ever closer to me. Terror and longing overwhelmed my senses. I wanted to reach out and pull her in, leaving no space between us, but my hands remained frozen to my sides.

"You grow more like your cousin each and every day. Your trust with Chiwa will be the end of you. I despise you for it." She spat the words in my direction, her voice torn between a desperate cry and a scream of anger.

I flushed with anger, longing instantly deserting me. *You should do away with her.* The thought raced through my mind, catching me off-guard. *You should end your weakness now and forever. It wouldn't take much. She probably wouldn't even put up a fight. You could make it look like the Governor's Guards did it.*

Hova took a step back as the idea floated inside me, shock all over her face. "You coward!" She said, choking back a sob. "Don't ever try to tell me of your love. Never again. From this day forward, you and I are at an end in every sense of the word." She turned and walked away, disappearing as she rounded the corner of the alleyway.

"What have I done?" I whispered to the empty alleyway. "What have I done?"

CHAPTER TWENTY

After wandering around the city until the sun went down, I returned home. Listening at the window entrance for several minutes I strained my ears for any sign of discussion regarding the run-in Hova and I had with Ava. Nothing but the hum of normal evening supper noise reached my ears.

Is Ava inside? I pondered whether to enter or leave - possibly forever. *Where would I go? This is all I have. This is my only chance at making a life of any kind. To leave would set me back years. I would have to set sail to the unknown or wander through the Woods to find another settlement where they don't know me.* Both thoughts were revolting. *Leaving would never grant me the satisfaction I seek of killing Aepep.*

I took a deep breath and swung myself inside the room. Quiet conversation continued with small interruptions from others to greet me. Hova sat in her corner, silently sewing a patch on a piece of clothing. She didn't stop or look up at me as I walked into the room, her eyes remaining fixed on the garment in her hands. All the children were at their homes which left only the original Shadows: me, Tyr and Hova, Hadithi and Shantha, Kaimbe and the twins.

"Yuvraj," Tyr said, pointing to the empty seat next to him. "Where have you been? Come, get some food. We have much to discuss tonight." His voice was light but the look in his eye was intense. *Did she tell him?* I thought as I nodded in his direction, grabbed a bowl, and went to the pot on the stove.

I dished out some thick bean soup loaded with potatoes, leeks, and carrots from our rooftop garden. The aroma of wild parsley, garlic, and rosemary wafted up from the bowl, causing my insides to rumble. Grabbing a chunk of bread and a wooden spoon, I sat down beside my half-brother, cradling my bowl in my lap as I devoured the food. In all the wandering and chaos of the afternoon, I hadn't realized how hungry I was.

"The time has come, Yuvraj." Tyr spoke quietly, his voice low enough no one else could hear him. "We need to start planning how we're going to take down Aepep. Every day he gets closer to us. We can't wait much longer. I fear one day he'll send his guards to destroy our houses or, worse, he'll send them to destroy the Slums entirely."

I nodded along, spooning soup into my mouth, and sopping up liquid with my bread. Glancing over at Hova, I tried to form my words tactfully as I mulled over what he'd just said. Hova did not return my glance. She appeared completely engrossed in her work.

"What do you mean he gets closer every day?" I asked, infusing my voice with as much curiosity and concern as I could muster. The back of my neck began to sweat as I contemplated what I'd do if I found out he was talking about Ava.

"I'm talking about the spies he likes to send around every once in a while. I know we haven't had any lately, but it's only a matter of time before we discover another one in our group." He paused to take a bite of his own unfinished food. "Or until Chiwa decides to give us up for personal gain. I doubt she's ignorant about where and who we are."

I took another bite of bread, scanning Tyr's face for any hint of deception. *Maybe it's a trap. Maybe he's baiting me to see if I'll confess to whatever Hova told him.* But his face showed nothing more than earnest passion.

"Are you alright, Yuvraj?" he said with creased brows of concern, setting aside his empty bowl and leaning forward to peer closer at my face. "What's wrong?"

I forced a smile to my lips as relief washed over me. "Nothing." I said, shaking my head. "I suppose I'm just tired from the day. Yes, we should absolutely begin to plan for how we'll take over. I agree and I'm all ears." I waited for Hova's voice to intrude on my thoughts. I fully expected her to rage against me, to call me a coward or a hypocrite or a liar. But my mind remained my own as the young woman continued to sew quietly in her corner. The silence did little to calm my unease.

"Come, let me show you the map I've drawn up." Tyr said, beckoning me to bring my food with. I stood and followed him toward the other end of the room to his cot. Kneeling in front of his bed, he reached underneath and pulled out a large piece of scrap paper with a map of the Governor's Grounds scrawled over it. Every entrance and building had been plotted out, along with a detailed schedule of the guards, Aepep's habits, and the servants who came and went. He laid it out on his cot as we kneeled before it, squinting in the dim light.

"I've been thinking through what worked and what failed when we went to get Chantrea. We were smaller in number, and our training wasn't nearly as good as it is now. Hadithi and Shantha - they were too young. We never should've taken them with us." Tyr's voice held regret as he spoke.

"But we're all older now, well-trained, and stronger. The Governor's Guards avoid us at all costs. Aepep knows of the magic running through your veins," He shifted his head back and forth as if mentioning our encounter with Aepep had irritated his scars. "But he doesn't know how strong you are or of Hadithi's existence. If we want to succeed and overthrow Aepep, then I think we need to act soon. The longer we wait the more chance we have of Chiwa turning us all in and one of his spies slipping past us."

My brother's sincerity caused me to both pity and envy him. *He has no idea.* I thought. *What must it be like to live trusting every single person who presents themselves as trustworthy?* I still wondered about Ava. Not whether Hova had told him about her - it was obvious she had not - but about where she'd gone when Hova told her to go home.

"If we start here," Tyr's voice drew me back to his plan. I followed his finger as he traced each step, nodding along to what seemed an excellently thought-out plan of attack. "No one under fifteen should be allowed to come with us. It's too dangerous. The younger children need some older children to help them, to take care of them." I agreed, though somewhat reluctantly. Even though they were young, their small stature and the sheer number of children we'd brought into our fold could be a wonderful asset in a surprise attack. But it wasn't a point I wanted to argue with Tyr, and I knew Hova would never allow them to participate.

"Tomorrow we will prepare for battle. We will attack in the wee hours of the new morning. What do you say, Yuvraj? Are you with me?" I could feel Tyr's eye studying my face. I nodded and met his gaze.

"Unto death, brother." I said without hesitating. I waited once more for Hova's voice to intrude on my mind and call out my lie. When none came, I turned to look at her as Tyr continued to bend over the map in silence. The little seamstress sat in the exact same spot as before, working away on the garment in her lap. A smile and a few words escaped her lips on occasion as she listened to Hadithi and Shantha talk quietly beside her.

'No condemnation, no words of warning or judgment?' I tried reaching out, tried to bait her. How I'd hated her voice in my head, constantly telling me how I was wrong. Now I wanted it? Her hand paused as if I'd reached her mind, but her eyes remained fixed as she returned to her activity after a few seconds. Her face remained passive and resigned, her silence complete.

As I turned back to Tyr to hear what he had in mind for getting ready, Hova's last words in the alleyway echoed in the back of my mind: *from this day forward, you and I are at an end in every sense of the word.*

In every sense of the word.

"I ALMOST DIED!" AVA screamed at the two men in the abandoned shack on the edge of the Slums near the great rocks. A single candle cast ominous shadows about the room as it flickered. Commander Jabez held one finger to his lips and his free hand out in the girl's direction, annoyed by her volume more than anything else. What she lacked in stature she made up for in fury.

"You promised me I would be safe! You promised that none of them would ever find out. Not the Shadows, not Aepep - none of them!" She stopped to take a giant breath.

"Ava, calm down." Commander Jabez said, his voice calm. "Please remember where we are. If anyone finds us together and reports back to Aepep, we could all face the noose. So please: shut up." His tone changed from gentle to dangerous. The girl took a step back and crossed her arms in front of her.

SON OF KINGS

"Why is he here?" She said, lowering her voice and pointing at the man leaning against the dilapidated wall. "What does 'The Gray Merchant' have to do with our plans?" She sneered at his nickname.

"Shut up, child or I'll finish the job Yuvraj promised." The man's voice was smooth and silky as he pushed himself away from the wall and brushed off his shoulder. Ava swallowed and took a tentative step backwards, her arms lowering to her sides as she made fists with her hands.

Walking up to her, he leaned down so she could see his face underneath the large gray hat. "The only way they could've found out is if you slipped. No one else knows our plans. I give you two choices, Ava. You can either do as we say and reap the rewards Commander Jabez promised, or you can die. Which would you prefer?" He smiled, as if inviting her to partake in a show of generous hospitality. The cold light in his bright eyes caused the girl to break out in a cold sweat as she tried to find her voice.

"Aruj," Jabez interjected resting a hand on the merchant's shoulder and squeezing it. "There's no need to threaten Ava. She's as loyal to our cause as the Shadows are to theirs." A smile twitched at his mouth as he said this. Aruj straightened and turned to face him.

"I swear, Commander," The girl stuttered, finally finding the voice that had escaped her.

"No need, Ava." Jabez replied, holding up a hand for her to be silent.

"If she didn't slip up, then how did Yuvraj and Hova find out?" Aruj asked. "And how can we be sure they don't suspect the real reason she was there?"

"You understand better than anyone of the inexplicable things that happen among their ranks. The tales told among my soldiers about Hova and her mind games are enough of a reason for me. My men may fear Tyr and his ability to defeat them, or Yuvraj's show of the same magic Aepep possesses, but they live in dread of that tiny woman. I do not think it wise or necessary to question how they found out about Ava." His tone was firm, resolved, and final.

The two stared at each other as Ava glanced between them, wondering what she should do or say.

"What's our next move?" Aruj broke the silence after a few minutes.

"We have no other move but to wait now. Ava will give us a detailed description of their talents, and she'll return to her house as Hova commanded. If she hears anything, she'll come and find us. If she doesn't, we'll have a plan in place anyway. We know the Shadows plan to attack and kill Aepep. When the time comes, my guards will fall back and allow them to breach our numbers without too much opposition. You and I cannot overthrow Aepep, but we can help those trumped-up gutter rats do the job for us before we turn on them and take Shantu for ourselves." Jabez paused, tilting his head from side to side as he thought.

"What of the witch?" Aruj asked.

"She wants nothing to do with Shantu. She wants the crazy woman in the dungeon. That's why Aepep keeps the woman locked up: as leverage against his niece. We give Chantrea to Chiwa and I guarantee we'll never see either of them ever again."

"And my daughter?"

The question hung in the air for so long Ava wondered if Jabez would respond.

"We'll find her, and you can take her home." The promise from Jabez came haltingly, as if he were unsure of his ability to issue such a promise. "I can guarantee her safety, but not her compliance. You know this, Aruj."

The Gray Merchant shifted uncomfortably from one leg to the other. "I know." He dipped his head in agreement.

"Then it is settled. We will go our separate ways tonight. Ava will come to warn me when they decide to attack." Jabez stared at the girl, waiting for her to nod her head. "Until then, we pretend everything continues as we discussed with Aepep."

"What if they never attack? What if it takes years for them to try?" Aruj asked.

"Years?" Ava scoffed. "Have you been listening to anything I've said over the past two months? Yuvraj and Tyr have been planning to attack all their lives. The others follow them like a group of hungry stray cats! I swear to you on my life, they will attack, and they will do so soon!"

The Gray Merchant clenched his jaw as the girl smirked in his direction, disgust for his questions plainly expressed.

"Ava, go home and keep quiet." Jabez commanded, pointing toward the door. "Stay out of the way, keep your ears open and your mouth shut. If Yuvraj comes around, hide. If Hova comes around, run. We'll wait for you to warn us."

The girl stomped off without another word, allowing the door to slam behind her as she disappeared into the quiet night.

SON OF KINGS

"I will not hesitate to get rid of her, Jabez." Aruj hissed at his companion. "If she accidentally gives us away, I will cut her down without a second thought. I'll make good on everything Yuvraj started to do."

"Don't be a fool, Aruj." Jabez snapped back. "We have waited too long for this moment to throw it all away. This is not one of your ships where you can torture and kill, and no one ever finds out. This is a city of people far bigger than any ship you've ever sailed. I've spent years finding children willing to even try to infiltrate the growing number of Shadows, only for each one to disappear on me - no doubt killed by Yuvraj."

He paused as he remembered the conversation Ava had reported to him. "You want to be governor and I want to rule this city with someone who has a brain for business. Aepep's mind is growing week with greed and lust. He's always been lazy, but his obsession with the Shadows and his inability to contain them has progressed the damage done by years of misused magic. His downfall will be of his own making. His children will be his undoing."

"Indeed. But you must understand that I am risking everything on this venture. I find with age that I'm growing weary of the Sea. I have kept my identity a secret for so long that the truth has become nothing other than myth and legend I use to my advantage whenever I can." He smiled grimly beneath his hat. "However, if the Upper Class of Shantu were to ever find out that the wagging tongues of the Slums and the Common Sector speak truth when they spread rumors about me, our plans would be hard-pressed to fall in place. The girl's silence is crucial to our success."

"Ava lasted longer than any of the others combined. I swear she will do as promised."

Aruj studied his companion for a moment. "Tell me, Jabez, what is your fascination with the child? Why do you defend her?" The two men locked eyes as The Gray Merchant waited for an answer.

"That's none of your business." The Commander spoke through clenched teeth. "I warn you, Aruj, the child must be left alone. If you harm her, I'll know. I guaranteed the safety of your daughter, you must guarantee the safety of Ava."

"Ah, so she's your daughter, is she?" Aruj prodded, hoping the most obvious answer were true.

"Swear to me no harm will come to Ava by your hand or by the hand of anyone you command." Jabez replied, neither confirming nor denying the assumption.

"Agreed." The Gray Merchant said. Soon the candle was extinguished, and the two men exited the broken-down shack to go their separate ways. The stars glittered above as a tall figure crept around from the side of the building, watching them disappear.

Efah walked briskly home, unnoticed by the few he passed. Upon entering the shack where Chiwa sat, he threw back his hood exclaiming, "My dear! I have such great news!"

Chiwa turned to face him, startled by his loud entrance into the quiet hovel. Her hands glowed red for a second as she tensed, ready for a fight.

"Efah," The witch's harsh voice growled at the excited man. "It would be wise of you to enter with more care next time."

"But my dear," Efah replied, bowing slightly and brushing away her comment with excitement as he sat down in the chair across from her. "This news is such that I cannot contain it." He proceeded to tell her of the conversation he'd overheard. Having seen Commander Jabez leave the Governor's Grounds unaccompanied, he'd followed him to the shack on the edge of town.

Chiwa's eyes grew brighter with each repeated piece of information. She sat for a few minutes, mulling over what this meant for her.

"You mean to say," She laughed quietly. "That Aepep has no friends left, and Yuvraj will help me get to Chantrea while Jabez looks on and happily hands her over to us so that he can go kill off the tiresome Shadows once they've completed their task in killing Aepep?" Her cackle was deep and loud as she reveled in the twisted nature of her foreseen triumph.

"Delightful, isn't it?"

"The stars are aligning, Efah. My destiny is calling. I am Chiwa. I am power and darkness and death." The words sent an odd chill up Efah's spine, a chill he enjoyed. He'd always loved playing with fire, and here was Chiwa: real, living and breathing fire.

"We will soon have that woman to ourselves," the witch continued. "This time will be different. I won't lose my temper." The promise was made to herself more than the man sitting across from her. "This time, I'll hold out. I'll weaken her mind until it's mine to manipulate and she begs for death. Just as my father broke the spirit of her friend long ago, so I will break her spirit. Tomorrow I will visit Yuvraj to see what he has planned. My time is coming, Efah!"

Chapter Twenty-One

The next day is forever seared in my memory as the longest short day I've ever experienced. We gathered the oldest and most skilled children within our care, outlining carefully what our plan of attack was for each one. Our numbers would be small in comparison to Aepep's army, but each of our fighters was skilled enough to take on at least two or three of his soldiers at a time.

We numbered twenty-five in total: me, Tyr, Kaimbe, Hadithi, Shantha, River and Ryder, and a slew of older children who'd been carefully picked and trained over the years.

Tyr remained true to his assertion that no one under the age of fifteen should be involved in the fight. When Hova agreed with him I remained silent, longing to argue that some of our most skilled fighters were just a year younger. I would never win that argument. Even if Hova could find it in herself to listen to me I knew I'd be met with cold silence. So, I refrained.

Hadithi and I remained at home as Tyr and the others left to notify their troops. None of those within our training were old or skilled enough to be of value in the upcoming revolt. Instead, we turned our efforts to organizing and sharpening the weapons we had at hand.

SON OF KINGS

Hova spent the day making a large amount of food and ripping up clean pieces of scrap fabric into strips. I realized her morbid expectation was that we would return to this hovel defeated and wounded rather than triumphing over Aepep to rule and reign over Shantu the way we deserved.

I wasn't sure if I should be thankful for her forethought and care or angry at her lack of confidence in us. Somehow, we made it through the day without ever speaking a word to each other. She kept her peace, and I kept my distance. Every time she interacted with Hadithi I bit my tongue and turned away. I did not wish to witness the gentle kindness in her care for him or the smile that broke across her face when she looked his way.

"What happened, Yuvraj?" Hadithi asked me quietly as Hova climbed through the window to get some vegetables from the rooftop garden. I paused and gave him a quick glance, wary of the question. We were wrapping ropes and tying them off, counting out to make sure at least half of us had a cord of rope for the fight.

"What do you mean?" I said, trying to make my voice sound relaxed instead of defensive.

"Between you and Hova. Neither of you have spoken to the other since yesterday morning. I realize you don't always see eye-to-eye, but this is extreme for either of you. Did you have a fight?"

My face flushed and my heart raced as I tried to control my impulse to slap him for his impudent question. The veins in my hands fought to turn red with fire, singeing the rope until a slight burned smell wafted up to my nostrils.

"Some things, Hadithi, are better left alone. I would advise you to keep your nose out of my relationship with Hova and focus instead on the battle at hand." I tied the rope off and dropped it in the pile. "I think you can finish up here. I'm going to gather some stones by the river."

"I'm sorry." His apology followed me as I sprang out the window and headed toward the river. It was mid-afternoon and the others would be arriving soon. I decided it would be best if I took a quick plunge to cool my veins before going back inside.

The water was warm but refreshing, shocking my body, and clearing my mind as I dove headfirst into the slow-moving rapids. A few minutes was all I needed. I climbed out and sat on the bank to dry off in the bright sunshine, the cool breeze causing my skin to prickle even as the sun warmed me through. Grabbing a small sack from inside my pocket, I gathered tiny stones as I'd said I would. They would work well in a slingshot as a last-resort weapon.

By the time I finished gathering the stones, the sun began to set. Pulling my tunic back over my head, I grabbed the sack and headed toward our home. The hazy red sky was calming, somehow displaying the fire I felt within me. I half-believed the sun and the clouds had read my thoughts and chosen to let me know they understood what desires lingered in my soul.

Taking a deep breath, I crawled through the window and dumped my sack of rocks on the pile of weapons. Glancing around the still, quiet room I noticed Hova and Hadithi were nowhere to be seen. Shantha met my glance with a look of concern and a tilt of her head.

"Yuvraj," Tyr greeted me in a whisper. "Have you seen my sister? Or Hadithi?" His voice was calm but the look in his eye betrayed an underlying anxiety.

"You mean they weren't here when you arrived?" I asked, frowning, my heart racing as I thought about all the possible reasons for why they might have left.

Tyr shook his head. "We thought the three of you were together, but then you came home without them. Hova never stays out so late in the evening and it's not like Hadithi to take off without telling one of us." I nodded along as my half-brother spoke, panicking that Hova had told Hadithi what happened with Ava. *Don't be silly.* I thought to myself. *Even if she did, he would never leave without Shantha.* My heartbeat slowed at this reassuring thought.

"I'll go out to look for them." I offered Tyr, curious to find out where they'd gone. Tyr nodded and followed me, pointing in the direction of the Sea as he turned to go west toward the great rocks. I walked along the road, turning down random alleyways as I went, winding my way through the maze of the Slums with ease. Finally, a familiar figure came into view: the mute woman whose home we'd patched. I sped up to meet her. She smiled up at me and ducked her head in greeting.

Smiling in return I greeted her and remarked on the fine sunset before launching into what I needed. "Have you seen Hova?" I asked, trying to keep the words calm. The woman tilted her head, still smiling, and turned to point in the direction of the Sea.

"She's over there?" I said to confirm what I believed she was communicating. The woman nodded and picked up a small stone, pointing at it and then gesturing with her arms. "Hova's at one of the large boulders beside the Sea?" I guessed, almost enjoying the charade of communication. Another smile and affirming nod were all I needed. Thanking the woman, I hurried down the street to reach the place indicated.

The light in the sky was fading by the time I drew close to the boulder. Not too far off to my left the muffled songs of sailors in their make-shift shore camp drifted across the sandy terrain. I crept around the boulder, searching for Hadithi and Hova, wary of any stray soldiers or sailors who might be out and about even though it was suppertime.

Soft voices reached my ears as I peeked around the edge of the giant boulder. The two of them stood side by side, faces pointed toward the water, Hova's small frame leaning against Hadithi's right arm as her head rested on his shoulder. My face flushed with envy at the sight, and I tried hard to listen in on their conversation.

"Make sure that getting what you want and getting what you deserve are the same thing." She said to Hadithi. She was staring out at the Sea, her face hidden from me. Her voice was sad, tired, and gentle. Gentler than I'd ever heard it before.

"Make sure that getting what you deserve," she continued. "That getting what's rightfully yours, doesn't rob you of what you want - of what you desire deep down." She sighed and turned to face Hadithi. Her hood was down, exposing her cropped fiery hair. I was shocked to see a tear glide down her cheek. A lump rose in my throat involuntarily, half empathy for the woman, half jealousy for the man with which she shared this vulnerable part of herself. A part I'd never seen before.

"Don't become what you cannot respect. Don't become someone you no longer recognize." She reached out for Hadithi's hands, staring down at them as she spoke. "You are born of royalty, a person of myth and legend whose story goes so far beyond the battle here. Tonight, as you face Aepep and fight for a cause you believe in, remember there are so many questions and battles in your life you have yet to confront. There is more to you and your story and your destiny than whatever bitter end tonight may bring.

"Do not give your life for the sake of a war not yours to fight. You are a Shadow of Shantu, but that doesn't mean you should become a shadow of the man I know you were born to be!" Hova squeezed his hands, went high up on the tips of her toes, and kissed him gently on the cheek. She walked quickly away around the other side of the boulder, wiping the tears from her eyes.

I wanted to scream, to run to her and hug her close, to receive the gentle kiss she'd bestowed upon Hadithi. *Why can't she believe in me the way she believes in him?* My mind swam with anger and bitterness, my veins burning with the desire to strike down Hadithi once and for all. I leaned against the giant boulder for support.

After all, I can defeat Aepep. No one will ever suspect I killed Hadithi. I can wait for Hova to be far enough away and then I can stab him in the back and throw him in the Sea! No one will ever know. The battle raged inside me, a cool voice reminding me Hadithi's magic was much stronger than my own and Aepep didn't know about him yet. I waged war within myself against what I wanted and what would be most likely to gain my desired outcome.

I am forever damned. I am forever alone, looking from the outside in on what could be, what might have been if I were only enough. If I were only good enough. Hot tears ran down my cheeks as I considered what it would be like to be loved by Hova. How heavenly it would be to be wanted and liked and desired by the woman I'd cared for since the day I met her.

Maybe he'll die tonight. Maybe I should make sure he dies tonight. She no longer reads my mind. With time and a little patience, maybe she would come to love me if Hadithi were out of the picture. Maybe when I am governor, and she sees how good I am at leading the people, perhaps she'll learn to love me. Once we're all comfortable and warm then maybe, just maybe, she could love me and be mine instead of giving her heart away to him with no hope of returned affection.

Hadithi continued to stand there, staring out at the water, still and silent. Gradually, he sank down to a seated position on the rocky beach. He was whispering again. Swallowing the bitter sobs that wanted to come out, I strained my ears a little more and closed my eyes to listen.

"Mama, I realize you can't hear me." He whispered, reaching out for a handful of coarse sand, and watching it sift slowly through his gloved fingers. "Your spirit departed from this awful place a long time ago. But I don't know what to do. I miss you. I've kept the secret you told me to keep. Not even Shantha knows. But I don't understand it." He paused for a second, shifting some small rocks around from one hand to the other. "You'd like her, Shantha that is. I wish you could meet her." After a few more minutes of silence, he began to sing in a bittersweet voice,

"Where wealth meets poverty
As the river flows to the Sea
There you'll find your destiny
There Zale will be."

I listened as he sang the verse on repeat a couple times through, wondering what the song meant. After another half hour, as the moon and stars grew brighter in the sky, Hadithi stood and brushed himself off. He left, following the same route around the boulder Hova had, which kept me out of the line of discovery. After a few minutes of numbness, I pushed myself away from the boulder and walked slowly back toward our home.

The sun disappeared as the moon rose in the sky. It was a bright night, full of starlight and cheerful rays from the still rising moon. I wandered down the street, deep in thought, paying little attention to the few who passed me.

"Yuvraj." The harsh whisper met my ears as I walked by an alleyway a few houses away from our home. Stopping, I backed up a few steps and entered the dark alleyway.

"Chiwa." I said her name in a flat voice, blinking to adjust my eyes to the darkness of the alleyway. I could just make out the outline of her figure. "What do you want?"

"I want an update, Yuvraj. Give me answers. I want to know when you're going to stop dragging your feet and do as you promised before some gutter rat you take in decides to betray you to Aepep."

I was instantly drawn out of my stupor, hyper-aware of the fact that Chiwa's words meant more than I cared to hear. "Don't threaten me, Chiwa. I'm in no mood."

"Then you might want to reconsider keeping information from me. You swore an oath." She hissed.

I stood silent for a second, gathering my thoughts and my wits. "I never promised you I would tell you all our plans. I swore I would deliver Chantrea to you in return for some helpful information from you from time to time. Have I somehow broken my oath? Do we find ourselves magically inside the Governor's Mansion?" I matched the danger in her tone, gesturing with my arms for her to look around at the dank alleyway we stood in. I knew I would lose in a battle against Chiwa, but I also decided I'd rather die at her hands than become her slave.

"Yuvraj," Chiwa came so close I could see the glint of her eyes. "I have asked you a very simple question and I want an answer before I lose my temper." The veins around her eyes glowed red as she spoke, indicating her self-proclaimed temper was ill-contained. "You swore to help me get to Chantrea. I told you *we* would attack. Now tell me the plan."

"Tonight, Chiwa. We attack tonight when the night is at its darkest. Two hours past midnight, when all are deep asleep and the guards are exhausted, we will attack." I paused, cautiously choosing my next words. "If you want to join us, then you can hide close beside the main gate. Once we're in, no one will be paying attention and you can come in after us. I can't afford to be seen with you, though. You must understand. The Shadows do not trust you and the Common People fear you. If any of them were to find out that we were allies, then all would be lost."

"Good." She sounded unexpectedly satisfied as the red veins in her face faded from sight. "I'll be waiting." Without another word, she turned and ducked out of the alleyway.

I sighed with relief and left the dark place, walking a little faster toward our home. To my surprise, I found Tyr sitting alone out front with his back to the wall. He hardly seemed to notice me as I approached. Wishing for my bed and a little peace and quiet I started toward the alleyway window entrance.

"Yuvraj." His voice was gentle but firm. As I'd done with Chiwa, I stopped and backed up.

"Yes, Tyr?" I asked him, leaning against the wall and looking down at him half-curious, half-apprehensive. "Did you find Hova and Hadithi?" I asked, trying to make light of whatever he wanted to ask me.

"Oh, yes. They went for a walk. They returned a bit ago. I apologize," he said, shaking his head. "I should have thought to send someone after you." He paused for a second. "What if the plan doesn't work?"

SON OF KINGS

The question caught me off guard. "It will. It must. We've worked so long and so hard for this. This is what we deserve, it's our time. Tyr, you planned this attack yourself."

He shook his head. "But we're outnumbered and young."

"We have Hadithi." I coaxed, trying not to choke on the words. "My powers aren't as strong, but you have me as well. None of the Governor's Guards can match your skill. None of the lesser soldiers can match the skill of those we've trained. This is our destiny, Tyr. This is our home and it's high time we took it back." I watched him with bated breath, anxiety beginning to tell me of the possibility he might lose his nerve.

"What if Hova's right. What if there's a better way, another way to win back what rightfully belongs to us?"

Fighting the panic building in my throat, I kneeled beside him. "Tyr, Hova is right about a good many things, but there will never be peace in Shantu as long as Aepep lives. Until our father dies, what you see around us and the way we live now will always be the legacy of Shantu. Only we can fix it. Only we can give the people of the Slums the life they deserve.

"What do the Upper Class gentry understand of life? They treat us as nothing more than rats. We: you, and I and Kaimbe and all the rest are the only ones who truly understand what it means to rule this city. The people of the Slums need us and so do the Common People." Passion poured out in my voice as I spoke. I believed what I said, and I needed Tyr to believe it as well.

"You're right, Yuvraj. Aepep needs to die. This is the only way to bring true reform." My brother took a deep breath and let it out slowly. "Don't worry, I'll be ready when the time comes. Leave me a few minutes longer out here to gather my thoughts." He glanced to meet my gaze, a half-smile breaking out on his lips. I nodded and squeezed his shoulder before turning into the alleyway to go inside.

My mind swam with the onslaught of conversations and emotions I felt had been pummeled at me since my interaction with Hadithi. Kaimbe sat in the alleyway, barely visible, staring into the darkness. He didn't speak to or look at me and I recognized he had no desire for me to interrupt his silence.

As I approached the window, I heard soft whispering from the roof accompanied by quiet crying. Climbing the ladder, I peeked over the edge to see who was up there. Hadithi sat at the other end of the roof, arms embracing Shantha as she cried gently into his shoulder.

"Why are we doing this, Hadithi?"

"It's the only way we can get to Chantrea. I have so many questions to ask her. I need her help. I don't know how to get to Zale. She's our only chance, Shantha." His face glowed faintly in the moonlight as he turned and pressed his lips against her head.

"I can't lose you. It's all too dangerous and it won't work to help Shantu."

"You don't know that."

"I do. Somehow, deep inside, I know the plan Yuvraj, and Tyr came up with is going to fail. Hova knows it too. She's so quiet, Hadithi. Quieter than ever. Her eyes look as if she gazed into the future of the Shadows and found nothing but a grave."

Hadithi remained silent. *I wonder if he told her about his interaction with Hova?* It seemed obvious he had not, and my tired mind worked to understand why.

"They're using you, Hadithi." Shantha said, sniffling and sitting up to look him in the face. "You know they're using you. Tyr justifies it because he desires so deeply to help the children, and he's never bothered to dig into who you are or what you want. But Yuvraj understands what he's doing, and he's doing it for his own gain. He doesn't care about you."

I gripped the ladder as her words made me flush with anger.

"He means well," Hadithi interjected quicker than I expected, catching me off-guard as I'd assumed he would turn on me in an instant. "Yuvraj may be misguided in some of his desires, but he means well, Shantha. Besides, it doesn't matter. I could've walked away a long time ago and I chose not to. I'm not sure if this mission will work or not but I agree with Tyr and Yuvraj that we can't afford to wait much longer. One can only hope our actions will bring some benefit to the Slums whether we succeed or fail. But I'm not here to defeat Aepep. I'm here to find Chantrea so we can go back to Zale and do as my mother asked."

Shantha nodded without another word, and they embraced again. I quietly descended the ladder and entered our home. My head swimming with exhaustion, I fell onto my cot and drifted away into a fitful sleep.

SON OF KINGS

A SMALL GIRL RAN through the streets in the direction of the Governor's Grounds, dodging in and out of alleyways as if trying to keep anyone from following her. One word from her to the guard at the gate and Ava was inside within seconds, heading straight for Commander Jabez's barracks.

"They came tonight to get the older children," she said, panting as she tried to catch her breath in the chair he pulled up for her. "They're attacking tonight. Before dawn breaks, I swear to you they will be here."

Jabez smiled and nodded. "So be it. No better time for Aepep to die than the present. Everything is falling into place. You've done well, Ava. You've done very well indeed."

Chapter Twenty-Two

THE MOON HUNG HIGH and bright in the sky as we all fell into place around the Governor's Grounds. Stars twinkled above us in peaceful silence as the world of Shantu slept. We numbered twenty-five in total, almost half of those we recognized as Shadows.

Tyr had entrusted me with the largest number of Shadows, five of the older children accompanying me in my attack on the front gate at the north-east corner of the Governor's Grounds. Hadithi and Shantha were down the wall from me close to the bridge, too far away to be seen at night. Four of the older children accompanied them.

Tyr had taken three of the older children to the wall opposite the gate. River and Ryder and three more children attacked from the same wall but closer to the river where Aepep had still not fixed the crumbling stones that once built up the wall. Kaimbe came last with the three strongest children from the river itself, swimming quietly down the summer current to the bank where we'd fought to free Chantrea all those years ago.

Hova remained at home with her stockpile of bandages and homemade salves to rub on the wounds with which she assumed we would return to her, defeated and broken. I found it offensive, but Tyr didn't even blink an eye.

SON OF KINGS

"Come on, Yuvraj." He'd said. "Even if we succeed it would be foolish to assume none of us will get wounded." I'd begrudgingly nodded and bit my tongue. I knew that wasn't her assumption. She knew something I didn't want to admit or understand. I had to believe her assumption was wrong, that we would win and defeat Aepep once and for all. If I didn't believe and Tyr gave up hope, then we'd fail for certain.

I shook my head and focused on the task at hand. *Forget Hova*, I thought. *She's safe at home and soon you'll show her a new home with a new life. You can't afford a distraction. Focus, Yuvraj, focus!*

A shadow moved to the right of where I crouched against the wall opposite the gate. Knowing all the Shadows accompanying me were to my left, I tensed and squinted into the darkness. My mind and body relaxed as the glowing veins of a hand flashed momentarily in the darkness then disappeared. *It's just Chiwa, you fool. Carry on.*

A quick survey of the guard towers at the gate yielded one guard facing into the Governor's Grounds while leaning heavily on the spear in his hand. My gut told me he was asleep. With a wave of my hand, we crossed the street to the gate itself. I formed a loop in my rope and easily hooked it at the top of the tower with the sleeping guard. Tightening the rope with a few quick tugs, I climbed nimbly up and peered over the edge.

The guard hadn't moved. One swift knock to the head with the butt of my sword, and he crumbled into my arms. I contemplated a quick stab to his heart or a slit to his neck before moving on, but the words of our motto echoed in my brain and kept my hand from ending his life.

Hit hard, but show mercy. Damn.

I stripped the unconscious guard of his weapon, and tied his hands and feet together with a short piece of twine. Pulling the rope up, I looped it back around my belt before cautiously opening the trap door to the narrow ladder below. Seeing and hearing nothing, I descended the ladder and cracked open the small gate at the bottom. Silence met my ears. No talking, no movement, all was still.

Creeping out of the tower, I closed the gate and latched it from the outside. I strode to the main gate to undo the bolts from the small door meant to let in one person at a time. The Shadows joined me inside the gate, and I closed it behind me with a swift glance outside. Remaining true to my promise to Chiwa, I didn't lock it.

My heartbeat quickened as I realized the first step had been accomplished without raising the alarm. *We're inside. There's no going back.* We dodged our way across the courtyard toward the main door of the Governor's Mansion, careful to remain within the shadows of the trees and the wall. I could only hope and believe that the others were on track and successful so far.

SHANTHA AND HADITHI CROUCHED with the four children entrusted to them beneath the bridge, waiting in the shadows for the drowsy pair of guards to turn around at the river and head back toward Yuvraj. Hadithi considered overpowering them. It wouldn't take much. The slouching guards walked in silence, grunting two-word sentences to each other as they patrolled.

"Nothing here."

"I know."

"Never is."

"Damn waste."

"Huh. Yah."

The mesmerizing conversation continued as they stood beside the rushing water, leaning heavily on their spears. The six Shadows pressed against the underside of the bridge, barely breathing. Overpowering the guards would be easy and wouldn't take much but their disappearance also ran the risk of prematurely alerting the rest of the Governor's Grounds to the presence of the Shadows.

"Let's go."

"Sounds good."

As the guards strolled away, Hadithi and Shantha peeked their heads out from around the corner to watch them go. As soon as they disappeared, Hadithi crossed the short distance to the grounds wall and detached the rope from his belt. Like Yuvraj, he hooked it to the top of the wall on the first try, signaling for the others to follow before pulling himself up.

SON OF KINGS

Reaching the top, he hoisted his shoulders over the rough stones to look over the wall. He was thankful for the protective leather Hova clad him in as the stones tried to dig in and rip his skin away. No one stirred in the grounds below. Pulling himself up to perch at the top of the wall, the Shadow undid the rope, re-attached it to his belt, and jumped. Tumbling through a somersault he crouched and surveyed the grounds as Shantha and the young Shadows followed his lead.

So far so good. He thought as everyone landed safely somewhere beside him. *Time to go find Chantrea.* He nodded to Shantha, and they all quickly ran through the thin grass to the wall of the Governor's Mansion. Two of the children spread out to keep watch as Hadithi lay down on his belly and removed his glove next to a grate. As he used his powers the way Yuvraj taught him, his conscience pricked him.

I'm still following the plan. I'm just taking a detour once we get inside. He argued with the annoying voice inside his head telling him to abandon his search for Chantrea. *I must find her. This is my only chance.*

Hova's word of caution from the night before came back to him. Her warning helped silence the weak voice of conviction that wanted him to abandon his plan and stick to the one Tyr and Yuvraj had laid out for him. Torn between loyalty to his mother and loyalty to his caretakers, the searing heat from his hand melted away one bar of iron at a time, faster than he'd expected. Realizing Shantha was lying next to him, staring at his face, he paused.

"Are you with me?" he asked as he tried to shake off the unsettling feeling in his stomach.

She squeezed his free hand, a smile breaking out across her face in the light of the moon. "To the end."

Soon the bars melted away, Hadithi propping them gently against the stone building as the faint stench of burned grass filled the air. The Shadow doused the red-hot stubs of the opening with ice, drawing on his powers once more before burying the sharp bottom ends in a thick layer of dirt. The top stubs would no longer burn, but the Shadows ducked away from the sharp ends to remain injury free.

"Let's go." Hadithi whispered and slid through the now gaping hole into the dimly lit corridor below. Shantha and the others followed.

ELLEN ES CEELY

The three guards at the front entrance to the Governor's Mansion were easy to take out. They were scrawny and half-asleep. Their mouths were soon stuffed with pocket handkerchiefs and their hands were bound with rope. Releasing the keys from the belt buckled around the waist of one of the guards made for easy opening of the mansion door.

In all his surveying, the one thing Tyr had been unable to discover was whether a key was kept outside the gate or if one had to knock to enter the mansion at night. *That was easy.* I thought. *But was it too easy?* I didn't have time to wonder. After all, our plan depended on moving swiftly.

After a few tries I found the correct key and inserted it into the lock of the door. Pushing it open gently, we all waited with bated breath. The hinges creaked eerily in the silence of the night and the moon cast a bright light through the entrance, illuminating the first couple of feet.

No one spoke. Nothing stirred inside. Waving to the other Shadows, I stepped inside with my knife drawn and one hand ungloved. I was ready to defend or attack if needed. Nothing happened. The others piled in behind me and my eyes adjusted to the torch lit stone entrance hall before us.

Being mere "gutter rats" none of us had ever seen inside the mansion. Only the Governor and the Upper Class were allowed inside unless you were a servant, a convicted criminal, or a soldier. Even then, only the very best of the best would likely ever see this part of the mansion unless they were going to be hung.

My mind flirted with the memory of the poor pregnant girl dangling in the courtyard outside all those years ago. *Focus, Yuvraj, focus!* I scolded myself and surveyed the hall. No one appeared. I'd expected to find resistance, to fight against half of Aepep's army as soon as we entered. Instead, I found silence. Nothing but the faint hiss of the torchlight met my ears.

From here on out, it was a guessing game. Without having ever entered the building, we had no idea which way Aepep's chambers lay or where he might be at this hour of the morning. With any luck, he'd be upstairs in bed asleep. That was my mission: find Aepep. Tyr and Kaimbe would take care of Jabez while Hadithi and I dealt with Aepep.

Three hallways lay before us. We could go left, right, or straight ahead. Squinting into the darkness I made out the outline of an impressive winding staircase about halfway down the hallway on the left side. I motioned again for the Shadows beside me to follow, and we moved soundlessly against the walls over the giant stone floor. Our soft shoes failed to cast an echo into the vaulted ceiling above. Footsteps approached as we neared the staircase.

We froze in unison, holding our breath as a single soldier marched by, his eyes fixed on the floor beneath his feet. One quick motion from behind him, and we had him unconscious, tied up and tucked away in the shadows of the wall. I nodded to my group and peeked around the staircase wall, realizing how calm I felt.

My heart beat steadily; my mind focused and clear. *I expected to be overwhelmed or anxious.* I thought as I drew my sword and crept up the staircase, two Shadows remaining below and the other three following me. *After all, it's not every day you try to assassinate your father.* My hands burned against the blade I held.

We reached the top of the staircase without mishap. I looked to the right and discovered one long hallway stretching all the way to the other end of the mansion. To the left lay several wooden doors that I could only assume were servant bedrooms.

Afterall, I mused. *The great Governor of Shantu would never live in such small quarters. He needs more than a feeble wooden door to protect him while he gets his beauty sleep and abuses his power over the young girls taken into his household staff.* Disgust turned into rage as my mother's face flashed before my mind's eye.

We slid down the walls of the flickering hallway with our swords unsheathed, hoping not to bump into any snoozing or patrolling guards. The doors we passed became more intricate and stunning with larger spaces between them. At random points we found side hallways with windows at the end of them. A gaping hole to the left turned out to be another dimly lit winding staircase. The more I thought about it, the more it made sense that Aepep's quarters would be on this side. He would be the furthest away from harm with a view of the river.

It's too quiet. My pulse quickened as I realized we could be walking straight into a trap. As far as I knew, Ava had done as Hova commanded her. But what if she'd gone to Aepep? *To tell him what? We might attack soon? How would she know it was going to be tonight?* I shook the idea from my head, hoping I was right.

The end of the hallway came into view. Two slouching guards stood beside the massive doorway before us. One awoke as we moved toward them. Before I reached him, he sounded the alarm with a hoarse yell and charged after us as his companion stood up straight, disoriented and confused.

Within seconds, they were both lying still on the ground, their blood spilling out onto the stone floor. The young Shadows stared at the still bodies in shock. *They've never killed before.* I thought, nervousness setting in as I realized there was no way we could have prepared them for this.

"Shadows!" I hissed at them. "We have no time for this. The Governor's Guards will be upon us in minutes. We must get inside that door." The three of them stared at me with wide, clouded eyes and then nodded. Holding my sword in my left hand I shot ice into the massive lock on the door before all four of us crashed against it. Within two tries the door splintered, and we tumbled into the room.

Darkness enveloped us. The flickering torchlight behind us made it difficult to see very far inside the room. The hair on my neck stood straight up as I took a tentative step forward, the younger Shadows falling in behind me.

The room was damp, the smell triggering my senses and pulling me back to my childhood. If cruel abuse and unwanted touch could have a stench, this would be it: the damp scent of roasted meat, smoking embers, dried blood, and spilled alcohol. *He's not alone.* The thought flitted through my mind as I took another step into the room. I closed my eyes to feel with my body rather than continuing to blink hopelessly into the darkness messing with my eyes.

"Why if it isn't the little gutter rat back to show me his tricks." Aepep's voice echoed throughout the chamber, making it difficult to pinpoint which direction it came from.

"It's over, Aepep." I choked out, surprised by the anger rising in my throat. *Where did the calmness go?* My hands burned against the hilt of my sword.

"Tsk, tsk." He clicked his tongue against the roof of his mouth before letting out a slow chuckle. "I took Chantrea away from you too soon. You have poor control over your powers. You care too much about emotion. Tell me, how did your mother die?" The chuckle continued to echo in the room as the words sank into my mind. *Focus, Yuvraj, focus.*

SON OF KINGS

"She died as most people in Shantu die." I answered, collecting my wits, and choosing my words carefully as I turned slightly to the right. "By your design. You alone are the plague of this land, Aepep. You fathered us and hoped we would die. Instead, you fathered your own defeat!" The more I spoke the more courage rose from deep within me. *How I wish Hova could see me now.*

Instinctively, I opened my eyes and shifted to the left as a stream of fire shot past my head, near enough to feel the heat before it dissolved into the wall.

"Bold words for a gutter rat." Aepep's voice was strained. "How poetic that your death will come at the hands of the one who gave you life." I heard the faint scream of a girl as Aepep jumped on me, his sword hitting mine before he kneed me in the stomach. Air escaped from my lungs, and I doubled over gasping for breath while the three Shadows behind me charged the well-built man wielding the sword. *Where is Hadithi?* I wondered, breathlessly. *He should be here by now.*

A light flickered from across the room, breaking through the darkness that gave us an obvious disadvantage. I looked up and saw a young teenager, no more than fourteen, her hand hovering briefly at the torch she'd just lit. Her right eye was adorned with pink and purple bruising, accompanied by a split lip. Her thin frame visibly shook with fear. Fire boiled up from the depths of my soul into my fingers, my breath returning with one final gulp of air.

Turning, I pulled off my remaining glove and threw it on the ground, sword raised, hand burning. I ran at Aepep as he shot fire into the ribs of the young Shadow nearest him. She crumpled over with a scream of pain and lay moaning on the floor beside the wall.

"Aepep!" I screamed at the man in front of me and swung my sword to meet his before he could finish off the wounded warrior at his feet. His eyes shot around to meet mine and our streams of fire met in the middle like some horrifying family connection. For a split-second I thought I saw the slightest spark of misgiving and fear in the Governor's eyes.

For the first time that night he considered the idea that he might not win. I had no doubt the Governor's Guards would soon be upon us. As the young Shadows tended to their wounds and gestured for the young girl to follow them, I pushed hard against Aepep with something I hadn't felt in a long time: hope.

Chapter Twenty-Three

'Hadithi, what are you doing?' The strong, Elven voice rang in his thoughts as he and Shantha ran through the long hallways beneath the Mansion, searching for where Chantrea might be.

'I must speak with you. I need to know. I need to understand. I need to go back. Please, tell me where you are.' He reached back out, the mind connection sparking a lump of grief in his throat as the lilt of her voice reminded him strongly of his mother's. He'd refused to engage in mind-speak with Hova, pretending that part of him had died even though her thoughts were sometimes so loud he couldn't help but notice. Hova knew, of course, but she never pushed it.

'I never said you shouldn't come this way, I merely asked what you're doing, dear one. You're headed in the right direction. Keep straight until the hallway diverges. Take the left fork in the hallway, the darker of the two. You will find me, and I will answer you.' The promise and direction gave new speed to his steps and the others struggled to keep up.

"Hadithi, you need to slow down." Shantha panted a few feet behind him. His pace slowed slightly, and he reached back for her outstretched hand. The fork soon came into view, and he bolted down the dark left corridor without hesitating.

"Trust me." He hissed back, sensing they were all about to question his choice. *There should be guards.* He thought as they continued to run unhindered through the hallway. *Even if only a few, there should be guards. This isn't right. Someone here knows what's going on.* A twinge of guilt festered its way up to the surface of his mind, reminding him he'd agreed to a plan he never meant to follow.

Stop it. I need to know. Shantu isn't the only place that needs help. His internal argument had begun the moment he met Chantrea. All those years ago he'd gone along with the plan and the training, teaching the ideals of a Shadow without knowing whether he considered himself a Shadow. Stronger light loomed ahead, breaking through the darkness of the hallway and the anxiety of his mind.

'Careful,' Chantrea said. 'You may have gotten here without much trouble but there are two guards outside the dungeon door and two more inside.' Hadithi slowed his pace and held up his hand for those behind him to stop. Creeping along the shadows of the hallway walls, he peered ahead.

Two guards sat on the floor in front of the dungeon door, their backs against the wall, eyes closed and weapons limp in their hands. He and Shantha stuffed thick pieces of cloth inside their mouths and tied their hands behind them before they could wake up. Two of the young Shadows with them finished tying them up and whispered in their ears how they would knock them out if they didn't stop struggling. Meanwhile, the other two stripped them of their weapons and armor.

"Hey, what goes on out there?" The gruff voice inside the dungeon chamber barked through the thin cutout window at the top of the door. Hadithi and Shantha stood on either side of the doorway and waited. "Lazy ass, good for nothin' guards probably took off." The man grumbled and fumbled with the key in the lock.

As the door swung outward, Hadithi slipped in behind the man and dealt with the second guard inside as Shantha and the other Shadows secured the one who had exited. It was a short-lived fight. The guards were tired and Hadithi's stature coupled with the number of intruders was more than they wished to deal with. The wrath of Jabez and Aepep potentially signing their death warrants later sounded far superior to the threat of dying now.

Hadithi turned to face Chantrea. Her new cell was much smaller than the one he'd found her in all those years ago. There was just enough room for a wooden platform on one side, a chamber pot in the corner, and the ability to stand near the iron gate.

Unlike the first cell, the room was windowless. The cruelty of the gesture made Hadithi's heart sink as he approached the cloaked woman sitting silently on her platform bed. *See,* Yuvraj's voice seemed to echo inside his mind. *This is why Aepep must be stopped. This is why we need to destroy him and take over as rulers of Shantu!*

Shaking away the rhetoric, Hadithi extended his palm through the gap between the iron bars. "I grant you peace." he said, lowering his hood in a traditional Elven gesture of respect and friendship. The woman sat still for a moment before pushing herself up to a faltering standing position. She gripped a bar with one hand, lowered her hood with the other hand and then covered his palm in return.

"Peace I receive." She replied. Her dark skin was wrinkled and dull, her blue-gold eyes flighty and blinking far too frequently.

"How many years since the light of the moon touched your face?" Hadithi whispered. Chantrea shook her head as a thin smile broke at the corners of her mouth.

"We have so little time, dear one." She whispered in return. "Please, release me from this cage and I will tell you everything you need to know." Her eyes pleaded with him, tears forming at the edge. Hadithi fumbled with the keys and soon had the iron gate open. She faltered as she took a step out, and he caught her, noticing her tall frame weighed far less than it should.

'I need moonlight.' She spoke inside his head again, gripping his arm for support. *'Take me back toward the open grate. Chiwa is coming. I cannot help you fight against her without the moon to revive me. If we stay here, we might neither of us live to see another day.'* Hadithi nodded in understanding as Shantha came to the other side of the Elven woman and supported her.

'We can talk as we walk.' She insisted. The four young Shadows deposited the guards into the iron cage and locked the gate behind them. As they exited the dungeon door, they turned the key and dropped it back inside to make it more difficult getting back in. Two of the young Shadows took the lead to fight off anyone who came before the group and two took up the rear to do the same.

'Who are you? How did you know my mother? I remember your face.'

They walked in silence for a moment.

SON OF KINGS

'She was my best friend. I served under her leadership as her scout. We were like sisters, Estel and I.' Hearing his mother's name for the first time in over eight years caused a lump to form in Hadithi's throat. *'Tell me, dear one, what did she tell you about your life and the land she came from?'*

Hadithi took a deep breath even though he wasn't using his voice to speak. Shantha eyed him from the other side of the Elf, frowning and wondering what was going on. *'She told me a lot of things.'* He began. *'She told me about her family and how much she loved being the Commander of the Elven army. She told me about that land - about Zale. We...'* His words drifted away as he lost himself in the past.

'We visited one time. I was so young my memories are vague and sparse. She took me there when I was three years old. I remember staring at the stars and the moon through the giant trees as she held me in her arms on an Elven walkway.' He paused. *'I also remember no one would touch me or look her in the eye and the Elven King told her to leave.'* Even in his head, his voice betrayed his pained anger.

'Do you know why he told you to leave?' Chantrea pushed. *'Do you know who your father was, Hadithi?'* The tone was gentle but firm.

"Yes." He whispered, causing Shantha to glance over at him again. "I know who my father was."

None of them spoke until they reached the open grate. Every time they passed a barred grate, Chantrea turned her head towards the moonlight the way a plant twists and turns to find the sunshine.

"Let me rest for a moment." She breathed in deeply as they propped her against the opposite wall, still standing. The Elf closed her eyes and sighed, a single tear dropping from the corner of her eye to her cloak. "If you know who your father was, Hadithi, then you know who Chiwa is."

He nodded to confirm her assumption. "Yes. She's my sister." The words came out quietly.

"What do you seek, Hadithi?" Chantrea's face was beginning to glow, her skin turning a deep, rich blue as Hadithi's glowed a much paler blue in the same moonlight.

"I want to go back. I want..." He hesitated.

"Dear one, you know I can force my way into your mind. Speak. Shantha deserves to hear it again."

Shantha started at the sound of her name. "How do you know my name?" she asked, slightly taken aback as she placed a hand instinctively on her knife. The other four Shadows shifted uncomfortably beside her, eyes moving from Hadithi to Shantha and back again, unsure of what they were doing standing in a dungeon hallway when the plan had been to find Aepep.

"You are beloved, my girl." Chantrea turned and smiled at her. "For your gentle spirit, your peaceful mind, and your kind joy. A love so pure cannot be hidden. It is betrayed in a single glance the way the smallest whisper can betray a secret."

Hadithi flushed, half embarrassed and half angry. "I want to make things right. I know about the...the Book." He said, disgusted by the word. Chantrea turned to eye him.

"What do you know about the Book?" She challenged him.

"My father brought a book, *the* Book of Nightmares to Zale and unleashed it on the land. I understand it plagues the people of Zale day and night. Sanity and decency are failing. I know it must be destroyed. *I* must destroy it."

Chantrea studied him for a moment, opening her mouth to speak a couple times and then hesitating. "Why you?"

Hadithi met her gaze for the first time since they'd left the cell. "Because, I am his son. His blood runs through my veins. It is my burden to right the wrong he brought into Zale." Pushing himself away from the wall he stood in the center of the hallway with his hands out to either side, gesturing in frustration. "It's his fault Zale suffers. As his son, as someone who possesses some of his magic, it is my responsibility to fix what he's done. I must make amends. It's the right thing to do."

The Elven lady's eyes were steady, her jaw set and her back straighter than before. The moonlight was giving her renewed strength. She opened her mouth to argue with him and stopped, compassion welling inside her.

"I cannot make you believe something different from what you choose. I swore to your mother the day you were born that I would care for you in whatever way I could if she were to ever die. I have not broken that oath and I plan to keep my word. Estel deserved better." Her voice cracked as she said the words, and she bit her lip. "Besides, I believe you can save Zale. It will not be easy. The road will be long and difficult, but I believe your destiny lies in that land, not in Shantu. Zale needs you and your unique talents."

SON OF KINGS

"But I don't understand how to get back. I don't know the magic. Mother never taught me. When I met you all those years ago, I wanted to ask you how I could get back. But we failed you. Please, can you teach me how to get back?"

The young Shadows were looking at each other in confusion, staring at Shantha to see if she could help them understand.

"Yes, child. I can show you." The Elf's tone was a mix of sorrow and joy, as if her ability to help him could not be reconciled with her desire to protect him. "But first, you must face another and I must fight beside you." The words had barely left her mouth before a flame flew past her head, hitting one of the young Shadows in the chest. The child cried out and sank to her knees, clutching the spot that burned as the others raised their swords. Hadithi covered his head and tossed a sword to Chantrea, who caught the blade in the air.

"Chantrea," The harsh voice echoed through the hallway, grating on everyone's ears as a small, cloaked figure approached with a much taller one close behind her. "It's been too long. Tell me, have you enjoyed living in the dungeon?" The witch cackled with glee.

"Tell me, Chiwa, how does it feel to have your own uncle betray you just as your father did?" The Elven lady's voice was even and calm. Hadithi stiffened and turned to look quizzically at Chantrea, realizing what this meant about Yuvraj and Tyr.

No time to think about that now. He thought, pushing the idea away as so many things began to make sense.

"How does it feel, Chantrea, to know that I killed your best friend?" The witch said unfazed by the intended sting. Hadithi froze, gripped his sword tighter and slowly turned to look back at Chiwa.

"You may have killed her," The Elf spoke through gritted teeth. "But you created a revolutionary to take her place. The best part is you have no idea."

"Is that so?" Chiwa asked, her laughter checked as she tilted her head to the right and continued to stare at Chantrea. "Who exactly is this revolutionary? Yuvraj? That boy sold his soul to me in exchange for information long ago."

Hadithi's chest burned with anger at the witch's words.

"Tyr?" The witch continued with another cackle. "He's hardly what I would call 'revolutionary'. The girl, I grant you, is quite the impressive little lady. But she's nothing to me and no match for my magic."

"You're wrong, Chiwa. Hova is the sweet nurture that will be the undoing of your sickening existence. Her kindness and wisdom combined with Estel's strength and character will become the cornerstone of your destruction." The Elf laughed unexpectedly, the thought bringing her joy. The witch took a step back and glanced over her shoulder.

"She's not here." Her harsh voice carried an undertone of annoyance.

"Do you know who I am?" Hadithi asked, his voice filled with quiet anger. Chiwa turned to look at him, glancing up and down his tall frame.

"Should I?" She cackled the question at him.

"Estel was a great warrior. She was captured by a man who tortured her and forced himself on her." Hadithi paused and took a step forward. "Do you know who I am?"

Chiwa took another step backwards, the veins of her pale white hands intermittently switching between bright red and deep blue. "Ah, the bastard child. I always wondered what happened to you. When I couldn't find you in that pitiful hovel of a house, I chose to believe you'd died in the fire or would die on the street like the little rat you are." She sneered. "Yuvraj failed to tell me he had you in his care."

"It appears Yuvraj failed to tell both of us a lot of things." Hadithi said, pulling a glove off with his teeth and lowering his hood. He tucked the free glove into a pocket as the jade undertones in his eyes grew brighter in the moonlight and his skin lit up with its pale blue hue. "I most certainly did not die." The veins in his hands brightened, mirroring the colors of hers. "And I don't plan to die today either."

Without another word, he shot a flame in the witch's direction and met the sword of her tall, silent companion Efah with his own sharp blade. The two men grappled against one another as the younger Shadows and Chantrea took on the witch. Chiwa began to rain down shots of fire and ice upon them, striking the younger ones easily as they whirled and dodged in confusion.

SON OF KINGS

Finding Jabez's barracks had been easy. Tyr climbed the wall opposite the gate with three younger Shadows much as Hadithi and Shantha had done by the bridge. It was safe to assume Jabez would be housed in the nicest looking barracks with two guards posted outside, closest to the front gate. It was also safe to assume that's where all six of the Governor's Guards were housed while the lesser trained soldiers were crowded into the other barracks on the Governor's Grounds.

The three young Shadows made quick work of the two soldiers standing guard. They were unconscious without even having seen their attackers. Tyr's choice of companion had been strategic: all older and well-trained by him to out-perform anything the Governor's Guards could throw at them.

It was risky to attack the six Guards and Jabez with only four Shadows. Tyr chose to rely on the element of surprise and the hope that one or two might not be present. He tried the door and found it unlocked. With a nod, the three followed him through the doorway into a dimly lit hallway. Six large semi-private cubbies ran along either side and a bright torch perched above a doorway at the opposite end. They walked down the hallway, swords at the ready, wary of each dark cubby opening, the doorway their main goal.

"You have to cut off the head of the snake if you want to stand a chance defeating the beast." Tyr had told Yuvraj as they planned. "I can take down Jabez and the Governor's Guards." Yuvraj had wholeheartedly agreed, anxious to have Aepep to himself.

Halfway down the hallway between the first and second cubbies, two Governor's Guards jumped out. The only sounds to be heard were the clashing of swords and the grunting of Guards and Shadows pushing against each other to overpower and kill the other. Tyr continued; confident his students could handle it. Two more jumped out as they reached the end of the hallway. The Shadow met both with a drawn sword in one hand and a knife in the other.

He eyed them as they pressed against him, their fear visible in the bright light of the torch. Twisting, he flattened himself against the doorway. His weapons clattered on the wood flooring beneath his feet as he grabbed hold at the base of their swords with his leather-clad hands. They exchanged a quick look of shock as he ripped their swords out of their hands and smacked them both on the head with the butt of each blade.

As the guards staggered backwards, the Shadow warrior made quick work of them, hesitating for a second before ending their lives. He grimaced and his stomach churned as he released the swords and bent down to pick up his own weapons. Unlike Yuvraj, Tyr had killed few in his life.

Don't think about it. He scolded himself, taking a deep breath and trying to ignore the fresh smell of blood filling the space. *You don't have time to think about it. Jabez is your goal. Freedom for Shantu is your goal. Their lives are a small price to pay in return for the lives of those you fight for every day. They have cast our people aside without a second thought time and again.*

Weapons back in hand he turned to the unopened door. The three young Shadows had finished the other two Governor's Guards and joined him without even a scratch.

Within seconds, they were inside the room. Jabez and the remaining two Governor's Guards met the Shadows with swords drawn. As Tyr's sword clashed against the Commander's, he noticed the small frame of a little girl dash out behind him. *Ava?* He wondered, leaning in as the distraction gave Jabez the opportunity to issue a swift rap to the Shadow warrior's knuckles. *Focus!* He thought, ignoring the smirk spreading across Jabez's face.

"Tyr." The Commander said, swerving around and dancing on his feet, testing the Shadow's training and talents. "At last, we meet."

Tyr pushed and shoved and danced as well, swinging his sword at the Guard Commander's feet to see how quick his reflexes were. "We've met before, Jabez." He growled at the man. "You helped Aepep give me this lovely patch, don't you remember?"

"Ah, that's right. The pesky little thief. I'm not entirely sure why he didn't cut your hand off instead." The Commander groaned as he turned, and Tyr's knife sliced through his arm. "But then again, he's always been a fool. I should've done us all a favor and cut off both your hands."

This harsh declaration caught the Shadow off-guard. Before he could answer he was distracted by the pounding of soldier's feet in the hallway. The thud of metal hitting skull on his blind side met his ears as his good eye went dark. The Shadow warrior fell limp on the floor as one by one, the young Shadows fought bravely for their lives to no avail. Rather than finish him off, Jabez bounded out

SON OF KINGS

the door and ran toward the castle in search of Aepep. Ava joined him as he exited the building.

Chapter Twenty-Four

Aepep and I battled relentlessly, locked in a winding circle of attack and counterattack. Our swords would clash as our veins shone bright and still neither of us appeared to be getting the upper hand. The Governor screamed for guards more than once, but to no avail. No one came clambering down the hallway to help him. One of the three young Shadows who had climbed the stairs with me ushered the petrified girl away from Aepep's chambers.

The Shadow Aepep had struck with fire in the stomach stopped breathing after a few minutes, and the remaining Shadow who had accompanied me looked on in terror. He stood beside his fallen companion unsure of what to do as the sword in his hand remained poised and ready to strike at any moment. I wanted to curse his brains out, to pop some fire at his feet and make him move. I wanted him to take a cheap shot and smack Aepep in the back, but the man before me demanded all my skill and attention.

Where is Hadithi? I wondered, realizing my backup might never come - might never have intended to come. *This was not the plan. He should have been here by now.* My breath became more labored, steadily increasing as I backed out the doorway. Aepep's eyes glimmered as he forced me down the long hall. He met each skillfully aimed stroke of the sword with equal skill, and each magical burst of fire and water with strengthening fire and water.

"Do you know how old I am, you little gutter rat? Do you imagine a few years of training with the stupid Elf and a bunch of gutter rat children could ever be a match for my inherited skill of magic from the old world? You don't even know where you came from." Aepep said, kicking at my stomach as he twirled with the sword and shot a flame at my feet. "I have practiced magic nearly twice as long as you've been alive, you fool. Give up this idiocy and surrender. I might choose to be merciful if you do." He sneered at me.

I danced around the flames and smacked the sole of his boot with the butt of my sword, blocking his sword with a shot of water. "What do you think Chantrea taught us? How to fight? Nothing more?" I landed a solid hit on his right leg, and hope simmered once more as a spurt of blood gushed from the wound. He grimaced in pain, anger consuming his face.

"I know who you are and who I am and how the magic flows through my veins." I continued. "I know who my grandfather was: a madman who destroyed a magical country to weaponize a book of nightmares. You don't know me. Don't imagine I'm ignorant."

"What do you want from me, bastard child of a prostitute? An apology? A word of fatherly advice?" He jeered at me, a smile coming back to his lips as we continued our dance down the hall.

"No, I want you to die." The words shot out of my mouth quicker than I expected. We twirled around, Aepep's eyebrows lifting as I continued to answer his question. "I want you to feel the pain of every person you've ever tortured as you bleed out on the ground, your blood-filled lungs crushing your breath as you die. I want you to rot for all eternity in a shallow grave, your flesh consumed by the wild animals that dig you up and leave your bones to grow moss beneath the trees of the Woods."

The anger consumed me, the desire to see him suffer growing steadily inside me like a suffocating fire finding oxygen. Magic burned in my veins, giving me newfound energy to fight.

"I want you to suffer."

I whirled again as we reached the stairs and caught him in the chest with a foot. Joyful satisfaction surged through me as the Governor's eyes grew large with terror right before he tumbled backwards down the stairs.

I bounded after him, sword lifted high, shooting fire from my veins, and shouting with delight as the flames met their mark on his back. Aepep howled in pain, groaning as he tried to push himself up from where he'd landed at the bottom of the staircase. A large gash had opened on his forehead, the blood dripping into his eye. His left ankle looked twisted or broken, and he'd lost his sword as he'd fallen.

"Stay down!" I screamed, delivering a swift kick to his ribs. He moaned in pain and collapsed again. The flickering torchlight illuminated blistering flesh on his back, the surrounding fabric scorched away by the fire streaming from my veins. Aepep turned over slowly, one hand raised as if in defense as he scooted his way backwards to lean against the wall.

"I'll give you anything you want." He groaned. "I'll make you Commander of the Governor's Guards, give you a house in the Upper Class where you and anyone you choose can live with you. Tell me, what do you want?"

I pressed my sword against his chin, visions of my mother lying on the ground bruised and bleeding passing through my mind's eye. Tyr's patch covering the sightless hole in his face, the mute woman with the leaking roof and the expression of that poor girl who'd hung from the gallows all came flashing before me.

I kneeled so that our eyes could meet, my sword still at his neck, my veins bright and ready. "Do you even remember their names?" I hissed into his face. "Do you understand what became of their lives? I'll grant you your life if you can give me one name. I'll cut off your hands and leave you to rot in the dungeon beneath us, but I'll grant you your life."

Aepep swallowed and licked his lips. "Surely you can understand how difficult it is for me to remember names. I know so many peo-." Fury surged through my free hand, my fist on fire meeting his jaw without hesitation knocking the back of his head against the wall behind him. He howled in pain but remained conscious. I stood up and dug the blade into his neck just enough to draw blood.

"It's time we were rid of you and your filth," my heart raced as I realized what I was about to do. "We told you once that we were coming. We warned you. You should've listened to us." I spat in his direction. "Shantu will thrive under a new

SON OF KINGS

Governor, a new way of living. We will destroy everything you've built. Your great weakness has become your devastating undoing. Who could've guessed that the bastard children you abandoned would bring about your end?"

Raising the sword with both hands, I prepared to plunge it into his chest.

"Aepep, Governor of Shantu, for the endless crimes you've committed against the citizens of Shantu, I find you guilty and sentence you to death by the sword. In the name of the Shadows, by the power that runs through my veins, and for the sake of all those you abandoned, I deliver your final judgment as judge and executioner, releasing you from the life you do not deserve to breathe."

"Yuvraj, no!"

I turned in shock at the voice behind me. "Hova, get down!" My voice was slow, the words tumbling out in surprise as a flame hurtled past me. Hova collapsed in front of me, her flashing eyes wincing in pain before closing as she doubled over and crumbled onto the floor. Turning, I found Aepep had stumbled onto his feet and was now leaning against the wall, his left foot hanging oddly as he avoided standing on it.

"You must choose between us, rat." He gasped. His breathing was labored. "Finish me or try to save her." His veins were completely devoid of color. With a scream of frustration, I turned away from him and ran to Hova. Gathering her up in my arms I pulled away her summer cloak. Her stomach gaped open, indicating where the fire had met its mark.

"Why, Hova?" I asked through clenched teeth, my mind racing as I tried to think up a plan of what to do. I could hear Aepep as he limped noisily off, clinging to the hallway for support. "I had him in my sight. I had him right where he needed to be, right where he deserved: ready to die and pay the price for everything he's done to us."

"You had him right where you were about to become exactly like him, Yuvraj." She trembled in my arms, squirming in discomfort. "Don't you understand? This was never the way to win the battle for the soul of Shantu." She paused and took a deep breath, coughing slightly. "The soul of Shantu is not found in a man who does irreparable evil. This place, this home we fight for cannot be defined by any one person. The soul of Shantu is in each child we train to live with integrity and joy and purpose. It's in the heart of each mute whose roof we repair and save from selling her body."

Her cough continued, interrupting her thoughts.

"Shhh, Hova, don't speak. I'll take you home, and we'll get you better and then you can tell me all about it." I tried to soothe her, hating every word coming out of her mouth and every word I had to silence her.

"I won't be going home, Yuvraj." She said, her laugh turning into a fit of coughing. "I didn't come here to live. I came here to save the Shadows, to try to save you from transforming once and for all into what you are not. This killing, would it have brought you peace?"

Her question hung between us. The hallway was silent, no soldiers came, and no servants stirred.

"It would have brought me satisfaction and pride." I choked, my own self-loathing festering as the sting of what had been robbed from me struck once more.

"That's not what I asked." Hova shook her head, shifting again in discomfort and groaning in pain. "How many more would you have taken out? How many more would have sufficed to quench your thirst for revenge? What of the women and children in the Upper Class who have no say in who their parents are or how they mistreat those of us without parents? What was your plan, Yuvraj? To make them all like us – gutter rats without home or love?" She coughed again, blood sputtering out of her mouth as she did.

It won't be long now. I thought. *Her lungs are filling. The blow was too severe for her tiny frame.* I wanted to run. I wanted to slap her face and scream at her to shut up and then run away. But I also wanted to hug her close to my chest and make her proud.

"Why did you do this, Hova? Why couldn't you just stay home like we thought you would?" Unwanted tears choked my words and ran down my cheeks. "Why couldn't you have told me all this before tonight? Why did you wait until now? Do you hate me this much that you had to choose to die in my arms?" I knew the question was unfair, but I couldn't stop it.

"Would you have listened to me?" she whispered, convulsing as she coughed up more blood. "Answer me, Yuvraj. I deserve your answer. Would you have listened to me?"

I closed my eyes and shook my head. "No."

SON OF KINGS

"This was the only way. This was my only shot at saving you and keeping the Shadows from dying and becoming something they are not."

I wept, quietly, holding her in my arms as she continued to cough. After a few minutes she touched my face with one hand and wiped away the tears on my cheek. I met her gaze as she began to sing.

> "Oh, faded days of life beyond the grave
> What do you see that I might face?
> Your light shines bright and beckons me
> To leave forever this dark place."

Hova choked and gasped as she finished her song, her hand grasping at her throat and her lungs making one final effort to cough up the blood drowning her. I turned my body, positioning her on her side so the blood could slide easily out of her mouth. It dripped down my pant leg and pooled on the floor. Her bright black eyes lost their shine as her deep brown skin continued to pale.

"Yuvraj," She whispered. "The world is so dark now. I think I'm dying. I wondered what it would be like. It's not anything like I'd imagined." She tried to laugh as if she'd told a good joke. Instead, she began wheezing as blood continued to dribble out the side of her mouth. "Tyr will be so sad." She continued. "Just like when our mother died. I wonder if I'll see her when I leave this place. She was so kind."

She coughed some more as I fought back the scream beginning in my throat and tightened my grip on her, wondering if it were possible to will someone to live.

"Please," She feebly grasped my hand with hers. "Tell Hadithi I love him." With one last cough her body convulsed and went limp in my arms.

AEPEP HALF-LIMPED HALF-CRAWLED DOWN the hallway toward the great meeting hall. The shot fired at Hova had taken every last bit of strength from him. His veins felt no fire or ice and black dots danced through his vision.

Where are all the guards? He wondered. *Jabez will answer for this with his life. I will make a public example out of him for his negligence in keeping me safe. They should never have even made it upstairs.* Different thoughts and theories flew through his head as he pushed against the heavy doors leading into the great hall. The door squished him as he pushed through, causing a rise in pain throughout his half-broken body.

At least a fire is lit. He thought, stumbling through the dark hall toward the opposite end where low flames danced against each other to break the deafening silence of the large room. Collapsing in front of the pitiful fire, he pushed himself up just enough to lean against the warm stones on the right side of the fireplace. His body was going into shock, shaking with pain and cold as his throat burned with thirst.

Two figures emerged from the shadows of the great hall. Jabez and Ava walked quickly across the stone floor and dropped to one knee beside the Governor. A tight rag was tied around Jabez's arm to stop the bleeding from the wound Tyr had inflicted upon him.

"Sire, what happened?" Jabez asked, his face portraying deep concern. "My Guards are all dead. I barely escaped the barracks with my life." He added as he peered at Aepep's wounds.

"Curse you and your life!" Aepep spat at his Commander. "Where are the soldiers? Where are the trained men you swore would always protect me? You'll pay for this, Jabez." If it hadn't been for his dry throat, the hissing would have been a scream. "Stupid child," he said, turning to Ava. "Bring me a drink before I die of thirst."

Ava looked at Jabez for direction. The Commander nodded toward the shadows off to the side where the girl found a goblet and an amber glass pitcher of wine. Uncorking the pitcher, she poured the goblet full and carried it back to the Governor.

"Here," she said, awkwardly holding out the goblet in front of him. "I poured you some wine."

Raising a feeble arm, Aepep pushed the goblet to his lips, Ava still holding it for support. Coughing as he drank, he didn't stop until he'd drunk every last drop.

"Get your hand out of my face, idiot child." He said, somewhat revived. He pushed her hand and the goblet away from his mouth and adjusted himself against the wall. Ava grimaced at his rough touch and bleeding hand but said nothing.

"Come close, Jabez." Aepep said, coughing slightly. "Let me tell you the story of the Commander who dies because he failed to protect his Governor."

Jabez didn't move. Instead, he smiled. "No, Sire. For once, you're going to shut up and listen to me. Do you feel that tickle in your throat?" He paused as Aepep coughed again. "Does it burn yet? Not with thirst, but with fire? Does it crawl up from your stomach, a fire consuming your entire being as you forget how to breathe?"

The Commander paused again and took out a small dagger, examining it as he spoke. "Tell me, oh great magician and wizard, oh powerful Governor of Shantu: how does the wine of an idiot child taste to you?" He laughed, his glance moving between Aepep and the dagger.

Aepep stared at Jabez with widening eyes, a hand going to his throat as his breathing became more labored. He opened his mouth to speak but nothing came out as he was overwhelmed by a fit of coughing.

"Spare me your words, you lecherous pig." The Commander's voice was steady, contempt rising inside him as he watched the man next to the fire claw at his throat and cough, gasping for air. "You promised me glory. You swore to me I would gain fame and comfort and more than I could ever wish for if I would only give you my life and my loyalty. Do you think anything I've done tonight or even in the past twelve years has been for you?" He motioned for Ava to sit beside him. "Do you know who this child is?" He waited as Aepep looked at Jabez then back at Ava and slowly shook his head, still choking and coughing.

"Then you must at least remember her mother, Ana." Jabez choked at the name. "She and I were to be married, remember? That is, until you met her. The day you met her you issued a command that all those serving as guardians of Shantu must refrain from marriage – including the Governor's Guards and the Commander of the Guards. You claimed our loyalty would be divided, and we would become incapable of truly defending this wondrous city if we married."

The Commander leaned in close to the choking Governor and locked eyes with him. "Ana told me what you did. She died giving birth to your child, Ava. Do you remember her now?" He hissed into the dying man's face.

"Yes." Aepep choked out the word.

"Good. Then die knowing that your own child killed you, and your trusted Commander helped her." Without another word Jabez plunged the dagger into Aepep's heart, twisting the blade back and forth as the Governor convulsed and went limp. After a few minutes, Jabez removed the blade and wiped it off on the dead Governor's shirt before sheathing it at his side. He stood up and brushed himself off.

"Come child. It's time you and I took our rightful places in this city."

Hand in hand, they walked through the great hall to rejoin the soldiers gathering outside the main entrance and readying themselves to march on the Slums.

Chapter Twenty-Five

"Shantha, get them out of here!" Hadithi cried to his companion as one of the young Shadow's moaned in pain from a strike of Chiwa's fire. Chantrea's strength grew with each passing moment in the moonlight. The hallway was crowded, but the moonlight was strong. Shantha dodged a shot from the witch and boosted one of the children up through the open hole.

"Run! Go find Kaimbe." She called up to the four as they limped off into the darkness and headed toward the river. She turned back in time to avoid a flame and land a nice smack of her sword to the witch's outstretched hand. Chiwa growled and turned to block Chantrea's descending sword.

"Chantrea," the witch spat at the Elf. "You know what I want. Tell me what I need in order to fulfill my destiny and I'll let you and these two gutter rats live." Pushing back against the wall, she shot ice in Hadithi's direction, barely missing him as he side-stepped and ducked away from Efah's sword. The ice hit the wall, caking onto it before slowly dripping down into a puddle on the stone floor.

"Whoever you are, this is not your fight." Hadithi said, twisting and turning with Efah, shooting ice at the man's feet to make him slip and slide as they pushed back and forth with their swords.

"Not my fight?" The man asked in a smoother tone than Hadithi had expected. "Do not pretend to know who I am. Chiwa and I are bound together forever. She is power and magic and deathly beauty. I, Efah, am her companion, her servant, and her protector. Where she goes, I will go with her. As a shadow falls behind the object that stands against the light, so I fall behind Chiwa as she stands against all that you believe is good and right in the world."

"Then you leave me no choice." Hadithi said, intensifying his strikes and gaining ground on the man before him. "As darkness is your name and you cling to it, so into darkness I must send you." His voice betrayed a hint of sadness within its resolve, his jaw set with determination as he advanced on the man. Efah backed up, slowly losing ground as the strength of the young Shadow warrior bore down on him.

"I know the land you seek." Efah said, pushing back forcefully. "I too, come from there. I was banished as a young man, sent here as punishment for my talent with magic and my affinity for the dark power that encompasses that world." His words slowed Hadithi's sword, the unasked-for information piquing the Shadow's curiosity.

"Then why are you still here? Why haven't you taken Chiwa back to Zale?" He asked, the two of them circling each other.

"Ah, I knew you would want to learn more about me." Efah crooned in his rich, smooth voice. "See, much like you I don't know how to get back. My father sent me here, but he did not teach me the way. This is why we need the Elf. She alone knows the way back."

Behind him, Hadithi heard Shantha cry out as Chiwa's sword sliced into her arm. Without even glancing back, he pressed harder on the man in front of him, firing off ice at Efah's feet and fire at his sword handle. Efah danced on the floor before dropping the blade that grew hot and heavy as it burned into his skin.

With one final twirl, Hadithi smacked the man across the head. Efah collapsed on the floor. He turned to face Chiwa and found her locked in a struggle with Chantrea. Shantha leaned heavily against the wall, her free hand gripping her wounded arm.

Though she was small, the witch was strong. The advantage Chantrea held in height had been weakened by lack of moonlight, hearty food, and practice.

"Chiwa," Hadithi spoke the name loudly enough for it to echo through the hallway. As the witch turned to look at him, he shot ice at her feet and took a step closer, his sword raised high. "You and I have unfinished business." He said through clenched teeth.

Pushing and twirling away from the Elf, Chiwa held her sword out toward Chantrea and her free hand toward Hadithi. Her hood fell to her shoulders, exposing the wild, golden curls cascading down from her head. Her silvery eyes bore into Hadithi's with a hatred he'd never known, the slight blue circle creating a chilling sensation as he met her gaze.

"You and I," the witch hissed at him. "Have nothing to do with each other. You are nothing more than a gutter rat, the bastard, unwanted child of royalty. I am an heiress, the rightful owner of a book so magical your pitiful brain cannot comprehend its significance."

"You killed my mother." Hadithi said, taking another step in her direction.

"Your mother chose her own fate. She wanted to die. She wanted to leave this world, to leave you alone in this cold, disgusting world." Chiwa sneered at him. "She chose death when I gave her the chance to live. She chose death over the love of her own child." She paused and took a small step backward as Chantrea also advanced a step in the witch's direction.

Hadithi's face flushed with anger as he took two more steps forward, making sure he stood as a wall between the witch and Shantha. "You destroyed the only family I had. Give it up. I swear you will not leave this place ali-."

Chiwa lunged at Hadithi, fire spewing, sword swinging to meet his counterattack. She twirled around, positioning herself closer to Efah and away from Chantrea. The Elf now stood beside Hadithi.

'This is not the way, Hadithi. This is not what your mother would have wanted.' Chantrea reached out to the Shadow warrior; her sword still poised in solidarity as she dodged the shots of fire. *'Think of Hova. Think of your mother. Think of Zale. Leave her here to rot. I will tell you what you need to know. Zale needs your help. Do not waste your time and risk your life trying to strike down Chiwa. Her soul died long ago.'*

Hadithi dodged the flames and returned the shots, refusing to answer the Elven woman beside him as he continued to advance.

'Shantha needs you. She needs help. If not for your mother or Hova, then leave the witch for the sake of the woman you love and the life of adventure you promised her.'

'That was cruel and cheap.' Hadithi reached back, his foot faltering slightly in his advancement as flames flew past his head.

'I speak the truth and you know it.' Chantrea replied as she ducked once more.

The witch reached her unconscious companion. At first, she nudged him with her foot, as if trying to revive him. Her meager efforts yielded nothing as the man continued to lie there in oblivion.

Hadithi's sword clashed against Chiwa's once more as his ice finally connected with her right foot. She screamed in pain and pushed against him only to lose her balance and topple backwards over Efah. Raising his sword above his head, the memory of her standing over his mother flashed before his eyes. The flames, the smoke, and the paralyzing fear struck him deep inside and froze his sword in place for an instant.

It was all the witch needed. Grabbing hold of Efah, Chiwa muttered something, and they both disappeared. Hadithi blinked and lowered his sword, taking a step forward to kick at the empty space before his eyes.

"Where?" He asked, turning to Chantrea. "I could've killed her. I could've avenged my mother." His voice shook as he spoke, and his hand trembled as if the shock of not killing Chiwa had been too much.

The Elf shook her head slowly. "No, dear one. You could not kill her. Not like this. You are too much like your mother to do that and she would never ask for you to avenge her death in the first place." She turned back toward Shantha. The young woman was sitting against the wall, fumbling as she tried to tie a bandana around her wounded arm. "Come, it's time we left this place."

Chantrea hoisted herself through the hole with Hadithi's assistance. He tightened the bandana on Shantha's arm and gently lifted her up to the Elf, shimmying his way up the rope behind them.

"Can you walk?" Hadithi asked Shantha, peering into her face, and lifting her hood up to keep her from view.

"Yes, I just need some help." She replied, smiling, and using her good arm to pull his hood up to hide his moonlit skin. Hadithi felt a smile break out over his face involuntarily and his jaw softened as she spoke. He nodded to Chantrea, pulled Shantha to her feet, and wrapped an arm around her waist to support her. The three began to run across the compound toward the river as quickly as Shantha could manage.

"Shantha!" A man's voice boomed behind them. "Wait, stop. Please Shantha, give me a chance to explain."

The young woman froze at the sound of her father's voice and brought her companions to a standstill. Like a bad dream long forgotten, his words sank into the deepest recesses of her mind, pulling out a mix of memories both chilling and nostalgic. Slowly, she turned around to face him.

Aruj stood there alone in his beautiful gray hat with the feather on top, a hand resting on his sheathed sword. He took a tentative step in their direction. "Shantha, it's time to come home." He said, reaching out with his free hand. "Whatever you believe I've done, whoever you think I am, I am still your father."

His voice was a mixture of grief, longing, and anger. "You belong with me. These people do not love you; they merely want to use you." He took another step forward. "Take my hand and come home with me, child. We will never speak of the past. We'll forget it all, let bygones be bygones. I will forgive your disloyalty and we can be a family again." He smiled and took another step forward.

"Stop." Shantha said. "Your words are poisonous lies. We were never a family. I was your pet not your daughter." She let go of Hadithi and patted his hand to let go her waist. Taking a step in Aruj's direction, she lowered her hood. "Tell me who my mother was. This time I want the truth."

The Gray Merchant paused for a second, his eyes shifting between Shantha and Hadithi as if estimating whether he could simultaneously fight the Shadow warrior and force his daughter to come with him. He chose caution as his eyes landed on Hadithi's exposed glowing veins.

"She was my wife." Aruj said, lowering his hand and forcing a smile. "My dearest, loveliest wife. You know this, child."

"No, I know what I saw on that ship, and I have met countless children who claim you as their father since I left your home. Tell me who my mother was and how she died."

"My dear," he said, nervously licking his lips and cocking his head to the right. "Come home with me and I swear I will tell you the whole story."

Shantha turned to leave without another word.

"She was a purchase I made while sailing the Sea." Aruj shouted in exasperation, his voice quivering as he spoke. Shantha turned back around, leaning against Hadithi. "She was unlike anyone or anything I've ever seen, even more impressive than," He paused, sizing Hadithi up once more. "This creature you're with. She was from another world." He paused again. "She claimed she was a star. Her hair was white and curly, her skin like porcelain and her touch was warm. She could heal a death wound with a single finger." His voice choked as he spoke. "I may have purchased her, Shantha, but I swear to you I loved her and took her as my own."

"Did she have a choice?" Shantha asked, her eyes frozen on his.

"I, she-" he looked down at the ground. "No. She did not." He bit his lip and looked back up defiantly. "But I treated her well, with kindness. I gave her everything she might ever want or need. She could've been bought by someone who would've thrown her in a hole for the rest of her life, chained her up and dragged her around like a freak show. I was kind to her." He was fuming.

"How did she die?" Shantha asked, ignoring his tirade of justification. "Did she die like my maid: beaten, hung, then thrown overboard for some small indiscretion?" Her voice trembled as she said the words.

"My child, I-" Aruj took a couple steps in her direction, arms outstretched. Hadithi grabbed firmly around Shantha's waist and pulled her back, his free hand outstretched with glowing red veins. The Gray Merchant stopped in his tracks.

"No. She died giving birth to you." He said through clenched teeth. "She bled out, unwilling to heal herself and too far gone for our doctors to do anything for her." His hand rested on his sword again. "So, I suppose you might say, you were the one who killed her."

Shantha stared him straight in the eye. "No, your cruelty and lies crushed her soul. I just wasn't enough to revive it. Goodbye, father. Forever." Without another word she turned her back to him.

As Shantha and Hadithi turned to leave, Chantrea waiting a few feet ahead, Aruj pulled out his sword and lunged at them. As if from nowhere, Kaimbe emerged from the darkness, grabbed Aruj's arm, and ripped the sword out of his hand while simultaneously flinging him to the ground.

"Run." Kaimbe shouted to the other three. "The attack has failed but I have unfinished business. Get away while you still have time." His eyes never left the

SON OF KINGS

man moaning in pain on the ground, cursing as he pushed himself up to his hands and knees. Chantrea, Hadithi and Shantha disappeared into the darkness without another word.

"This is not your fight." Aruj screamed at the giant man in front of him. "This is between me and my daughter." He stood up and pulled the whip off his belt. "You and I have nothing to do with each other. Leave now and I'll spare your life."

Kaimbe eyed the man. "You don't remember me," he said, twirling the sword in his hands and taking a step in Aruj's direction. "But I have never forgotten you." He spun toward Aruj, nicking him on the cheek as the lash of the whip cut into his ankle. "Maybe if you don't remember my face, then you'll remember my scars." He said, ripping off his shirt to reveal rippling muscles covered in thin scars from long ago.

The Gray Merchant eyed him as he ran through all the possibilities of who the Shadow before him could be. "Are you some good for nothing ships boy that ran away?" He asked, hoping this preferred theory was correct.

Kaimbe smirked. "You know who I am, *father*." He choked on the word. "I am as much your son as my sister is your daughter. Her you treasured, I you tortured. If the fight of the Shadows must end in failure, then I will at least keep you from continuing to torture another."

As Jabez marched out to meet his soldiers, ready to take charge of Shantu, he noticed two figures off to the side. He paused for a moment as the tall, shirtless man caught the end of the whip with his bare hand. He smacked the Gray Merchant on the back with the flat of his sword and threw the man to the ground in one smooth motion.

The Commander considered, for a moment, whether to help Aruj, but quickly put the thought aside. He continued with his business as Kaimbe grasped the handle of the whip and rained lashes down on the man at his feet.

I STUMBLED ACROSS THE grounds toward the bridge and the river where Hadithi was supposed to enter the Governor's Grounds. Hova's limp body weighed heavily in my arms. I had no plan, no direction or big idea. Having gathered Hova up, I'd exited the main entrance and heard soldiers marching in the direction of the front gate.

My only hope for saving myself was to move in the opposite direction toward the bank of the river and float downstream. I didn't know what to do with Hova, I only knew I couldn't leave her there. Reaching the water without conflict, I sank to my knees and held Hova in my arms, rocking back and forth as I stared at her empty, lifeless eyes.

"Please, tell Hadithi I love him." Her words haunted me, ringing in my ears on repeat.

"Why, Hova? Why?" I wept; my jaw clenched in anger. "Why couldn't you have just stayed home?" Guilt welled inside of me as I remembered her speech, her effort to save me, her strange words about trying to save the Shadows. *I wouldn't have listened.* I thought to myself. *I wouldn't have done as she asked or stayed home. I still would have attacked, would have followed Tyr and planned our attack. I wouldn't have listened to her.*

"Yuvraj?"

I looked up, startled by the hoarse voice calling my name a few feet down the bank. Tyr came into view, blood dripping down the side of his face and soaking into his eye patch. He held his sword loosely in one hand.

"Tyr?" I said, trying to wipe away the tears on my face. He approached me slowly, the blade of his sword dragging along the ground.

"What...how..." He stood there unable to finish his question, staring at his sister laying limp in my arms.

"I'm sorry, Tyr. I, that is Hova, she followed us in. I didn't see her. I didn't know she was coming. She came in and distracted me and I was about to kill Aepep but she told me not to and then he killed her and I-" the words came tumbling out in a blubbering fashion. "Hadithi never showed up, I don't understand where he went, he wasn't there to help me." I found myself fighting for control, clinging to some semblance of perceived virtue, trying to make sense of what had happened.

"Shut up, Yuvraj." Tyr's voice was deep and dangerous. "Get away from her." He said, taking a step toward me. I sat there, shaking, trying to gather my wits, and let go of her. "Now!" Tyr screamed, raising his sword.

Survival instincts kicked in as I found myself rolling away from my brother, barely escaping his swinging sword. I crawled and stumbled, trying to stand up, fumbling for my own sword at my side. *Whack!* His sword smacked into the back of my legs, pushing me back down to the ground.

"Tyr, stop, please let me explain." I gasped, rolling over onto my back.

"Explain? Explain what?" He shouted at me, standing over me with his sword raised. "Explain your obsession with my sister? Explain how you failed to kill Aepep? Explain why you couldn't protect the best person to ever walk among us? What is there to explain?" He screamed down at me, spit dripping from his mouth as he shook with rage. "Hova's death is your fault and your fault alone! She should be alive!"

"Please, Tyr, we planned this together, we decided this was the best time to try. Something must have gone wrong, Jabez must have found out somehow what was going on."

"Shut up!"

Before I could move, he plunged his sword into my left palm, pinning it to the ground. I cried out in agony, writhing as the pain shot up my arm and into my chest. *This is how I die.* I thought, my memory going back to that rainy day in the stinking alleyway when Tyr, Hova and I first met. *This is my end. Today is not the day my father sees justice, but the day I die at the hands of my brother.*

Tyr stood there for a moment, watching me, his hand still gripping the sword. Finally, he pulled it out. Blood spurted out of my hand, and I screamed once more. Grasping it with my free hand, I tried to wrap it up in a handkerchief from my pocket. My brother walked away from me back to Hova's body and kneeled beside her.

"You failed." He said quietly.

I could barely hear him. My ears rang as I tried to maintain consciousness and tighten the already soaked handkerchief.

"You failed and so did I." He paused, picking up one of Hova's hands and holding it between his own. "She never liked you. Never trusted you. She always warned me that things would end badly if I continued with your obsession over our father. She was right. I should have listened to her. As long as I'm alive, I will never forgive myself."

He dropped her hand, stood up and walked back to me. I thought for a moment he would end my life. Instead, he extended his hand and pulled me to my feet. "I will never forgive you either, Yuvraj." He said, locking eyes with me. "Leave, and never speak to me again."

With that he turned away from me and kneeled beside Hova. I stumbled to the bank and fell into the water, allowing it to float me down stream toward the next bridge. As the sun rose over Shantu, I watched from beneath the stone structure as Jabez led the soldiers in turning out every person in the Slums from their home and burning down half of them. As noon struck, the soldiers filed back to their barracks under the command of the new governor of Shantu: Jabez.

I made my way into the Woods to hide from the wrath of Chiwa and the grief of Tyr.

EPILOGUE

Do you curse me now, Reader? Do you loathe me with the same hatred that runs through my fire and ice veins? Perhaps you should.

To my knowledge, Kaimbe and the twins escaped and kept their mother from being harmed. They roam the streets of Shantu as Shadows, ever out of reach of Jabez's men. The Gray Merchant has not been seen since the day he met with Kaimbe. Whether he's dead or merely maimed and in hiding is unknown.

I have not seen Tyr since that night on the bank of the river. However, I hear from time to time of the one-eyed Shadow who brings food to children and patches roofs. The young Shadows that accompanied us, and those we left behind, all scattered when the soldiers marched on the Slums. What was once a family of strength and power, known and beloved by all Commoners, has become a secret only spoken of in hushed tones.

Jabez rules Shantu with Ava sitting beside him as his daughter. Whether she actually is his daughter is doubtful. As she grows in stature, she also grows in resemblance of Aepep. I do grant Jabez's rule is neither as cruel nor as terrifying as Aepep's. However, Shantu remains much the same. The people who live there fall under three categories: the very rich, the very poor, and those who just try to scrape out a living in order to not become the very poor.

ELLEN ES CEELY

When I go into town for supplies, I hear rumors of a witch and her companion who wander the streets looking for a woman most believe to be nothing more than a ghost or a legend. I have not seen Chantrea since that first failed rescue, and yet from time to time I feel as if someone were watching me from the trees.

Of Hadithi and Shantha I know not. I assume they left this world in search of Zale, following whatever directions Chantrea gave them to get there. I curse their names and their lives and wish them nothing but the very same death they brought upon the Shadows.

For their betrayal, I have no forgiveness.

For their love, I have no understanding.

For their lives, I have nothing but contempt.

Here I live in the Woods as an outcast Shadow, the rightful ruler of Shantu in a shelter made from branches and no other company than that of the memories that haunt me.

So, judge me, Reader. But judge me fairly. Either way, cursed are you for you do not know what it is to be me.

Yuvraj: *Commander of the Shadows; Exile of Shantu*

"GATHER 'ROUND CHILDREN, AND I will tell you of the greatest myth to ever exist; of the prince who never became king." The tall, cloaked woman lowered her voice, causing the wide-eyed children to lean in closer as they sat around the fire in the Slum alleyway of Shantu.

"I will tell you of the power of love, the strength of light over darkness, and the importance of hope in the midst of fear. I will tell you the legend of the Shadows: brave men and women who walk among you. I will tell you of selflessness, pain, consequence, and the ability to rise above what your enemy would have you become. I will tell you of the illegitimate hero, and the need to live to fight another day rather than dying as a martyr for a cause you cannot save.

"Once upon a time, there was a beautiful land in a faraway place called The Deadlands. This land had been cursed by a horrible wizard. Waking or sleeping, nightmares followed you wherever you went, coming to life to taunt and torture even the youngest and most innocent of minds. The Shadows of Shantu discovered this place by accident, traveling there and back as they tried to save the people of that land."

The eyes of the young, pale faces around the fire lit up. They were hungry for more than food and affection. They were hungry for adventure, love, and hope. *Stories can change the world.* Chantrea thought as she wove myth into the history of Zale. *Stories can change the course of one's destiny.*

TO BE CONTINUED

MANY THANKS

To my husband, Brian: this book would not exist without you. Thank you for never giving up on me and never allowing me to give up either. No one else knows how much of myself is poured into the stories I write or how much they mean to me. No one else witnesses the bad days, the crazy times, the obsessive hours, or the distracted looks. You're the only one who sees just how much my writing takes out of me while simultaneously bringing me life. I love you forever.

To my Alpha reader, Sarah: I am forever grateful. Thank you for being honest, constructive, and trustworthy. I'm honored to have you as the first set of eyes.

To my sister, Gracia: your encouragement and insight never fail me. Thank you for being one of my biggest champions.

To Samantha: thank you for taking time every time I pop up and ask you to read! You have been such a good friend to me.

To Lisa: you're a wonderful Beta reader. I couldn't do this without you.

To my Mommy: thanks for loving me and keeping me going on hard days. Thank you for reading everything I write and recommending it to everyone you know.

To my Mother-in-law: you're the best bonus mom a girl could ask for. Thanks for always reading my work and encouraging me to keep going.

SON OF KINGS

To my Aunt Kathy and my Aunt Trish: you both are my heroes. I love you.

To my author twin, Ellen Vandever: thanks for adopting me as part of your found family.

Last but not least: to my Patreon community: I have accomplished more with your support than I could have ever dreamed. Thank you, thank you, thank you!

ABOUT

As a child, Ellen dreamed of writing books, acting in plays, and going on adventures. She read books, played in the dirt, and sewed herself costumes as she got older. Adulthood took over for a while and creativity took a backseat. One day she recognized the longing to write again and picked up an old story. 18 months later *Child of Shadows* was born.

Ellen currently lives a quiet life in North Carolina with her husband, Brian. In her spare time, she enjoys sewing, spending time with friends, and watching TV. Her current dreams include renovating an old house, making a full-time living with her writing, and learning to garden.

To watch her journey, access full color maps, character name lists, and learn more about her, check out her online presence below.

www.authorellenceely.com
Instagram: @authorellenesceely
TikTok: @author_ellenesceely

BOOK THREE

Dear Eliora,

There are so many stories I have not told you. So many names and legends I have buried deep within my soul. And now, I fear, their stories will never be told. At least, they will never be told by me.

I'm tempted to say I'm sorry for dragging you into this world, into a mess you didn't create. However, I believe I saved you as much as you have saved us. For that, I am grateful.

I have made many mistakes in my life, the regrets of which follow me everywhere I go. You see me as strong and infallible and I let you believe those things because it brings me some sense of relief. But I am not who you think I am. At least, I have not always been who I am today.

As we draw nearer to Castle Island, I believe we draw nearer to my death. My dreams are dark these days, but truthful. They speak to me of my end. If you're reading this now, then I can only assume my dreams came true. So I leave you with three final thoughts.

First: you are the best thing in my life; my pride and joy. You have always been what no one would expect; forever underestimated. I cannot overstate how proud

I am of you, how dear to my heart you have become, or how sad I am to leave you. Thank you for being the closest thing I have ever had to a daughter.

Second: you are not a nobody. If your time in Zale has taught you nothing else, please know that you are far more than "nobody". Ask questions. You will find out the truth, or at least a piece of it. If Einar survives this journey, stay close to him. He will guide you and guard you until one of you dies, and he will help you find some of the answers you crave.

Third: create the family you have always wanted. Sadiki will keep you safe. Trust him. His soul is tied to your own. I know Hardwin will come to live with you someday. Keep him by your side. Together you will accomplish so much.

Do not grieve my passing for too many years, dear one. Your life has been lived in the shadows for too long and you deserve to live the rest of it free, basking in the sunshine. You are brave and strong and full of light. Carry on with your stories and your shining eyes. Your heart is too bright to stay hidden from the world. Zale needs you. Do not be afraid of disappointment and failure. These will only make your heart stronger in its illuminating power of truth.

Never forget what Chantrea told you: you are your name and your name is you. You are a child of light, a dream whisperer, and a warrior for the oppressed.

I do not believe this is the last time you will face darkness in this land. When that day comes, remember how much more lies ahead than behind.

All my love,
Hadithi, *Child of Shadows*

"Eliora..." The whisper met my ears, tugging inexplicably at my heart. Light blue eyes with a circle of dark silver flashed before my mind.

I was on the side of a snow-covered mountain, icy wind whipping my hair into my eyes as it froze the hairs inside my nostrils. I struggled through the snow, at times sinking knee deep. Finally, I leaned against a tree, gasping for air, my teeth chattering and my warm breath creating clouds of steam in the air.

"Eliora..." The whisper came to me again as someone passed by in the shadows.

SON OF KINGS

"Hello?" I cried out, half afraid it would be an enemy, half hopeful it might be a friend. But no answer, only the sight of a short man in a long, regal robe strolling through the trees. I stumbled after him, crying out once more in hopes that he might help me. But he never looked around, never seemed to even notice my existence.

Up ahead the man stopped, bending over something beneath the shelter of the trees. As I neared the spot I stopped short in horror. A woman in a black cloak lay still beneath the trees, something clasped tight to her chest. Her face was white with cold, her brown eyelashes causing a stark contrast against the deadly pallor of her skin.

"Look closer..." The whisper echoed through the wind as I leaned in, the light blue eyes flashing before my own as I did so. I watched as the man pried the woman's frozen arms away from her chest and opened up her cloak. Blinking in amazement, I rubbed my eyes and looked again. A tiny baby lay in the embrace of the dead woman, the small puffs of mist revealing it was still alive.

The man stared at the child for a moment, his right hand poised over its face. There was something dark and sinister about the way his hand hovered. Uneasy, I took a step forward, reaching out to pick up the baby before he could grab it himself, but I was too late. He picked the child up, turning its face toward me.

The baby's eyes opened and the air caught in my lungs as the vision of those pale blue eyes flashed through my mind, aging backwards to meet the look on the child's face.

"Eliora..." The whisper danced over the wind once more. "Help me. Please."

TO BE CONTINUED

But even in death a story is never truly at an end...

An evil witch thirsting after unlimited power. A magical book that controls nightmares. An orphan with a knack for storytelling. A warrior determined to make amends for the actions of his father.

The Slums of Shantu run rampant with poverty and crime. The orphans survive, protected by the mysterious Shadows who tell them stories of a faraway land where nightmares come to life.

The dog's eyes burned red, its bared teeth glinting in the moonlight. A spiked chain connected to the building was wrapped around the dog's neck, digging into its obviously starved body. It growled dangerously and lunged at me.

Screaming, I held my arms out in front of me, trying to hold onto the idea that it was a dream. I wondered if I would be torn to bits by the only living creature we'd seen on this island. As I pushed forward with closed eyes and clenched teeth the barking died out.

Eliora, an orphan of Shantu, soon discovers her quest is far more dangerous than she imagined. But she is also more powerful than she believed.

Made in the USA
Columbia, SC
20 October 2023